WHITE FLAG OF THE DEAD

Book 1: Surrender of the Living

Joseph Talluto

Author's Note

I first became interested in zombies when I read a borrowed copy of Max Brooks' <u>Zombie Survival Guide</u>. From there I dove headfirst into the genre, and have never looked back. After reading several good books about zombies, I began to realize I wanted to write a book of my own. I threw together a first chapter, showed it to a couple of friends, and they encouraged me to continue. As I kept writing, the project sort of took a life of its own, and the original outline I had created is nothing like the finished project.

What fascinates me about the whole zombie theme and zombie apocalypse is not the living dead themselves, but the reaction of people to the sudden shift in their world. Nothing is the same, nothing will ever be the same, and a daily fight for survival is something many people are not willing to come to grips with.

What I have tried to accomplish with this first novel is to show how one man deals with not only the zombie threat, but the threat from others who would take advantage of the end of the world, while trying to protect his son and his sanity. In the end, he makes the adjustment from ordinary man to survivor, but the journey is a long and hard one. I would like to think that should the worst happen, most people would be able to make the adjustment, but my understanding of human nature doesn't hold that hope for long.

This project has fired a long dormant interest in writing, so it is not a stretch to think that the crew of <u>White Flag of the Dead</u> series will be called upon to ride out to save the day.

I hope you enjoy the books as much as I have enjoyed writing them

Acknowledgements
I would like to thank my family and friends for their support of this project, especially Dottie and Jason, who opened the door to the zombie genre for me. I never would have finished this book had I not had their continued support.
I would most of all like to thank my wonderful wife Jodie, whose tolerance of my eccentricities let me fulfill one of my dreams, which hopefully may allow me to fulfill all of hers.

1

"Ugh."

"How's that?"

"Ugh."

"Come on caveman, your son is calling you." My wife of six years poked me in the ribs and pushed my feet off the bed. In the background, soft music played through the monitor, indicating that Jake, our son, was awake and had activated the toy.

"I'm too tired to play daddy today. Get someone else." I groaned, rolling over and burying my head in my pillows.

"Move it or we'll never play at making another one," she threatened.

"Empty threat. I'm too good for any woman to give up cold turkey."

Ellie grabbed my pillows. "Fine. How about it's your turn since I got up at 2?"

I rolled out of bed and lay on the floor. "I'm nothing if not fair."

The words "Have fun." floated over the bed and down to my ears as I started my morning routine of pushups and sit-ups. I barely felt them anymore, since I had been doing them since I was a kid. But habits are habitual, and it woke me up in the mornings.

I walked down the dark hall, feeling very much like a zombie. I am sure I looked it, too. But things needed to be done, and as the wife said, it was my turn. 5am was waaaay to early for anything, let along getting up from a very sound sleep. Jake, my five-month old, was wiggly and wanting to move out of his crib. He was just learning to sit on his own, although he couldn't push himself to a sitting position yet. He rolled all over creation, and dragged himself along in an attempt to crawl. We thought he was the greatest thing, being new parents, but even we were surprised at how happy he was all the time, and what an easy baby he was, if judging by the grousing my brother did about his kids.

"Hey, buddy." I said stepping over to his crib. Jacob had activated his plastic fishbowl, which had alerted us to his state of wakefulness. Jake looked at me and smiled through his binky, swinging his arms in excitement. How these little guys remained so cheerful all the time was a mystery me. If I could bottle it I would be rich.

I picked him up and headed downstairs to make a bottle for him, since Ellie was not breast feeding. She had tried, but it just seemed to not be in the cards, so here we were, spending lots of money on formula. I didn't blame Ellie, how could it be her fault? She felt bad enough as it was, since she believed she was not getting that special "bonding time" that so many people say is so important. On the plus side, it allowed both of us to have some special time with the little guy, so we enjoyed it for what it was.

Downstairs I made him a bottle and a small bowl of oatmeal cereal. The doctor had said he could start it, so we got some and he really seemed to enjoy it. I tasted it once and it reminded me strongly of glue, but I didn't let Jake know that. I turned on the television to see what news there could be had. I generally watched Fox for news simply because it was slightly harder to spot the bias. Ellie liked the local stuff and once in a blue moon I turned on CNN. Most of my news came from the internet, but it was good background noise.

"...incoming reports remain sketchy, but there seems to be some sort of outbreak in New York City on the lower east side. We go to Hannah Graves at the scene of Angel of Mercy Hospital. Hannah, what can you tell us?" I glanced at the screen, but Jake decided to make a grab for the food bowl, so I lost the reporters comments.

"Okay, thanks, Hannah. We're going to our interview with Dr. Rafik Narwal, from the Center for Disease Control. Dr. Narwal, what can you tell us. Are we looking at a pandemic?"

That got my attention. I picked Jake up to give him the rest of his bottle and stood in front of the television. Dr. Narwal looked bad, like he hadn't gotten a lot of sleep lately.

"Nothing of the sort. We have taken precautions, like we normally do, when we have a situation where an infected person comes down with symptoms we haven't seen before in this country. In Africa, this sort of thing is routine and would not even be a story." Something in his manner was not sitting right with me. I had spent the last four years of my life as an administrator in public schools, and I knew when someone was lying to me or when they were trying to cover up something.

Right now, Dr. Narwal was lying, and worse, he seemed scared. When the CDC spokesman looked scared, check your antibiotic supply because things were not good. I started to think about what I had read recently, where estimates of the death toll from a pandemic avian flu outbreak could reach 150 million. I started to pay very close attention

"What kind of symptoms, so we will know what to look for?" Darla the commentator asked. I called her Darla because I didn't know her name and she looked like one, anyway.

Dr. Narwal looked nervous. "The symptoms are relatively flu like, with profuse vomiting, diarrhea, sweating and salivating. If anyone comes down with these symptoms after being infected, it is a very good idea to isolate them, as they are very contagious."

"Is this a new disease?"

"All reports indicate we have not seen this strain of virus before, no."

"Where did this begin?" Why people cared about this I wasn't sure, but maybe it gave them some sort of relief blaming someone else.

Dr Narwal explained. "One of our colleagues was doing research in a remote village in the Congo Basin. Nothing out of the ordinary there, many of our diseases and cures come from largely unexplored regions like the Congo and the Amazon. Dr. Roberto Enillo was researching a new virus outbreak and discovered this new disease. We are currently running tests as to what kind of virus this is, what the incubation rate is, its survival rate in the open, what kills it and what feeds it.

I noticed he used only the past tense when talking about Dr. Enillo.

"What can we tell people to do.?" Darla asked, leaning forward, looking concerned for the camera. I felt her concern, and appreciated the glimpse down her shirt.

Dr. Narwal relaxed a bit, as this was familiar ground. "People should not panic. If a relative comes down with the symptoms, isolate them and call the authorities. If you feel you are sick, go to a hospital or clinic and they will take care of you." Something was ticking in the back of my mind, but I didn't pay close attention as I knelt down to change a dirty diaper. Jakey was finished with his bottle and gave me a satisfactory belch to complete his morning routine. I laid him on the floor and smiled at him, which got a full smile and arm flapping in response. *What you don't know about the world, buddy.* I thought.

"In world news, England mobilizes its Territorial Army for a possible containment operation near Wales. Details are sketchy at this point, but there appears to be rumors of some sort of patient uprising in a local hospital. Further details as reports come in."

"Okay, thanks, Hannah, in other news..."

I turned off the news as my wife came down, yawning and stretching. "Anything on the news?"

"Something about a new virus going around that seems to be hitting hard in a lot of places." I said, placing a few toys about for Jake to play with while I got my breakfast.

"Really? Anything I need to know about?" Ellie stayed home with Jake three days a week, taking a year off from full time work. We did the math and realized that she would be working just for day care for Jake, so what was the point? She worked as a cardiac nurse for a hospital in the city, so she generally worked the shifts no one else wanted, Saturdays being one of them.

"Just keep an eye out for flu-like symptoms, and call the authorities if anyone has been infected. They didn't say anything about transmission, but that it was very contagious." I replied.

"Any reports of outbreaks around here?" Ellie asked, her eyebrows rising.

"Nothing on the local news, but I am sure things will get out as needed, information wise." I assured her. The internet eliminated information dissemination by the media, everyone had a camera, video recorder, or some combination which allowed them to post immediately exactly what was happening. You Tube was a great source of information, but it was better to watch with the sound off, as the posters tended to think they were trained cameramen.

"All right. We'll stay close to home, but I need to go to the grocery store. Jakey is running low on food. We are starting him on level two foods this week." Ellie seemed pretty excited. "He's getting to be such a big boy."

I grinned "Takes after his daddy."

"Right. Nice fishing for compliments." Ellie walked over to rescue Jake, who had managed to drag himself over to the vent and got his sleeper button stuck.

I smiled and got myself breakfast, thinking about what I had heard on the radio. That old feeling was ticking in the back of my head, and for once I decided not to ignore it.

"Hey, babe?" I said.

Ellie looked up from Jake. "What?"

"When you go shopping, could you pick up some extra bottled water? I kind of want to ease back my pop intake."

Ellie shrugged. "Sure whatever. Anything else?"

I thought for a minute. "D and AA batteries. I think Jake's fishbowl is sounding weak, and his musical dragon is not so musical."

"Okay."

I went back to my breakfast, and thought about things before I went upstairs to get ready to go to work. I couldn't shake the feeling that there was a going to be a lot more to this virus, and as I put on my shirt and tied my tie, I decided that prudence was the better side of caution. I reached into my closet and opened the small safe I had hidden behind my Chicago Bears jersey. I pulled out my Walther PPK and checked to make sure it was fully loaded and a round was chambered. I took it to the side of the bed where I had a thick book hollowed out to accept the little pistol. I placed the book on my nightstand, and hoped that everything would be all right.

2

Driving to work at my usual pace, I barely listened to the radio, focusing more on the unusual amount of traffic that seemed to be on the road. The Governor of my state was likely going to be indicted, he said he was innocent, the president was meeting with other world leaders about the new threat, and someone was having a sale on last years model cars. Blah, Blah, Blah. I really didn't listen until I heard the word virus and Chicago. All of a sudden, I was interested, since I lived only thirty miles outside of the city proper. The talk show was discussing the new virus that seemed to be on everyone's mind. They said there have not been any cases yet reported in the Chicago area, but New York seemed to be having a difficult time containing it. A sound bite from the mayor of Chicago reassured everyone that precautions were being taken, and antibiotics were being stocked up. I laughed at this. Antibiotics are useless against viruses, but it made the masses rest a little easier.

I pulled into work, and the first thing I noticed was a general lack of activity. Usually there was a group of kids running around, but today it was quiet.

I went to my office and spent what was essentially a normal day, dealing with the normal problems of running a school. Kids showed up, we taught them, and they went home. It wasn't until later when I started to get that old familiar feeling again.

Ellie called me on my cell. "Hey you! Just wanted to touch base with you. I'm at Cost Go and wanted to know if you wanted anything special for dinner." I could hear Jake squeaking in the background, like he always does when he rides in a shopping cart.

I thought for a minute. "Just stock up on everything you think we need. Get a lot of canned goods and dry goods, stuff that we don't need to refrigerate. Extra toilet paper, batteries, everything. Don't worry about paying for it, just use the credit card."

Ellie seemed baffled. "What's going on, John? What are you preparing for? I am *not* going to be acting like some lunatic Y2K fear monger."

I knew I would lose a protracted argument, since I tended to lose them all. But I also knew that Ellie was nothing if not practical. "Just taking some precautions. If the virus spreads, people are going to panic, and then everything will be up for grabs. Why not get what we need now, and not worry about it later?" I stood by my office window as I spoke, and that allowed me a good view of the surrounding neighborhood. I watched an old man stumble a bit around his yard, like he didn't know where he was. *Alzheimer's*, I thought. *Too bad.* Judging by the bandage on his arm, he had managed to injure himself.

Ellie's voice cut off my observation. "All right, but don't complain to me if you get tired of soup and rice." she said.

"Thanks," I said, looking out the window again. The old man's caretaker was coming out into the yard. "I'll see you soon. Love you!"

The caretaker walked out into the yard and I could see the old man turn his head and look at her. He reached out with one arm, and the other one hung limp. *Stroke victim*, I thought, feeling sorry for the old guy. Staggering steps were taken to the caretaker, who walked forward to give him a hand. When she reached him, his hand grasped her shoulder, and his head snapped forward to her neck. "Jesus Christ!" I yelled, watching as blood sprayed over both of them. My secretary poked her head around the door.

"What's up?"

"Call 911 right now!" I yelled at her, not being able to take my eyes off the scene across the street. "A woman is being attacked on the other side of Hampshire Street!" The man had dragged the woman down and was furiously chewing on her neck and face. She was struggling, screaming, trying to get him off, but I could see she was weakening from the loss of blood. The old man bent down and tore another chunk out of her neck, and the woman shuddered once, and then was still. I watched in horror as the old man tore at her stomach, ripping the clothes and skin open and tearing out hunks of flesh, barely chewing the meat, just forcing it down. I couldn't believe what I just saw. There was no way that just happened. I looked around to see if anyone else had seen or heard anything.

I yelled at Janet "Where the hell is 911?"

"They said they are busy at the moment, but call back in fifteen minutes."

My mind reeled. I looked out again and saw the old man had gotten up from his kill, the front of his shirt completely covered in his victim's blood. He began his shuffling around again and I could not believe he was staying near the body. I watched as a neighbor came out and walked over to the fence. The old man made a moaning sound and lurched toward the neighbor. *Get out of there!* I silently screamed at the neighbor. The neighbor held out a hand to the old man over the fence and when the old man got close enough, he grabbed the hand and promptly bit the arm it was attached to! The neighbor yanked his hand back, and ran towards his house, screaming bloody murder all the way.

"Jesus Christ!" I yelled again, not understanding what I had just witnessed. Janet again poked her head around the corner.

"What now?" She asked.

"The old man who just killed that woman, was eating her and the neighbor came out and the old man bit him, too!"

"What?"

"I'm serious! Right there! Look!"

Janet came over to the window. She glanced out and nearly gagged. "Oh, God!" she said, covering her mouth with her hand. The woman's body wasn't pretty. Her face and neck were covered in blood and bites, and there was a raw open wound in her stomach. Entrails were hanging by her sides like blue-grey ropes.

"What did 911 say?" I asked, turning her away from the window. "Exactly, what did they say?"

Janet refocused, "They said that they had received numerous calls, and were dealing with them as quickly as they could. If it was not a life-threatening emergency, then we would have to wait."

I looked at the scene across the street. I guessed the waiting for help to arrive had just started. I decided I needed to get home and get with my family right now. I said as much to Janet and suggested that she leave right now as well. She didn't argue with me, having three children of her own waiting for her   at   home.

As I packed up to leave, I looked out the window again. The old man was gone, and so was the woman. Blood was all over the grass, turning brown in the sun. I guess 911 came to the rescue after all. Hope the guy with the bite on his arm was okay.

As I walked out into the parking lot, I was struck by how quiet everything was. I didn't hear any trains going by, I didn't hear any kids playing. Unusual for this neighborhood. I did hear an odd moaning, but I figured that was the wind. As I got to my car, I thought I heard several pops, like someone lighting off fireworks. It came from the east, where the hospital and clinic were, but I didn't think anything of it.

As I drove home, I kept the radio off. I kept replaying what I had seen in my head and nothing added up. What would make an old man attack someone like that? Alzheimer's did not turn people violent, and most certainly did not turn them into cannibals. I was so lost in thought I barely felt my cell phone vibrating. It was Ellie. I snapped it open, not sure of what I was going to tell her. "Hey, you!"

"Hey, John. Just wanted to touch base with you. I'm still at Cost Go right now and have picked up a lot of things, is there anything else you think we need.?"

"Off the top of my head, just extra batteries for the flashlights and the toys, some extra medicine stuff like aspirin and baby cold medicines for Jakey." My voice shook a little as I spoke to her.

"Are you sure? That seems like a lot." Ellie seemed skeptical and reluctant to spend so much."

"Trust me, I'd rather be on the safe side. Look at it this way, you won't have to go shopping for a while." I tried to be humorous, but I kept seeing that old man attacking that poor woman. Jesus, what the hell?

"All right." Ellie said. "I'll see you at home."

A thought occurred to me. "I may be home a little later, I want to make a couple of stops."

"Right. Pizza okay for dinner?"

"Sure."

"Bye now,"

"Bye."

I looked to see where I was and I realized that I needed to get over quickly to catch the interstate. I had three stops to make, and would need to move fast to get home in time for dinner. As I merged on the interstate, I noticed there was a lot of traffic leaving the city, but that seemed normal. It was a Friday, and people generally left the city for relatives and other places. I caught the ramp to another highway, and moved towards the street I needed. I briefly hoped that I would be able to get through the traffic quickly, but one never knew.

My first stop was a little shop tucked away behind a gas station. It had two floors, and the first floorwas devoted to fishing gear. Anything you needed for fishing except boats could be found there. I wasn't interested in fishing gear, I needed what was on the second floor. I went up and found the place to be slightly more crowded than usual. Racks of rifles and shotguns lined a display behind the counter, which held a wide variety of handguns. As I worked my way to the back of the store, I caught snippets of conversation.

"Heard its spread to three cities now…"

"What's this I hear about London and dead people?"

"What's the damn government gonna do, set up another committee?"

"Can we waive the waiting period?"

I stopped in front of the reloading supplies and looked around. Guns, I didn't need, but ammo was another story. I grabbed two cans of powder, two boxes of primers, and box of 1000 180gr HP 40 cal bullets. I worked the supplies over to the counter and waited for a salesman to notice me.

An older gentleman came by and asked me if I found everything I was looking for.

"Sure did. You guys are doing a good business these days?"

His eyes glanced into mine briefly. "Never seen nothing like it. Something's got folks jittery."

"Yeah, something." I said, lamely.

"Follow yer gut, I always say." said the old man, grabbing a couple of bags for my purchase.

I winced inwardly. What if your guts were being ripped out? Chase after the bastard who did the ripping?

I signed the receipt and headed out to the car. As I was putting the supplies into the trunk, I noticed several more cars pull into the parking lot. Maybe we all are following our gut this time.

I pulled back onto the interstate and headed south. I needed to make another stop before I headed home, and I wanted to make as much time as possible. So I ramped it up to 80 and rocketed down the highway. The main mess of traffic had left at the interstate junction, and only people heading downstate or across the state were on the road. I finally decided to turn the radio on.

"*In world news today, there is a state of emergency in Africa. The Enillo Virus has already claimed 3,000,000 lives, and more are expected to drop as countries which up till now have been focused on military matters, now turn their attention to this growing crisis. In Europe, Spain and Portugal have closed their borders, and England is no longer allowing any international flights to land. Thousands of French have fled the country to the north, hoping to cross the English Channel to perceived safety. French officials have denied reports that Paris is being overrun with infected persons, but several videos have surfaced on the internet. The grimmest scenes are filmed, posted on the internet and viewers are cautioned as they are highly graphic. In Asia, China and North Korea have officially closed their borders, and North Korea has issued a statement that any foreigners will be shot trying to cross into their country. President Trottman is expected to address the United States this evening. In business news, the stock market took a sharp turn as investors began a big late afternoon sell off. Gary?*"

I switched the radio off. What the hell was going on? Was the Enillo Virus as bad as all that? I began to worry about Ellie. She worked at a hospital in the city and would have to go to work tomorrow. If viruses hit the US, she'd be right in the crosshairs.

Lost in my reverie, I nearly missed the exit. A truck was pulled over to the side of the road and blocked my view of the sign nearly before it was too late. The driver was sitting behind the wheel, but as I flashed past he raised a hand to the window. I waved back and zipped down the exit.

At my next stop, I decided to buy ammo directly, and to hell with the cost. I grabbed up all of the hunting ammo they had for the 30 carbine, and the target stuff too. I left two boxes on the shelf, figuring to be kind if anyone came after me looking for it. I noticed the shelves were empty of .223 ammo and 5.54x39 ammo.

The clerk's eyes didn't even flicker when I brought the ammo to him. "Will that be all?" he asked, reaching for my credit card.

I tried to make small talk. "Selling a lot of ammo these days?"

He smiled. "Quite a bit. Must be a competition or something coming up."

"Could be." I said. "Could you double bag that, I'd hate to have it spill all over the parking lot.

"Sure."

I thanked him and took the ammo to my trunk. As I backed out of my spot, I noticed an older employee come to the door with a sign that read "Cash only for sales, please." I thanked God for my timely purchase and headed back to the road. One more stop and I would head home. I turned the radio back on.

"...reports are coming in from Africa that infected people are reportedly falling into deep comas, then reviving and getting up. They are allegedly attacking anyone around them, except for other victims. We have heard reports of horrific violence, and the entire continent seems to be on the verge of collapse. For exclusive videos and uploads, please visit our website for the latest information."

I turned the radio off as I sped down the back roads to the last gun shop I wanted to visit. I felt an almost overwhelming urge to get back home as quickly as possible. Every warning bell I had was clanging as loudly as possible, that if I did not take this seriously, there would be no second chance.

I stopped at the gun shop which happened to be on my route home. It was more crowded than the others, and several people were trying to buy more guns than they had money for. One guy, who came in to sell his gun, received four offers from other customers. I watched as two men nearly got into a fight over an AR that one wanted to see and other wanted to buy right then. Everything was selling, from .22 pistols to big 7mm Magnum rifles. Ammo was flying off the shelves, and I was relieved when I saw that no one had picked up the 30 Carbine ammo yet. Pays to have an unusual caliber gun, I thought.

I signaled man behind the counter who was waiting for a customer to make up his mind on shotguns.

"Can I help you?" He asked. I noticed he was wearing a .45 on his hip. Prudent, I thought.

"I need to get some .30 carbine ammo." I said.

"Right. You want it by the box, or case?" He asked, reaching behind him.

I was surprised. "You have cases?"

"Sure thing. Cheaper to buy a case then sell it piecemeal, but we just got an order in yesterday, so if you want a whole case, I'll sell it to you discounted. Bigger discount if you pay cash."

"Deal." I said, reaching for my checkbook. I kept emergency money there, and something told me this was definitely an emergency.

"Let me go get it." He walked off to a back room that had a large padlock on it. As the door opened, I could see stacks of various ammo in a wide range of calibers. Bet a lot of people would like to see that room, I thought.

As I finally headed home, I thought about what I had seen and heard. I thought about what I had in the trunk and hoped to God I was wrong. If I was, I was going to have a hell of a shooting day at the range, the next time I got out. If not, well, I did what I could to protect my family. I just wish I had a clue as to what I was protecting against. If the virus was airborne, there was little I could do. If it was spread by contact, that was something else.

A raindrop hit my windshield and I looked at the darkening sky. Storm. Great. Maybe I'll get home before it hits. With any luck, it'll all blow over.

3

"...in related news, the Enillo Virus has claimed millions of lives worldwide, and scattered reports of victims returning from the comatose state and attacking their caregivers are on the rise. In Africa, a veritable army of infected people are slowly marching their way across the continent, ravaging every village and city they come across. Their numbers seem to swell from each attack, and nations across the globe are scrambling to counter what many have called the worst crisis mankind has ever faced. Infected individuals seem to be impervious to pain or even what some might consider debilitating injuries. New reports coming in from New York and Chicago and Los Angeles indicate a heavy population of infected individuals. Official reports are debunking the somewhat popular notion that the dead have come back to life. YouTube videos abound on the internet, and officials warn self-styled "Zombie Hunters" that they will be prosecuted within the fullest extent of the law. Anyone caught looting will also be prosecuted. Individuals are urged to stay in their homes and avoid all contact with infected individuals. They are to be considered extremely dangerous. If a loved one or family member exhibits any symptoms of the virus, they are to be isolated immediately, and the family is to place a white cloth on their mailboxes to alert emergency personnel to the presence of another victim."

I switched off the television and looked out my front window. I could see three houses with white towels on their mailboxes, and I wondered how many more will there be? Will there come a time when all the houses have white flags on them? If your house doesn't have a white flag, will the officials think you're immune and want to take you away for testing? Who knew?

The last week was a blur. I went to work and tried to keep things as normal as I could, but the kids were scared. Some were talking about how their mom or dad or sister was sick, and they didn't know what to do. Many of my students were absent, their parents taking them to relatives in Mexico or other states, trying to get away from the large population center of Chicago. I worried about my brother, who lived downtown with his family, but I spoke with him the other day and he seemed fine. I called my parents in Virginia, but was only able to leave a message. Their house was fairly isolated, and my father was an ex-marine, so I figured they would be all right.

Two days ago, the governor of the state called for a suspension of attendance of public schools, the thought being that if a student were infected, he could easily spread it to many families due to the close nature of classrooms. For once the governor actually had a decent idea. So for the last two days I have been busy reloading ammunition, cleaning my guns, and stocking up on foodstuffs. Pickings were getting a little slim at the grocery store, as people began to see the wisdom of hunkering down and waiting out the storm.

I was very grateful Ellie had managed to get to the store before the real storm of public awareness hit, and I managed to make a few runs myself. I had gone to the bank and withdrew as much as I could, figuring to replace it should the worst pass. I didn't want to be caught up short without cash, and yesterday they announced on the news that credit cards are going to be suspended to try to prevent people from going overboard and end up losing everything when the crisis passed. I bought everything I could think of, and my basement was pretty well stocked. I was going to feel like a class A fool if this thing blew over quickly, but the little voice in the back of my head said we were in for a rough ride.

Ellie was working today, and since I was home, I was doing the house thing with Jacob. He was such a little joy to have around. All smiles and not a worry in the world. His eyes, the little "chocolate browns", as Ellie liked to call them just sparkled and when he looked at you it was if he was saying "I trust you with my world." More than once I found myself just looking at him for a long time, wondering how in the hell I got so lucky.

Jake was playing in the living room when I got a call from Ellie.

"John?"

"Yeah, babe. What's up?" I moved over to the kitchen table so I could keep an eye on our little one. He couldn't crawl yet, but he was pretty good at a military crawl and rolling got him into trouble more times than not.

"Not a whole lot. We've been seeing a lot of patients today, and I might be later than usual." Ellie sounded nervous.

"All right, I'll feed Jake and get him bathed." I tried to sound nonchalant, but inwardly my concern just skyrocketed.

"Thanks. And John?"

"Yeah, babe?"

"Are your toys loaded?" Ellie asked.

That sent my concern into the stratosphere. Ellie never asked about my guns, letting me have my little hobby as long as didn't advertise it and kept my guns in a safe away from Jake. "Not yet, why?" I asked.

"You might want to think about having them handy." Ellie said cryptically.

"Ellie, what is going on?" I said, more forcefully than I intended.

"John, just do it. Please. There's more to this virus than people have been told." Ellie said. "I gotta go, they're paging me to the OR. Love you!"

"Love you, too." I said, but the line had already cut out.

I wondered what the hell was going on, but I didn't question Ellie. She had sources of information that did not have anything to do with the media. The cops that brought the victims in to the EMT's that treated them at the scene to the victims themselves. Ellie often knew days before anyone else about things that were happening. She knew about a tuberculosis outbreak three days before the news reported it. But in all our years together, she had never told me to load my guns and have them handy. I decided maybe this was the event that was prickling my senses

I went down to the basement, after putting Jake in the Pack 'n Play and putting on a baby video for him. Gotta love the electronic baby-sitter. I went down to my secret room, an area which was an expanded crawl space under the garage. It was large enough to stand in, and it was there that I had my gun safe and reloading equipment, and various other supplies and things. A casual glance would never reveal that there was anything there at all. Since no one ever expected there to be any usable space under a garage, if at all, it was the perfect hiding place. So I went down there and surveyed what I had and what I might need.

I had a modest firearm collection, around ten handguns and rifles. I didn't have any theme to my collection, just bought what I wanted at the time, selling it when I wanted something else. I also had a few guns inherited from my Grandfather, so that added a bit. I had played at Cowboy Action Shooting for a while, owning a couple of six-guns, a lever-gun, and a pump shotgun. After that I got into IDPA, which was a lot less equipment oriented, and owned a Springfield XD in .40 and a SIG P226 in .40 caliber as well. I reloaded for a number of calibers, and lately had been reloading for .40 S&W. On the rifle front I had an old Enfield No4 MkI, and a couple of .22's. I had an Auto-Ordnance M1 Carbine replica that I had recently purchased, this was the one I had stocked up on ammo for. I had three additional 15-round magazines and two 30-round magazines for the little carbine, so that gave me 105 rounds without needing to reload a single mag. Thanks to the case and extra boxes I bought, I had 2000 rounds of ammo for the M1.

I took the two semi-auto pistols and grabbed all the extra magazines I owned for each. I grabbed four boxes of ammo and put all of this in a little backpack I had. I put all the magazines for the carbine in the bag, and put in three boxes of ammo for it. I put a box of .22 ammo in the bag and grabbed the carbine and one of the .22 rifles. At the last minute, I threw in a box of .380 ammo, and the extra clip for the Walther PPK.

Slinging the now very heavy backpack on my shoulder, I ran upstairs. I checked on Jake and went into the office. I needed to think about what I was doing and where would be the best placement for armament. My IDPA days were serving me well at this point. I was looking at my home with new eyes. Where were the weaknesses, where were the bottlenecks? Where was the best place to store a gun for easy access? Do I shore up the windows, or do I block the stairwells? If I was determined to get in, what would stop me?

I sat at the desk and decided that the best way to ensure a forceful response to a crisis was to be armed at all times. I loaded my SIG and put on my competition holster. I placed spare magazines in the kitchen and in the front room for the gun. I went back and forth as to what rifle I wanted on the ground floor, and decided on the .22, figuring if things got bad on the ground floor, I wanted superior firepower on my back up locations, which was my basement and my bedroom. The basement had the shotguns and the Enfield, so anything coming after me down there was going to earn it. I loaded the magazines for the M1Carbine and inserted a 30-round clip into the gun. Best to start off with a hail of withering fire, as my dad used to say. I loaded the .22 next, having only two magazines for it, but each magazine held 25 rounds, so I did not feel under gunned. The .22 rifle I had was a GSG-5, an MP5-looking .22. Mostly for plinking, but as I loaded the hollow points, I found myself hoping it would be enough. I placed the rifle on the top shelf of the pantry, figuring it was the most central location and gave me access to the hallway and basement stairs if needed.

I took the XD and carbine and brought those upstairs, placing the pistol on a shelf in the hallway linen closet. The door of the linen closet swung outward, effectively blocking the hallway if needed, but only as a temporary measure while the pistol was retrieved. I placed the two extra magazines on the dresser near the door of my bedroom and two more in the master bathroom; the final stand, if it came to it. I prayed it never did, but I did the best I could think of.

I went back downstairs and looked at my doors and windows. If I had to hole up here, how would I block them? What would I use? I figured the first floorbeing brick was very comforting, and I needed to think of some way to board up my windows and doors. I needed to go to the home improvement store.

I packed up Jacob and started out to the store. Immediately leaving my driveway, I felt something was wrong. It was in the air, something out of kilter with the world. It didn't feel bad or scary, but your senses were on alert. Maybe I was just reacting to what Ellie had told me, but as I drove through my neighborhood, I began to see signs that things were not right. Doors to some homes were open, and there was a large stain on the porch of another home, as if something had been killed there. I saw several families packing as if to leave on vacation, putting as much in their cars as they dared. In each case, the mailbox had a white flag on it. Were they taking their sick with them? I couldn't tell, and I really didn't want to stop and ask. One house had the garage door wide open, belongings scattered around, and the door to the house open, as if they just ran in the middle of packing up the car. I wondered if the city was the same way. If this virus was that bad, was anywhere safe? Were these people just running to bigger problems?

I thought about these things as I made my way to the home improvement store. There were a lot of cars on the road, and many of the ones I saw had a lot of belongings in them.

Turning onto the major road, I was stunned at the amount of traffic. At this time of day, there should not have been the hundreds of cars I saw. I joined the southbound lane and noticed that the northbound lane was heading south as well. Everyone was heading south. I began to wonder what the hell had happened to the city, and whether or not my brother was safe. Every business along the road was closed, and I seriously doubted I was going to find any store open. As I slowly passed a parking lot, I saw two men arguing over a water jug, and just as they passed out of my line of sight, I saw one man take a swing at the other man's head. People were going nuts.

I pulled off the main road into the drive of the home improvement store, and I immediately saw it was the wrong thing to do. The store was a madhouse, with people rushing in and rushing out, grabbing supplies from each other and racing off without tying down their loads. There was no way I was bringing Jacob into that mess, even being armed as I was. I had forgotten to take off my gun when I went out, so my SIG was still with me, under my coat. I pulled out of the parking lot, narrowly missing an elderly woman rushing out with what looked like fifty feet of heavy chain. Weird.

I headed west to a street that would take me to a road back north, and it was packed as well. It took me twenty-five minutes to go two miles, and everyone was on edge. I decided to get off the main road and head through the subdivisions and get home that way. I wound my way through the first subdivision, noting once again the signs of hurried leaving. Jake was starting to act up, not liking being in his car seat for any length of time. I reached around, trying to find his binky, and managed to poke him in the eye while I searched. Naturally, he hated that, and let me know it. Good set of lungs on that little guy. I looked back and found his binky between his legs, so I grabbed it and placed it in his mouth.

WHAM! The car jerked and slewed sideways, and I fought to control the vehicle as I brought it to a stop. I checked my rear view mirror and saw a body lying in the road. *Oh God, Oh God, No, no, no, no, no....not good at all.* I got out of the car and ran back to the body, a middle-aged man who was lying on his face in the street. "Help!" I yelled, hoping someone in the houses would hear me. "Somebody call 911!" I yelled to the unresponsive houses. I kneeled down and turned the man over, hoping he was still alive. I immediately stepped back, as the man had a gaping hole where his throat used to be. His shirt was covered in dried blood, and his face had dried blood all around the mouth. His eyes were closed, as if he was sleeping, and his left leg looked broken at the ankle. What the hell was this? Did I run over a dead body in the road? If I had, how the hell could he be there without any police or ambulance? I started to walk back to the car, and I saw another man approaching the vehicle from the passenger side. I shouted at him.

"Hey! Hey, buddy!" He looked at me and starting walking towards me, his eyes fixed on me. Something wasn't right. He opened his mouth, and instead of saying hi, he let out this hideous groan, like he was in serious pain. I stepped back and he raised his hands towards me, as if he wanted to grab me. I backed up and placed my hand on my gun. "Hey, pal, you better back off. What's the matter with you?"

The man didn't answer, he just let out another groan, and lunged for me. I backed up and drew my gun, hoping the sight of the weapon would stop the guy. I circled to the left away from the car and the guy never even acknowledged the gun. He followed my movements and I could see his nose flaring, as if he was smelling me. For a brief second my mind flashed to the old man I watched tear apart his caretaker.

I raised the gun and tried one more time. "Mister, if you do not stop I *will* shoot you." I was nearly shouting at this time.

No response. He just kept coming. I thought for a second to just wound him, but nobody can shoot like that. I lined up his chest in my sights and pulled the trigger.

The shot seemed unnaturally loud in the subdivision, and struck the man squarely in the chest. The .40 caliber slug knocked him backwards and onto his back. Exhaling heavily, my breath caught as I watched in horror while the man slowly scrambled to his feet and come at me again.

Thinking I must have hit something in his clothes that stopped the bullet, I took careful aim this time at his chest and fired another round. The man staggered backwards a few steps, but managed to stay on his feet. I could see the holes in his shirt, and they were both centered on his heart. No blood came out, nothing. It was like the man was already dead, but how the hell could he be walking around? I heard another groan as the man came at me for a third time. I raised my aim and fired a shot that entered his right eye, exploding brains and dark matter out the back of his head. The man dropped instantly and was still. My brain spun for a moment. A noise snapped me out of my reverie, and I looked up in time to see the man I had initially hit with my car shuffling up to me. He moved slowly, and I could see his foot was broken as he dragged it along the ground. His leg bone clicked as it hit the ground in his advance. A rasping gargle came out of his ruined throat as he reached for me with one hand, the other hanging loosely at his side.

I didn't waste time with any more body shots. I centered my sights on his face and fired once, the bullet smashing through his nasal cavity and erupting out the back of his head. The man's head snapped impossibly far back, largely due to the fact that he was missing half his throat. Overbalanced, the man fell straight back like a tree falling and smacked onto the road.

I took a step back, holstered my gun and looked around me. Two men were down, killed by my gun. But were they killed by me? Or were they already dead? Ordinarily that would be a crazy thought, but I had just seen for myself a man rise after being hit by a car and having his throat torn open. Did the virus do this? Were all those people who were reported as "comatose" actually dead, and coming back to life? Way too many questions and this was not the place to think about it. I could see other people starting to come from houses and around buildings, attracted to the noise I made. By the way they were walking and the groans I was starting to hear, no one living came to investigate, which I think scared me worse than anything else. Was this whole area just dead? I needed to get out of here and get home. I turned back to the car just in time to see a teenager clawing at the back window, trying to get in at Jacob. Jacob was screaming at the noise I had made, and his screams must have attracted this nightmare. The teen was grayish in color, and his face was ripped up. One of his cheeks was torn open, giving him a horrific leer. That face was pressed against the back window, and I could see the teeth working, wanting to get in and tear at Jake's tender skin.

Something in me snapped. I ran over behind the teen, grabbing him by the scruff of his neck and the belt that held up his sagging pants. I screamed "NO!" as I bodily lifted teen and slammed him down head first into the pavement. His head cracked and dark fluid began leaking out. I didn't wait to see if he was dead. I drew my gun again and fired eight shots rapidly into his head, splattering brains and bone and everything else all over the road. Bullets skipped off as they ricocheted off the road. The slide on my gun locked open, indicating an empty gun, and still I pulled on the trigger. I was breathing heavily, and couldn't see very well. I heard noises around me, but nothing registered. I didn't want this thing dead, I wanted it destroyed.

Jacob's crying penetrated my fog, and I managed to look around. At least ten more people were coming at me, and I did not have any more rounds. Time to go. I ran to the driver's side of the car, jumped in and started the engine just as another one came at my door. It was a housewife in a robe, and the robe was open to reveal a ripped-open stomach cavity. What horrified me was her organs were missing. I could see her backbone as her bloodied hands pounded on my window. That was a close-up I didn't need.

I started the engine and pulled away, bouncing another woman off my fender and swerving to avoid three more people. When I cleared the area, I looked back and saw a mob of about twenty slowly following my car. To my horror, I saw a young woman run out of her house, waving her hands and trying to get my attention. She didn't notice how close the mob was. They reached her quickly and she was dragged back screaming as fetid mouths began to tear chunks of flesh from her arms. She was swallowed up and taken down by the crowd, and I could see just a single foot drumming the ground for a second, then she was still. It was like watching a pack of hyenas kill an animal. I shook my head and gunned the engine, trying to get out as fast as I could. If I had gone back, I would be dead and so would Jake. *Please forgive me*, I prayed, wondering what kind of God I was praying to, and wondering if prayer would ever matter again.

I drove home without incident, paying very careful attention to the road and side streets. There were several cars on the road that looked like they had been abandoned, at least I could not see anyone in the cars. I moved through my neighborhood without incident, although I swear I could see something moving in the backyard of the guy who lived at the end of the block. I pulled into my garage and quickly closed the door. I pulled a now-sleeping Jacob from his car seat and moved him quickly inside. I carried him upstairs and laid him in his crib, then went downstairs to close the blinds and drapes on the ground floor. I didn't want to announce my presence to anything unfriendly, not until I had taken some precautions. As I closed my front drapes, I noticed a dark figure moving down the street towards my house. My heart skipped as I thought, *He knows someone's here.* I ran to my ammo store and reloaded the empty magazine in my SIG. I went to the pantry and retrieved the .22, checking the magazine and making sure a round was in the chamber. I went back to the window and surreptitiously watched the dark figure slowly become more recognizable. It was a man, roughly my age, limping slowly down the middle of the street. His mouth hung open and his hands were swinging at his sides. He walked with an almost hypnotic gait, edging ever closer to my house.

Suddenly, Jake started crying. I ran to his room and picked him up, trying to get him to go back to sleep. His cries were unusually loud, and as I peeked out the window I saw the man move closer and closer to the house.

"Please, baby, please be quiet." I whispered as I bounced Jake gently. "Sleepy time, daddy's here." I wondered if he had a nightmare about that horrible face trying to get through the back window of the car.

I looked out again and the man was closer, his head cocked to the side as if he was locking in on my home. Christ, if he started pounding on the doors he was going to attract more of them.

"Jakey, sleep honey, sleep." I tried to sound as calm as possible, but an edge was getting into my voice. *We're so dead.* I thought.

Jake finally quieted down to subdued whimpering and I snuck a look outside. As the dead man came within ten yards of the front of my house, out of the east came a kid on a bike, pedaling like the very demons of hell were on his tail. He swerved away from the corpse on the street and headed west, dodging an outstretched hand and groaning mouth. The corpse turned to follow the biker, completely losing interest in my house. I nearly fell over in relief.

That was interesting. They follow what they want until distracted, then they follow that. Might be useful to remember.

I stayed at the window, looking out and managed to see what the kid on the bike was running from. A crowd of about twenty of those things came shambling down the street, in various states of decay and disrepair. Several had large amounts of blood down the front of their clothing, others were missing fingers and eyes and pieces of flesh. One particularly gruesome specimen had his lower jaw ripped off, and his tongue lolled around in the air under his face. Where were they all coming from? Why wasn't the news reporting this? I had to resist the urge to run out and hose down the mob. I knew I would be overwhelmed and killed, and what would happen to Jake then? No, caution was better. Besides, I needed to think about reinforcing my windows.

Where was I going to find enough wood to build a barrier? I certainly was not going back to the home improvement store, and I sure wasn't going to leave Jacob. What to do? I pondered this as I looked out my back window at the bike path that ran along the power line easement behind my house. The condominiums across the way looked peaceful enough, but part of me wondered what nightmares awaited in the halls. I hoped I would never have to find out. For a moment I considered my fence as a source of lumber, but dismissed that as foolish. I might need that seven-foot barrier if for nothing more than to be able to move unseen in my yard. I was never so glad that I insisted on reinforced support posts than I was right now.

My eyes fell on my porch, and all of a sudden I had a flash of inspiration. My porch was made of two by sixes of various lengths. All the wood I needed was right there. I just had to pull it up and bring it in. I ran downstairs and grabbed my drill, pausing to put the extra battery in the charger. Thankfully, I had made the deck with screws, so I just needed to back out the screws and pull the boards up. I figured I had only an hour before Jake woke up, so I needed to move quickly.

I brought my .22 outside with me and slung it across my back. I needed to move all the stuff off the deck first, and do it quietly, since I wasn't ready to withstand a siege. I moved the chairs to the fence, giving myself firing positions if I needed them. The back of my property dropped off four feet. The table I moved to the fence door, and jammed it into the ground. The door opened outward, and I needed to be able to block it if got pulled open. I hoped it never came to that, but then the dead seemed to be walking, so here we are.

As I went back to my porch to take off some boards, I was struck by how quiet it was. My house was in the landing pattern of the nearby airport, so there was usually a plane or three overhead. I listened to the wind and could faintly hear distant sounds: intermittent pops that I figured was gunfire, a groan or two, and the screeching of tires. I hoped all the noise would distract any infected from whatever noise I made.

The first few boards came off easily with no serious sound. I removed about three feet of boards and brought them into the house. The hard part was going to be cutting them, but I had hand saws for that. As I placed the boards in the house, I noticed the curtains move on my neighbor's house. As I straightened up, the curtain was pulled aside and I saw my neighbor's daughter Erica in the window. She waved at me and I waved back, happy to see another person in this crazy world. All of a sudden she was jerked back and the curtain was shoved forward. I hoped she was okay. I didn't hear any screams, and so I figured it was just her parents trying not to attract attention to their house. They were just as scared as I was.

I went inside and heard some happy baby noises coming from upstairs. After I put the rifle back, I went up and found Jacob sitting up in his crib, playing with his blanket. He smiled a huge smile when he saw me, apparently no worse the wear for the experience we had over the afternoon. I picked him up and changed him, able for a brief second to forget the world and the crisis we seemed to be in. I took him downstairs to the basement, transferring his pack 'n play. I went back upstairs and measured the windows, figuring on using the deck screws to fasten the boards to the window frames. I went back down and began cutting boards. For whatever reason, Jake thought this was fascinating, and smiled and laughed the whole time I was cutting boards.

I took him back upstairs, and brought up the boards I had cut. I figured only to cover the front windows at this time, since they were the weakest point of entry, and there were only two of them. The good news was there was a hedge in front of the windows, and my house was raised off the ground by several inches, so direct access was difficult. It could be done, but not easily. I decided to cover up the windows but leave the top six inches open to let in light and give me a firing opening.

If I needed to close the whole thing, I could just drop the drapes.

I was just attaching the last board when the phone rang. It was Ellie.

"John?"

"Hey, Babe!" I said, trying to sound cheerful, in spite of all that had happened today.

"How are you doing?" She sounded like here was something seriously wrong.

"I'm fine." I said, moving over to where Jacob was.

"Have you been watching the news?" Ellie asked.

"Actually I've been a little busy." I understated things, since I didn't want her to worry.

Ellie sounded exhausted. "Just to let you know, whatever you hear on the news about this crisis being localized and that the government is handling things, is a flat out lie."

I actually wasn't so shocked by this, giving what I had been through. "What are you talking about?"

Ellie sighed and told me. "We have been working non-stop on infected people. They don't go into comas, they die. They die and then they come back. The morgue is a nightmare, full of walking dead and they are trying to get out. Several patients who didn't get transferred in time came back and attacked staff members. John, I watched my shift boss get eaten by two patients. Eaten!" Ellie sounded more panicked. "Jesus, God, what the hell?"

I didn't know what to say, so I was quiet for a minute. I was having a hard enough time wrapping my head around the events of the day to really hear what Ellie was telling me. Ellie seemed to shake herself and asked me "Did you do what I asked, earlier?"

I told her, yes, and I went into detail about my preparations, about where I had guns and ammo, and the boarding of the windows.

"They're that far south, are they?" Ellie asked.

"What do you mean?"

Ellie sighed again. "We had a Chicago cop in here and he said the city was complete anarchy. Thousands of those things were in the streets, attacking anyone they saw, and transferring the virus. If they aren't killed, eventually they become one of them. Sometimes it's fast, sometimes it's slow, and it all depends on the individual. The cop said they can only be killed by destroying the brain."

"I know." I said inadvertently.

Ellie paused. "How do you know?"

I told her about my little excursion, not leaving out any detail. I figured I would catch nine kinds of hell, but she just was quiet and then said, "Thank you for saving my baby."

I tried to be reassuring with a little false bravado. "Any zombie coming after him has to go through me first, and hell hasn't made a zombie yet to match me."

Ellie began to cry, and I immediately regretted my words. "I'm sorry babe, I know this is serious."

Ellie managed to bring herself together, and asked me where Jakey was. "He's over on the floor, trying to figure out why he can't put a ball that's bigger than his head in his mouth."

"Can I talk to him?"

"Sure." I brought the phone over to Jake and held it to his ear. I could hear his mother speaking to him, and he smiled as he recognized his mother's voice. He squealed and laughed, and I could hear Ellie say how much she loved him and she would watch over him. That was odd.

I brought the phone back to me and said, "Hey, I'm back, he rolled away."

Ellie was crying again. "John?"

"Yeah?"

"Take good care of my baby, please.?"

"Sure thing. What's going on? When are you coming home?"

Ellie paused. "I'm not."

"What? What are you saying? Why aren't you coming home? If things are that bad, you need to get out of there and come home." I was getting very concerned.

"John, please listen to me." Ellie begged.

"Okay." I said suddenly worried.

"I've been infected with the virus."

My world suddenly crashed. The sinking feeling I had in my gut became a hole in my chest. My heart sank and I could not focus. I started breathing heavily and I nearly dropped the phone.

"John? Please talk to me." Ellie said. "I need you to talk to me."

"Jesus, no, Ellie. Not you. Please not you." I started to choke up, cursing a God that would do this to my family. "How?"

"An accident. An infected patient was brought in, and he hemorrhaged in the OR. Two of us got blood in our eyes."

All I could do was shake my head. "No, no, no, God, please, no."

"John!" Ellie cried. "I need you to strong for me. I need you to take care of Jake for me. Please!"

"I'll come get you." I said, knowing deep down it would be suicide. "Just wait and I'll come get you." I could barely talk.

"No, John. Please don't. This is hard enough as it is. If I know you and Jake are safe, it will make things easier. Please don't come for me. I don't want you infected. Promise me, John, please."

Watching Jake with tears in my eyes, I promised my wife I would not come to her rescue. "I won't. You're right."

"Thank you, John." Elli sounded relieved. "John?"

"Yeah, babe?"

"Could we just talk? The phones have been going in and out and I don't know how much time I have." Ellie sounded like she did when we first started dating. My eyes watered up again, and I almost couldn't talk.

"Sure, babe. Sure."

So Ellie and I talked for the next hour about everything we had done, all of our happy memories, our regrets at not being able to do the things we wanted to do. I must have told her I loved her a thousand times, and she did the same. I brought the phone over to Jake again, and with the phone on the floor, I tickled Jake so his mother would have a memory of her baby laughing as she went into the long night. I asked her about what was going to happen and she told me that the doctors have been giving massive doses of morphine to anyone who was infected so they would die peacefully. I found this to be of some comfort, morbid as it seemed.

Suddenly the phone started to have static and Ellie and I realized we did not have much time left.

"John, please remember me as I was." Ellie asked

"Of course," I said. "Nothing else."

"Take care of my baby."

"He'll grow into a fine man." I said, my voice catching.

"Just like his daddy." Ellie said, starting to cry again.

The phone buzzed again and for a second I thought I lost her. "Ellie? Ellie?"

"I'm here, John. We may as well stop, as I'm not feeling well, and I need to go see the doctor."

"I don't know if I can do this without you, babe." I cried, trying to hold back my sobs.

"John, be strong. You're much tougher than you give yourself credit for." Ellie tried to console me, but it was hard. "Jake needs you."

That brought me back into focus. "I miss you already." I said.

"Me, too." She said.

I didn't know what else to say, except, "I promise you, Jake will survive this. On my life, he *will* survive this."

Ellie cried again. "Thank you, John. I love you."

"I love you, too, babe."

"Give Jakey a hug for me."

"Will do. Ellie?"

"Yes, John?"

"Thanks for all the joy you've given me."

"My pleasure, sweetheart. Good bye, John. Love you."

"Love you." I started crying again. "I'll see you again."

"Promise?" She asked, crying herself.

"Promise." I said, and I meant it with all my heart.

The line crackled once, and went dead.

With that, I never saw my wife alive again. I went over to where Jake was, sat down, and just started crying.

4

For the next week I was on auto-pilot. I woke up, I fed Jake, I changed his diapers, I ate, and I went back to sleep. I couldn't think of anything past what I was immediately doing and Jake's needs. I didn't try to go anywhere, and I didn't even turn on the news. I was in a fog, lost in a pit of depression and self-pity. All I could ask was why? Why did this have to happen? Why did I have to lose my wife? Why did Jake have to lose his mother? That depressed me a lot, that eventually Jakey will not remember his mother in a little while. I was all he had.

I was all he had. That thought began to stick into my head and I began to realize that I *was* all Jake had. I was all that kept him alive, all that prevented him from maybe turning into one of those things. I remembered a line from a very good movie once, and it stuck in my thoughts, so much so that I wrote it on a piece of paper and placed in on my fridge so I would never forget its truth. Very simple and more poignant than ever these days. "Get busy living, or get busy dying." I thought about Jake and remembered my promise to his mother. Time to get busy living.

I turned on the computer and fired up the internet. I was stunned at what I had missed over the past week. Headlines of "The Dead are Walking" and "Dead Consume Living" were all over the place. Talking heads were discussing the end of mankind and things like that. One of the sites had a list of cities to avoid, as the number of walking dead far outnumbered the living. People were in a state of panic, and martial law had to be declared. Videos were all over the net of people being attacked by mobs of zombies. One had a video of an attack, then the cameraman was attacked and the last shot of the video was of a mess of blood on the ground as two bloody feet slowly walked away.

Realizing I could be overwhelmed with information and none of it useful, I decided that if I was to survive this, I needed to know what I was up against. I spent the next three hours learning about the virus, how it was spread, how long it took to incubate, what the symptoms were. I read survivor stories and got bits of information from there. I learned that the infected victims hearing and smell seemed to be heightened, while their sight remained normal. I learned that they weren't particularly fast, and were extremely limited in problem solving. I watched a video of a zombie trapped in a small room because it couldn't figure out where the door was, let alone work the knob. I began to wonder how in the world everything had gotten to be such a mess, with an enemy that was pretty much stupid.

I got my answer a lot closer to home than I intended. While I was on the computer, I happened to see a man out on the bike trail behind my house. He was walking on the trail when another man came out from between the garages by the condominiums. The second man walked slowly and directly at the first man. The walker held a baseball bat and waited for the first man to arrive. The second man was an older gentleman who clearly was infected. His skin had a grayish pallor, and he groaned into the wind. The walker waited until the zombie was close enough, then struck him on the shoulder, clearly breaking his arm. The zombie didn't even slow down and barreled into the walker, knocking him down and biting whatever her could reach. The first man screamed and kicked shoved the zombie off, losing his hold on his bat. The zombie took repeated kicks to the face with no effect, and continued to bite and tear at the walker's legs. The man screamed again and kicked with his feet, dislodging the zombie and scrambling backwards. The zombie rolled up and grabbed the man's leg again, dragging him back within biting range. The walker's legs and hands were bloody from bites, and he was obviously weakening. But he gave one more effort and threw the zombie off of him. The walker got to his feet and stumbled away, pursued by his attacker. The encounter had attracted the attention of another zombie, a woman with a torn shirt, who came out of a doorway, saw the walker, and started after him. I thought two things at this point. One was the man who was bitten was going to die anyway and become a zombie, and two, the zombies never stopped coming. They didn't feel pain, they didn't do anything but attack, attack, attack. My own experience was testimony to that.

Part of me wondered why I didn't try to help the man with the bat, but as I was learning from the internet, the less attention you attracted to yourself the better. I was grateful I had covered the front windows with boards. They kept things out and let me move about my house without fear of being seen from the street. They likely muffled sounds as well. I was probably going to have to board up the back windows at some point, but for now the light was nice to have.

I checked on Jake and he was happily playing with some blocks, smacking them together and startling himself with the sounds he could make. I went back to the internet and surfed a few boards, taking in some survivor stories and tips on living on your own. I was interested in the groups that talked about "bug-out-bags" and what they needed for those leaving in a hurry. That seemed like a good idea, so I learned about that for a bit. I watched a few more videos, and I was struck by how many people made so many mistakes. If you kept your head, didn't take chances you didn't need to, didn't do anything stupid, and kept your guard up, you could stand a reasonable chance of survival, if you weren't trapped somewhere with no way out.

I wondered about my brother and his family in the city, and with a small pang I realized that I probably wouldn't see him again. He was a pretty smart guy, and had guns of his own, but he also had kids to look out for, so his choices were limited. I had tried to call him earlier, but the lines were all down or limited to official use only. I had left an e-mail with him, but had not received an answer for two days. Likewise with my parents. That was probably the worst part, not knowing. At least with Ellie I knew, and had a chance to say goodbye.

I decided to turn on the news for a bit, and after making sure the volume was down low I sat on the floor with Jakey and took in the news.

"...government agencies urge people to not use the phones as they are to be for official use only. All citizens are urged to stay away from hospitals and clinics, and people are urged to stay away from heavily populated centers. Infected people are everywhere, and no city is safe. Road congestion has stalled traffic in all major areas, and citizens are being attacked in their cars by roving infected. People are urged to stay inside, do not make undue noise, and try to stay out of sight. The president will be speaking later today regarding the situation. In world news, Australia has been overrun with infected, and small pockets of humanity have fled to the deserts and the outback. Europe is on the edge of collapse, and Russia has sealed its borders to prevent the further spread of infection from refugees. China has fallen to the infected, and India is said to have fallen as well. North

Korea attempted a nuclear solution, however their missile misfired and destroyed the compound which housed it. The crisis has reached pandemic proportions, and experts now seriously doubt whether the surviving humanity will be in sufficient numbers to take over should the virus be contained. In local news, people are urged to stock up on water and supplies as there is no indication how long water or power might last. Congress is holding emergency sessions as all National Guard Units are called to active duty. At the bottom of the screen are the cities in the United States which have been deemed unsafe for people to travel to. Anyone with loved ones in these cites are urged not to try and reach them. If you are to travel, safe centers have been set up in each state to provide shelter and safety to those who arrive."

It took me a minute for my mouth to close. Holy crap. If this was what they were willing to tell us on the news, what were they hiding? I had grown up with a healthy distrust of news media, but I guess when the world ends, bias goes out the window in the interest of self-preservation. I was curious as to what the president had to say, but I was hypnotized by the stream of cities and towns that were scrolling across the screen. I wondered if there was a place on the internet where I could get a list of towns in my state that were overrun. As I watched the list go on and on, I realized that the safest course of action was to assume *all* population centers were dangerous, and you should not go out if you could avoid it. I felt sorry for anyone who was trapped in towns and cities. Where could you go? How could you get out? If the roads were clogged, you had to walk, and then you were a sitting duck.

I turned off the news and played with Jake for a while. There wasn't much else to do, and it allowed me to forget what was happening for a while. After the tenth game of Where's Jakey?, I saw that it was time for his lunch bottle, so I made the meal and quietly fed Jake on the couch. He was a good boy about his bottle, not pushing at it like he had done in the past. His little brown eyes closed, and he was fully asleep when he finished. I carried him upstairs and placed him in his crib, closing the shades and door. I needed to make sure that I heard him as soon as he woke up, as I did not want his cries to attract attention.

I went downstairs and took stock of my supplies. Water was still running, so that was not a problem. When it finally turned off, I had a natural supply, but it was a long walk across open ground to fill up. Not an option if I could avoid it.

Food was in plentiful supply, I did not have too many worries there. I figured I was good for two months if I was careful, and Jakey was good for at least that long. Thank God we had stocked up before this mess came to a head.

I had plenty of ammo, and since the attack I saw outside, I was keeping my guns within easy reach. My .22 was now on the kitchen table, and my SIG never left my side. I wandered into the garage and looked for what I could use as backup weapons. I had a pickaxe, but dismissed it as too unwieldy. I had an axe and a hatchet, but figured those would have to be last-ditch weapons. I brought them near the door, since you never knew, especially now. I took down my bicycle and thought about it. I had seen the videos of the clogged roadways, and wondered if biking was a better option. We had a bike cart that Jake could be strapped into, and there would be room for other things. Food for thought. I attached the bike cart and inflated the tires of both it and the bike. Just to be ready.

I went back inside and brought my backpack out of the basement. I spent the next hour putting things in, taking things out, testing the weight, seeing what I could carry. I learned that water weighs a *lot*, and I needed to figure out what I was going to do with Jacob if I had to ditch the car or bike.

I have to admit, at first the thought of being completely on my own was daunting, but as I began to pack and prepare and pray, I realized that I was comfortable with the tasks. It didn't seem as strange to me as it might have seemed to others. It began to feel like this was something that I was meant to do, like I was meant to survive. I felt no panic, just a calm determination. Maybe it was because I had someone to live for, someone who needed me, but I think it may have been more than that. For a long time I had felt like something wasn't getting done in my life, that I was supposed to be doing more. Maybe this crisis was a wake-up to see what I could do. Heck of thing, but I didn't roll the dice, I just laid my chips on the craps table and hoped seven didn't show up.

I went back online after I checked on Jake and went on with a purpose. I wanted to find out everything I could about the zombies. I already knew that they couldn't feel pain, and they were driven by hunger. I knew if they bit you, they spread the virus which turned you into a zombie. What I needed to know was details. How fast were they, how were their senses affected? I remembered the one zombie acting like he was smelling me, and I wondered about their sense of smell.

After another hour of furious research and video watching, I came away with a much better picture than I had before. A decayed, rotting, smelly picture, but a picture nonetheless. I had watched several videos of people engaging zombies in combat, and the successful encounters involved people who kept on moving, who did not stand and try to take on a horde. Keep the fight to one on one, and you stood a pretty good chance. I saw one video where a person ran from zombies, only to be taken down after he ran out of breath. Lesson learned, they never tire. I read a report of a guy who said he tried to cross a street with ten zombies fifty yards away. He had stepped on gravel and they came after him. Lesson learned, their hearing seems to be heightened. Another story related how three people hid in a building, and two of them made it to the second floor and hid in a janitor's closet. The third had hidden herself in an office. The zombies had gotten in, and zeroed right in on where she was. The only explanation was their sense of smell seemed heightened as well. I wasn't so sure about that one yet, but it seemed possible.

I heard a little voice upstairs, and I ran to get Jake before he started to cry. He was talking to his fishbowl again, and smiled his sweet little smile when I came to get him. I felt a pang again when I thought about his mother, since he looked so much like her. But I pushed those thoughts down. *Get busy living*, I thought. I changed his diaper, and checked the supply. We were good for a while, but one of the things I overlooked was diapers for when he got bigger. I was going to have to think about what I was going to do about that.

Suddenly, it all came into focus. There was no more running to the local store because you happened to run out of something. There was no more store. You could run out to try and find something, but you stood a good chance of getting killed. There was no more manufacturing, no more deliveries, no more anything for a long time, if ever. We were lucky to have power right now, but it wasn't going to last forever, since it was likely on autopilot. Water was eventually going to run out, and food was unavailable as grown supplies. Everything we knew or accepted as our world, was done. Would we come back from this? Not for a long time. It was going to be awhile before we would even feel safe to go outside. Who knew how long zombies lasted? Who knew how long the virus survived? I needed to think long term, not just here and now. With everything on the brink of the abyss, I had a lot of time to do just that.

I took Jakey downstairs to play for a while. The sun was still bright in the sky, and for all intentions the world looked like a pretty normal place. I didn't bother with the news, since it was all the same. I didn't bother with the internet, since there wasn't much more I could learn. After a while you started to get used to the images, and that was something that truly disturbed me, given what I had seen.

I watched Jake play a bit, and decided that I wanted to bring in all the rest of the wood from the deck. I didn't know if I was going to need the lumber, but I'd rather have it inside on the windows than on the deck when the zombies came calling. That was a big part of the change in my thinking. I assumed that the attack was coming, I just didn't know when, and was going to do everything I could to keep me and mine safe.

I went outside and looked carefully around. I didn't see anything out of the ordinary, but at this point I wasn't taking anything for granted. I took my drill with me and carefully began removing the screws that held down the boards of the deck. I had my hammer as well, as some of the boards needed persuading. I took several boards inside, making sure Jake was where he was supposed to be, and I put a video on for him. I figured we may as well use the power while it was there. He liked the music baby videos, especially the one that had water as the focus.

I went back to get more boards and heard a knocking at the gate of my fence. That was weird. No one in their right mind would be roaming around if they could help it. I went over to the gate and heard the knocking again. I decided to take a peek first, so I grabbed one of the chairs that was near the fence and put it close to the gate. Stepping on the chair, I slowly peeked over the fence.

There was a man standing there, staring at my fence, and I recognized him as George Galos, my neighbor from two doors down. He stood there and seemed to be waiting for me to open the gate. I climbed down and opened the fence.

"Hey, George. Good to see someone from the block is still safe. How are you and Marlene doing? Do you need anything?"

George didn't say a word. He just looked at me. More to the point, he looked right through me. That was wrong. My warning bells went off and I was just about to shut the gate when he lunged for me, his mouth opening and letting loose a hideous groan. I backed up and he grabbed my shirt, trying to pull me in to bite. I pushed at him, but he had a grip on my shirt and wouldn't let go. I got forced back, and tripped over the chair that was behind me. George landed on top of me and brought his head in to bite at my face. I barely got an arm under his head in time and his teeth clacked an inch from my nose. His breath was horrific, and I could see large amounts of drool and bile in his mouth, which was starting to run down his chin. I forced his head back to try and keep his teeth and spit from me, and managed to twist him off of me. I wrenched his hand to get it to release my shirt, and I pushed away from him and dove to the side, rolling and getting to my feet. George was slowly regaining his footing, and he looked around to find me. When he saw me his lips retracted, showing me his teeth as he began to come at me again. I drew the SIG from my holster and was about to shoot when I realized a shot would bring all of these things within earshot to my house. Not a smart way to survive by calling zombies to dinner. I holstered the weapon as George came for me. I climbed onto the skeletonized porch, hoping the lack of boards might slow him down.

George climbed the porch, and immediately fell between the boards, his body wedging in between the support beams. He thrashed and groaned, smacking his head on the boards, trying to free himself to take another shot at food that was nearby. I looked around for a weapon and spotted my hammer.

Not liking what I had to do but knowing it had to be done, I grabbed the hammer and reversed it, so the claw end was forward. I moved over to George, who was still flailing about with his free hand and kicking with his feet. I worked my way around to his head and looked into the eyes that found me and locked on. His struggles increased, and I could see he would eventually free himself if I left him alone. Not wanting to let that happen, I raised the hammer, and with a genuine "Sorry, George." I brought the hammer down and split George's skull. He immediately stopped moving and went limp. I pulled the hammer out of his head and noticed that the blood was mixed with some blackish material which I assumed was a serious concentration of the virus. I wiped the hammer off, and tossed it into the grass, resolving to put some flame to it to kill any remnants.

I went inside and grabbed my gloves, stopping for a minute to make sure Jakey was okay, then came back to get George. I grabbed him by the collar and pulled him out of the porch. I dragged him to the edge of the fence and tried to figure out how I was going to get him outside the fence. I could throw him over, but I didn't want to make too much noise. I could drag him out, but I was worried about attracting more attention.

A shuffling noise turned my head and I managed to see another zombie walking through my open gate. *Dammit!* I forgot to close that thing. *Here we go again,* I thought. This one was a smaller female, probably a teenager, although her gray-blue skin and bloody clothes made it hard to tell. She stumbled towards me and was halfway across the yard when I moved.

I ran at her and ducked under her hands, scooting by her and knocking her a little off balance. I felt her hands brush my back as I bolted for the fence and secured it shut, making sure no more surprises wandered through the gate. The zombie followed me, reaching out and lurching towards me. I grabbed up the chair and using it like a big fork, rammed it into the teen's chest. Her teeth slammed together at the impact and she flew backwards. I ran with her and when she fell, I was on top of the chair which was on top of the zombie. The legs of the chair imbedded themselves into the soft ground and when I jumped off, I realized that I had pinned the girl to the ground, and she couldn't get up. She struggled like a turtle that had been tipped over, but she lacked the strength to pull the chair out of the ground. I'm sure I could probably have gone inside and she would still have been there in the morning. I went over to where I had thrown the hammer and picked it up off the grass. I went back to the zombie who was still struggling, and finished her off with a well-placed hammer blow to the top of her head. A twisted part of me wanted to yell "Fore!" before I swung, but I hadn't gotten that far gone yet with my humor.

I went inside to check on Jakey and found that he had rolled under his swing while I was outside dancing with the neighbors. I washed my face, hands and arms, just in case anything had gotten on me, and then retrieved Jake from the swing. He was still happy, but needed a change, since he smelled slightly worse than the girl I had just killed. I changed his diaper and put him in his saucer, where he was able to bounce around and play with toys, while pretending he could stand up. It was one of his favorites, and I used to spend a good amount of time just watching him and marveling that I had helped bring such a joy to my world. I set my teeth and swore once again I would not allow anything to happen to him. I had nearly bought it out there, and if I hadn't moved fast enough, I would have been infected and Jacob would not have had a chance. I realized that what had happened out there was probably how a lot of people bought it. A neighbor or relative was infected, managed to get close to the living without them thinking anything was amiss, and just like that, they were infected or eaten. Either way, they wound up dead.

I went to the counter and pulled out a large garbage bag. I pulled it over my head after I had made holes for my arms and head. I went back out and pulled the chair off the dead girl. I dragged her over to where George lay and grabbed her by the ankle and wrist. Swinging her around, I heaved her over the fence after I had gained enough momentum. I then grabbed George and did the same, although it was a lot harder, since he weighed a good one hundred-seventy. His head hit the top of the fence and he cartwheeled over, landing with a thump on the other side. I briefly wondered what it must have looked like to see two bodies suddenly sailing over a fence in the middle of the suburbs. Shaking my head at the way the world had become, I stripped off my big baggie and went back inside, retrieving my hammer from the grass again.

Putting the hammer in the garage I figured it was about time to give Jake his dinner. I put him in his high chair and fed him his baby food. He looked so small in his big chair, but we had recently moved him out of his bouncy seat, as his legs were hanging off the sides. I put the TV on to see if there was news, and not just more of the same. I managed to catch the President in mid-speech.

"...a crisis which could not have been predicted or prevented. We simply did not know in time to save the millions of infected. We do know that the infection is spread through bites of infected individuals, and fluid transfers as well. You have all heard the reports that individuals infected with the Enillo Virus are dying and coming back to life. I cannot deny this inexplicable phenomenon, and experiments by our scientists bear this to be true. We do know that those returned to life can be stopped by severe trauma to the brain. It is apparent that the virus needs the brain to operate the host, and when that no longer functions, the individual ceases to be a threat. Our scientists also note that because of the length of time between death and reanimation, infected individuals do not possess any intelligence, and are unable to complete simple tasks and complex motor functions. We do know they can climb stairs, but ladders are beyond their capabilities. However, we urge all citizens not to underestimate them. They exist to spread the virus and feed on living flesh. This has been proven time and time again in our experiments. We therefore urge all citizens to go to protection centers set up in each state. National Guard units have been recalled in each state to protect the citizens of each state. State Governors are called upon to pool all necessary resources for the survival of the citizens of their states. Federal help at this time is unavailable. Congress has been released to states with functioning governments to help coordinate rescue and survival efforts. If citizens are able to travel to these centers, they are encouraged to do so for their own safety. We do not know who is capable of hearing this message, but please remember this. If only one American survives, America and what she stands for will not die. May God watch over us and deliver us from what is our darkest hour."

I gave Jake his fruit and turned off the television. "I don't think we need to go to a center, little buddy." I said to Jake as he grinned at me. "I get a bad feeling about things like that, and it sounds more like a situation rife with potential problems. When was the last time the government took over something and didn't make it worse?"

Jake waved his arm at me, a signal that I wasn't shoveling the fruit fast enough. He only warns once, then he yells at me. He should be a load of fun when he becomes a toddler. He wasn't a great conversationalist, but as a listener, he had no peer.

We finished eating, and feeling a few pangs myself, I went to the fridge and made myself a sandwich. I figured the power was probably going to last only a few more days, so I needed to eat the perishables before they went bad and were worthless. The freezer had a decent amount of food, since when I had stocked it I thought two people were going to be eating it. Hopefully it would last.

After a little while it was time for Jake to get his bath and get his jammies on. We went up stairs and I drew his bath. He was big enough to have a bath seat, so after soap and washing, I added some water and let him sit for a while. He enjoyed splashing and feeling the water, and was genuinely happy. I used the time to change into my comfy clothes and take a look at the neighborhood from my windows. I kept the lights off, as I didn't want to advertise my presence, although it was still light enough outside for it to be difficult to see an interior light.

I saw activity across the street and realized my neighbor Rich and his wife were making a run for it. They had opened the garage door and were throwing what they could into the back of their Tahoe. Rich was standing guard at the door with a scoped rifle in his hands. Not much good in a close fight, but at least it was a gun. His wife Beth was loading the vehicle, and when she was finished, she shouted to him and he jumped into the car. They rolled out quickly and sped off into the evening. I couldn't figure out why they were moving so fast.

I got the answer a second later, as their two daughters came stumbling out of the house. They were obviously infected, and their parents were running for their lives. The girls started after the car, but stopped after it turned from their sight. They stood there for a few minutes, and then the older one started walking off to the north, following the street. The other one stood in the middle of the street, swaying slightly from side to side. She was dressed in pajamas and was barefoot, her eyes sunken into her head and surrounded by dark circles. She looked around and I saw her eyes drift over to my house. I didn't move, fairly certain that she couldn't see me. I remained stock still, wishing with all my might that she would turn away or something would distract her. If I moved and she sensed I was there, she was going to come to the house.

A dog barked in the distance, and her head snapped around. She began a slow shuffle towards the sound, moving as if she wasn't quite sure how she was supposed to walk.

I released the breath I didn't know I was holding, and closed the blinds. I angled them until it was impossible for anyone in the street to see into the house, but light could still get in. I went and got Jake and dressed him, taking him downstairs and we played on the floor for a little while. I tried not to turn any lights on, as I didn't want anyone to notice us. I wondered who else was doing the same thing, trying to survive by not being noticed.

I decided I needed to barricade the rest of the downstairs windows, just in case, and resolved to take care of it tomorrow.

It wasn't like I had anything else to do. Jake started to get a little cranky, so I made him a bottle and he went to sleep grasping my hands and putting his little head on my shoulder. I laid him down as the sun went down, putting the world into darkness. Figuring on tomorrow being a long day, I decided to go to bed myself. Reflecting on what the day had been like, tomorrow was likely to be lively. I wondered about the rest of my neighborhood, who was alive and who wasn't. These days, it was hard to tell, and you couldn't exactly stroll up to the door. You ran the risk of getting shot or eaten, neither of which was a fun way to go.

I placed my SIG on my nightstand and drifted off to sleep.

5

The next day was just busy, with me playing with Jake and putting boards up in windows. I tried to leave a little open area at the top, and I left a little two inch space about head high (on the outside) to "repel boarders" as it were. I had enough boards to cover the back windows, and I was thinking about covering the outside of the windows as well when I got a surprise. Without warning, my cell phone rang.

"Hello?"

"John?" The voice whispered.

"Mike?" I asked, not believing it could be my brother. I had figured him for lost like Ellie. Relief flooded over me at the sound of his voice. "Where are you?"

Mike sounded panicked. "We're trapped in our house on the third floor. We held out for a while, but they're everywhere! I got separated from Nicole and Annie, but I have Logan with me. I think Nicole and Annie are in the basement, but I can't get to them!"

I tried to calm him down. "Have you spoken to them at all?"

Mike took a deep breath. "We're talking through a vent. I don't know how long they're going to last. They don't have any food and the zombies know they're there because Annie keeps crying. I can hear them pounding on the door!"

I thought fast. "Mike, listen to me. Do you have a radio or anything on your floor?"

Mike paused. "Uh, yeah, there's a little battery-powered one in the bedroom here. Why?"

I explained. "These things are attracted to sound. Turn it on as loud as you can, find some noise on it, and throw it onto the roof of your garage behind your house. You're going to have to move as fast as you can, and tell Nicole to be ready to move as well. Grab what supplies you can and head out. Do you still have your 9mm?"

Mike grunted. "Stupid thing is on the first floor with the zombies."

I rolled my eyes. "Get it if you can. Grab a crowbar and your backpacks and get out. I know you guys have all that camping crap in your house. You gotta move as fast as you can, and don't stop for anything."

Mike sounded unsure. "Where can we go? I look out my window and there's twenty of these things on the street at any given time. I watched a guy get eaten yesterday who tried to make a run for it."

"You're smarter than that, bro. Look out your front window. Your escape is right there. Get on the el tracks and you'll be able to move pretty quickly. These things can't climb, and you need to get out of the city." I tried to sound reassuring.

Mike sighed. "Thanks bro. I needed this. Once we're on the el, then what? We can't walk to the country."

I tried not to sound harsh. "The world as we knew it is over. We're back in the middle ages and there are monsters all around. You gotta get busy living or get busy dying."

"Wasn't that from a movie?"

"Makes as much sense now as anything. You need to make a choice. Walk out of the city or try to get to the lake and get a boat. You might be safer on a boat." I thought that one out and it seemed logical.

Mike sounded skeptical. "How do I get a boat?"

"Get your gun and you'll get a boat."

I could almost hear Mike mulling *that* one over. "All right, we're gonna try to get out of here. I'll try to call you back once we are out of here and on the el."

"Keep moving. Don't stand and fight if you can avoid it. If you have to face one of these things, always aim for the head." I tried to give as much useful last minute advice as I could.

"Since when did you become an expert?" Mike was curious.

"Since Ellie died and I killed two of these things in my back yard yesterday."

Mike had nothing to say to that. He at least still had his family.

"Good luck, brother." I said. "Call me when you're on the move if you can." I didn't want to waste his time talking. I also had no idea how the hell he managed to call me, but I was still amazed.

"Talk to you." Mike said.

And that was it. Mike hung up and I prayed with everything I had that he and his family was going to be safe. If he managed to get his gun and get to the tracks, he had a chance. Not a strong one, but a chance. I went back to my windows and spent the rest of the morning reinforcing the wood that was already there and checking the rest of my defenses. I decided to play a little game with myself. What would I do if the zombies managed to get in here? I figured that the best place to be would be on the second floor, as the basement, although convenient, only left one way out. Deciding this, I went down to the basement and retrieved all my weapons and ammo that were still down there. I brought them upstairs and stashed them in the bedroom. I went back and retrieved my tools and supplies and brought them upstairs as well. I began bringing as much food as I could upstairs, leaving only a little bit downstairs as necessary.

I looked at my stairwell, and figured it was the weak point in my plan. I needed a way to secure the stairs, but I also needed to think about escape. Mike and his family brought that into focus. What if they got in here and I was trapped upstairs? What could I do? I thought for a bit and realized that I needed a ladder. Fortunately, I had an extension ladder in the garage. It was a real trick to maneuver that thing upstairs, but I did it. It was long enough to reach to the roof of my neighbors, so I figured I could go from roof to roof if I needed to.

Getting back to the stairwell, I needed a way to block it. Nothing was jumping out at me so I decided to worry about it later.

I fed Jake and put him down for his nap, and thought I saw movement outside. I went to the window and watched for a bit. Sure enough, something was moving in the field behind the houses. I had three guesses as to what it was and the first two didn't count.

I went downstairs and picked up the .22. I was curious if a .22 would be effective at all against a zombie's head, and since there didn't seem to be any more out there, I figured it would be a good time to see. I went outside to the fence and stood on one of the chairs. I didn't see anything right away and looked around. For the moment, all I could see were the two corpses I had thrown over the fence the previous day. They didn't look too good, as the flies had done a number on them.

As I was looking at them, another zombie stumbled into view. It was walking along the ditch, and was hidden from view by one of the trees I had near the fence. It was a young man, about twenty-five as near as I could tell, and he was in rough shape. His clothes were nearly gone, hanging in shreds from his body. Raw wounds covered his torso, and his left leg sported a six inch gash that went completely around it. Maggots covered the wounds, and fell off every time he lurched one way or the other. He hadn't noticed me yet as I hadn't moved, and I began to wonder about their sense of sight. If you didn't attract attention to yourself, and they couldn't hear you or smell you, it seemed you were just part of the scenery.

I checked the clip and chambered a round, the bolt sounding loud in the stillness. The zombie's head turned my way, and he groaned when he finally saw me. I lined up the sights on his head as he came closer, and when he was no further than fifteen feet away, at the base of the hill my fence sat on, I fired the round at his head. The shot echoed off the condominiums across the way, and a neat little hole appeared in his forehead. He collapsed without another sound.

"That worked well." I said to myself as I heard answering groans coming from across the way. Three more zombies came stumbling out from the condo's parking lot, seeking the source of the noise. I waited until the first one came near and then dropped it with a shot to the head. I was still hidden in the tree branches, so they hadn't quite zeroed in on where I was. The second was a bit further out, about twenty yards, but I tried it anyway. It too, fell with a round to the head. I wondered what the true effective range was, and tried a shot at about fifty yards. The zombie's head jerked, but he didn't go down. I waited for him to get closer, then I hit him again. This time he went down for good. I could see that the first shot had hit him, but the bullet had not penetrated the skull, but traveled around the skull under the skin. Not pretty, but a lesson learned. .22's were good for close in work, and they had to get hit straight on.

I didn't hear any more groans, so I stepped off the chair and started back toward the house; as I did, a figure suddenly appeared in the window of my neighbors' house. I was startled enough to raise my weapon and get a sight picture before I realized it was Erica, my neighbor's daughter. She raised both hands and her eyes got really huge. I lowered the weapon and gave her a thumbs- up, hoping it was reassuring. She smiled and waved, and retreated from the window. I went back inside and spent the rest of the day trying to figure out what I was going to do about my stairs.

6

During the night, the gas turned off. I didn't realize it until morning, when I went to take a quick shower that hot water was gone. This was not convenient. Not unexpected, but still inconvenient. Well, it was only a matter of time. Jake was going to have to get used to some room-temperature baths. I filled a gallon jug and placed it in the sun, figuring it would help a little. Jake was a little trooper; in his world, as long as daddy was around and somebody, didn't matter who, changed his diapers, his day was golden.

Speaking of diapers, I realized that things were critical when it came to diapers. I needed to get another supply and do it today. I didn't want to have to leave the homestead, but I needed some things and I needed to go as soon as possible before everything had been looted and taken. I wasn't sure about the looting, but with police pretty much non-existent, and the National Guard pulled back to the safe center, if there was one. People were pretty much on their own. And as any disaster survivor will tell you, calamity brings out the best and worst in people. That's just the way it was. Besides, I needed to get out there and see just how bad things were. For all I knew, it wasn't too bad. Yeah right, and maybe I'll be named king next week.

I packed Jakey up in his car seat and got myself ready. I had my big crowbar out in the car, and I had my ever-present SIG. I took my Winchester with me as heavy firepower, figuring that if I couldn't get it done with full power 45 Colt loads, it couldn't be done. I had eleven rounds in the gun and put ten more in my pocket. If it came to a firefight, I was bugging out. I had Jake with me and couldn't take chances. The lever gun had been a faithful companion, and I felt more secure in taking a shot with it than most of my other guns. Besides, with my Cowboy Action Shooting practice, I could empty that gun fairly quickly.

I checked the street before I opened up the door, as I didn't want to have to engage a zombie right off the bat if I could avoid it. I unlocked the door and rolled it up as quietly as I could. No one was in sight, so I re-engaged the lock and started the car. I pulled out of the garage and headed out into the street, closing the garage door behind me. I had locked the door leading to the house, so I wasn't worried about zombies breaking into my home if they managed to get into the garage.

I drove through the neighborhood, again noting the signs of violence and hasty exits. No cars blocked the way, which was good, so I was able to head to the main road fairly quickly. I did see a few zombies, and they turned towards me, but lost interest after I pulled from their sight and they saw they couldn't catch me.

I drove down to the crossroad, a small highway tucked away from the main roads. It had a couple of cars parked on the side of the road, and a car was in the ditch by the local body shop. All the businesses were closed, and the golf course on the west side of the street was deserted, except for some zombies strolling around the eighth green. They were interested in something in the water, so I didn't think it was polite to disturb them.

I turned up towards the main road and found a few more abandoned cars. Some had blood in the interior, and more than one had a corpse in it. Several had movement, and I could see that the zombies were trapped in the cars, unable to figure out how to free themselves. I drove the car into the small lane that went between a gas station and a bank, and led to the drug store around the back.

Immediately, I sensed something was wrong. A car had been forced to the side of the lot near the back, two other cars bracketing it and preventing it from moving. I drove to the side of the building and parked it under the drive-through. It was out of the way and in the shade, and gave me a chance to hide the car and Jake. I was not going to bring him with, as he was safer in the car, and if I needed to move quickly, I didn't want to have to worry about him. Besides, he was falling asleep, so he wouldn't miss anything important.

I got out of the car and cautiously approached the other vehicles. The forced car had its doors still open, and I could hear the faint dinging of the open door warning. The other two cars were closed, and I could see a lot of beer cans and cigarette packs in the back of the vehicles. As I went closer, I could see a pair of legs by the front of the vehicle. Bringing my gun up, I eased the hammer back and approached the legs, not happy about what I might find. As I reached the front, I could see that the legs belonged to a man, probably in his thirties, lying in a semi-fetal position. He had not been killed by zombies, that much I could figure out by the way his throat was cut. His blood had spilled out over the pavement and pooled at the edge of the drive. There was nothing I could do for him so I turned back the way I came. That's when I saw the woman.

She was lying face down in the ditch, and was naked from the waist down. Dirty hand prints covered her legs and ankles. What clothes were on her were ripped and torn, and her hands clawed the dirt. A single knife stuck out from between her shoulder blades. She had died hard and in pain. I began to realize what had happened. This couple had been trying to escape, and been forced off the road by these marauders. They dragged the man out and likely forced him to watch his wife being raped. They then killed them both. Since there was no hope of police action, this was done for the pure pleasure of it. My jaw tightened and I breathed out heavily. As I turned back, I saw something that made my blood run cold. In the back of the car was an empty car seat. If there was a child, where was it now? Was it even alive? Anything left with animals that would do this would surely suffer.

I walked back to my car and checked on Jake. He was still sleeping, but wouldn't for long. I needed to get what I needed and get out of here. As I stepped back to the lot, I realized I needed to make sure I wasn't followed. I ran back to the cars and, using my knife, slashed the tires on all three vehicles.

I went to the side of the building and walked carefully to the front. I began to hear voices from the opening, which I could see had been smashed open. I had no idea why I was going in the building, how many I was facing, or what I planned on doing. But there was a child in danger, and no matter how badly I wanted to cut and run, I could not give up on that child.

I held my rifle at the ready and walked inside. The aisles had been trashed, and a lot of stuff was all over the floor. I stepped carefully around a waterfall of makeup, and headed towards the back of the store where the voices were. I stayed at the edge of the store, trying to stay out of sight of the big mirrors on the back wall. I could see at least three people near the pharmacy, and could hear more grabbing things off the shelves.

As I moved closer, I cocked the hammer back on my SIG, loosening it in its holster. The hammer was still back on my Winchester, and I moved closer to the pharmacy.

The three punks I could see were leaning on the counter, talking to the ones in the back. I figured there were five of them, and I could see they had been busy. Even in the relative darkness of the store I could see them sporting several gold watches and chains, and I could see guns tucked in the waistbands of two of them. They were all about eighteen years old, and were relatively well-dressed. It didn't make sense what they were doing, and their crime was even more horrific for it. I worried even more about the child. Where was it? I slowly angled out to the left and raised my rifle. I could see out the drive-up window, and thanked God I hadn't parked further back, or they would have seen me and Jake.

I didn't waste time with small talk. "Where's the child?" I said.

The reaction was immediate. As one, the three spun around and two hands streaked for their waists. "Don't!" I yelled, stepping into the dim light of the window and showing them I had the drop on them. "You'll never make it." I heard some muttering coming from the pharmacy and called to them. "You two in the back! Come out now and have your hands up!"

The closest one, an oily bastard if I ever saw one, sneered and said, "You a cop?"

I shook my head as the other two made their appearance. "You're not that lucky. I don't have rules to play by like cops do." I noted that one of the ones from the back had deep scratches on his face, like someone had been fighting him. I could guess where he had gotten them. "Where's the child?" I asked again.

Oily sneered. "Fuck you."

I didn't say a word. I just shot him in the chest. He flew back from the impact and slammed against the counter. He fell onto his face and his companions could see the four inch hole the heavy slug had created as it exited his body. They all stood stock still and raised their hands higher.

My face was stone cold as I pointed the gun at the next one in line, a slender blonde kid who looked like he had just started shaving a week ago. "Where's the child?"

The blonde started to shake, and couldn't answer. His partner, a heavy kid with greasy hair and a bad complexion, reached for the gun at his waist. I swung the rifle on him and shot him in the mouth as he screamed. The back of his head blew all over the pharmacy, and he fell back like a tree, thudding into the ground.

I pointed the rifle again at the blonde, and kept my eyes on the remaining two kids. "Where?"

The blonde kid shrugged and I brought the gun to within an inch of his face. The .45 inch hole at the end of the barrel must have seemed like a garage from that vantage point. "I'm not going to ask again. Where is the child who belonged to the father whose throat you cut and the mother who you raped and stabbed? *Where?*" I screamed in his face.

The blonde kid said nothing, he just looked up towards the camera counter. I didn't look but I was afraid of what I would find. At that moment, the blonde kid said exactly the wrong thing. He smiled at me and said "Did you want her for yourself?"

I lowered my rifle and casually shot him in the gut. He folded in half and crashed back, landing in a heap by the counter. He shrieked and grabbed at his stomach, trying to hold in his guts and screamed himself to death at the same time. His companions looked in horror and one of them managed to wet himself. I kicked them back to the counter to sit amongst their dead and dying companions. "If either of you move, I will kill you." My voice was ice and I could not imagine myself with more anger than I felt at that moment. They nodded their heads and tried to shift away from the growing pools of blood. The blonde kid continued to scream, but he was running out of steam. I grabbed their weapons and threw them towards the front of the store.

I had to move. The shots and screams had likely attracted attention, and I needed to get out of here as fast as possible. I moved to the baby aisle and grabbed bags of diapers. I headed to the back of the store, pausing to fire a shot at one of the kids who tried to move. He ducked as the bullet clipped near his head, then he held stock still. I went out the back door and loaded the trunk of the car. Jake was still sleeping, but I didn't have much time. I ran back in and grabbed more diapers, pausing to snare a small first aid kit as well. I threw the items in the trunk and went back in one more time. I needed to know something and know it now. As I made my way to the front, I could see shadows in the parking lot, and I didn't have any more time. I reached the camera counter and looked over, afraid of what I would see.

A small girl was one the floor, no older than 18 months. Her brown hair lay in small rings around her face. A large bruise was on her forehead, and she looked to have other bruises due to some rough treatment by the scum at the back.

As I reached down to check to see if she had a pulse, her eyes popped open and she jerked away from me. She immediately started crying and tried to crawl away behind the photo machine.

"Hey, sweetie! Don't cry. I'm not going to hurt you. I'm going to take you out of here. Okay?" I tried to be as reassuring as I could, although I could feel a rising anxiety as some low groans began to start at the entrance of the building. "Come on, sweetheart, we need to go." I can only imagine what I looked like in the darkened store, but I held out my hand, and as trusting as kids can be, thank God, she took it and came to me.

I scooped her up and ran back to the back door, just as the first zombies came walking in the smashed front entrance. I passed the two on the floor, who were just starting to edge away from their companions. "Good luck!" I shouted as I bolted out the door and ran for the car. The little girl started crying again, and I buckled her in faster than a NASCAR pit crew member. I jumped into the car and drove away, checking the building and seeing about ten zombies wander in the front door. *Better than you bastards deserve*, I thought, as I passed the three cars. *Much better.*

I made it back to my subdivision without incident, and the little girl had stopped her crying and started sucking her thumb. Jake had awakened and was fascinated by the new child in his life. He tried every method of flirting he could think of, from smiling to drooling to expansive farting. The little girl seemed oblivious. As I headed down the street I saw my neighbors, Todd and Naomi and their daughter coming out of the side street. I flagged him down and he stopped.

"We're heading out, John. You and Jake want to come with?" Todd asked me.

I shook my head. "I think we'll be fine here, thanks anyway. Where are you headed?"

Todd shrugged. "We're going to try to see if the state center is safe. If not, we'll head to the cabin outside of Jacksonville. We can live pretty well there till this blows over."

I looked at him. "Todd, I need a huge favor."

Todd got serious. "Sure, what do you need?"

"I need you to take this little girl with you. Her parents were murdered and I managed to take her away from the murderers." I didn't see any need to explain further.

Todd looked at me for a long moment and then at his wife. Naomi answered for him. "Of course we'll take her, John. Erica always wanted a sister."

That settled it. I went to the car and got the now-sleeping little girl from the seat. I carried her to the other car and Nola helped me put her in the back seat. "What's her name?" she asked.

That threw me. I had no idea. I looked at her wrist and saw a little bracelet. In little letters, the name "Ellen" was spelled out with flowers. My heart caught in my throat and I couldn't speak; I just pointed to the bracelet.

Nola gave me a hug and went back to the front seat. I went around to Todd and shook his hand. "Good luck, and thanks."

Todd smiled. "See you again sometime."

I smiled back. "You bet."

They drove off and I headed back to my house. Once inside I unloaded the car and took Jake back in. As I lay down beside him I thought about what I had done. I had no remorse, no regret. I felt absolutely nothing. Was this part of who I was becoming? Was this someone I wanted to be? Was this someone I wanted Jake to see as his father? I didn't have the answers. But a small voice in my head told me I had done the right thing. If I had let those animals go they would have preyed upon others, likely leaving that poor baby to die. Part of me scolded myself for taking such a risk, but a much larger part simply accepted it as what had to be done.

My cell phone rang, interrupting my reverie. It was my brother.

"We made it! We managed to get out while they were going after the radio! We're on the el, heading towards the lake. I don't know what we're going to do when we get there, but at least we're moving."

I felt a huge relief flood through me. "Sounds good, Mike. Did you get your gun?"

"Yes, I grabbed it right before they saw us and came back in the house. Two more seconds and they would have had us."

I exhaled at the close call. "Keep moving and trust no one. Get a boat and get away."

"Done. Where are you going to be?" Mike wanted to know.

"I'm staying here for a while. No reason to leave." I was serious, too. Unless I had to, I was not leaving.

"Maybe we'll head your way. Check the canals for us! Gotta go!" Mike hung up and I was left looking at my phone.

I thought about the events of the day and suddenly I was very tired. I went outside and got the sun-warmed water to give Jakey a bath. I needed some normalcy in this crazy world, but I couldn't shake the feeling normal was a thousand miles from where it used to be.

After Jake was put to bed, an odd thought struck me. Could zombies swim?

7

We had power for another week before it finally let out. I had been expecting it every day since my run to the drug store, so it was not out of bounds. It was going to be hot, since it was June, but I was able to open the attic vents, and open the second floor windows for ventilation. The first floorwindows, being covered and boarded up, did a really good job of keeping the first floorcool. I was never so grateful for a brick ground floor. It was kind of dark, but it was cool enough that I didn't worry about Jake getting too hot. We had enough light to see by, and the water still worked, so we were doing okay, all things considered.

I spent a lot of time working out and staying in shape. We had a treadmill in the basement, but since I never really used it much to begin with, I didn't really care about it when the power went out. I liked jumping rope, so I did that in the basement. I hoped that I wasn't making enough noise to be noticed, and so far I had been lucky. I really had very little else to do. If it wasn't for the zombies, and the constant threat of being infected or eaten, I might actually have enjoyed myself .

I had no illusions about being able to withstand a siege. I knew eventually the zombies would get in if given enough time, and time was all on their side. I had to hope to try to remain under the radar and get through this as best I could.

That was a sobering thought that kept recurring to me through the days. What if there was not an end? What if this was the world we had to get used to? Zombies on the prowl, degenerate humans preying upon survivors, God knows what else waiting for us out there. Government control seemed to be lost, what government there was, in all likelihood, was hiding out and waiting for the day when someone else saved their asses.

So what then? I could accept the fact that I was on my own. I could accept the fact that no one was going to save me, and the only way I was going to survive and Jake was going to survive was to find a place that was secure from the zombies, had a source of food and water, and wait for the eventual rot and decay of the infected.

As much as I hated to admit it, Jake and I were going to have to leave. I did not like the thought of leaving my home and all the memories behind, not to mention a lot of resources that might be useful. But I needed to be realistic. This place was defensible, but against a large scale attack, it was going to fall, myself and Jake going with it. The attack might never happen, but I was not going to take the chance.

I began to see more zombies on the street. At one point, there had to be about thirty of them, and they just wandered down the street, not paying any particular attention to anything. They did get animated when a cat ran out in front of them, but they followed it to a house that had a cat door and began pounding on the doors. In a very short amount of time, they had broken in and all hell broke loose. I could see zombies wandering the downstairs, and they seemed to be still chasing the cat. I figured that little tabby was going to be a meal in short order. I was about to turn away from the window when I heard a scream come from the house and I could see a man and a woman trying to climb out their bedroom window. They had tied a sheet to something, and were trying to shimmy down and get away from their house. I watched the woman slide down and fall on her back, but she got up and seemed unhurt. The man was halfway out the window when a grey arm reached around his neck and pulled him back inside. The woman screamed for her husband, then committed suicide by running back in her house in an attempt to try and save him. Her screams didn't last long at all.

It all happened in the space of a minute. In an ironic twist, I saw the cat that caused the death of its owners run out of the house again and disappear between two other houses across the street. I felt bad for the couple, as they obviously were laying low and hadn't been noticed, but they had to have seen what was going on and didn't take even the most rudimentary precautions. I promised myself to shoot that cat if it even came *near* my house.

I just shook my head and went back to my business, which was taking care of Jake and getting ready to go. I needed to make sure I had everything ready and would not leave anything behind that was important. I also wanted to make sure that I would still have important stuff to come home to, if this mess ever managed to work itself out.

I packed my "bug-out-bag" with the essentials, and made sure I had enough ammunition. I needed to make sure I had a weapon for silent kills, and my three foot crowbar was enough to foot the bill for that. Plus, it would be a great help if I needed to break into anywhere for shelter. I packed my saddle bags as well, concentrating food for Jacob and water. I made sure they were balanced and placed them in the garage.

I spent a good deal of time figuring out what I was going to take and what I was going to leave behind. I had to re-pack and re-think what I was going to do several times, and it was two days before I finally had everything together.

I decided not to use my car as an escape vehicle. Sure it could go further faster, but it was also a magnet for zombies and others. If I used my bicycle and child trailer, I should be able to move relatively undetected.

Jake was oblivious as I ran around the house getting things ready and making sure we had what we needed. The weather worked for us, as we didn't need to worry about cold weather clothes, but I packed some footie pajamas for Jake just in case. He was going to need to be strapped in to the bike seat behind me, something I am sure he was going to love. He always enjoyed going for walks and having the wind in his face. I thought about having him in the trailer, but I wanted to make sure I could get him out in a hurry if I needed to. And if I needed to ditch the trailer, I didn't want to have to figure out how to strap Jake on the bike on the run.

As I looked at my weapons, I realized I had only my SIG, my knife, and my M1 carbine. I wanted to take another weapon, something with serious firepower. I dismissed my shotgun as too unwieldy, and my .22, though handy with a lot of rounds, didn't make it in the serious firepower department. I decided to take my Enfield, although where the heck I was going to put it was a mystery to me. It weighed quite a bit, and was fairly awkward, although no one who saw it doubted its effectiveness at long ranges. Looking around my garage, I saw my bungee cords, and with a moment's thought, managed to bungee the Enfield to the center post of my bicycle, with the muzzle pointing forward. The action was still free, and I could easily manipulate the bolt and trigger without too much worry. This gave me a mounted gun I could get into action quickly. I thought about adding the spike bayonet, but figured that would be overkill. I stuck the bayonet in my backpack, just in case.

As an additional measure, I wrapped the gun with a towel to hide what it was, but still kept the action loose.

I couldn't shake the feeling that I needed to go and I needed to go now. It was like something was coming on the horizon and if I didn't get moving, things were going to get bleak in a hurry. There was no explanation for it, it was just a feeling I had. Maybe it was the increased zombie activity in the area. I don't know. I just knew I needed to get moving.

I began moving things into my den under the garage. The guns and ammo I was leaving behind were already there, so that wasn't an issue. I brought down anything of value or use, including my tools and clothing. I didn't bother with Jake's clothes, as he would have outgrown them by the time we came back, if ever. When I had filled the room, I closed off the opening with a piece of polyurethaned lumber I had cut for that purpose years ago. I took out my caulk gun and sealed the edges. I then put another piece of lumber in front of the opening and caulked that in place as well. That was about as much as I could do as far as keeping water out. With no power, a good rain was going to cause some flooding, and I was trying to save my keepsakes as long as I could. Part of me figured it was an exercise in futility, but a more stubborn part of me refused to accept the fact that this was it, and I was never coming home again.

I went back up stairs to check on Jake, and he was still taking his nap. I checked my bags again and looked out in the garage at my preparations. I figured to move first thing in the morning, and I needed to move quickly. I was headed south, and hopefully I would be able to put some serious distance between me and the troubled spots. With luck, I might be able to find a town that had not been infected, and Jake and I can settle into some sort of life while the rest of the world went crazy.

8

The next morning I got up and checked on Jake. He was still asleep, so I went down and got some breakfast. Cereal bars weren't exactly the greatest of breakfasts, being a milk and cereal man myself, but with the power out, the only milk I was going to get was from a cow, and I hadn't seen one of those is these parts. I thought about the route I needed to take, and I figured to avoid main roads altogether. I planned on using the bike trails as much as I could to head south, but I was eventually going to have to cut through populated areas. Hopefully, I could avoid zombies and other ilk on my way.

I went through the house and really looked at it for what might be the last time. I looked at the hardwood floor I had installed last summer and the new bathrooms I had put in for Ellie. I ran my hand over the granite countertop she loved so much, and glanced at the curio cabinet which was now empty, everything being moved downstairs. In the darkened rooms I let my grief go a little, and cried one last time for my wife. After a moment, I heard Jake crying upstairs and hurried to go get him.

As I took him out of his crib, I looked out on the bike path and was relieved to see it was clear. I didn't need any obstacles this morning, and the sun was bright and inviting. I had no clue how hot it was supposed to be today, and in all honesty, I didn't care. I had sunscreen for Jake and a hat with a strap for his little head. He was good to go. Breakfast was a quick affair, and then I made preparations to move. I filled all of our water bottles and then turned the water off in the house. I turned on the faucet in the slop sink next to the washer in the basement and let the water in the pipes drain out. I went back upstairs and opened the faucets in the sinks and bathtub and shower. If I was going to be gone for a while, I didn't want the pipes to freeze and I came back to more of a mess than I needed.

I went into the garage with Jake and strapped him into his seat. He was thrilled to be moving and he gave me a baby thumbs up with some arm waving and squeals. I put sunscreen on his arms and legs, strapped his hat on, and went to the garage door. Fortunately, we had windows on the garage door and I was able to look out. There were two people down the street, and I couldn't tell from a distance whether they were infected or not. They moved slowly, but it was hard to tell if they were zombies or just trying to be careful. I decided to wait and see, rather than run the risk.

As they got closer, I could see they were not infected, they were just trying to avoid being seen. They were a man and woman, and they had backpacks loaded with materials. They walked down the center of the road, and carried makeshift weapons. The man, about twenty years old, carried a length of lead pipe, and the woman, closer to thirty, carried a police baton. They both wore knives on their belts and had a hard look about them. I decided to let them pass and go their way, and I would go mine. No need for getting together at this point. They turned to the west and headed off. I silently wished them luck.

I gave them about ten minutes to clear the area, during which I entertained Jakey. He was such a good boy, he didn't care what we did, as long as I smiled at him and changed his diapers.

Checking the road again, I slowly opened the garage door, keeping an eye on the street. Those zombies from the other day were still out there somewhere, and I didn't need a protracted battle at this point. The sun was starting to heat up the day, and the bright light made everything stand out in stark contrast. I had a brief thought about the length of the lawn, then shook it off as stupid. I put the padlock on the garage door leading to the house and locked it, then moved the bike and trailer out onto the driveway. Closing the garage door, I padlocked it as well, knowing that it would not do much for someone determined to get in, but I wasn't planning to give anything away. I hung the key around my neck and with a last look at the house, got the bike and went towards the trail out back.

I followed my fence towards the trail, then turned towards my neighbors' yard. The ground sloped more gently behind his house, and wouldn't subject me and Jake to a four foot drop at the edge of the property. I glanced briefly at the two zombies I had disposed of earlier, and they were not a pretty sight. The heat and humidity, as well as incessant flies had done a number on them. George was missing an arm, and the girl's face was completely torn off. I found that interesting.

Apparently the virus only was harmful to humans, animals could feast on the dead without ill effect.

We crossed the field and hit the trail. The trailer was heavy, but moved easily. I kept to an easy pace, not wanting to tire myself too much in case I had to move quickly. My senses were completely keyed up, and I found myself listening harder than I had ever before, and staring longer at unidentified shadows and shapes much more than I had ever before. I smiled to myself. *So this is what prey feel like.*

We rode without incident to the Turtle Head crossing, and I was amazed at how quiet everything was. I had heard a few groans and such as I passed some yards, and at one point I could see some dark figures huddled over another on the ground through the slats of a fence. I could see many zombies in windows as I passed, and more than one beat on the windows of their prisons in futility. I kept moving and never looked twice. I didn't need those images haunting me as I rode quietly past.

Turtle Back Lake was quiet, and I decided to rest for a minute and check on Jake. I stopped near the water and parked under a tree. My legs protested as I got off, not being used to this kind of riding. Jakey smiled as I got him out, and one whiff told me why he was smiling. He had managed to fill his diaper and was waiting for a change. I got the towel off the Enfield and laid it out on the ground. I put Jake on the ground and started to change him.

As I was working on Jake, I noticed a car slowly pulling into the Turtle Back Lake parking lot. It was a small compact car, and looked to be crammed full of stuff. There were two men in the front, and they seemed to be running on empty. From where I was, I could see them fairly clearly without being noticed. The tall grass hid the brightly colored trailer, and since I was kneeling by Jake, I was hidden as well. The car had numerous dings and dents, and the front fender looked as if it had been dented then fixed with a baseball bat. Dark stains were on the grill, and I could imagine how they got there.

The two men got out and looked around, and I could see they were both armed with Glock pistols. They were of medium height, one slightly taller than the other, and both were dark haired. One had a tattoo on his left arm, but I couldn't see what it was. They looked like they had been running for a while and needed to rest. I didn't get any bad vibes off them, and I needed to stand at some point. But I didn't want to get shot for my trouble.

I figured the direct route was the best. I stood up and placed myself behind the tree, Jacob on the towel behind me. The two men had passed me and were making for the lake. Unholstering my SIG, I said loud enough to hear, "Don't do anything stupid, you're covered and I really am not in the mood for a fight today."

The effect of my words was interesting. The two men stiffened and spun around, hands streaking towards their guns. Their hands stopped when they saw I had my gun out and as one, they placed their hands up in front of them, keeping a wary eye on me.

Tattooed man looked me over and spotted my bicycle behind me. "Thanks for not killing us, you sure had the opportunity. Nice ride, by the way."

"Thanks." I said. "I figure there's not enough of us left to be shooting each other, so there's no reason not to try to get along. But everybody is jumpy as hell, so you can understand my precaution."

"No problem." Tattoo said. "Can I put my hands down?"

"Sure." I safed my SIG and, looking Tattoo in the eyes, holstered my weapon. The move was not lost on Tattoo or the other man. By holstering without looking, I was showing them I knew where my weapon was and knew how to use it.

"Where you guys from?" I asked, curious as to the situation in other parts.

"We rolled out of Los Platos this morning." Tattoo said. "The wave had hit us a day earlier and if we didn't get out when we had the chance, we weren't going to make it."

"Wave?" I asked. Lack of power really had limited my informational sources.

"Wave of the dead. Many of the infected that were in the city started moving to the outlying areas in search of prey. They would kill or infect, people would die and reanimate, and move on to the next. House by house, they broke in, killed and consumed. Duncan, there," Tattoo indicated with a flick of his thumb, "Saw two cops surrounded and killed by a mob of over a hundred of the things. They never had a chance to even fire their guns." Tattoo sighed. "But I gotta give the man credit, he went back to the carnage after the zombies had left and got the cops' guns for protection. We figured we needed to bolt as soon as possible, so we threw everything we had into his car and made a run for it."

I thought for a second. Maybe this was what I had been dreading and was running from. Something had warned me to go and this just confirmed I did the right thing for me and Jake.

"Sounds like you did the right thing. Name's John, by the way." I said, holding out my hand.

Tattoo shook it. "Tom Carter. My friends call me Tommy. At least they would if..." His voice trailed off and I got his meaning loud and clear. He had lost everyone as well.

Jacob chose that moment to introduce himself by babbling fairly loudly. He did that from time to time when he felt he was being ignored. I went over to him and picked him up. He smiled at the two men, and buried his head in my shoulder again.

Tommy got over his shock to see a baby to say, "Holy shit. You've got a baby with you."

Duncan seemed shocked as well, but he didn't say anything. He just stared for a second, then went back to the car. He sat on the other side of the vehicle, away from us. I cocked an eyebrow in question at Tommy.

"Don't worry about Duncan," Tommy said, "He's gonna be quiet for a while, but then he'll be all right. He lost his brother and his brother's family to the dead, just so you know."

"That's too bad." I said. "Seems like everyone left alive has lost somebody."

"You, too, it would seem." Said Tommy, indicating Jake.

"Yeah, me, too. This is Jake, by the way." I said, my tone of voice telling him I was unwilling to go into it further.

Tommy changed the subject. "Where are you headed? You can't be going too far on a bike."

"I figured to head south, maybe hook up with other survivors or a town that hasn't been infected. Find a place to settle into while this whole mess works itself out." Even as I said it, it didn't seem realistic. But it was all I had at the moment until something else came up that sounded better. "What about you two?" I asked.

Tommy shrugged. "We had planned to hole up at my house after his house got overrun. But when they started just going house to house looking for people to eat, it was time to leave. I saw a family that had boarded up their windows get attacked, and in no time, at least a hundred of those things were tearing at the windows and doors. The boards didn't last long, and the family was eventually slaughtered. These things would beat their hands off trying to get into a house if they thought there was meat in there."

"Sounds like you guys have seen a lot." I said, shifting Jake, who was testing his "twisty" powers.

Tommy sighed. "Sometimes I wonder what the point is. Why bother to go on? Be real simple to just eat a bullet and join everyone who's died, you know?"

I nodded. I had been there, and the only thing bringing me back from the brink was the little guy in my arms.

We got lost in our own separate thoughts, so much so that we jumped when Duncan leaped up. "We got company!" he yelled, pointing towards the entrance to the preserve.

9

Tommy and I both craned our necks to see what Duncan was pointing at, and we saw a group of people slowly making their way down the lane towards the lake. There was about fifteen of them, and it was obvious they were not among the living. Their shambling, disjointed walk was the first clue, and the second was when one of them stumbled, his arm, which had been hanging by a tendon, snapped off, and he didn't seem to notice.

Tommy and Duncan fingered their weapons and looked at me. I took the situation in and made a decision. "If we stay, we might get them all. But a battle will attract a lot of attention. I'm taking off back on the trail. I'll fight on my terms." I said, taking Jake back to the bike and strapping him in.

Tommy called to me, "What about us? Our car can't take ramming any more of them, and we don't have enough ammo to get them all."

I looked at Tommy. "Your car can fit on the trail. Get moving and follow me."

Tommy didn't need to be told twice, especially when the zombies caught sight of us and started groaning, their pace increasing at the sight of food. Duncan was already in the car, looking anxiously over his shoulder and mentally calculating how long it will take for the zombies to get to us. Tommy ran to the car and started the engine. I pushed the bike and trailer back to the trail and guided Tommy and Duncan over to the path. Their car was just narrow enough to fit comfortably on the trail, but if we had to cross any bridges or go through any tunnels, we were going to be in trouble.

I rode quickly, putting as much distance between the zombies and myself as I could. I knew they were going to follow, but hopefully they would lose the trail after a little bit. The nice thing about the trail was it curved frequently, so the zombies were going to lose sight of us fast.

Their groaning faded into the distance as we headed back to the trail crossroads, and I took the south fork. I figured to stay on the trail as much as I could, and avoid population centers. Eventually, I figured to hit Interstate 57,and be able to head south with the hope that other towns had survived and would welcome other survivors. That was the plan, anyway.

After riding for a while, Tommy honked his horn and got my attention. I pulled up and he got out of the car. He was holding a length of rope and I eyed it curiously.

"Feel like taking it easy for a bit?" he asked, tying one end to the rear bumper of the car.

I got his meaning and grinned. "Sure, thanks. The trail just heads south for a while. It will cross two roads, then merge with a main highway for a bit. That will be Oak Lawn Ave. It might get a little snarky there, so we're going to have to be careful." I took the other end of the rope and tied it to my bike, leaving about twenty feet of space.

"Try not to go too fast, hey?" I asked

"No worries." said Tommy, as he got back into the car.

We started off with myself and Jake in tow, and it was a great relief not to have to pedal. We had a few moments where I nearly ran into the back of the car, but that was because I wasn't paying close enough attention. Jakey loved it. We were going fast enough to get some wind in his face, and he laughed nearly the whole time.

Tommy managed to get to Oak Lawn Avenue without a problem, but I could see things were not going to go completely smooth. The road had quite few cars on it, and we could see several were occupied. I untied the rope and coiled it back up, tucking it into the bumper. I eased up to the car's windows and Tommy poked his head out.

"Where to, chief?" he asked.

I looked at the road ahead. There were several cars in front of us, and it looked to be difficult for the car to get past. On the bike, I would have no trouble, but I really couldn't leave Duncan and Tommy behind. I thought for a minute, then said "We can push some of the unoccupied cars out of the way on the left side, and that should let you through. Watch the occupied ones, though. They might not be fully dead."

Tommy ducked back inside, and after a moments discussion and a game of Rock/Paper/Scissors, Duncan got out of the car and started moving vehicles. I left Jake with Tommy, who got out to talk to him, and helped Duncan shove several vehicles out of the way. We moved three of them, and headed for a fourth when Duncan suddenly yelled.

"Shit, its got me!" A zombie had reached out of the back window of a sedan and had managed to grab his belt. He tried to pull away but its grip was too strong. His struggles were starting to pull the zombie out of the car, and I knew we would have real problems if he dragged it out. "Get it off!" He was starting to sound hysterical, and I didn't need to attract any more attention. Tommy looked up from his playing with Jake and started forward.

I waved him off and, unslinging my crowbar, went up behind the zombie. It was a hugely fat woman, and upon inspection, I realized there was no way she was going to fit through the window. But her very ugly head, topped with brilliant orange hair, had managed to get out of the window, and her mouth was snapping at Duncan's waist.

"Help!" Duncan yelled, straining to break her grip.

I lined up behind the woman and took a two handed grip on my crowbar. I raised it and smashed it down on her head. She slumped down, then raised her head and looked at me, hissing in frustration at a meal about to get away. I swung again and cracked her skull, causing her to droop and slide back into the car. The motion caused Duncan to slide towards the window, and his shoes squealed in protest as they were dragged over the pavement "Shiiiitt!" he hollered.

Part of me wondered if he was going to be pulled into the car like a cartoon character. But he stopped and I used the hook on the crowbar to pry the fingers from his belt.

"Thanks, man." Duncan said. "I thought that bitch had me for sure."

"No problem." I said. "Was your belt buckle stuck?" I asked.

Duncan stared at me for a second, then slapped himself on the forehead. "Don't tell Tommy," he said. "I get enough shit as it is."

"Deal. Let's get moving." I headed back to Jake and mounted up.

Tommy was able to move around the cars and I could see other zombies trapped in vehicles, pawing at the glass and moaning. Some were stuck in their seatbelts, and the summer heat was not kind to those in cars. One looked to have very nearly liquefied. I shuddered at what *that* had to smell like.

We moved down Oak Lawn Avenue towards the office center, and didn't see any more activity. Part of me wondered where everyone was, the other part was grateful it was quiet. I saw more evidence of hurried exits, and in a parking lot several cars looked like they had been broken into. We moved past a tanning spa and saw two police cars sitting in the parking lot. I waved Tommy to a halt and rode over to investigate. Checking the windows, I didn't see anything in the vehicles. Trying the door on the first one, I found it unlocked. The car had nothing of value in it, so I decided to pop the trunk and see if there was anything in there.

My eyes widened at the sight of the trunk. There was an AR style rifle, extra magazines, extra ammunition for the rifle, plus 9mm ammo. There was shotgun ammunition, but no shotgun. I found some gloves, a balaclava, and some goggles. I guessed this was some kind of riot gear. What they needed it for in Turley Park, I could only guess. I grabbed what I could and brought it back to the car. Duncan's eyes nearly bugged out of his head when I brought up the booty, and he jumped out to help me. Tommy jumped out to check the other car, but it was locked. He smashed the window and popped the trunk. He didn't find another AR, but he did find some 40 S&W ammo, another set of gloves, and a bulletproof vest. He took it all and headed back to the car, stopping to give me the ammo for my gun.

We were grinning like idiots when the wall fell in. Literally. Tommy's smashing of the window must have roused the local zombies, because they managed to cave in the section of fence of the yard they were stuck in. There had to be fifty of them, and they came boiling out of the yard like a fetid, pus-filled avalanche. Their groans chorused as they saw us and started to give chase. They were ten yards from us and closing fast. I ran to the bike and hopped on, throwing the gear and ammo on top of my carefully piled stuff.

Duncan froze for a second, then drew his weapon and fired at the mass. His bullet stuck a man squarely in the chest, knocking him down, but causing no real damage. Jake screamed at the noise, and the zombies groaned louder.

"Save it!" I yelled, pedaling away. "Get moving, there's too many!"

Tommy gunned the engine and Duncan barely closed the door as zombies slammed into the car, clawing at the metal and glass. The car shook off the zombies and caught up to me, with the crowd in pursuit. Tommy leaned out the window. "Where now?"

I shook my head as I pedaled for all I was worth. Jake was crying, and I could hear groans all around me as the moans of our pursuers called forth the minions of hell. I was thinking furiously of where we could go, when the answer came literally around the corner.

I spotted a gas station down a crossroad and headed for it. It was one of those large stations with a big convenience store. It was out of the line of sight of the zombies chasing us, and I hoped like hell they wouldn't see us going for it.

I sped into the station and zipped around to the back of the building. There was a wall behind separating it from a subdivision and little else. A dumpster was nearby, but it was empty. I jumped off the bike and tried the back door. It was locked. *Naturally*, I thought. I grabbed my crowbar and went to work on the door, trying to open it as quickly and quietly as I could without damaging it.

I managed to pry the frame just enough to get the door open and I pushed the bike and trailer inside. Just as I got the trailer in I was wondering where my new friends had gone off to. I got my answer as a now-quiet car coasted to the back of the station, and Tommy and Duncan both jumped out, grabbing weapons and ammo.

As they jumped inside, Tommy said breathlessly, "Would you believe we ran out of fucking gas?"

I just shook my head at the irony and closed the door, using the crowbar to bend the frame back and secure the door. Tommy had run to the front door to make sure it was locked, and came skidding back to the counter, unlimbering his rifle and spreading out the clips on the counter. Duncan set up a position by the soft drinks section, after being shown how to use the rifle by Tommy, and I stayed over by the drink machine. I still had a crying Jake with me, and pulled out a bottle for him to take for lunch. I prayed it would keep him quiet until the worst of the danger had passed, if it did. I laid my carbine on the floor in front of me and sat back against the machine. I pulled out a spare magazine and placed it nearby.

We were actually in a better position than I could have hoped for. The glass windows were mostly covered in advertising posters, and stacks of water softener salt reinforced the windows up to chest height. Shelving units further obstructed anything looking in, and the place was in sufficient disarray that we would be hard to spot if we held still. The only thing that might give us away was sound, and my big concern on that was Jake. He was generally a happy baby, and liked to hear himself. Unfortunately, in our current situation, that could prove fatal.

We waited in silence for the ghouls to show up, the only noise was Jake slurping on his bottle. He fussed a bit from time to time and my heart was in my throat. We didn't have long to wait. The first one, a bald zombie with a hand missing, slowly walked through the gas station. His head turned slowly from side to side, and I could see his nostrils flaring. Right behind him was another man, this one a grayish color, and in an advanced state of decay. Skin was hanging off him, and in more than one place I could see bone showing through. A woman came next and she gave us the worst scare. She came around the corner, with a ripped up shoulder and bite marks down one bare arm. She was right up to the window, and we all froze in place. She slid along the front, leaving a greasy trail on the glass, and stopped right at the door. She faced the door, and looked right into the store. None of us dared to move, and we all wondered how to get her to move on. Her dead eyes just stared, and I could see her nose flatten a little as she pressed her face to the door.

I suddenly realized what she was doing. She was trying to sniff us out, and if we had passed through that door, she would have found us. We waited in silence, and I was afraid to even look in another direction. She stayed at the door, and one hand rose to scrape against the glass. Another zombie saw what she was doing and came to investigate. He wasn't in as bad shape, and I couldn't see any trauma on him. He must have turned from internal infection. He walked up to the door and put both hands on the glass. I was getting anxious. Jake was about to finish his bottle and was going to need to burp. If I didn't move him, he was going to get fussy and loud.

The zombies stopped moving and slowly put their hands down at their sides. I was stunned when I saw them actually close their eyes. What the heck was up with that? I wasn't about to question their motives, I just decided to use the opportunity. I slid down further towards the floor and sat behind a shelving unit. I couldn't see the zombies, and hoped they couldn't see me. I shifted Jake, and he let out a small but forceful belch. I couldn't see the zombies, but I saw Tommy tense.

"Their eyes just opened again" he whispered in a barely audible voice, not daring to move even his lips.

"Christ, they have good hearing," I whispered back, just as quietly. I was silently praying that Jake would not make any more noise. I had to assume the store was currently surrounded, and we would be in serious trouble if they found out we were in here. For right now, I had to assume they knew we were somewhere, they just didn't know where.

"How many are out there?" I whispered to Tommy. I couldn't see from my hiding place behind the shelves.

I could see Tommy's eyes darting around the station, and he hissed, "At least fifty that I can see, God knows how many more." I felt bad for him. Being at the counter, he was directly in the line of sight of the zombies at the door, and couldn't move at all. I felt Jake shift, and looked down to see that he was starting to get sleepy eyes. The fresh air and the excitement, not to mention the recent bottle, had done a number to put the guy to sleep. I held him to my shoulder and rocked him gently, praying he would go to sleep. Knowing my luck, he'd probably snore for the first time in his life.

I heard a scratching at the glass again, and figured the two ghouls were still trying to figure out if food was available in the store. I just hoped they wouldn't decide to smash the glass and find out.

Tommy suddenly let out a breath and whispered, "They're leaving. Something distracted them and they're heading away."

Duncan slid away from his position and went back by Tommy. "Thought that woman zombie was going to find us for sure." He said, shaking his head and placing his rifle on his shoulder.

"Same here." I said. "I thought a burp was going to be our undoing."

Tommy shrugged, "We'd have figured something out."

We were still speaking in whispers, as we could see dozens of zombies in the streets. The risk of one coming to investigate was still high, so we decided to retreat to the back areas of the convenience store. Jake had fallen asleep, so I brought him back to the manager's office and laid him on a Mexican blanket I found in the store. I closed the door most of the way, and went to exploring our new home. At least for a while.

I checked the back area, and found the storeroom mostly intact, save for a scattering of towels and such on the floor. I found a box of energy bars, and added it to the supplies I had in the bike trailer. Duncan found a supply of batteries that would be useful, and some cheap two-way radios. He unpacked them and put batteries in, giving me one of the radios when he finished. Tommy was checking out the bathrooms, making sure there weren't any surprise visitors waiting for us.

Duncan and I were sitting in the employee's break area, enjoying a lunch of Ho-Ho's, peanuts, and stale Doritos's, when Tommy came back and sat with us.

"Well, we're alone, thank God, no surprises in the building. I was able to look out the window of the women's bathroom and see our car. The zombies were crawling all over it like sniffing dogs, but they didn't break in or anything." Tommy said, picking up a Ho-Ho and having some lunch himself.

"Any idea what might have distracted them? Not that I'm not grateful, but if there's someone else out there, we might be able to help them." I said, opening another package of Doritos's.

"Not a clue. Anybody willing to change the focus of so many Z's has to be slightly crazy." Said Tommy.

" 'Z's'?" I asked.

Duncan piped up "Z for Zombie. Like calling them Zack or Zed."

I shrugged. "Works for me." I looked around our little haven. "Well, gents, what's our next move? I personally would rather not spend the rest of my days in a gas station. Kind of lowers your ranking when you finally head to the Great Divide, you know?"

Tommy laughed. "I hear that. So what's the plan?"

I pointed at the ceiling. "We should probably send someone up top to get a look at the situation, and see if there might be a break in the Z migration for us to make a run for it. We should also fortify the front windows, as they are our weakest point. If we can't fortify them, we should at least find a way to keep from being seen from the outside."

Duncan spoke up. "I can handle that. I saw some advertisement posters in the back area, I can tack them up without too much trouble."

"Sounds good," I said, "Just make sure our girlfriend doesn't come back."

"No joke. I swear she looked right at me." Duncan stood up and headed to the back to get the posters. Tommy looked at me.

"You want to go climbing, or should I?" he asked.

"I'll go." I said. "Jake's good for a while, and I am curious to see what kind of hole we managed to dig for ourselves."

"What do you mean?" Tommy asked, his face scowling.

"We stopped here, but we could have kept going and put more distance between them and us." I said.

Tommy shook his head. "You might have, but we would have been meat. We ran out of gas, remember?"

It was my turn to shake my head. "I forgot about that." I said sheepishly.

"Yeah. When I saw you had just the bike, I thought you were nuts. But right now, you look like a freakin' genius."

"Got it. I'm going to head up. I'll be back in ten minutes."

I headed to the back room, where the ladder was to get to the roof. I had already found the key to the padlock in the office where Jake was sleeping, and it was a simple matter to climb up, unlock the lock, and get on the roof.

Once up there, it was different. I had to stay low so as not to be accidentally seen by the zombies roaming around the area. The roof was covered in tar paper, so I was able to move quietly to the edge and peep over at the car. The zombies had abandoned it as uninteresting, and I could see them starting to shuffle down the street towards the east. Their walk was mesmerizing, the slow, steady gait, swaying from side to side as their virus infected brains worked at remembering basic motor functions. They had no direction, just wandering where they would until something attracted their attention.

I rolled to the center of the roof, then crawled up to the front. A four-foot false front afforded me a good bit of cover. I slowly raised my head over the top and looked about. There were still about twenty or so zombies wandering around, but none seemed interested in the store. They seemed to be heading in circles, and some were just standing still, waiting for stimuli to motivate them. I was curious enough to try a little experiment, and I looked around the roof to see if there was anything I could use. I spotted a tennis ball at the corner and belly crawled over to get it. Bringing it back to the front, I positioned myself and using a hook shot throw, lobbed the ball to the middle of the intersection.

The outcome was amazing. Even before the ball hit the ground, zombies had already zeroed in on it and were chasing it. Those that had not seen it, spun around at the sound of it hitting the pavement. The group as a whole converged on the bouncing ball and became a tangled mass of arms and legs. Several zombies fell to be stepped on by their comrades, and the group only lost interest when they realized there was nothing for them to eat. I did manage to move most of the zombies away from the gas station, and they were now focused primarily on the parking lot across the street. *Useful bit of information, that*, I thought. I didn't figure a tennis ball would do any distracting if they were chasing live prey, but if they didn't know you were there and got distracted enough to move, that could buy you some very precious seconds.

I turned around and as I made my way to the ladder I happened to look over the stone wall and into the backyards of the subdivision behind the gas station. I saw a lot of white flags on mailboxes and shook my head. I also saw a lot of zombies milling about and couldn't figure out why they were there. That was until I looked at the second floor windows and saw what had to be thirty people looking at me. To say I was stunned stupid was an understatement.

The people had rigged together four homes by the upper floors. Ladders extended between the houses, and I shuddered to think what it must be like to crawl on an extension ladder suspended over a sea of hungry ghouls. I raised a hand in greeting, and got twenty in return. There was no way to communicate outside of hand signals, and I needed to get back inside. I went back down the ladder and met up with Tommy and Duncan.

Duncan had effectively managed to cover the front windows, so we were okay with anything looking in. We still needed to be as quiet as possible, since sound seemed to attract them in droves. We sat down at the employee section again and I had Jake in my lap. He was playing with some stuffed animals I had found in the store, and taking turns hitting them on the table, trying to eat them, and talking to them.

"So how was the roof? I saw the Z's go running after a tennis ball. That your doing?" Tommy asked, sipping on a warm bottle of water.

"Yeah, that was me. Just running a little experiment." I said.

"Well, it was exactly the right thing to do at the time. Duncan couldn't put up the posters without attracting attention, so you gave him just the opening he needed."

Duncan nodded. "I had everything taped and ready to go, but couldn't move because three of them were too close. Thanks."

I nodded back. "Speaking of close. Have either of you taken look out back, over the wall?"

Tommy shook his head. "Can't see anything over the wall unless I stood on the dumpster, and I sure ain't one to try that right now. Why?"

"Well, you're not going to believe this, but behind the wall, there's a subdivision of houses, and at least three of the houses are occupied with a number of people."

Tommy and Duncan just stared at me. If I didn't know better, I would swear Jake stared at me, too.

I continued. "They are living on their second floors, and have connected the houses with extension ladders on the roofs. It looks like several neighbors came together and have created a sort of refuge, but I can't imagine they have enough food for all those people.'

Duncan halted in his eating of a granola bar. "What do you want to do?"

I thought for a second. "We need to communicate and see what their situation is. For all we know, they're fine and just enjoying the show of three lunatics trying to make a run for it. Duncan, do you remember where you put those radios you found?"

Duncan nodded. "Yeah, I remember. Are you thinking on tossing one over?"

I shook my head. "I don't have an arm like that. We need to think of some way to launch one over without attracting too much attention."

It was Tommy's turn to shake his head. "Why worry about attracting attention? Why not just throw it in the yard?"

"There's about thirty zombies wandering around the yards, and likely as many in the houses on the ground floors. We'd be witnessing a slaughter if they tried to get it." I said.

Tommy looked down. "Hadn't figured on that." he murmured. Then he brightened. "What if we tossed the radio into the yard, distracted the zombies from the roof here, and they could get to it."

I thought about it. "What about the zombies on our side? Won't they hear us?"

Tommy got more excited. "Yeah, but if we're on the roof, near the false front, they'll never know where the noise is coming from, and lose interest in a little while. All we need to do is get the ones in the yard to see us, and they'll be wandering over to the fence in no time."

"Works for me".

Duncan got the radio ready by wrapping it in a towel and putting it in a coffee can. We didn't need to throw it too far, but a good fifty yards. Tommy said he'd give it a throw. I had no problem with that. Jake was getting antsy, so I needed to spend some time with him before I gave him his dinner. Duncan and Tommy would let me know how it went.

They were gone for half an hour, then came scrambling back down the ladder. Duncan was slapping Tommy on the back and Tommy was grinning like a loon. I looked up from feeding Jake and asked, "So, Mrs. Lincoln, how was the show?"

Tommy slumped into the seat and took a swig of water. "I've never felt so wanted in my life. We climbed up on the roof and waved to the people in the houses, and then Duncan whistled. Holy shit. You would have thought he just farted in church. Every zombie in the yard came limping over and clawing at the wall. I saw several come out of the houses and join the group." He took another drink. "After that, we just sat there and let the group see us. Duncan would occasionally wave at the zombies, but it gave me time to throw the can." Another sip. "I had no idea I could throw that far."

I glanced over. Jake was nearly done. "How far?"

Tommy grinned. "I bounced it off the porch and it landed near a smashed-in sliding glass door. I have no idea how they're going to get it, but we did what we could."

I couldn't argue with that. We had no real obligation to those people in the houses, and they had no obligation to us, either. But since the dead seemed to be outnumbering the living these days, we kind of needed to try to stick together. Duncan clicked the radio on and we waited. I gave Jake a bath in the big sink in the back area, and he loved it. He played with the faucet and laughed when I used a bottle of water to wash his hair. I really envied his inability to understand the situation he was in. Yeah, we had a scary moment there, but we recovered and now just needed to plan our next step.

10

The sun was starting to set, and that was when the radio crackled to life.

"Hello? Hello? Anybody there? Are the guys who threw the radio to us still there? Hello?" The voice sounded frantic.

Duncan picked up the radio. "Hello, we read you. How are you all doing?" He looked at Tommy and me when we came over to hear.

"We're okay for now, but we're running out of food. We've been rationing for a week now, and are nearly out. Any way you can get some to us?"

Duncan looked at Tommy , who shook his head. "Negative, it's too risky right now. How many people are up there?"

The answer stunned us all. "We've got sixty-two people on the second floor of four houses. We've been going back and forth with the ladders. The zombies know we're here and won't leave."

It was my turn to shake my head. "Can't get them out without serious help. Do they have vehicles?" I asked.

Duncan asked the question to the person on the radio. "No, our vehicles are gone. A group passing through took them two weeks ago." the voice said sadly.

I ground my teeth in frustration. *People suck*, I thought. A thought occurred to me. We could get them out, and moving, but we were going to have to do it soon. I reached over for the radio.

"Hello?" I said.

"Yes?" came the reply.

"Do you have any weapons?" I asked, formulating a plan as I spoke.

"Yes, we have about fifteen guns and everyone has a weapon of some kind"

I raised my eyebrows. That was a lot more that I ever had expected. "Do you have any ammo?"

"We have about four shots each. We used a lot when we set up our little forts." the radio said back.

I hoped it would be enough. "I have a plan, but it's going to take a serious concentrated effort. We'll talk again tomorrow. Can you hang on until then?"

The voice sounded determined. "We've made it this far. What time?"

"I'll call you back at 8 am. Turn off the radio so you don't waste batteries. Out."

"Will do. Out." The voice sounded off.

Tommy and Duncan looked at me. "We have some planning to do, and I for one, am tired of playing nice with these decaying bastards."

"What's the plan then?" Tommy asked.

"Simple." I said. "We kill them all."

Planning became lively after that, and we talked and long into the night.

11

The next morning, at precisely 8am, the radio crackled to life.

"Hello? Is anyone there, hello?" The voice seemed calmer, but I could hear other voices in the background. I picked up the radio.

"Hi there. How are you all holding up?" I asked.

"People are pretty excited, I have to say. They figured they were going to die up here either through starvation or suicide." The voice said.

I could understand that. Tommy and I had talked about such things as well. "Can you hang out for a little while longer?" I was curious about our time schedule. If we could wait until it rained, that would be so much better for trying to move a large group of people without attracting so much attention. My plans were shifting away from hiding, but even I knew when to cut and run. We could be running into thousands of zombies, we just had no way of knowing.

"We can hold out for about a week, then things will get ugly."

"Understood. Listen, we think we can get you out and moving, but it's going to take some coordination." I outlined the basics of the plan, and heard some exclamations from the other end as the voice responded.

"We don't have much choice, do we?"

I waited a second before responding. "I'm not going to lie to you. We're going to have a running fight the second we get this going. If you don't want to go through with it, that's your choice. We'll leave the door open to the gas station and you can try to get your food from here after we leave. But we are going. You need to decide if you are staying."

The radio was quiet. I could almost hear the arguments going on. Then the voice came back on. "Okay. We're with you. What do you want us to do?"

I spoke for about fifteen minutes, and then signed off. They had promised to be ready whenever we were, and we had no real idea when we were going to go. I was hoping for rain within the time frame, but the best laid plans always seem to go wayward, as I had already seen.

I fed Jake and then spoke with Tommy and Duncan about being ready to move as soon as possible. They had already been to their car, and managed to get most of their essential gear, as well as the rest of the ammo, back into the gas station. They had also moved the dumpster right next to building as needed.

Duncan had found some duffle bags in the back room, and he and Tommy both filled two of them with gear. I still intended to move with the bike and trailer, so I was good. I looked around the store and selected a few items I thought might be useful, but for the most part, a lot of the stuff was useless. I saw some magazines near the front, so I wandered up that way. I looked over the selection, and picked up two of them that looked interesting. A gun magazine and a news magazine. Both were a month old.

I stood up and looked straight into the eyes of a zombie. One of the posters had fallen, and I hadn't noticed it until I had stood in front of the store. The zombie looked at me, then opened its mouth and moaned loudly. It was a nasty one, with no shirt and huge tears in its flesh. Its skin was stretched over its skull and bared teeth snapped at me as I stepped back, my hand going for my SIG, then the zombie smashed his head into the glass. The window held, but a crack formed and grew longer as the zombie moaned again and struck the glass with its fist. Behind it, I could see more zombies coming over to investigate.

Crap. Well, we needed to go, why not now? I bolted back to the back room and grabbed Jake, getting him in the seat of the bike and giving him a toy to play with. I put some hearing protection in his ears, as it was about to get very loud.

"Duncan, Tommy! We got company! We gotta start the plan NOW!" I yelled

Duncan didn't hesitate, he grabbed his rifle and extra magazines and headed to the roof. Tommy came running out of the back area and grabbed up the radio and hollered for them to get moving, we're bugging out.

I grabbed my carbine and an extra magazine and headed back for the front. The zombie who had been pounding on the window had broken a large portion out of it, and was starting to climb through, like a big greasy worm. I raised my gun and blew his head in half, shifting my aim immediately to the zombie behind him. I shot that one down as well, and saw many others begin walking my way. I cleared away another one, then heard Duncan open up on the roof. It was gratifying to see several of the shuffling dead go down for good, head shots taking the unlife out of them. I shot another one that was close to the front, too close for Duncan to see. It was a young boy, likely no older than twelve, with a hideous neck wound. Black fluid leaked out of the big vein in his neck, and he dropped with a coughing moan.

Tommy was not sitting idle. He went out the back door and shot two zombies that had been around the side, out of sight of the roof and front. He dashed back inside for his and Duncan's duffle bags and brought them outside.

Two minutes into the fight I heard a crashing fusillade of shots, and then another. I smiled grimly to myself. *Looks like the squatters are rebelling against the landlords*, I thought. I looked out into the street and saw that Duncan had done his job well. He had waited until the zombies had reached his 'killing zone', then proceeded to drop them systematically. Thirty corpses were stacked on each other in a wide semicircle like a grotesque fence. Damn fine shooting.

I heard Duncan jump off the roof onto the dumpster, then push it over to the fence for the wave of people we were sure to have. I pushed the bike and trailer out of the gas station, and checked on Jakey. He was fussing and his bottom lip was out, indicating he was about to cry, he started squirming a little and wanting to get rolling, but I needed to make sure we had everybody first. I pushed the bike out to the center of the station and looked around. Down the street towards the west was a lot of movement, and we were going to be in serious trouble in about ten minutes.

People were starting to stream over the fence. They had backpacks and duffle bags, some were even carrying garbage bags of stuff. I pointed at the gas station's back door. "You have two minutes. Grab what you can then get out here." I wasn't going to let anything go to waste if these people needed it. Tommy and Duncan were helping people over the fence, and protecting their rear. Several zombies had come for the noise and more than once I heard the crack of their rifles.

I rolled to the street and scanned the road. God, there was a lot of zombies to the west. We had no choice but to run south and hope for the best. I checked the north road and saw several zombies coming out of the subdivisions. I shot one that was getting too close, and added to the fence Duncan had created. We needed to move.

I looked back and saw Tommy and Duncan running towards me, their duffle bags banging around their hips. They were followed by a crowd of people, ranging in age from one to fifty years old. I got on my bike and rode ahead, figuring with my mobility I would act as scout. We headed south on Oak Lawn Avenue, passing by several burnt-out homes and businesses. I made a brief stop at a small gun shop on the way, but found it to be looted of guns and ammo. I did find two crossbows and a bunch of bolts, so I passed those out to two men who did not have guns.

The group had organized themselves well, with those who had firearms on the outside, protecting those on the inside who were unarmed. There were about ten children on the inside, corralled by their mothers and older children. Tommy and Duncan led the way, and I rode point.

Behind us, the dead followed. We were able to keep ahead of them simply by walking, but if we got delayed, we were going to be in trouble. I hoped to hell we would be alright. I was trying to make it to the junior high school at the end of the road, figuring it would make a great place to make a stand and regroup.

It wasn't until we had gone about a mile when we hit trouble. I was coming out of a side street and heading down the main road when three men stepped out of a building and blocked the road. I was so busy looking for zombies I didn't notice them until I was on top of them.

The leader of the trio, a scruffy-looking specimen, held a shotgun casually in the crook of his arm. His wide face split into a grin as he looked over my gear and my son. His comrades, two smallish individuals with several pierced body parts, had each a rifle and two pistols shoved into their belts. Tommy and Duncan were too far behind to be of any help, so this was my mess to deal with. Perfect.

I stopped my bike about ten feet from the trio, and was immediately covered by the two riflemen. I dropped my hands to my lap and sat back. My SIG was holstered and my carbine was slung over my shoulder. This was going to take some negotiation. Jakey had recovered from his grouch and waved his arms at his new friends, not realizing they were actually enemies.

The leader walked towards me and straddled my front tire. He placed a hand on my handlebars and kept smiling that stupid grin of his. "How's it going?" he asked, his eyes lingering on my sidearm and carbine.

"Just fine, thanks." I moved my hand ever so slightly, unlocking the safety on my Enfield, which apparently, Smiley hadn't seen.

"Good." He said. "You realize you're on my road, now." His smile never reached his eyes, and I could see this was going to get ugly. I didn't have time for diplomacy, but I also had Jake.

"That's too bad." I said, thinking to myself, *Are you kidding me?* "But I am in a hurry and didn't know it was your road. Any chance of letting me and my son and the people behind me just heading on our way?"

Smiley laughed, and his two sidekicks laughed with him. "Oh, no, no, no. What kind of businessman would I be if I just let any asshole who wants to get away without paying?"

My eyes turned hard and Smiley stopped smiling. "What do you want?" I said, already knowing the answer.

"Your gear, your ride, your weapons, and..." looking over my shoulder at he approaching crowd. "Oh yes, your women." Smiley was grinning again at the thought of the haul he was going to score.

I pretended to think about it and Smiley removed his hand from my handlebar. He grinned at his companions while jacking a round into his shotgun. He already had a round chambered, so a live round went spinning off over his shoulder. His friend, a short blond with a tattoo on his neck, snickered, and Smiley glared at him.

That was the opening I needed. I pulled the trigger on the Enfield, and the booming report echoed off the buildings. The bullet punched through Smiley's crotch, blowing open his scrotum and severing his testicles in the process. The bullet entered his lower abdomen, exiting through his ass. Smiley screamed and dropped to the ground, clutching his ruined manhood and bleeding profusely through is fingers.

I didn't wait for his companions to realize what had happened. Right after I pulled the trigger on the Enfield, I was drawing my SIG and punched two holes into Smiley's companion to my left. I ducked down as the one on the right fired his rifle more in surprise than anything else, and the bullet passed harmlessly over my head. I swung the SIG around and fired twice more, the handgun's crack sounding puny after the military gun. The second thug dropped to the ground, his life's blood pouring out of the two holes in his chest.

Smiley kept on screaming. He tried crawling to his knees, but the pain knocked him down again. I had no pity. How many people had he robbed, possibly killed? He would have killed me and Jake without a thought had I not been able to get the drop on him. For his part, Jake was letting me know he was unhappy by screaming his head off.

By this time, Tommy and Duncan had caught up to me, their rifles at the ready.

"What's up?" Tommy asked, looking at the now-whimpering Smiley and his two dead companions.

"Would you believe this moron wanted to charge a toll?" I ejected the spent round in the Enfield, chambering a new one. I turned to Jake and tried to comfort him.

Duncan snorted and gathered up the weapons and ammo from the dead and dying. He took it back to the group and distributed it. Some people looked curiously at the scene and then at me. I decided to make sure there was no misinterpretation.

"This piece of shit wanted to rob us of the ability to defend ourselves. By his confidence, I figure he and his friends had done it before. I changed his mind." I was not in the mood to be judged. "Let's keep going. The dead are catching up."

And indeed they were. We could hear their moaning now as they got progressively closer. We moved away and heard Smiley's screams cut off as the dead caught up to him and reduced him and his companions to bones.

We headed down the street and I was hopeful about holing up at the school, but when I got closer to check it out, I realized it was not going to be an option. The school had apparently caught fire at some point and large gaping holes were in the burned out roof. I waited for the rest of the group to catch up, and discussed options with Tommy and Duncan.

"Well, we need to keep moving, and I was hoping this place could provide us with a little respite." I said, indicating the burned building behind me.

Tommy looked doubtful. "I'm not from this area, so I have no idea what's around here."

Duncan piped up. "There's a concert place nearby, with fence all around."

I thought about it. I knew the place, and initially it sounded good, but long term would not be useful. "Not defendable enough if they come in force, and they will."

Tommy spoke up. "So where then? We can't walk forever."

I racked my brain. All of a sudden, I knew where to go. There was a two story school nearby that had been built within the last ten years. The windows were high enough off the ground that entry would be difficult, and there would be plenty of room for everyone. The doors were all steel, and there were only a couple that might prove problematic. We'd fall off that bridge when we came to it. Right now we needed to get moving.

"Come on, I know where we're going." I said, mounting up and moving out.

"Where?" asked Tommy.

"Another school." I said, giving him my best smile. "Trust me."

Tommy sighed. "Why not? You've been good so far."

Duncan punched him on the arm. "He just took out three armed men. You want to argue?"

Tommy shook his head at me as he began walking again. "Not really."

12

We headed down a west-bound street, toward a huge intersection. There were a lot of cars, and I could see many of them were occupied. We needed to be careful. I led the small procession down the left hand side of the road, there were fewer cars on that side, and we could stick to the shoulder much easier. We passed the convention center and hotel, not bothering to stop and check it out. I had heard they used that area for treatment of early infected people, and I really did not want to wander into a zombie convention if I could avoid it.

There was a scream behind me and everyone tensed and spun around. I looked and saw a woman who had gotten too close to a car managed to get grabbed and bit before she managed to pull herself free. One of the other armed men finished off the zombie, but the woman sat down on the ground, staring at the bite mark on her arm. Her husband sat down next to her, tears forming in his eyes. Tommy spoke to both of them, and then came up to me.

"She got too close to a car and got nabbed. Zombie bit her before she could get help. She says to leave her, and her husband wants to stay with her." Tommy sounded sympathetic.

I sighed. *How many more?* I thought. *How many have to die?* I made the decision. "We need to keep moving. Ask if she wants someone to end it for her, talk to her husband, and see what he wants to do. But we need to keep moving."

Tommy nodded. "Will do." He headed back to the couple, I waved to Duncan to keep moving. We needed to get to somewhere safe and do it now. The dead were still following us, and it looked like they were growing in number.

There was a commotion behind me. The man had pulled a gun and was waving it around. "Don't come near me! You can't kill her! Stay away from her!" Tommy was backing up with his hand up, the other still holding his rifle.

I called from where I was. "Leave them! We don't have time!" I realized I had grown a little cold, but all of a sudden I was put in charge of dozens of people, and I was not going to risk them for this.

Tommy ran from them, and the dead started to close in. I saw the man holding his wife, then I turned away. I had a bad feeling about what was going to happen next.

Sure enough, a shot rang out. Then another. I looked back briefly and saw two forms lying on the ground, blood pooling beneath their heads. Jake started crying briefly at the noise, and I realized he was going to need to eat soon. What a mess. I got back on the bike and headed back to the front of the procession, passing Tommy and the rest. We crossed the intersection without further incident, and headed towards another intersection. As we passed the mental hospital, a man came running out. Duncan ran out to intercept him and the two had a brief conference. Duncan ran back to me.

"What's up?" I asked.

"Man says he has about seventy people holed up in the hospital, but they're nearly out of water and food, and need to move on. Can they join us?" Duncan asked with a lopsided grin, like a boy asking if he can keep the puppy he just brought home.

"Why not?" I said. "See if you can get a small detail to help them get moving, and form an armed perimeter around the group. We have enough guns for that. But they have to move." I pointed to the small army of living dead that slouched along behind us. "They have five minutes, otherwise they aren't going to be going anywhere."

"You got it." Duncan ran to the main group and soon six armed men headed off. Looking at the hospital, it would have been ideal if they had a source of water and food. The building didn't have a first floorsave for one access door, and if that was blocked, the dead had no chance to get in. Something about that nagged at my mind, but I pushed it back for the time being.

I rode up to the front again, and Jakey was starting to get really fussy. I knew I was going to have to stop somewhere and feed him. Trouble was I couldn't stop until I knew we were safe, and we still had a little ways to go. I quieted him with a binky and rode on.

I passed the Turley Park Police Station and quickly rode around the building. I wanted to check out the armory to see if there was anything worth taking. Tommy caught up to me and started checking the cars in the parking lot. After about two minutes, he had broken into three of them, and the unarmed men in our group managed to secure more AR-15's , more ammo, and a couple of shotguns. I couldn't find a way into the building, but I figured we'd be back.

I turned south on the next cross street and headed for the I-80 overpass. I felt a little like Moses leading people to the Promised Land, although unlike Moses, I wasn't exactly happy with God these days. I swung back to Tommy and gave him some directions.

"I'm heading to another school. It's roughly a mile down this road on the left. If you can get the people moving quickly enough, the dead might just pass us by. If not, we'll be in a pretty defensible position. I'm going to scout it out and try to open a way in for us. The place is Watson School. The homes surrounding it have fenced back yards, so there hopefully won't be too many on the welcoming committee." I said quickly, spinning around and heading back over the bridge.

I rode as quickly as I could, and for the most part the passage was nearly silent except for the sound of my tires on the road. In a way it was kind of nice. In another way, it creeped the hell out of me.

I spun down the driveway to the school and headed towards the back of the building. I didn't see any signs of activity or damage, so I was hopeful that the inside was undamaged as well. I pulled up to the garage door and pulled out my crowbar, snapping the padlock that secured the door shut. I pulled it up and scanned the garage with my SIG out. Lately, I have learned I do not like surprises. Seeing it clear, I pulled the bike inside and pulled the door down. I picked up Jake out of his seat and grabbed a bottle. He was getting really antsy. I decided to feed him now while I knew this area was safe and just listen for a little while. I figured I had about half an hour before the groups showed up.

Jake immediately became quiet when I started to feed him, and I sat back on a pile of bags of sidewalk salt. I reflected on the past two days, and I just had to shake my head. All I wanted to do was head south and start over. I never expected to be trying to save a hundred people in an abandoned school.

Jake finished his bottle and promptly fell asleep. I wasn't surprised, given the morning we had. I unwrapped the towel from the Enfield and laid him down on it. I took several of the salt bags and made a little fence to keep him safe in case he woke up when I wasn't there. I needed to check the building and I hoped like hell I wasn't walking into a crowd of infected dead. I reloaded my magazines for my SIG, and topped off the magazine for my M1. I made my way to the door and stepped into the hallway.

Immediately I smelled something. It wasn't heavy, but something was definitely dead in here. Great. Here we go. I decided to work my way from the back to the front, so I went down towards where I thought the gym was. I passed a glass doorway, which let in a lot of light, and went towards a commons area. The smell was stronger, but I didn't hear anything moving around. I checked the bathrooms on the way, but they were clear. The commons was clear, but the smell was definitely coming from the kitchen area. I moved towards the door and opened it, jumping back to give myself room.

Nothing came out, and I poked my head around the corner. It smelled awful, but the room was unoccupied. Weird. I moved towards the fridge and noticed the smell was coming from the refrigerator. I smiled to myself and figured some teacher's lunches had gone bad. I opened the fridge and jumped back cursing as a body fell out at me and thudded to the floor.

"Jesus!" I said loudly, quickly sighting the corpse's head with my guns. I needn't have bothered. This one had been seriously dead for a long time. It was a young girl, probably about fifteen, but it was hard to tell. How she managed to get into the fridge, I had no idea. I watched her for a second to see if there was any movement, then I grabbed her shirt and dragged her to the door. There was an awkward moment when I tried to throw her outside, but after a little heaving, I managed to toss her out.

The gym and locker rooms were clear, and I worked my way through the building. I didn't find anything out of order and I was more and more impressed with the building as I went through it. We had a lot of room for all the people we had with us, and there was minimal access to cover. The weak point was the front door, being all glass, but could be secured with materials in the building.

Circling the outside of the building, I was thrilled to see a creek off to one side, so our water supply would be assured. I headed towards the back of the building and got a shock. The corpse I had thrown outside was gone.

I spun around with my carbine at the ready and saw nothing. *Did she get up on her own, or did someone come and get her?* Her walking away actually made me more comfortable than the thought of someone coming to get a corpse. I thought about Jake and ran towards the garage. If someone had seen me enter, they might have gotten in the same way. I skidded to a stop in front of the door and opened the garage. Light flooded the garage and I ran in to check on Jake. He was still sleeping in his area, and relief flooded through me.

To be completely replaced by adrenaline when a voice behind me said "I didn't know there was someone with us. I wish I had."

I jumped and spun around, rifle coming up. In the corner near the door, a thin figure was sitting on the floor, the corpse of the girl cradled in his lap. He was all pale skin and bones, and his black hair hung in greasy strips on his head. His clothes were filthy, and his long nose accented his rat-like face. He was stroking the dead girl's hair, and ran a hand down her chest.

"She got away from me, but I got her back." His voice was a whisper, but it carried to my horrified ears like he had shouted. I had to get this thing away from my son.

"Maybe you two need to go for a walk, and get reacquainted." I said lowering the carbine but keeping the barrel on him.

"No, no, no, she might run again, make me chase her again, make me be mad again." He looked up at me and I saw in his eyes he was completely insane. He had a feral look about him, and every instinct was screaming at me to kill him.

I decided to skip being nice. "You need to leave. Take your girlfriend and go. By the way, she's dead. Get out." I raised the gun again to punctuate my words.

He hissed at me and bared his teeth. "She's not dead, not dead, not dead. No, no, no, no. Not dead, not like the walking sleepy ones, not like them. No, she's sleeping, my beautiful is sleeping, sleeping, sleeping."

I was out of patience. This thing had been too close to my son for too long. I stepped forward quickly and punched the lunatic in the head, stunning him. I then grabbed the girl by the ankle. I moved fast and dragged her outside again before the freak realized what I had done.

When he came around, he howled and lunged at me. I was ready for him and slammed the stock of my carbine in his face. His nose spurted blood and he went down in a heap. I grabbed him by the hand and threw him outside on top of his beloved. "Good luck, slick." I said as I closed the door. I threw the deadbolt and went to the front of the building in time to see a large group of people moving across the parking lot.

Opening the door I waved to Tommy and Duncan. They waved back and started to jog towards me.

When they got close I shook their hands and smiled. "You guys make it okay? No more losses?"

Tommy smiled. "We got 'em all. This place secure?" he asked.

I nodded. "Good to go. When the people get here, get the women and kids upstairs, with two men at the top of the stairs to make a stand if needed."

Tommy looked at me. "You expecting trouble?"

I pointed over his shoulder. It looked like a thousand dead were coming down the lane after the group. A shuffling, shambling mass of moaning, wheezing dead.

"Here it comes now."

13

We were out of time. Tommy, Duncan and I managed to get one hundred and thrity-two people to the relative safety of a school building, but right on our heels was a small army of undead. We had five minutes before they were on us, and we had no where else to go. *So this is it*, I thought. *Here is where we stand.* I made some quick decisions.

I looked at the group assembled before me. Most were tired from their long walk, and in no shape to fight. But we had no choice. We had to stand here, or we wouldn't stand at all. I was not going to go out this way. I was not going to end here, not going to break my promise to my son or to my wife.

"Listen up! Listen people! I don't have time for a long speech. The dead are coming, and they will be here shortly." I saw some nervous looks towards the doors and windows. Thankfully, no one screamed. "We need to get the children upstairs to safety with their mothers and fathers. Each family gets one gun. If they get past us, you decide what you want to do." I pointed to two men who held rifles. "You two will guard the stairs. Don't waste ammo on anything other than head shots. If the dead get past us, you'll need to choke the stairs with bodies to buy yourselves some time." I threw some large zip ties at them. "Secure the doors at the ends of the hallways. If you need to get out, use the north stairwell. Get through the window at the bottom of the stairs. There's a creek out there and it will slow down any Z's coming after you."

The men nodded and started herding the families and children to the main stairwell. I stopped a young woman heading away.

"What's your name?" I asked, shifting my carbine to my other shoulder.

"Karen." She said, her eyes wide with fear. She looked to be about 20, with thin blonde hair and summer clothing.

"Karen, I'm John and this is Jake." I held up my fully awake, squirming son. "I need you to take care of him until I come for him." I said, handing him over.

Karen held Jake but shook her head. "Oh, no, I couldn't. What if those things get through, what if they come up, I can't..."

I gently held her face and looked into her eyes. "Karen. I know you can do this. Just play with him like there's nothing going on, and I will be back for him in a little while. No matter what you hear, you keep it together. Keep him safe, and I will keep you safe. I promise."

Karen nodded and took Jake away. I steeled myself that I would see him again and turned to the task at hand. A slow fire was starting in my gut and my jaw clenched at the coming fight. In a strange way, I welcomed it. I wanted the fight, I wanted to kill and kill and kill. I wanted revenge on these things that had taken away my wife, my life, and destroyed my world. I would fight today and not go quietly.

I ran to the garage and retrieved my Enfield and crowbar. If it came to close quarters, I wanted every tool I had. I grabbed my extra carbine magazines and ran back to the group, which numbered around 75.

I motioned Tommy and Duncan over. "Take five men each and cover the front entrance. That's the weakest point. Take them down close to the building, make the rest slow up. Each shot has to count. Make sure everyone has a blunt weapon in case they get in. The stairwell at the north end of the building is your fallback point. Good luck." They ran to the group, quickly selected ten men, and ran to the front door. I could see through the windows that the zombies were halfway through the parking lot.

I turned to the main group and assigned ten men to cover the back door, which was also glass. I told them to hold their fire and make every shot count. Create choke points and buy themselves time. I didn't expect trouble from there, but who knew? I grabbed five men and took them to the small hallway near the gym. There was another door there that led outside. I gave them the same advice. Don't let too many get through, make them work for it.

I took the remainder and spread them out in the hallways in groups of two. Any more together and they would likely hit each other. They didn't have guns, and were nervously fingering their makeshift weapons. They were to act as backup if someone went down. They were also to guard against any zombies making it through a window. Not likely, given the nature of the windows, but it was possible. One of them, a big guy I had heard someone call Charlie, positioned himself in front of the main stairwell doors. He held a length of lead pipe that had a t-junction attached to one end. In the other hand he had a small hatchet. I mentally gave him a *Good luck, brother*. I stationed myself near the south door. It was another weak point, but I figured it was as good a place as any. I went to the door and looked out the window. I had a stairwell to the second floor nearby, but I knew the doors had been secured with a zip tie.

Holy shit. We were in serious trouble. More zombies had joined the original crew from the subdivision surrounding the building, and I figured there had to be at least eight hundred of the bastards out there. We didn't have nearly enough ammo. That slow fire in my gut began to burn a little hotter and I had to restrain myself from throwing myself outside to do battle. Where did this come from? Why was I so eager to jump into the fray? I advised caution at every turn, but here at what could be my last act, I wanted to just engage my enemy, to rend and smash. My hand gripped my carbine tighter and I shifted my crowbar to be within easy reach.

I jumped back from the doors as a rotting face slammed against the glass. Broken teeth cracked against the upper window of the door. It was so torn and rotted I couldn't tell what it used to be. It moaned loudly and began pounding on the door. Since the door opened outward, it would be a while before this was a serious threat. But the message was clear: The dead had arrived

I could hear pounding echoing throughout the building, and glass crashing. Shots were being fired, but I couldn't tell where they were coming from. Shouts could be heard, and I could hear Tommy yelling "Kill them, kill them! They're getting in! "Kill them! Aim for the head, damn you!" I desperately wanted to run down to see what was happening, but things were getting interesting on my end. The window of the door had been smashed in and two arms were reaching through the opening. They belonged to two zombies that looked relatively fresh, although they were cut up badly from putting their arms through the glass. The center of the door was about chest high, so they couldn't quite climb in, but I hesitated at killing them. I didn't want to give the ones behind them a step up to get in the door.

More shots and shouts. I couldn't take my eyes off my door, since all it took was a second and you were done. I chanced a glance behind me to check on the other guys in my hallway and found myself alone. *Fuck it*, I thought. Oh well. At least I didn't have to worry about getting shot by accident or clubbed by somebody. All I had to worry about was being torn to pieces by zombies and consumed, or infected by the virus and turning into a zombie myself. Spiffy.

With my back clear, I decided to slow things down at my door. I shot the two that were hanging in and they slumped to the ground. They were immediately trampled by the zombies behind them and because these were able to stand on the first ones, they were able to leverage more of themselves into the window. I was astonished at their tenacity, especially when they jagged glass tore open their abdomens and ropey intestines spilled out over the door. I didn't waste any time on introspection, and shot them as they raised their dead faces and groaned at me. They slumped over the window and effectively blocked the next two, which were pushing forward. I shot them as well, trying to block the door as much as possible. But the crowd outside was surging, trying to get at the prey they knew was within, and the door started to bulge and strain. The first zombies to fall were pulped as others trod on them, and the windows of the doors were full of grasping, groping arms.

I realized that piecemeal wasn't going to work. I needed to go on the offensive and really make trouble. I shouldered my carbine and went to work. I shot every head I could see, whether it was trying to get inside or if it was outside. I missed a few shots, but hitting such small targets in such circumstances was miraculous at best. I reloaded my carbine with my second thirty round magazine and stepped closer to the door, trying to hit more of them outside. I had made a pile about three feet high of corpses, but more were crawling, tearing, groaning to get in. I looked at a sea of dead faces, bloated stomachs, and reaching arms and hands. I had the wild urge to throw my carbine aside, draw my knife and crowbar, and dive into that morass.

I fired again and again, killing and killing. I started to have difficulty seeing my targets, as the corpses piled higher and some of the zombies were shorter, managing to stay out of sight. There was a lull in the firing, and I could hear sounds down the hall. There were shots and screams, cursing and crying, and over all the constant sound of zombies on the prowl.

I looked over my shoulder and received a shock. Two zombies were shuffling their way towards me, their slow, shambling gait evident in the low light of the school. Beyond them, I could see many more zombies walking and littering the floor. As I watched, I saw a zombie's head slam sideways and bounce off a wall, struck by something and someone unseen.

I shifted my attention back to the two in the hallway. There were two classrooms between myself and the Z's, so I darted into one of them, the zombies shuffling in pursuit. I kicked a couple of desks towards the door and shoved a few more for good measure. The two zombies came into the room, scanned the area and saw me standing there. They immediately started towards me, and crashed into the desks, falling to the floor. I stepped up quickly and smashed one on the head with my crowbar, ending its killing spree once and for all. The other, twisting on the floor and getting to its feet, rose slowly and locked eyes with me. Its lips peeled back in a snarl and a high pitched wheeze came out of a hole in its throat. I didn't waste time and smashed the crowbar's business end onto the top of its head, slamming it to the floor where it lay still.

I ducked back towards the door and quickly peeked out. The exit door was still holding, but I could see that it was not going to hold out much longer. I needed to see what else was going on. I didn't want to think that everyone else had bugged out and I was in here all alone save for a few hundred zombies. I ran towards the front door, jumping over several corpses along the way. When I reached the main foyer, I could see the door had been smashed open, and there were dozens of downed zombies, each one having some sort of head wound. I could see a mass of blood in the area, suggesting that someone had been caught by the zombies and killed. I didn't see where Duncan and Tommy had gotten off to, but I hoped that they had fallen back to the rally point. I heard bunch of shots coming from the commons area, so I turned and headed that way.

As I moved over a neat ring of dead-for-good zombies surrounding the main stairwell, I looked back down my hallway and saw that the door had caved in, and the zombies were pouring in the opening. Great.

I chanced a glance over my shoulder at the front door and ducked as a decayed hand swept towards my head. I dove forward and sprang to my feet, spinning around and facing my attacker. Correction. Attackers. About five of them had come in the door while I was ruminating, and I nearly got nailed for it. I whipped my carbine up and shot down the first one, snapping off a lucky one-handed shot that entered through its chin and blew the top of its head off, spraying brain all over the ceiling. I didn't have time to shoot the second one, he was on me too fast. I kicked him backwards and he fell over another corpse that was on the ground. The third came from the side and I swung the crowbar viciously at his head, connecting with his neck and breaking it. He went down, but his mouth still snapped, his eyes tracking me as I moved. I shot the second one as he got up and nailed the fourth to the ground. The fifth moved slowly enough that I was able to sling my carbine over my shoulder and get a good two-handed grip on my crowbar. It came within reach, a decaying woman with dank hair and half her cheek missing, along with her nose. I swung hard and literally took her off her feet, tossing her aside and slamming her into the wall. She wasn't dead yet, so I needed to smash her again to finish her off. I was running out of room on the floor. Literally most of the floor was covered in some sort of gore or decaying flesh, or eaten flesh, by the looks of some of it. We were losing people, but the question was, where were they, and how many had we lost?

I quickly checked the doors to the upper floor and saw they were still secured on the inside by zip ties. Good. No one had been that way. I briefly wondered where the big guy Charlie was, but I realized I maybe didn't want to know if the worst had happened.

I ran towards the firing and skidded to a stop by the atrium. Three zombies were feeding on a corpse, and they were so engrossed in their task they didn't know I was there. I looked at the body and to my horror, the hand on the ground closest to me was still moving, the fingers curling into a claw of pain. It may have been reflex, but part of me was sickened by the notion that this poor person was still alive as these creatures were feeding on him. I unslung my carbine, and placed my crowbar up against the wall. I clicked off the safety and got busy. I killed the three in short order, then shot the downed man as well. If he was still alive, he was coming back as one of them, and I could only hope someone would do me the courtesy should the need arise.

I saw more corpses of our survivors as I moved towards the gym and commons. I didn't see Duncan or Tommy, so I still held out hope they were still alive. Moving quickly I looked back over my shoulder and saw a steady stream of corpses from my old post. They tripped and stumbled over the bodies in the hallway, falling and getting up, never ceasing in their movement towards me. I realized I needed to keep them coming, so they wouldn't try to get upstairs. I fired at the closest ones, dropping two and causing the rest to head my way. I backed towards the commons, and got my first look down the hallway by the gym that led to the outside of the building. It was choked with bodies, most of them zombies, although I could see a limb here and there that was not grayish in color. *My God*, I thought. *Who's left?*

I didn't hear any more shots, so I was fearing the worst as I opened the door to the gym. I was immediately assaulted by the smell of dozens of decaying bodies, and the coppery smell of blood that no one ever mistakes for anything else. There were corpses everywhere, and small pockets of men were making a final stand in several places in the gym. I could see Tommy and Duncan on a small stand in a little alcove in the gym, and they were elevated enough that they could stand and smash zombies that came to them without danger of being grabbed. I saw that guy Charlie standing with three other men, swinging his length of pipe like a medieval mace. Every time he connected with a skull it was caved in and the zombie went down. But I could see he was going to be overwhelmed by the sheer numbers of zombies that were reaching for him. I had to do something, or all of these men were going to die.

I raised my carbine and began firing. I killed ten of the zombies before the noise began to register with them and most of them turned my way. *Oh, brother.* I backed up a step and took aim at another Z. Click. I glanced at my gun and realized I was out of bullets. I quickly switched my 30 round magazine for a 15-round one, and again took aim. I fired ten more times, and dropped nine more zombies. The tenth round was a straight miss, and Duncan jumped as splinters flew from the furrow the bullet dug in the bleachers he was standing on. Whoops. "Sorry!" I shouted, as I lined up another ghoul. That one went down as well. I fired my remaining shots, then switched magazines again. I killed several more, then began backing towards the door.

"Finish the rest, then get out of here!" I yelled at the groups. "There's a huge group coming in any minute!" I screamed as I fired, knocking down several more zombies. "I'm going to try and draw the rest outside! Head for that door and meet me outside!"

I spun around and ran back for the door, shoving it open and knocking down a zombie that was on the other side. I stepped out of the gym into a foyer choked with zombies. I didn't hesitate, I just ran for the hallway, scrambling over the corpses and gagging as my foot slipped in something I would rather remain unidentified. The horde behind me howled and gave chase, stumping along in that rhythmic gait that never stopped. I reached the door and fell as something tripped me. I looked down and saw a greenish-grey hand clutching my pant leg. I pulled on it, but only managed to free a length of arm that was attached to the clawing hand. I pulled harder and managed to pull out the head of the zombie who was grabbing me. It had a bullet hole in its head, but it must not have been a killing shot. The decaying face moaned and tried to bend down to bite my leg. I kicked it in the face with my other foot, trying to dislodge it. No luck. My hands were slipping on the floor, and I couldn't get away from the ghoul.

I was getting panicky, pulling on my leg and trying to get out, all the while a gang of undead was slowly making their way over the pile of corpses, moaning and tripping.

The zombie that had my foot was freed further by my struggles and started to bend down to bite at my leg. I pulled again and unholstered my SIG. Enough of this. I drew a bead and pulled the trigger, putting another hole in its head and causing a dark splotch to appear on the wall behind it. The hand relaxed its grip, and I managed to pull away, just ahead of the grasping crowd. I went outside, and glancing around, saw there weren't any moving zombies out here. There were a great many lying around, but all were permanently dead. Cautiously looked around the corner and found myself kissing the barrel of Tommy's gun. I backed up as he sheepishly put his gun away.

"Sorry, man. Thought you was a Z, you know?" Tommy shrugged.

"No troubles, brother. I'm glad I smell better." I said looking at the men he had behind him. Out of the 75 that we had started with, at least 20 were missing. The good news was the remaining men were more battle hardened and would stand if needed. I looked at Duncan and said, "Take half the men and sweep around to the other side of the building. Hit this group from behind and deal with any outside. Keep moving, don't let them bottle you up. Make them come to you, make sure you have an exit.

I motioned to Tommy. "I'm going to act as bait and stand out there." I pointed to a spot on the grass. "Give me five men to place on the other side of that wall there, and put the other five over there by that wall." I indicated spots out of sight of the doorway. "Get set, and hit them hard from behind as they come out. If your weapon sticks, let it go, next guy in line steps up. Got it?" I got several nods. "Okay, follow me."

I headed out to the grass and immediately heard several groans and moans as the dead caught sight of me. They came stumbling out in twos and threes and we killed them in twos and threes. The ones on the left side were wiped out by the men on the left and the ones on the right were wiped out by the men on the right. The ones that came straight on or were too bunched together got dispatched by my carbine until I ran out of bullets, then I switched to the SIG. There were growing piles of zombies and I was amazed that they just kept coming. If they were on the roof, I bet they would just keep falling off if there was something they saw on the ground they wanted.

We lost one man to a zombie who came around the corner a little too fast and managed to get a bite out of his arm. We killed the zombie, but the man just sat on the ground staring at his arm. It was a death sentence, and he knew it. He looked at us and with a look of quiet dignity coming over his face, he raised himself up onto his knees and placed his hands in his lap. He stared out into the distance, and with a final look at me, nodded his head. I nodded back and moved behind him, drawing my SIG. I waited ten seconds and then put a bullet into the back of his head. The rest of the men just looked on and I saw some nods. I knew what they were all thinking. If something like that happened to them, they would want someone nearby to end it for them as well, rather than submit to being a zombie.

After ten minutes, we ran out of zombies. There were corpses everywhere, and from the sounds I heard coming from the other side of the building, there were many more. I reslung my carbine, hefted my crowbar, and started to move back through the corpses and back into the building.

Tommy stopped me just as I started back inside. "What are you doing?" He asked. "Why don't we swing around back?"

I shook my head. "We need to hit them from behind while they are busy in the front. Surprise can get us ten zombies, easy." I started back inside with several men following me. Tommy just shook his head and followed suit.

Back inside the building the stench was nearly overwhelming, but we pressed on into the gloom. There were signs of battle everywhere, with splatter on the walls and corpses creating a grisly carpet on the floor. At any second, I kept expecting a ghoul to come around the corner, snarling and biting. But none came, and we moved cautiously towards the next battle. I could hear the distant groans of the dead as they moved towards their prey, but I didn't hear any screams that would indicate they had found any.

Glancing around the corner of the atrium, I saw a crowd of zombies slowly pushing their way out the back door. Over their heads I could see weapons coming down and smashing them as they came into range. Figuring I could even up the odds a little, I motioned for Tommy to take the rest of the men into the commons, and I waited behind. When I got a hand signal from Tommy, I moved towards the center of the room, then I whistled as loud as I could.

The zombies at the back of the pack spun around and immediately began moving towards me, I slowly walked towards the commons and stuck my crowbar through the door. Immediately someone struck it with another bar, causing a painful vibration to pulse through it. I heard a "Whoops! Sorry!" from the other side of the door, then I stuck my head through.

"They don't carry weapons." was all I said as I moved into the room. I didn't even look at the man who struck my crowbar. Tommy had arranged men by the door and men in the bleachers. Two more were acting as bait, and we were going to have our hands full in a minute. I took off my Enfield, and placed it on the top of a milk cooler. I put my carbine next to it and limbered up my crowbar. It was when I looked around that I got my flash of inspiration.

Along the west wall of the commons was about twenty large lunch tables, folded in half for easy storage. I grabbed one and wheeled it over to the entrance, and unfolded it so it was perpendicular to the entrance. Tommy looked at me strangely, but I just grinned at him. I motioned for three more tables to be put along side this one, and signaled the men on the bleachers to move higher. They looked at me the same way Tommy did, but didn't argue. I told him to grab another table and put it near the entrance, but don't open it.

I told the other men to act as bait on the end of the tables and had a few more wait by the sides of the tables, ducking down so as not to be seen easily.

The ghouls walked in slowly, never taking their eyes of the men on the end. They shuffled and groaned and stayed where they were supposed to, between the bleachers and the tables. They groaned loudly, and hurried as best as their infected legs would take them.

When there was about twenty of them, I yelled "Push!" and I shoved the table from the other side. The men all pushed and managed to pin all the zombies against the bleachers, effectively immobilizing them. The men on the bleachers worked their way down the line, smashing in heads and crushing skulls. Tommy had moved the last table in front of the door, and was desperately holding it against the horde that was behind it.

"Hurry!" he shouted as the table lurched and a grey arm reached around to try and grab.

"Pull back the tables! First positions!" I pulled on the table and repositioned it, seeing that the other tables were in the same spot. Tommy pulled back the upright table and allowed twenty more zombies into our killing zone. We pushed the tables and trapped the next ones, and the killing began again.

By the time we had finished, we had used the tables eleven times. Tommy pulled back the upright and looked out. There were no more zombies in the hall. He looked at me and I shrugged. Maybe we had won. But we couldn't know for sure.

I ducked out into the hall and worked my way to the back entrance. There weren't any ghouls lingering back there, so I cautiously looked out. Duncan and his men were sitting on the ground, taking a breather. I stepped out into the sun and several men jumped. I could only imagine what I looked like. Goggles and balaclava, gloves and crowbar, and covered in zombie goo up to my elbows. GQ all the way, baby.

"What's the status?" I asked, sitting down next to Duncan.

"Well, with you out here, I think we may have actually done it." Duncan said, to the half-hearted cheers of the men on the ground.

"You might be right." I said. "But if we want to live here, we need to clean out the corpses."

Duncan groaned and fell back on the grass. "Come on, mom, I'm tired. No wanna got to school!" Considering where we were, that was actually pretty funny.

I laughed with the rest of the men and got to my feet. Duncan followed suit and the crowd of us headed back to the piles of corpses we had made. I instructed the men to use their tools and drag the bodies to that baseball diamond up on the hill. It was a distance, but a necessary chore. We couldn't risk the virus getting too close. I then went to the janitor's closet and gathered up as many cleaning supplies as I could. We would need to wash down everything as best as we could. I sent two men to the creek with buckets to get water while I rummaged around the garage. Finding a can of gasoline, I gave it to the men dragging the bodies away and told them to burn what they could. With any luck, that would stave off any chance of infection.

I went back to the garage and rummaged through my trailer. I reloaded my SIG magazines and my carbine magazines, mentally wondering how many I had shot. *Not nearly enough*, I thought, as I went back into the hallway. Tommy was supervising the cleaning of the gym and the commons, and we were doing well. I wandered over to him and asked what I thought was a dumb question. "Did you go upstairs yet and let them know we had been successful here?" I asked, expecting him to confirm that he had.

Tommy laughed out loud. "I thought you did. Oh, geez, they must think the worst!" He laughed again.

I chuckled with him. "I figure they must have looked out the window at some point and saw us dragging bodies out of the building."

Tommy nodded. "You're probably right. You want me to go up?"

"No," I said. "I'll go up. We need to get some more help down here anyway. Did you send anyone to sweep the building on the outside for stragglers?" I asked

"Duncan's with them now, although they haven't found any yet."

"Good enough. See ya."

Tommy waved me off and I headed to the stairs. As I went past the atrium, Charlie was there, dragging two dead ghouls by the collars of their shirts. Our eyes met and he nodded. I nodded back, the understanding between us clear. He was saying 'thank you' and I was saying 'you're welcome' in that expressive way men had.

I reached the stairs and stuck my knife through the crack between the doors. It took some work, but I managed to sever the zip ties holding the doors closed. I stepped into the stairwell and shouted up the stairs. "Hello?"

"Hello! Who's that?" Came the reply.

"It's John! We did it! Can I come up?" I asked, poking my head around the stairs and smiling at the two nervous-looking gents at the top of the stairs.

They both relaxed visibly, and waved me up. When I reached the top of the stairs, both men insisted on hugging me. While I wasn't much on displays of affection between guys, I found I didn't mind this so much. I grinned at them and went into the hallway. One of the men ran down the hall, shouting that we had done it and people streamed out of the classrooms. I shook a lot of hands and received a lot of hugs. There were a lot of questions, but I raised my hands for silence.

"Hey all! Listen up! We have a lot of cleaning up to do before we can call this place home, so anyone with gloves or a crowbar head downstairs and help drag the bodies away for burning. Anyone who wants to help with the cleaning of the floors and walls, go see Charlie by the atrium. Just so you know, this is not the last fight we will have, but we won this time and learned a lot, so we will be more ready when they come again."

Someone asked, "When will they come again?"

All eyes turned to me. "Could be tomorrow, could be today. We learned a few tricks, so next time we won't lose as many.

"How many were lost?" came the question. I knew it was coming, but that didn't make giving the answer any easier.

"We lost 27 to the zombies, so we will need people to help bury them." I let that sink into the silence that followed. "But their sacrifice is not going to be in vain. We *will* survive and we *will* beat these zombies. I have no guarantees except my word. I promise you that we will survive."

I saw several nods and sent all the men downstairs to help with the cleanup. I was going to go shortly, but there was something I needed to do first. I scanned the crowd and saw Karen standing at the far edge. I caught her eye and she nodded, motioning me to a classroom. I followed her in and she pointed to a small bundle in the corner. I went over and sat down next to my sleeping son. I picked him up gently and held him to my chest. I couldn't stop tears from flowing and I held his sleeping form tighter. *I did it, Ellie. I kept my promise.* I thought to myself, bending my cheek to Jakey's head and dampening his hair with tears.

I held him quietly for a while, just taking him in, then I put him back down. He shifted in his sleep, turning on his side and letting out a long fart. I grinned. *Just like Jake.*

I headed out of the room and thanked Karen for watching him. She smiled and said "Anytime. He's a good boy." and went back into the room. I went back downstairs to lend a hand with cleanup, and it was nearly dark before we finished. We could hear several moans out in the neighborhoods, so we knew we had more work ahead of us.

I sat down in the teacher's lounge with Duncan, Tommy, Charlie, and several others. The families and the rest had been assigned rooms on the second floor, and most people had just collapsed from exhaustion. Hauling corpses was surprisingly tiresome. I had chosen a room on the ground floor, and Jake was sleeping there for the night, surrounded by his blanket and favorite teddy bear. We had spent a good deal of time reinforcing the doors that were broken in, and I was confident that they would hold in the future. I didn't think we would be facing another horde like we had repelled today, but we had a plan to deal with it if we did.

Tommy told the rest about using the tables, and they all thought it was a great idea to trap them like cattle and slaughter them likewise. To that end, we prepared the commons as a killing zone, leaving the tables in place for use at a moments notice. We agreed to try to keep them out as much as possible, but if we were breached, it would serve as a focal point for killing.

The rest of the conversation was a going over of what the rules of the community should be. I advocated that everyone be trained in the use of weapons, and everyone attend training on a regular basis. One of our survivors was ex-military and said he would be happy to set up a training program.

Someone brought up the notion of what to do if the rules had been broken. Several ideas were fielded, but I held out for removal from the community. "Given the state of the world, I would think that people would rather simply behave than risk fighting for their lives for whatever time they have left. I think the rules need to be simple. Help out however you can. If you have usable skills, we'll need them and use them as best as we can. Everyone works, everyone defends." I didn't see any disagreement.

"What about food and supplies?" Duncan asked, voicing a concern that was likely on the minds of everyone. I had actually thought about this a bit.

"We are surrounded by houses on all sides. What we need to do is start raiding those houses for whatever we can find. If they are occupied by the dead, we take them out. If they are occupied by the living, we invite them to join us, or leave them alone. We take nothing from the living. I figure we could do quite well if we took our time and were methodical.

"I know these are tough times, but I also know we will get through this. For God's sake, gentlemen, we killed over eight hundred zombies today. Yes, we lost a few, but the majority survived. We survived. And we will continue to survive. I refuse to accept any other way." I finished my little speech to quiet faces.

"Last thing." Tommy spoke up. "We need a leader, someone we can count on to make decisions when things go rough. Someone who will be fair, but focused. Any nominations?"

A man whose name I didn't know spoke up. "Why do we need a leader? We could have a group or council to make decisions, and we could have elections and such."

Duncan put that idea down. "That would work for a huge group of people in a large, organized community, but we're barely hanging on as it is. What do you do if something comes up that needs a decision right away? What do you do if the Z's attack in force again? Do you tell them to wait until you can make decisions as a group? Sorry, friend, but if there is one thing history teaches us, a single leader can save a society where a council can stagnate it." The man who spoke nodded with understanding.

It was quiet until Charlie spoke up. "I nominate John. He saved our asses in the gym, and continued to lead attacks on the zombies. All I heard from him was 'Follow me' as he went in to fight. I know most of us wouldn't be here if he hadn't found us in the gym, and led the zombies away." Charlie spoke directly to me. "You need someone to watch your back, you let me know. Whenever, wherever." Charlie leaned back in his chair and folded his arms across his broad chest. His demeanor challenged anyone to say otherwise.

I have to admit I did not expect to receive any endorsements. I simply did what needed to be done, and took charge when someone needed to step up. I would be the first to admit that I have my faults and would be surprised that anyone would want me as leader.

Duncan spoke up. "You guys that we picked up when we were on the road, you don't know what Tommy, John and I went through to get where we are. But I would have to say John made all the right moves, and he can fight like hell when he needs to. He's slow to get started, but stay away after he does."

Tommy spoke next. "I second the nomination for John. We need someone who keeps a cool head, stays focused, and is not afraid of a new idea." He looked around the table. "Seriously. Would any of you have thought of using the tables to herd the Z's like cattle to the slaughter?" Several shakes of the head and rueful smiles provided his answer.

"So let's vote. All in favor of naming John Talon the leader of our so-called group, raise your hand." Tommy called the group to make a decision.

I have to say, I was surprised when all hands went up. But, someone had to do it, so I guess I was as qualified as anyone, even though I felt like a goofball standing up and acknowledging the vote.

"Thanks everyone. I appreciate your support. I don't really know what to say except I will never ask anyone to do anything I wouldn't do myself. I have a son here, as most of you know, so the survival of the community is top of my list. We have a lot of work to do, but I think we made a good start today, and in the next few days, we're going to see our little compound come together and we will be happy to call it home for a while." I sat back down and we hammered out a few more details regarding what we had here and what resources were available. I felt positive about where we were, and felt pretty good about the chances we had in this place. We had created a fort, and we now had a duty to defend it.

God help us all, as the living dead moaned into the night.

14

The next morning, I woke up with a headache. I initially didn't remember where I was, and it took a few minutes of looking around before I realized where I was and what had occurred the day before. It was dark in the room, with a little morning light coming in through the single window in the room. I sat up, and looked around. My bike and trailer were in the corner, and my carbine was near the door. Jacob was still sleeping, snoring softly in the little crib I made for him using blankets and desks turned on their sides. I stood up and stretched, working out the kinks that accompany sleeping on a hard surface. I went back to the floor and did my morning routine of sit-ups and pushups, idly wondering when I might actually work out with weights again. Part of me wished we had made for the junior high, where they have a full workout room, but there isn't a water source for a mile.

I dressed quickly and belted on my SIG. I had been wearing it for so long it was like an extension of me. I felt weird when I wasn't wearing it, like something was missing. I imagine that's how the old gunfighters of the West felt. The gun just became part of them that they couldn't function without it. I wondered when I would be able to put my guns away, to bring them out when I just wanted to enjoy them. *Lemons and lemonade*, I thought as I went into the hall. I had about ten minutes before Jake started to stir, so I wanted to see if anyone else was up.

It was still pretty dark in the school, but enough light filtered through the windows to give a twilight effect. The school did not look as threatening as it did yesterday. The day before, the dark hallways and echoing moans punctuated by occasional shots and screams, presented a much more foreboding atmosphere. I could see where the cleanup missed a few spots here and there, and there were some scorch marks were we had burned some of the remains to remove any threat of infection.

As I walked towards the commons, I could see small piles of brass here and there, and sunlight streamed in through the back doors, giving an orange tint to most of what I could see. I could hear voices in the commons, so I headed that way.

In the commons, I had to navigate through a little maze of tables, but Tommy and Duncan and a few others were discussing some options regarding supplies. They were in the kitchen area, and had the door open to let in some light. One guy was standing watch for zombies that might have been attracted to our battle the day before. Way out on the grass, just at the edge of the property was a corpse of what looked to be a young girl and a mess of blood and bones. Decaying meat was scattered around, and a couple of carrion birds were picking at the corpse. I didn't remember anyone being caught outside, so I was confused as to who that might be.

Duncan saw me looking and walked over. "I meant to tell you about that. Right before the zombies hit us yesterday, there was a weird little guy dragging a girl around out there. We yelled at him to get inside, but he spit at us and then proceeded to try and have sex with that girl until the zombies came and ate him. Wonder why they didn't eat the girl?"

"That's because she was already dead." I told the story of what I had found here when I first arrived, much to the shock and chagrin of my listeners.

Duncan shook his head. "Good riddance, then. No ones needs a loony pedophile roaming around. Fitting justice would be if zombie kids had got him."

I smiled. "Truth to that. What's up for this morning?"

Duncan indicated the group. "We were talking about heading out to see about some supplies, but we had a little disagreement about where to start and what to do about safety, and what not. Usual stuff."

"I can understand that. It's not like anyone's actually had experience with this sort of thing. But we can sort it out based on what we know about the zombies. What do you have so far?"

Duncan outlined the overall plan, which was to start searching the nearest houses for food and supplies. They would take only what they needed, no looting of non-essential supplies. If the house was occupied, they would deal with the zombies first.

After hearing the plan, I had a few questions. "Do you have a fallback plan, in case you get surrounded? How far do you plan to roam? What will you carry your supplies in? How many men do you think will work? When are you leaving?"

Duncan answered all the questions except for the last. They figured they would head out around 11:00am, and be back by 2:00pm. That seemed to be the time we saw the fewest zombies on the move outside. Maybe it had something to do with their eyesight, like maybe the bright light hurt them. Who knew?

"All right." I said. "Assemble your team, I'll see you at 11:00."

Tommy spoke up. "You coming, too?"

I looked at him. "Of course. You two can't have all the fun." I left them smiling as I went back to feed Jake and get ready for the raid.

The building was stirring a bit as people started to arrange their assigned rooms into more livable space. We had enough rooms so there wasn't going to be any crowding. We decided to leave the gym as a play area, and the garage would be a staging area for raids and·such. The science room on the second floor was to be the food pantry, and there was an effort underway to use the water in the school's boilers. The library was to be used as a meeting room/reading room, and the teacher's lounge was the training area. The main office wasn't really needed, so we were just going to leave it. The band room was a good observation point, and Tommy and Duncan thought it would make a neat little room for themselves. The room was octagon in shape, and attached to the northwest end of the building. There were two little offices, which would work as bedrooms. The weak point was the room had two sets of doors leading outside, but they could be secured.

Jake was stirring and rolling around his makeshift crib. He usually woke up happy, and today was no different. I made him a bottle and changed his diaper. I checked on our personal supplies, and realized I was going to need to make some acquisitions for Jake. We had enough food for about two weeks, but after that I was going to have to get creative. I racked my brain regarding the area and remembered there was a store down the way. I'd have to check it out later.

Jake finished his bottled and gave me a very satisfied burp for my trouble. I dressed for the raid and had to think about what to wear, since I hadn't done something like this before. I dressed in long pants, and put on my work boots. I decided on a long-sleeve shirt, and tucked my gloves and balaclava in my belt. I picked up a small backpack that I had found in the school, and packed some emergency supplies. In case things got nasty, I could hole up for a bit without worry.

I picked up Jake and went upstairs, pointing things out to him and just talking to him in general. He seemed interested in the stairs, and laughed when I ran up the last four to make him bounce in my arms.

I went to the first door I found and knocked on it. A sleepy head poked out and I asked if there was anyone they knew of who could baby-sit my son.

"You're the new leader, hey?" the disheveled head murmured.

"Umm, yeah. That's me." I said, not clear as to why this was relevant.

"Pleased to meetcha." A hand came out. "I'm Paul Yates. My wife is Elizabeth. We were in the mental hospital when you folks came by."

I shook the hand. "John Talon, nice to meet you as well. Listen, I need to find someone to watch my son while I go looking for supplies. Any suggestions?"

Paul scratched his head, "Can't say for sure, but there is a family down the way with a couple of teenage girls. They might be able to help."

"Thanks, Paul." I said as I headed down the hall

I knocked on the next door and a woman answered. "Can I help you?" she asked, sounding like she was not thrilled with the prospect of actually helping. She was disheveled and wearing a long t-shirt, which did double duty as pajamas. Her middle aged faced showed nothing more than impatience.

I decided to try a different tactic. "Yes, get in the hall. Now." My tone took her aback, but she stepped into the hallway with her arms crossed.

I walked to the middle of the hallway and raised my voice to what I liked to call "principal level", guaranteed to reach every student on a playground. "Everyone out in the hall now! This is John Talon! Everyone out! Go! Go! Go!"

I smiled to myself when people began spilling out of their rooms. Some were holding weapons and others were holding bags of stuff. Mothers were holding onto children and fathers were looking grim and determined.

"Thank you." I said to the assembled mass. "I am sorry to have awakened some of you but I need a couple of favors and have not been able to find anyone to help." I looked around and there were many frowns looking back at me. Good. "I am going on a raid in a couple of hours and need a babysitter for my son Jake, here. Second, I need a couple of good organizers to take over the food storage and distribution. We are hoping to have a working pantry this afternoon, so anyone familiar with food storage and such, please let me know. Also," I added, "We need help with the burial of those we lost yesterday in the fighting. The north field is the designated graveyard, and the men there could use help."

The looks around the hall got less hostile and two girls no older than thirteen raised their hands to watch Jake. I got two more women to organize the pantry, then went back down to my room, after thanking them for their assistance. Several men got dressed and headed down to help with the burials. I thanked them as well and I reminded myself that we needed to have a meeting to discuss the rules of the community.

At 11:00, the two girls came down to my room, and I introduced them again to Jakey. I could tell they were experienced baby-sitters when one of them sat down immediately to play with him while the other checked out where his supplies were. I put on my backpack and extra magazine pouch for the carbine. I had a double magazine holder for my SIG, and put on my knife as well. I felt like I was gearing up for battle, and in all seriousness, I guess I was. There was no second place winner when it came to battling the undead.

I picked up my rifle at the door and said goodbye to the girls. I smiled and waved at Jake, and he gave me a smile in return. He was almost at the point where he could sit up by himself, and was trying it out as I left.

I went back to the garage and met up with Tommy and Duncan and the rest. Everyone was ready and there was quite a variety of weapons, ranging from crowbars to AR-15's. We had a wheel barrel filled with makeshift sacks, and some backpacks. Duncan noticed my pack was full. "What's in the pack?" He wanted to know.

"Some food and water, and emergency supplies" I said.

Tommy was curious. "How come? We don't plan on being out longer than three hours."

"Never hurts to be prepared. If it goes down hard and we get separated or trapped, I want to be able to hold out as long as possible. Why, you think I'm nuts?" I asked sincerely.

In response, both he and Duncan left the room to get their own packs, and several of the other men as well. I guess it was a good idea after all.

When the rest of the group came back, we headed out into the day. Immediately, we could see several zombies wandering around, and they began moving in our direction. I motioned for Tommy and Duncan to follow me, waving the rest back. "Come on, let's get to them before they bunch!" They quickly followed and we ran up to the first zombie. She was a tall female, stumbling slowly forward, but she increased her pace when we got closer. Her milky eyes locked on me, and she raised her hands to grab and tear. That was when Duncan nailed her in the gut with his pipe, and when she doubled over from the impact, I brought my crowbar up in an uppercut swing which slammed into her head, imbedding the hook into her skull. She immediately dropped to the ground, and I ripped the bar out of her head. Tommy was already running to the next one, a fat guy with rolls of grey flesh swaying as he stumbled towards us. When he came within reach, Tommy slammed him in the head with his straight bar, knocking the fat man to the ground. The zombie seemed stunned but he was still alive as he slowly tried to right himself. When he got to his knees, Duncan was already there, and pounded Fatso on the back of his head, cracking his skull and putting him down for good. I moved past them both and kicked a smaller zombie in the chest, knocking him to the grass. I stepped onto his chest and held him down as I crushed his skull with the chisel end. The last two were dispatched the same way, and we jogged back to the group who had watched us take out the zombies.

"Why did you guys run to them?" one of the men wanted to know.

I answered him. "It just occurred to me. Think of it this way. One on one, we can take any zombie out there. They're stupid, they're slow, and don't really think outside the box. But when they come at you in twos, threes, or fours, then you have trouble. If your weapon sticks or you drop it, you can get to your backup. If you have two on you, you're screwed. If you keep them from their greatest strength, which is attacking in force, then they can be dealt with pretty easily. Just keep your head and smash in theirs." Anticipating the next question, I said "And we didn't shoot them because shots attract them like politicians to money. They can hear better than we can and their sense of smell is better, too. We learned that in the gas station." I told them about the woman smelling the door, looking for us.

Several nods occurred around the group as they took this in. Tommy, Duncan and I cleaned off our weapons and moved up to the front of the crowd. We headed towards the closest houses to the school, figuring to start there and just work our way down the street. I didn't expect to find much, but we didn't have much choice. If we went through everything people brought with them, we had two days at best.

We approached the first house slowly, looking in the windows and trying to see if it was occupied. I assigned four men to watch the street, and three more to stations outside the door. I figured to lure any zombies outside where we could control the killing and have room to move. I went up to the door and tried the knob. I expected it to be locked and it was. I knocked on the door and waited, listening intently. I didn't hear any movement, so I worked my crowbar on the door, easing it open as quietly as I could.

I pushed the door open and stepped back. Nothing came out at me so I poked my head in. It was neatly furnished, and I could see no signs of struggle or violence. I immediately thought that this was a household that went straight to one of the state centers which was subsequently overrun. Poor choice there.

I moved into the home, Tommy and Duncan coming in behind me and spreading out. Duncan moved to the kitchen and immediately began checking the pantry and cabinets. There seemed to be a decent store of dry goods, so he went out and got a sack from one of the other men. He filled it and sent the man back to the school, to drop it off and come back to get some more.

I went through the house, looking for anything of use, and came out with linens and towels and a good supply of toilet paper. All this went to the wheelbarrow and back to the school. I found the basement stairs and went down slowly, whistling softly to stir any zombie that might be down there. I got no response, so I kept going. The basement held the usual bunch of junk, although I did find a small area that held a little promise. There was a box of pictures and mementos, and it seemed the owner of the house may have been a vet of some sort. Digging deeper, I found a cherry wood case that held a pristine Colt 1911. A little searching found an old box of shells, and I figured the old gun had not been fired much, if at all. I tucked the box and ammo into my pack, to give to another member of the community, since I was comfortable with my SIG.

Finding nothing else, I went back upstairs. Tommy and Duncan were waiting for me, and I joined them on the lawn.

"Anything good?" Tommy asked.

"I found an old .45 and some ammo." I said, flipping a thumb towards my pack. "I know you guys have your Glocks. I'll give it to someone familiar with guns."

Duncan nodded. "Ready for the next one?"

I waved him on and we went to the next house. This one was definitely occupied, although not by anyone living. The zombies had made a mess, stumbling around and knocking things over, drooling over things, and bumping into the furniture. They came out when we opened the door, and were easily dispatched as they tumbled to the ground.

I went in, and found a large cache of canned food and bottled water, and a good supply of batteries. I didn't find any guns, but we did find the keys to a large pickup truck in the garage. Expecting the worst, I turned over the engine and was amazed when it coughed and came to life. I opened the garage door and surprised the hell out of everyone assembled out there. I pulled it out to the street and starting filling the back with the supplies. It was a huge truck, with a crew cab and full size bed. I grinned at Duncan and joked with him. "You need to come up with something pretty cool to top that."

Duncan mumbled something about the luck of fools and we went to the next house, one of the other men driving the truck.

At the next house we got really lucky. Apparently the owner was a sort of survival nut, and there was a large supply of canned food, bottled water, water purification tablets, first aid kits, and emergency blankets. I idly wondered where the owner was, since he had enough to survive a long time. I got my answer when I went into the back bedroom. The owner was lying on his bed, pistol in his hand, and a large portion of his brains splattered on the wall. I figured he may have gotten infected and chosen not to be a zombie. Either that or the reality of the true end of the world was too much for him to handle.

I relieved him of his gun and stored it in my pack along with the other gun. Heading to the lower level, I bumped into Tommy, who was carrying a large bundle of military surplus rifles. Another man was carrying metal cans of ammo. Two other men had two handgun cases each, and another was carrying a box full of assorted ammunition.

"Guy had a regular gun room in the basement." Tommy said, hoisting his load for a better grip. "We found a lot of useful stuff and a shitload of ammo."

I nodded my head. "Good deal. The owner won't want it anymore, and I'm sure he'd want us to have it."

Tommy arched an eyebrow at me. "You find him?"

I nodded. "He's upstairs in bed. His brains are on the wall. Must have been infected and ended it before he turned."

It was Tommy's turn to nod. "I'd probably do the same if I got nailed. Or hope someone would do it for me."

"Yeah." was all I said.

Tommy and crew hauled their load out to the truck and went back to get more. Duncan cleared out the kitchen and by the time we were done the truck was fairly loaded. I told the driver to head back and unload, but I had Duncan ride along and told him to store the guns until we could sort out what we had and make sure it was divided evenly. No one was to get anything until we got back. Duncan understood and hopped into the passenger side.

I watched the truck head back and looked toward the long line of houses. We had a lot of work to do, but I think we were going to be all right. At least for the time being.

A low moan on the wind was a poignant reminder that it was going to be a long fight. But we had gained a foothold, and were going to take it from there.

15

<u>Six weeks later</u>

I awoke to the sound of activity. It was roughly an hour before sunrise, looking at the sky outside my window. I could only see through the top six inches, the rest being reinforced by wood slats. But it was enough to let in a little light, and that was all I needed. I crawled out of bed and checked on Jake. He was still sleeping, tucked into a little ball with his butt in the air. I wondered for the hundredth time if that was comfortable, promising myself to try it sometime. But I covered him anyway, and got dressed, belting on my sidearm and field knife. Cleanup days were a bitch.

Essentially, the idea of a cleanup day was to remove all zombies killed the day or night before, burn the carcasses, and take out any that had been attracted by the noise of fighting. Thanks to my having to use a high-powered rifle, I figured there were lots of Z's aimlessly wandering outside, bumping into each other and seeking a way in.

I went over to the window and climbed onto the small ledge that was part of the structure. Not being stupid, I very slowly raised my head to look outside. Zombies are attracted to movement, and if something in their vision suddenly moves, they will focus on the source. I didn't worry about one trying to get in, but fifty could do some damage if they all focused on the same spot.

Peering over the boards I got a clear look at the outside grounds. There were about fifteen milling about the parking lot, and three or four strolling the grounds. Most of them were in pretty sorry shape, and one had somehow lost the use of its legs, dragging itself along the ground. There were some kids in the group, and I always felt bad for them, since they never really got a shot at life before it was taken from them. Two kids were dressed alike, making me wonder if they were brothers. I thought about Jake and swore once again he would never revive into the walking dead.

I was lost in my reverie when a zombie lurched into view, right in front of me. I had to resist the urge to step away, because again, the movement would have marked me. He was a young black man, his dark skin turning a deep grey with half of his scalp torn off. His left eye was missing and the other traveled around in lazy circles. His shirt was torn at the neck, and deep gashes, like claw marks, could be seen through the torn material. His right hand was clutching something, and what I thought was a stick at first was really a severed human finger. Lovely. I had to take all this in and remain motionless. If it was just me, I'd say to hell with it, and move, but I had Jake to worry about. So I got to watch Stinky shuffle on past. A small part of me wondered what had happened to me, how I managed to become so steeled at the sight of the living dead so close. I wasn't always this casual. No, this wasn't comfort, it was survival. If I let these walking corpses get to me, I'd be dead quickly, and my son right after. I guess that's what made me so determined; I had something to live for and someone who needed me for their life.

When the danger had passed, I stepped off the ledge, making sure I moved slowly. This was one of the reasons why we put the newcomers and families on the second floor. They could leave their curtains open and look out all they wanted. Unless zombies learned how to fly, they didn't have much to worry about. If zombies did learn to fly, we were all pretty much screwed, anyway. I was never any good at skeet.

Jakey was starting to stir, I was going to need to get out and get the clean up organized. Not really sure how I managed to become a kind of de facto leader of this little band of survivors, but since I used to be a school administrator, the leadership role wasn't new.

I opened my door and literally bumped into Nathan Coles, one of our "trainers". He was ex-National Guard, ex because his unit had been wiped out defending a last-stand position for the Governor of the state. On one of our raids, I had found him holed up in an attic, sick with flu and about a dozen zombies stumbling around the house wondering where the sneezing was coming from. Nate took in our newbies, taught them rudimentary judo and hold-breaking, and basic weapons use, from firearms to knives to improvised weapons. He was the one who taught me how to use the knife I had on my belt.

"Hey Nate! Good Morning!"

"Hey, John. How's Jake?" Nate always asked about Jake. I think he may have lost his son in the Upheaval, but he never talked about it.

"Fine. Getting bigger." I saw Nate's eyes cloud over briefly and again figured there was a story there. "What's the status on our cleanup?"

Nate grimaced. "We're getting ready to head out. Tommy is on the roof and figures there are about thirty-two in the area. We have squads of shooters and squads of cleaners suited up and ready to go. Also, we've got some of people who aren't happy that the families are exempt from cleanup."

That surprised me. "Who's making noise?" I had a feeling I knew what the answer was, but I have been wrong before.

"That new guy, Frank." Nate said, with an irritated glance down the hallway.

I followed his look. Frank Stearns was talking to about three people, making a lot of hand gestures and faces. I made a mental note to deal with Frank later.

"Leave him to me. I'll have a chat with him later." I reassured Nate.

"You sure?" Nate asked. "He could have an 'accident' out there, you know."

I looked at Nate. "Not my way, but I'll keep it in mind. Maybe I'll get lucky, he'll screw up, and some zombie will have fresh Frank for dinner."

Nate grumbled. "If you had luck like that I'd marry you."

I laughed, "You're too ugly for my taste."

Nate walked past, shouting for the squads to assemble and check their gear. I hopped up the stairs and knocked on the door to Kristen's room. A very sleepy head poked its way into the hall. "Hmmm?"

"Do me a favor and see if anyone is up enough to dress and feed Jake. I need to get out onto the grounds for cleanup." I said to the blinking head in front of me.

"I think Kristin's already downstairs, and Jessica's still sleeping. I'll ask Dawn, she's up." The head yawned.

"Thanks. Ten minutes?"

"'Kay." The head withdrew. Process of elimination made Janice the girl I was talking to. Nate had found her on the roof of a gas station, having climbed there to escape a mob of zombies that had chased her out of her house. She faced death by dehydration or being eaten by zombies, so when Nate came charging in, she was more than willing to come along.

Nate was a demon when it came to killing zombies. He was calculating, methodical, and deadly. He never panicked, and was silent as a ghost when he wanted to be. Just the man I liked to have around when raiding.

I headed down the stairs, thinking about out situation. We had a decent thing here, but there was no real life, no actual thought about the future. Was this the place I wanted Jake to grow up? Was this the place I wanted to grow old and die in? Off the bat, the answers were no. But I didn't have a solution that was acceptable. Sure, I could say lets build an army and go kick ass, but logistically it was impossible. If most of the world was zombie or dead, that left roughly one million zombies per survivor. Not good odds by anyone's standards. I did have some notions to work out, one being going back to my house to retrieve items left behind, if they hadn't been stolen by looters, bad memories not withstanding. Another was an idea I wanted to float by Nate as soon as I could. But I had work to do now.

I walked into the commons area where the cleanup and eradication crews were assembling. Cleanup consisted of four squads, four people in each. Two people were chosen by flipping a coin and they were the ones who dragged the bodies to the burn area to be disposed of. The other two people in the squad provided cover and protected the unarmed draggers. The draggers had six-foot-long poles with large hooks attached to them. The dragger just had to shove the hook into the dead body's collarbone or neck, and drag it off. Sometime the bodies were in weird places, and required careful manipulation of two dragger hooks. Eradication groups consisted of six squads, four people in each. One of the squad members each had long poles with larger hooks on them, the notion being to trip up the zombie and get him on the ground. Two other members had shorter poles, about six feet long that had a flattened rod attached perpendicular to one end, which then was rounded at the ends, creating a kind of "crescent moon on a stick". One member would pin the zombie down around the torso after he was tripped, and the other would then pin the zombie by the neck. The fourth member had a short rod with a heavy pointed weight on the end which was used to bash in the zombie's head when he was pinned to the ground. This method was invented by Nate when we realized we needed a relatively quiet and safe method of disposing zombie that strolled into our yard. It worked most of the time, sometimes there were problems, like when there were many of them and they began swarming. Then it came down to the Shooters – six men armed with rifles to hold a line and start eliminating. Every squad member has a sidearm, only to be used when things got overwhelming. Then one member was to drop his pole and then use his gun. The other members would use their poles to hold the zombies at bay until a head shot could be taken. All told, there would be 46 armed people out there, ready to do battle if needed. Sometimes they were needed, and more than once, they weren't enough.

I looked at the group assembled, and found my Shooters. There were four of them, I made up the fifth. We had two jobs. We were to shoot the Z's if they got too swarmy, and we were to act as decoys to get them to the eradication squads. Not too hard, but accidents happened. I looked over at Nate, and he nodded toward Frank, who was looking very glum as a Dragger. He held the pole as if he expected it to bite him, and I saw him looking over his shoulder at the other three members of his squad. Something tickled the back of my mind and I went over to Nate, who was checking the gear of an Eradicator whose pole seemed shaky.

"Heads up, Nate."

Nate glanced at me. "What's that, bro?"

"I think we're going to have some runners today."

Nate's eyebrows went up. "Really? Your buddy?"

"Yeah. I get the feeling he's wanting to wander off, not liking the rules of this place."

"Some people are stupid that way. I kind of figured him for an opportunist."

I thought about that. "Let's just hope he doesn't get anyone killed."

Nate grunted. "If he does I'll stake his sorry ass out on the lawn and cover him in ranch dressing for the Z's"

I laughed. "Roger that. Just giving you a gut feeling."

Nate smiled. "Your gut ain't been wrong yet."

I clapped him on the shoulder and went back to my shooters. I rounded them up and sent them to their assigned doors. I would head out the front door, and with luck, we should wrap this operation up quickly. Cleanup crews would head out when we called them, and we would all head for the baths for washing after.

I found my squad and we went through the routine of checking gear and tightening straps. No loose clothing was allowed, and guns were checked to make sure they were loaded and chambered. I lowered my goggles and jacked around into my carbine. For this work I preferred the AR-15 over my M1 Carbine. Thirty rounds of .223 was enough for this work. I saved the M1 for serious work. I checked the window and made sure there were no surprises waiting outside the door. We had taped over the windows and had a thin slit for viewing. No Z's were close to the door, although there was a middle-aged guy about ten yards out. He was first.

I flicked the safety off, braced my foot on the release bar of the front door, and shoved the door outward, moving into the morning light. I didn't have far to go, and was immediately the center of attention of about seven zombies that had been milling about the parking lot before I popped out at them. They must have thought dinner was about to be served because as one, they started to move towards me and my group. We quickly fanned out and went towards the closest zombie. He reached a mangled hand out to take hold of the first guy he saw, only to go crashing down to the dirt on his face. The hook had taken out his legs. Immediately the two pinners jumped on him before he had a chance to get back up. One leaned in with the pole on his back and the other pinned his head to the ground. The basher ran in and with one hard swung to the top of the head, the zombie was finished. I focused on the remaining zombies and figured the teenage boy with the mutilated face was next, he was moving a little faster than the rest and would be closest. The other five were a little more spread out, and would not get to us in time.

My squad fanned out again, giving the Z multiple targets, which confused his poor virus-infected brain. He stopped and looked around, then focused on the pinner which was taunting him with a pole. He reached out and grabbed at the pole, which allowed the tripper to hook his ankles and drop him on his ass. The pinner then jumped on him, keeping his body down while the other one danced in to try and pin down his head. Trouble was, he was too slow, and the first pinner stepped too close. The zombie managed to grab hold of the pinner's ankle and start to drag his foot closer to his gaping mouth. Chipped teeth bared and the other hand tried to grab the pole that was pinning him to the ground.

"Shoot him!" cried the pinner, grabbing my attention from the encroaching zombies, two of which had my undivided attention, as they were moving way too fast for comfort. "Shoot him!"

I had to move to get a shot, which was becoming difficult as the pinner had let go of his pole and was trying to rip his leg away from the zombie. The two other members were paralyzed, not sure of what to do.

"Please God, Shoot him NOW!" Screamed the pinner, kicking at the zombie who was grabbing now with both hands and trying to bring a flailing leg in for a bite. I stepped to the left and fired a shot, the report extremely loud in the morning. The round slammed into the zombie's shoulder, knocking him off his victim, but definitely not out of the fight. His teeth ground together as a new moan erupted from his mouth, and he rolled over to get to his feet.

I was about to deliver another shot when my basher stepped in, and swinging his weapon like a baseball bat, crushed the zombie's skull and dropped him like a bag of crap. I looked at the saved pinner and pointed to the gun on his hip. The idiot could have shot the zombie himself.

Two down and holy shit! I looked back to the other zombies and found two of them were way too close together for the squad to be effective. I lined up the head of one in my sights and just as a pulled the trigger, the son of a bitch ducked. What the fuck was that? It was like he knew I was shooting at him. He stayed in a crouched position and actually sped up to what I considered a fast walking pace. I dropped my sights and fired again, nailing him in the forehead and killing him for good. I switched my sights to the second one, but my squad had recovered their wits and moved in to kill this one. They actually surrounded the teenage girl zombie and the two pinners held her head up from the sides while the basher moved in from behind. Her moans were pitiful as she grabbed at the poles which held her head immobile. Her shirt was shredded, and her back was missing chunks of flesh where she had been attacked. Her neck was a raw open wound, and likely was how she died.

With the girl dead, we had two left to deal with, and they were coming at more leisurely pace. I directed the squad to the closest one, while I moved out to keep the other occupied. I thought I heard a scream from the other side of the building, but I was not about to go look just yet. Standing rule was you finish what was in front of you before you went looking for seconds.

As the zombie got closer, I was amazed once again at the virus that continued to animate these corpses. This guy must have been dead for a while, as he was shirtless and his mottled grey skin was torn and hanging off in various places. I didn't see a wound which meant he likely caught the virus through secondary contact. His mouth was a bloody ruin, and one eye was missing, as if he had been in a nasty fight for his last meal. He lurched towards me on legs that had seen too many miles. His femur was showing through a hole in his pants leg, and he reached out with claw-like hands to grab hold as he moved slowly closer. I backed up a few steps, keeping an eye on him, but also stealing a glance around for any others.

My squad killed the other zombie, a small Hispanic female with only one arm, then moved over to mine. They dropped the man, pinned and bashed him in short order, then we all looked around for more targets. None in sight.

I breathed a sigh of relief when the screams started again, this time they were more like shrieks, and there were several gunshots coming from the side of the building.

I yelled at the squad as I ran to the side of the building "Weapons out, weapons out!" I didn't know what I was going to find, but we were not going to be unprepared I stopped them about ten feet from the edge of the building and motioned them to stay behind me. I had the heavy firepower so I was going to go first. I angled away from the building and started forward, "cutting the pie" as the term was called from my old IDPA days. Never thought I would actually be using those skills, but I guess that was the point of the competition.

I rounded the corner and saw chaos. Two members of a squad were down, and each had four or five zombies on them, eating whatever they could tear off. The other members of the squad were in a small group, facing outward with their poles, pushing zombies away that got too close. They couldn't take their eyes off the Z's long enough to draw their weapons, which explained the standoff. I could see the poles of a pinner and a basher on the ground, which made sense as to why the remaining members could not deal with the zombies in front of them. I briefly wondered where their shooter was, but then I heard a shot coming from the field just west of the road that led to the parking lot in the back of the building. Time to work.

"Take out the feeders! Heads shots! Now!" I yelled, earning me grateful looks from my team. They spread out and four guns barked as one, dropping the zombies feeding on the basher from the besieged group. They ran to the next group and their guns barked again. I went to work on the standing zombies, and I shot like a metronome...aim, fire, aim, fire, aim, fire. I shot four zombies and the fifth turned his head to look to me. That was wrong. They don't ever take their eyes off prey. What the hell was going on? First the ducker, now this. The zombie, a guy about thirty, turned from his attack on the small group and came at me, his legs moving quickly. I didn't have time to line up a killing shot when he was on me, knocking me to the ground. My rifle was between us and that was likely the only thing that saved me. His head reared back for a bite, his mouth opening wide. I shifted the gun's muzzle and jammed it into his mouth. His yellowed teeth clamped on the barrel, and two of them chipped to jagged points. His hands clawed at my back and arms, trying to get me in for a killing bite. I pushed at him, trying to get my hand on the trigger to blow his head off, but his clothing had gotten in the way. I rolled to the left, pinning the zombie beneath me, still keeping the rifle between us as a way to keep from being bit, my back was hurting like hell where the Z had been clawing at me. The good news was scratches didn't turn you into a zombie. Bad news was you nearly died from infection from the rotting things.

"Fuck this." I said, taking my hand off the rifle and shoving it into his throat. That was a risk. I had seen other guys do that only to shove their hands into waiting mouths. I got lucky. I pushed back and sat up as I straddled his struggling form, keeping my hand on his throat. A gargled moan came from his lips as he struggled and thrashed at my arms. I drew my sidearm and, shoving the barrel in between his eyebrows, fired once, ending the zombie once and for all.

I stood up and surveyed the damage. Two members were definitely down and finished. I walked over to where the bludgeon lay and picked up the heavy stick. I went back to the two still forms, and with two very swift swings, ensured that they would not be coming back for dinner. Sometimes the virus reanimated people killed by zombies, sometimes it didn't. Better to be sure, I always say.

I went over to the survivors and spoke with the other pinner. "What happened?' I asked.

The pinner, Bill Cross, shook as he looked over his dead squad members. "I'm not sure. One minute we were doing just fine, then all of a sudden this trio of fast moving zombies comes out over the hill and jumps our Shooter. He got one of them, but the other two split up and came at us while we were dealing with that fat one over there." He indicated with a wave of his hand the large corpse laying a few feet away.

"Wait. You said they split up?" I asked, not sure I had heard correctly.

"Yeah. One of them went after the Shooter and the other came at us from behind. Christian never knew what hit him until the thing had dragged him down. That bought enough time for the rest of them to swarm and hit us as a mob."

That made sense. Not a lot, but it did. "Where's your shooter? Where's Steve?"

Bill looked out over the hill. "He's down that way. Looks like he's coming back."

I followed his gaze. Sure enough, I saw my other Shooter coming back. He walked a little stiff, like his leg was hurting him. I walked over to the top of the embankment and started towards him. He stopped me with a raised hand.

"Sorry, John. That's as close as you get." He said, keeping me about twenty feet away.

"What happened, Steve?" I asked, not wanting to hear the answer.

"Fuckers came out of nowhere, moving faster than I ever saw these bastards move. Just wasn't expecting it, you know?"

I knew, having seen a couple of them myself. "Yeah, I dealt with one myself."

"Was it the guy in the red shirt?" Steve asked.

"That's the one."

"Never saw nothing like it. Four of them came fast, only managed to get a lucky shot off that dropped one of them. The other three charged, but only one attacked me. The other two stopped for a second, looked at me, and then went off to the squad. It was like, like..."

I finished his sentence. "Like they were thinking things through and made a choice."

"Exactly!" Steve thought for a second. "It was like he knew I would kill him, so he went after easier prey."

"Need to think about how this changes things, don't we?" I said.

"You will. Not me." Steve showed me his hand. It was bloody at the wrist and a chunk was missing.

I didn't know what to say. Steve was a great guy, not prone to panic, and hated zombies with a passion for killing his wife and children. He knew he wasn't going to make it and didn't want to risk anyone else. "I'm sorry, Steve."

He waved me off. "Don't worry about me. I've avenged my family a dozen times. At least now I can go be with them." His voice trailed off as he looked around him. I knew what he was doing. He was taking a last look around and just appreciating all the good things he could see. I did that myself, once, when I thought all hope was lost and it would be better just to end it all for Jake and myself. It was different for Steve, though. His family was gone.

"Do me a favor?" Steve suddenly said.

"What's that?" I asked, although I already knew the answer.

"I can't kill myself. Thought I could but a while ago knew I couldn't. Guess that's what made me such a badass with the Z's. I wasn't fighting so hard to kill them, I was fighting so hard so I wouldn't have to kill myself."

I understood where he was coming from. Steve was my friend, and I had to kill him before he got sick and turned. My heart was heavy as I answered him. "I'd be honored."

Steve locked eyes with me. "Thanks. I'm glad I found a friend like you in this mess." He put his guns down and made a pile of the gear he took off. His guns would go to another shooter, his clothes would be burned, and his body would be buried on the hill overlooking the creek. He would join the 27 others up there, killed in a battle that some, even myself, were wondering why we bothered.

Steve walked away from his gear and stood facing the field. I could see the other corpse out there, the one that Steve killed; the one that killed him.

I walked a little to the right until I was about fifteen feet behind him. I had a hard time with my sights, because something got into my eyes. But I knew what he wanted and as a friend I could not do less. I would want someone to end me the same way should I get bitten. I said a quick prayer for Steve and quick request for forgiveness, and pulled the trigger.

The high powered round took Steve in the back of the head, killing him instantly. His body fell straight over, not bending or crumpling in any way. I smiled slightly to myself. That was just like Steve. No compromise. I looked skyward, raging inside at what I had become, what I was forced to do. But nothing was going to change what had happened that day. I lowered my rifle and walked back to the groups waiting for me. I picked up Steve's weapons and slung them over my shoulder. My mind went back to the days when I had to kill another person, when the all the killing began.

16

Cleanup went fairly smoothly, although there was a definite pall in the air. People were angry that three of their number were down, and more than once I had to stop people from going "hunting" on their own, looking for some kind of revenge. When you were angry, you didn't focus, and when you lost your focus, especially against this kind of enemy, you were killed. It didn't get any simpler than that. Screw up and die, there were no second chances.

A large pile of corpses was dragged to the baseball diamond, where we had dug a hole in the pitcher's mound a while ago. Bodies were unceremoniously dumped, covered with gasoline siphoned from cars, and set on fire. We have a pastor who once wanted to say a prayer for the dead, but after a particularly scary moment where his wife was nearly bitten, his prayers usually consisted of "Fuck you and burn." I didn't think that helped morale any, so we stopped the practice.

Frank was the consummate complainer. He whined about how heavy the bodies were, how bad they smelled, how much his back hurt, are we sure they were completely dead, why can't he be a pinner, why can't he be a shooter. Nate Coles was about ready to shoot the little bastard. Can't say as I blamed him. I fully expected Frank to go completely childish and ask "Are we there yet?" each time he dragged a body over the bridge.

I was busy myself, hunting a lurker that had managed to avoid the eradication crews by falling into the wooded area on the north side of the creek. Two of the groups had indicated that they were sure something was in there. I hated the woods, because it was hard to see. The leaves hadn't fallen yet, but there were enough on the ground to make silence impossible. What made it worse was the trees were small and close together, so rifles were hard to use. Yippee for me. I positioned two other shooters to cover the woods on the north and south, and I was going to enter through the west side along the creek. Why the thing hadn't come out yet was a mystery. Did it catch a stray round that had luckily put it down? Who knew? All I knew was I had to go get it. Part of being a leader,

I guess. Never ask someone else to do something you wouldn't do yourself.

I edged along the creek with my gun out, held low. My senses were on hyper alert, and I strained to hear anything that might give me a clue as to where he or she was. I stopped at the edge of the woods and called out, "Here, Stinky, Stinky, Stinky!" No response except a snicker from one of my shooters. I tried again. "Come on out, you cute little pus-bag, you!"

No luck. I started to think there was nothing here. But I still needed to check the woods to be sure. I went in slowly, stepping along the creek. The bank of the creek was steep, and footing was difficult. The water was noisy, covering any sound Stinky might make. I walked a little bit further, and still saw nothing. What the hell? I could see the end of the woods a little further ahead, and no sign of any zombie. If they knew I was here they'd be out already, so my guess was nothing was here.

I turned to head out and the creek exploded upwards behind me. The ghoul had apparently fallen in the creek and was lying on its back. The rushing water must have masked any sound, causing it to go quiet. My shadow on the water had made it react and lunge.

I spun around and took a step back as a dripping zombie rose up out of the water with arms outstretched and mouth open with a gurgling groan. Talk about your B-movie moments. Water flew everywhere as it fought to get out of the water, and I nearly shot it then and there, I was that surprised. But figuring that dragging that sucker, who looked to weigh two hundred pounds, out of the water would be a little much to ask of anybody, I decided to bait the bastard to drier ground.

I walked backwards out of the woods, trying to keep Slimey in sight. He was a big guy, pretty much my size, except he was completely bald with an eye and ear missing. His shirt looked to be a security uniform, and his belt was a police issue. I noticed he had a couple of magazine holders, so I made a note to have the draggers check his belt for ammo once he was down. Every round counted in this war.

He stumbled after me, moving slow, but steady. Water dripped off him in little streams, and even more water came out of his mouth as he tried to groan, keeping his eye locked on me.

I led him out to a small lawn, and when he came close enough, I put a round through the hole he already had in his head, just making it deeper. He dropped immediately, slumping into a ball on the grass. I holstered my weapon and signaled my shooters to draw back, keeping an eye on the houses and bushes. You never knew when one action will lead to a reaction. Most of the areas around the school were cleared out, but drifters were everywhere. In all seriousness, I probably should have saved the bullet, but hugging a wet zombie while sticking a knife in its ear didn't rank high on my list of things I enjoyed on a regular basis.

I went back to the building, waving to a cleanup squad that there was another one to pick up. By the way one of their number's shoulders sagged, I knew it was Frank Stearns. *Poor baby*, I thought. *It's tough making a living in a dead world.*

I went inside and got cleaned up. Things were always busy on cleanup days. I passed through the gym and waved to the kids who were playing basketball. In all, choosing this place as a safe haven wasn't so bad. There was enough room for all of us, we had a water supply, food was still plentiful, and we could feasibly grow food out on the grounds if needed. We hadn't been through a winter yet, but it was coming. I personally was curious about what cold weather did to zombies, and whether or not it killed the virus. If so, there was going to be a lot of cleanup in spring, and people could actually go home.

Home. Hadn't thought about that place in a while. Wouldn't mind going back and seeing if anything was left. Especially some of the ammunition I had to leave behind. We were getting short on a lot of it, and I was down to five boxes of ammo with my M1 carbine. Something to think about. I couldn't go now, but it correlated with another idea I had, which I wanted to run by Nate before we made any decisions. It was going to take agreement from the group, because there was going to be some serious changes. We'll see.

I stopped by my room and looked in on Jakey. He was working on a bottle with his sitter, and she shook the bottle at me to remind me that we were running low. I nodded.

"I'm going shopping today." I said, as I put on another pair of pants and shirt. "Anything you and the girls looking for?" I asked.

"If you could find magazines, we would appreciate anything." Holly said, giving Jake a pat on the back. He rewarded her efforts with a huge belch, which made all of us grin. She handed him to me and went out, and I rolled on the floor with him for a while. After about an hour, I saw his eyes starting to drift, so I put him down to sleep. He nodded off slowly, and I stayed with him until he slept. I tried to stay with him as much as I could before he went to sleep. Some strange part of me wanted to make sure he knew I was protecting him even in his sleep.

I went out and watched the rest of the crews come back in. They streamed in by twos and fours, and the shooters never let down their guard until they were inside. Even though there was no threat nearby, they were trained to never assume anything. The equipment went into racks, and people got cleaned off. I waved at Nate, and he strolled over, glaring daggers into the back of Frank Stearns' head. I figured Nate would have happily killed Frank several times over, and I was beginning to wonder why not? But everything in its place and I am sure there was a reason he survived long enough for us to find him.

Nate strolled up. "What's up?"

"Not much. We need supplies, and I need a crew to go and get some." I told him.

Nate nodded. "I can get you Tommy Carter, Charlie James, and Sarah Greer. They should be ready to go in an hour."

I thought about the choices. "I need to add Kristen to the group." Nate's eyebrows shot up. I countered his look with reason. "She's been a solid member, and she wants to prove her worth. Sarah will look out for her." Nate still looked skeptical. "Look, I gave her a weapon and I think she's ready." Nate didn't say anything. I tried guilt as a last resort. "Okay, if you think she should stay behind, then you tell her. I guess since you trained her, you would know if she's ready or not. Not saying anything about your training, of course."

That did it. Nate scowled at me and said "If I knew my mother in law was going to live here I'd join the zombies."

I laughed. "That bad?"

Nate snorted. "She'd scare off these zombies with one withering screech, followed by a round of phlegm-filled coughing."

"Ew." I said. "Must have made Christmas fun."

Nate eyes darkened. "Don't go there. I still have waking nightmares."

I nodded. Who didn't these days? "One hour. Ready to roll."

"Taking the truck?" Nate asked over his shoulder as he walked away.

"Have to." I replied.

"One hour."

"Thanks." I went back to my room and looked over at Jakey, who was still sleeping. He was usually good for an hour or so in the afternoon, so with any luck, I'd be out and back before he woke up. I put on a long sleeve shirt, grabbed my extra gloves, and put on my denim jacket. I opted not to wear my boots, figuring if I needed to be stealthy, my sneakers would do the trick. I belted on my knife, holster for my SIG, and my Gerber multi-tool. You never knew what you might need. I opted to bring my carbine, even though I was getting low on ammo. It worked for me, and it was a comfort to have that kind of firepower in close combat. As power went, it hit as hard at one hundred yards as a .357 magnum did at ten yards.

I grabbed my spare balaclava and headed to the garage. We had one vehicle that we used for supply runs, and it wasn't anything fancy, just a full size pickup with a crew cab. It sat four comfortably, five not so comfortably, and five with weapons and gear rather uncomfortably. We found it on one of our runs through the neighborhoods, and since the owner was not going to use it anymore, it went to the cause. Finding gas wasn't a problem, since there were lots of vehicles to siphon gas from. Luckily, one of our people was a gear-head, so he kept things running pretty well.

As I turned to the door, our pastor stopped me and reminded me about burying our dead. I told him to go ahead, get it done as soon as possible, I wasn't going to be there since I was on a run.

Inside the garage my fellow scavengers were checking each others gear and loads. Tommy was wearing his assault vest, complete with a cross draw holster and a small loop which held a two-foot crowbar. Useful in many ways, not the least of which was crushing a zombie skull or two.

Charlie James was wearing clothing similar to mine, but his weapon of choice was different. He had two tomahawks that he had found somewhere, and had fashioned a harness that allowed him to keep them on his back until needed. It worked pretty well, considering he was already swinging them pretty hard just when he drew them out. At 6 feet and two hundred pounds, Charlie was a good man to have on a raid. He was absolutely fearless, and even-tempered even when things got bad. His backup was a 9mm Glock, useful for all domestic disputes involving the undead.

Sarah Greer was a veteran of many zombie battles, and her favorite weapon was a little semi-automatic Ruger MkIII. She was deadly accurate with it, and liked to get the zombies in the eye when she could, in the ear when she couldn't. When the Upheaval started, her husband had gotten sick, turned, and killed her two children before she could put him down. We had found her in a long-range recon going house to house, killing any zombies she could find. Looking at her slim five-foot-five frame, auburn hair and fierce green eyes, one would never suspect she was a Public Relations Director in her former life. Strapped to her belt was her backup weapon, a hand pickaxe which was amazingly effective.

Sarah was helping our last member, Kristen, settle her gear and was giving her a lot of advice on zombies. Kristen was taking it all in and nodding. I figured there was no better mentor than Sarah for Kristen. Sarah was like the older sister to all the "orphaned" girls we found, a tough but fair mother hen. Kristen had her Glock, and a three foot spiked pole as a primary weapon.

I looked over the group and checked my SIG. As I holstered it I asked "Does any one need to be somewhere else? I can get a replacement if you need it." I always asked, letting people know they had a choice to risk their necks.

No one answered. I said, "I know we lost a few good people today, and no one feels it more than me. I had to put down Steve Tarnette today, and to be honest, I'm not really feeling too good about it. But those of you who knew Steve would know he would be the first to tell us to quit whining and get the damn job done." There were smiles at this. "I just want to relate a few things before we head out. The rumors you may have heard about some zombies moving fast and seeming to think things out are true." There was a collective eyebrow raising at that. I needed them to be aware of what transpired. "I don't know what it means, other than we are going to need to be on our toes that much more. The fast ones aren't that fast, but if you're expecting your usual Shuffler, he's going to be on you faster than Nate on a slacker. Just be careful, and take nothing for granted until we learn more. Any questions?"

Sarah spoke up. "John, why do you keep going on these raids? You don't ask any family man to go, yet you have Jake and you keep going."

The group looked at me. The only answer I had was, "I need to do this, because like it or not, this is the world we have right now. I need to be as skilled as possible, so I can teach him to survive. Besides", I added, "Every Z we put down is one less he has to kill later." That got a grim collective nod. "Let's mount up. Kristen, you're riding the in the truck bed."

Kristen looked at the bed and its relative discomfort. "Why me?" she asked.

Sarah gave her a slap on the back. "You gotta earn the cushions, little girl. Get moving!" Kristen frowned but jumped into the bed anyway. It was clear she did not like being exposed, but we all rode there at one time or another.

Charlie got into the driver's seat and I rode shotgun. Sarah and Tommy shared the back seat. The truck was comfortable, but we had added a few things as needed over the months. The mesh on the back of the front seats had extra loaded magazines, and the center console had two extra pistols and spare magazines. There was extra food and water stored in the cab, as well as matches and a first aid kit. There was a flare and a blanket. All the comforts of home. The bed of the truck had two hatchets to repel boarders, and swing up sides to increase the height of the edge of the bed. The added height made it impossible for zombies to reach in, and the boards locked together at the edges for additional strength. Pretty useful if you get swarmed, to buy yourself enough time to regroup and fight back.

I signaled to the teenager by the garage door that we were ready to head out, and he radioed to the roof for the all clear. When the clear signal came back, he grabbed the door and heaved it skyward. Charlie started the engine and rolled out. As soon as we cleared the door, the kid hauled the door back down and locked it tight.

As we rolled out, I looked at the neighborhood. You'd never know today was any different than any other day. The houses looked normal, cars were parked in driveways. If you had just awakened from a five month nap, all would seem normal. If you looked closer, however, you would see different things. Shadowy figures moved slowly past windows, and several homes were burned down. There were some cars run into the sides of the roads, and former occupants were still inside them, unable to figure out how to release themselves from the seatbelts. We dodged a few of these as we went down the road. We were headed to a large shopping center to see what we could salvage. I had my doubts we were going to find anything, but you never knew these days. On the way to our current residence, we had found a gas station that was unlooted. I figured the odds of us finding useful foodstuffs was becoming slim as the days wore on, and we were going to have to range much further to bring home the bacon, as it were.

We headed north, and turned at the first big intersection. There were a lot more cars on the road here, and Charlie had a bit of a time weaving through the abandoned vehicles. I knew why they were there, left like that. After Chicago fell, the resulting wave of zombies spread out to the suburbs, and overwhelmed anything in their path. People caught out in the open were devoured instantly, and people trapped in their cars were eventually dragged out and eaten. More than once I saw cars with smashed in windows and dried blood all over the interior. I tried not to look too closely at the cars with child seats in them, as I really didn't want to imagine a child stuck in a seat screaming for its mother as dead hands reached to rip it apart.

We didn't see many zombies, just a few stuck in cars and the occasional drifter. I could see Sarah mentally calculating how tough of a shot it would be, and more than once I saw her hand drift to the window button to open it and try a shot. But she always stopped, maintaining her inner discipline. More than once I was thankful I never had to put Ellie down, and that I got the chance to tell her how much she meant to me before she died. Not many people in the Upheaval got the same opportunity.

Charlie dodged a big truck in the road and had to go for a ways on the shoulder. I could hear Kristen bouncing in the back and cursing the whole time. I grinned and remembered my first time in the truck bed. I had bounced so high at one point the driver thought I had fallen out.

Charlie turned at the sign for the Big Circle store and headed to the back of the large building. We figured out a while ago that the front of the store was nice for picking, the backs of stores is where they had everything neatly boxed for you, and in greater quantity. Who needed three cans of beans when a crate was available?

Charlie backed the truck up to the door, and Kristen jumped out of the bed. She waited for Sarah to get out and followed her to the front of the pickup. She and Sarah were on lookout duty. I could see Sarah motioning to Kristen to keep her eyes open and to check the area constantly. Tommy, Charlie and I got out and immediately scanned the area. No Z's were in sight, but that didn't mean they weren't there. There was a retention pond over to the northwest, with a lot of water and high grass. A hundred could be hiding there and we'd never see one before it was too late. Charlie drew his tomahawks and stood back about ten feet from the door. I stood off to the side and flicked the safety off my carbine. Tommy went to work on the door, first checking to see if it was open and then using his crowbar to pop the handle. He didn't open the door right away, and placed his ear to the door to see if there was anyone on the other side. Since noise attracted them, we wanted to make sure we were ready when they came calling.

Sarah and Kristen were staying back, Sarah watching the grass and sides of the building. Kristen stuck close to Sarah, but seemed eager to prove her worth.

Tommy raised his hand and signaled that he had heard something. He tapped on the door and was rewarded with a loud thump that nearly opened the door. Tommy jerked back and yanked the door open, keeping it between him and the opening.

Two zombies came spilling out, and one went to his knees as he fell. The other one, a female, stepped around the fallen one in a slow gait, seeing Charlie and stepping towards him with arms coming up and a slow groan emerging from her torn lips. Charlie stepped back and waited for the zombie to come to him, his eyes impassive under his hood. When the zombie girl came within reach, Charlie whipped his hand around and planted a tomahawk on the top of the girls head. She dropped instantly, taking the weapon with her. Charlie was experienced enough to know to leave the weapon until the Z was dead. People had been lost who held on to weapons thinking they had killed a zombie, only to realize the critters weren't dead yet.

Tommy wasn't idle. As soon the first zombie who had fallen through the door started to get up, he stepped up behind it and slammed it in the head with his crowbar. The zombie went down, but wasn't out. As it struggled to re-orient itself, Tommy smashed it again with the crowbar, this time cracking the skull. One more hit put it down for good.

Charlie retrieved his 'hawk from the fully dead girl and wiped it off on the Z's shirt. He dragged the body over to the side of the lot and left it there. Tommy was a bit more creative, hooking his kill with his crowbar under the collar and dragging it out as well. Sarah didn't even look at the bodies as they were dragged past her. Kristen looked at the bodies and narrowed her eyes, but she held up well.

I waited at the door, listening for any more sounds, but I couldn't hear anything distinct. I thought I heard footsteps, but they stopped and didn't resume.

Charlie was about twenty feet from the door when a zombie burst out of the doorway headed right at him and headed fast, like a speed walker. I had but a glimpse of his face as he strode past me, and that was enough. His lips were torn from his face, exposing his yellowed teeth. If that was how he got it, it was a nasty wound to die from. His neck and shirt front were completely covered in blood, and his hands were vicious claws he was extending to reach Charlie with.

I didn't want to shoot for fear of attracting more of them, but Charlie looked like he was not going to be able to defend himself. I swung the carbine and was about to squeeze off a shot when Charlie moved. It happened so fast the zombie never knew what hit it. Charlie waited until the zombie's hands were nearly on him, then he ducked and pivoted out of the way, sweeping the zombie's legs from underneath him with one of his tomahawks. As the zombie landed flat on his back, Charlie jumped over its flailing arms and swung at the zombie's head, intending to nail it from the top. The zombie had other ideas, rolling away and letting the tomahawk slam into its shoulder. Charlie left it there and the zombie stood up with the 'hawk sticking out of it like a big toothpick on a rotten hors devours. It started for him again and Charlie sidestepped the lunging arms and swung at the back of its head. The axe blade bit deep with a sound like a watermelon being dropped, and the zombie stumbled forward, falling on its face, dead for good.

Charlie approached the zombie with his gun out in case the damn thing didn't know it was dead. But it was and Charlie retrieved his weapons. Tommy and I exchanged looks, and Tommy said "Looks like that was a fast one."

"Yeah." I said. "I hope they all don't get like that or we are going to have serious trouble."

Charlie joined us. "Thanks for the warning on the fast ones. That little bastard nearly threw my timing off."

"Dead is dead. You did fine." I said. I looked at the zombie he killed. Something was wrong about it. "Hey, guys. Look at that Z over there. What's wrong with him?

Charlie looked at him and shrugged. "He's a born-again corpse. What's *right* about him?"

Tommy looked. "You're right, why doesn't he look like the others.?"

It took me a minute to figure it out. "The blood. The blood on his shirt is fresh. He just killed something recently." I said.

Charlie looked at Tommy and they both looked at me. "So?" they said.

I sighed. *You gave them eyes, Lord, but they refuse to see,* I thought. "Fresh blood means fresh kill. Fresh kill means there might be more survivors."

That changed their expressions. Charlie looked at the dark opening and hefted his tomahawks. Tommy followed suit and gripped his crowbar tighter. I signaled to Sarah to watch the vehicle as we closed on the door and stepped inside.

The interior was dark, but the light spilling in the doorway provided a decent amount of light. The storeroom was filled with boxes, pallets, and assorted crates. I signaled Tommy to head to the left while Charlie broke off to the right. I went straight ahead staying in the light. I could see the wall of the storeroom in front of me, and I edged my way towards it, checking the aisles as I went by. Every ten steps I stopped and listened, and I could see Tommy and Charlie doing the same. I could see a body in the shadows on the left side, but it wasn't moving. Tommy bent down to check it, and shook his head at me. Dead for sure.

Passing the third aisle, a small hand shot out and grabbed my foot. "Whoa!" I whispered loudly, causing Charlie to pause and Tommy to straighten up. I looked down and it was a small child, about three years old. It was a girl, judging by its clothes, but that was where the resemblance ended. Her hair was mostly torn off, like it had been trying to escape something that had grabbed it, and its legs were mostly gone, save for some bones sticking out in awkward positions. That's why it hadn't come to greet us, it couldn't move.

I shook off the grasping hand and stepped back before she had a chance to get close for a bite. The pathetic creature let out a groan and dragged itself closer. I drew my knife and finished it off, closing its eyes forever. Part of me was sad at the necessity, but all it takes is a moment of pity and these things will rip your throat out.

We finished checking the storeroom without further incident, and regrouped back at the door with Sarah and Kristen.

"We still need to check the rest of the store, but I want to send supplies back now." I told the group.

Charlie looked skeptical. "Don't know if we want to split our forces, chief. Could be a hundred of those things in there."

Tommy concurred. "He's right. Could be a death trap, with no way to retreat."

I nodded. "You're right, it could be all that, but I don't plan on going in just yet. We've got a lot of food here, and the truck will take too many trips. I'm sending Sarah back with a loaded truck, and she's coming back with the bus for the rest. Besides, if there are survivors, we'll need the extra room."

Charlie and Tommy agreed with me on that point, so for the next fifteen minutes we spent loading up the truck with as much as we could without running the risk of spilling anything. Sarah got in the truck and I handed her the radio. "Let Duncan know what's up when you're on the road, so he can get the bus ready for a quick departure."

Sarah nodded. "You want anyone else to come back with me.?"

I thought for a second. "See if the doc is available, and if she is, haul her along, just in case."

Sarah rolled her eyes. "And what do I tell her is she doesn't want to come?"

"Tell her that we've busted a place that has a pharmacy, and would she like to do a little shopping?" I figured that little incentive might go a long way.

Sarah shrugged. "She won't wear a gun, you know that."

I nodded. "I don't really care. Give her a stick if you have to, just get her."

Sarah smiled. "Done." With that, she rolled away carrying the first of what I hoped to be many food trips. We were going to attract a lot of attention, but it was worth it. I had winter to worry about, and I still needed to talk to Nate about some new plans.

Tommy and Charlie and Kristen watched the truck roll away, and Charlie was the first to speak up. "We just gonna wait here, then?"

I snorted. "Hell, no. We're going in. They won't be back for half an hour, and I want to see the situation inside."

Tommy nudged Kristen. "Told you." He said conspiratorially.

Kristen grinned at me. I flipped Tommy off and brought my gun up to the ready position. "Let's go, we don't have much time."

Back inside, we stopped at the swinging doors which led to the store area. There was a window in the door, but it was useless in the dark light. I could see some light coming in the front windows, but as it got closer to the back where we were, the light was noticeably less. We had two options, bust through and let whatever was in there come at us, or creep in and hope we could gain some advantage. I looked at the aisle directly in front of me and saw it was clear. The good news was we could hold off quite a few if they had to funnel into the aisle to get us. The bad news was we could be overwhelmed if there was sufficient numbers. Always a risk, anyways.

I signaled to Charlie to hold the right, and Tommy to hold the left. Kristen was to come behind me and stay close. We pushed through the doors and headed to the middle of the aisle.

The first thing that struck me was the smell. It was nearly a physical thing that I had to wade through. Rotting meat and produce from the grocery section gave the air a sickly kind of stench. There was a smoky smell I couldn't identify, and a definite coppery smell, like there was a lot of blood somewhere. Something had died here, and had died recently. I stopped in the aisle to get my bearings and to listen for anything attracted to the noise. I heard a thumping sound, and some groans, which told me we weren't alone, but since the thumping hadn't stopped, whatever it was focused on something else. I went down to the end of the aisle and peeked around. The store was surprisingly not a mess. Sure there were things on the floor, but I expected a lot worse. We worked our way down one of the center aisles, checking each row carefully for zombies. Nothing so far.

We got down to the end of the main aisle and regrouped at Lawn and Garden. The thumping sound continued unabated, which helped mask our presence. It was pretty creepy, knowing they were there somewhere, yet they didn't know we were there.

We moved towards the outside wall, picking our way through some debris scattered on the floor. The Camping section seemed to be pretty well picked over, but I motioned Charlie to grab some karabiners, which are always useful for securing doors and gates. The next couple of aisles brought us to the sports equipment and it was interesting to note the baseball bats were all gone. Nice thought, but in the long run, not effective enough. Human heads were hard, and you needed penetration, not just force.

We passed quietly to the electronics section, and this area looked to have been looted. Not exactly sure why anyone would want anything electronic when the power was out, but some people didn't care about that. The thumping was getting louder, and I thought I heard a voice amid the pounding. I looked at Charlie and he nodded his head. He heard it, too. Someone was alive in here.

We gripped our weapons a little tighter and moved our way towards the pounding. There was a lot of light coming in the front, and I could see why. A car had smashed through the front doors, opening up the building to anyone. A look at the car gave a grim picture as to what had happened. Someone had tried to find refuge here, and were attacked by local zombies. Dried blood covered the outside of the driver's side of the car, and there were dark bits of flesh scattered around. On the other side of the car a body was laying on the ground, most of it had been eaten away. I could see ribs sticking out of the torso, and the organs were all missing. The flesh on the arms was shredded, and I could only imagine the fight, as what had once been a man tried to fend off his attackers. Behind me I could hear Kristen gag a little as she saw the corpse. I wondered about the little girl I had put down in the storeroom and if she had come from this car.

Pushing these thoughts aside, I raised my hand and ducked down by the car. Tommy moved to the side and Charlie covered the rear. About twelve zombies were gathered around an office door, and one of them was pounding on it, trying to break it in. The rest were hitting the door when they could reach it. During a lull I definitely heard someone scream at the zombies. Tommy and Charlie heard it, too. Definitely alive. We had to move. I figured the noise had attracted all the zombies in the store, which was why we hadn't seen any elsewhere in the store.

I signaled to Tommy and Charlie and they drew back, allowing me a clear course of fire. We couldn't risk getting swarmed, so the rest of the team fanned out and watched the aisles and the door. I heard Kristen curse as she slipped on the blood by the car.

I waved to Tommy and he turned on his flashlight, lighting up one of the zombies. I took quick aim and shot it dead. The loud report inside the building froze the zombies for a minute and I was able to drop two more that Tommy highlighted for me. The rest turned and with various degrees of mobility came at us. Tommy kept lighting them up and I kept putting them down. In short order, all twelve had been killed for good.

The silence was nearly deafening, and we held our collective breaths, waiting for any more noise or movement. Kristen broke the silence from the door.

"We got movement out here!" she shouted, adjusting her grip on her weapon and checking the magazine in her Glock.

"How many?" I yelled back.

"Six at least, headed this way."

"Placement?"

Kristen glanced out the door. "All individuals, moving regular."

I did a quick calculation. The bus should be here in ten minutes, if everything went well. We needed to be out back ready to go in five. "Charlie, head outside left and engage. Kristen, go with Tommy and see what's left of whoever is alive in here. Tommy, give me your weapon, I'm going out with Charlie."

Tommy handed over his crowbar and Charlie headed out the door, tomahawks at the ready. I handed the carbine to Tommy and he slung it over his shoulder.

I headed out to the parking lot and headed right. Charlie had already taken out one zombie and was heading for his second. I ran toward the closest one on the left and as soon as he was within reach, I smashed the crowbar across his forehead. His head caved in and he crumpled without a sound. I ran toward the second one, a medium-sized man who was missing most of his face, ducked under his hands and planted the hooked end of the crowbar in the back of his head. He went down with a small sigh, as if he was grateful I had ended his miserable existence. Charlie was working on his third one, an elderly woman, judging by her dress, hooking the legs out from under her with one 'hawk and caving in her face with the other after she hit the ground. I left the crowbar and faced the last one, who had managed to close the distance while I was dealing with the little guy. She was a woman in her thirties, roughly, and looked like she had been through some tough times as a zombie. Her skin was tight against her skull, and her eyes were sunken. Her lips were black with dried blood, and her teeth were chipped and jagged. I could see a line of something coming out of the corner of her mouth, and made a note to stay the hell away from that disease-ridden spittle. I didn't have time to retrieve the crowbar, so I drew my knife and waited, holding it in a reverse grip. As Drooley got close, her face turned into a snarl and she reached up with both hands. I pushed her arm away to the right with my left hand, pivoting on my waist and turning her to the left and profiling her head for a second. As her dead brain tried to re-orient itself, I reached high and slammed the knife down onto the top of her head, the tanto point punching through her skull like a bullet. She dropped without a sound, and the knife slipped out of her skull without my having to let go of it, making a slurping noise on the way out. *Some things you never get used to*, I thought, grimacing at the sound.

Charlie came up to me as I wiped off my blade and retrieved Tommy's crowbar, wiping it off as well. He didn't say a word, I didn't feel the need to talk either. We just nodded to each other in that way men have, and looked around. The area was strangely quiet of zombie activity. I would have figured there to be more around here, it was oddly still. Usually that was when the floor fell out from under you, so Charlie and I jogged back to the store.

Inside, Tommy and Kristen were talking to a group of survivors. They jumped at the sight of us, but relaxed when they saw we weren't zombies, and Kristen was reassuring the group. There were five of them, three females and two males. One of the females was openly crying, stealing glances at the body by the car. They looked like they had had a rough time. Small wonder, given what they thought might have been their last moments. As we got closer, I told Charlie to head to the back to wait for the bus. I walked over to Tommy and drew him aside, handing him back his crowbar and he gave me back my carbine.

"So what do we have here?" I asked.

Tommy shrugged. "Typical story, really. They were three neighbors that had banded together after everything had gone south. After a while, they ran out of food and water. They decided to go see if they could re-supply, and when they stopped to check out the store, they got jumped by what the blond woman says was a fast moving zombie. The thing had an arm in their car before they knew it, and Bill, the guy who got grabbed, panicked and hit the gas, crashing the car into the store. Before they could react, other zombies had dragged Bill out and were ripping him apart. Jason, the bigger guy there, he figured they needed to get out and use the distraction, so he pulled the rest out of the car and got them to the office before one of the zombies saw them and went after them. He's pretty shaken up, and feels guilty he didn't help his friend, but I figured you'd talk to him about that. That's pretty much it, I'm sure there's more, but I personally don't need details."

I smiled. Tommy was a great fighter and friend, but don't ask him to give rat's ass about your problems. "Thanks. Charlie's out back, the bus should be here. We need to get loaded and get moving."

"What are we taking?" Tommy asked, looking around. He wanted to know so he could tell the crew that had come back to help.

I looked at a virtual warehouse of items we could use. Clothing, tools, bedding, food, toys, everything. It coincided perfectly with what I wanted to do with the survivor group, so without hesitation, I said, "Everything."

Tommy did a double take at me and looked around. "All of it?" he said incredulously.

I nodded. "All of it. We have a lot of work to do. When you get back, rouse everyone and get the gym ready, we're packing it in there until we can get it sorted out. And Tommy?"

"Yeah, John?"

"No one takes anything until its all back and I have a chance to talk to everyone."

"Got it." Tommy jogged back to the rear of the building to tell Charlie the good news.

I turned back to the ragged group of survivors. Kristen was holding one of the women, a petite brunette who couldn't stop crying. I went over to them and introduced myself. "My name is John Talon, and I'm part of a group of survivors who have managed to live in this mess for while now, and we are living in a school not far from here. There's enough room for all of you if you want to stay and contribute to the group. If you want to go out on your own, we'll supply you and see you on your way. Your choice. We're going to clean out this store and take everything of value back with us. You can head back with the first bus load."

I didn't expect much in the way of conversation, but the one called Jason raised his hand. "How many people do you have?" he asked.

"Over a hundred. If you decide to stay with us, we'll ask you to contribute in some way to the group. We'll train you to defend yourself, and be part of the cleanup and eradication crews we have. If you show serious aptitude, you'll become a raider if you want to. If not, good bye and good luck." I learned a long time ago that honesty never hurt in the long run.

"What about Bill?" Jason wanted to know about his friend.

"Well, there's not much I can do for him, since there isn't much left of him, but we'll do what we can later. He's not a priority at this point." The brunette glared at me for that, and would have said something, but Kristen squeezed her arm and she stayed quiet. "If there's nothing else, you all should head to the back." I said.

I walked over to the car and took a look at it. Except for some minor damage, it should run decently. It was a Subaru Outback, and it had only crashed through the doors, scratching the hell out of it. I stepped around Bill and looked into the car. No blood inside that I could see, and the doors were all closed. The keys were in the ignition, so I figured, what the hell? I reached in the window and turned the key, expecting nothing like I had found in so many vehicles before. Imagine my surprise when the darn thing turned over and started! I hopped in the car and pulled it out of the store, hoping the tires would not be punctured by the glass. I grinned like a kid at Christmas as I pulled the car into the parking lot and drove it around to the back. It had nearly a full tank of gas, and might be very useful as a scout vehicle, having four wheel drive capability.

Charlie shook his head as I drove up and grinned at me. "Twenty car dealerships within a ten mile radius and you think that POS is worth keeping."

I laughed. "Its ugly but it has style, just like me."

Charlie laughed. "True that. The first bus load is gone, along with your survivors. Tommy says you want to take it all."

I looked at the building. "Indeed I do. We have a lot to talk about, but for right now, we have a shitload of work to do."

"What are you going to do with that car?" Charlie wanted to know.

I looked sideways at him. "After I clean it I figured on outfitting it for a recon squad. Know anyone who might want to take part in that sort of thing with a customized vehicle?"

Charlie's eyes lit up as he considered the possibilities with the little car, and he turned thoughtful as the potential sunk in. I left him circling the car and watched as other members began hauling out the second load of supplies to be carted back to the building.

Not a bad day, I thought. *Not bad at all.* I needed to hop on the next run back to get to back to Jakey. I had been gone nearly an hour and a half. Almost too long. I wasn't worried, as I knew Nate would check on him, and Kristen would, too.

As the sun crept higher in the sky, I could see some movement here and there as the occasional Drifter wandered around. I'd deal with them when they got close. But the time was coming when we were going to change our ways, and we'll see how our luck held then.

17

We managed to move the majority of the supplies from the Big Circle store into the school. We had a few skirmishes with zombies who came to investigate, but nothing major. Everyone was extremely happy at the clothing that had been doled out, and the extra foodstuffs were a welcome addition as well. Jake was set for a long time in terms of food, and he was starting to be able to handle things like cheerios and soft foods. He was so funny to watch with the cheerios. I would put a handful in front of him, and he would smack them with both hands, then eat the ones that stuck to his hands. I thought about my own food and wondered if it would work with sandwiches.

The weather was starting to turn colder, and we needed to think about making it through the winter. I personally was curious as to what effect winter had on zombies. Would they freeze to thaw out later? Would they keep moving through the snow and cold? What about the rest of the people who might still be out there trying to survive? With the power out and water available only through natural sources, how would they survive? We were in a pretty good position here, having food and water nearby.

My thoughts were interrupted when someone knocked and Sarah stuck her head in my door.

"You decent?" she asked.

"No, why?" I grumbled, not really sure I wanted to hear what problems we had today.

"You might want to get down to the training area." Sarah said cryptically.

"Why?" I wasn't in the mood for trouble.

"Just go. You'll see. I'll be in the library if you need help." She said as she closed the door.

I looked at Jake, who was just finishing his cereal, and said, "We should just go live in the woods." Jake didn't answer, he just looked at me with his 'chocolate browns' and grinned. That always lifted my spirits. I picked him up and brought him upstairs to the 'day care'. That was what we called it. It was a classroom that was used for teaching the kids we had, and also for watching the kids that were not old enough for school. We had been extremely lucky that we had managed to have two elementary teachers and one high school teacher among the survivors. They taught the kids, and two moms watched the little ones when their parents were on duty or chores or whatever. I brought Jake up there as much as I could, since he loved to play with the little kids. I figured it was good for him, and the workers liked him there since he was so good-natured.

After I had left Jake, I went back to my room and decided to go for a walk. I knew I needed to see what was happening in the training room, but I also wanted to take a look around the neighborhood. I was curious as to the habitability of some of the homes, and I was also curious as to who might have some stores of firewood in their yards. I also wondered if there was still anyone out there, or if they had all been infected.

I suited up for combat, putting on my black cargo pants and boots, my long sleeve shirt and black field jacket. Thanks to our recent raid, I had a lot of new clothes. I especially appreciated the new underwear. I belted on my knife and SIG, and made sure I had a few zip ties in my pocket, as well as a couple of karabiners. I put on my backpack, which held three days worth of food and water, as well as a radio, first aid kit, two foot crowbar, and emergency blanket.

I put on my gloves and balaclava, and put my goggles on my forehead. I slipped two extra magazines for my carbine in my side pocket, two extra magazines for my SIG in the breast pocket of my jacket, and slug my M1 over my shoulder, attaching it to its clip on my backpack.

As I passed my window, I looked at myself and wondered for the hundredth time how the hell a school administrator managed to get himself into this mess. Although I had to admit the effect of the outfit was a bit thrown off by the bright red backpack on my back. Oh well, it worked, and in this world, that was more important than looks.

I headed down the hall to the training room and I could already hear a spirited exchange.

"Jesus Christ! Will you shut the fuck up! Why can't you just do what you're told without opening your stupid mouth?"

That would be Nate. I guess training was in session and somebody didn't want to be there.

"I swear to God, if you open your dumb fucking mouth one more fucking time I am going to shove this fucking stick so far up your fucking ass you will be the world's ugliest fucking popsicle!"

That was a good one. I hadn't heard that before. As I reached the door I could hear the object of Nate's anger, and shock of shocks, it was Frank Stearns. His voice was like nails on a chalkboard. Some people could stand it, others couldn't get near it. I tolerated it because I had to, not because I wanted to.

"You don't have to shout at me and I am really offended by your language. How dare you single me out in front of everyone else." Frank nasally voice sounded really indignant, and I realized Nate was going to murder him if I didn't intervene. You did not question Nate and his methods. He wanted you to survive. If you showed aptitude, he trained you privately to hone your skills and make you better. If you just didn't get it, you were shown rudimentary skills and assigned to group tasks. You never went on raids or recons. Nate and I were near equals in skill with firearms, but he could take me eight out of ten times with a knife. We practiced unarmed combat three days a week and worked out five days a week. Sounds like a lot, but in all honesty, there wasn't much else to do besides read. I trained as much as I did so I could teach Jake when he was old enough.

I stepped into the room just as Nate, with his face red, stepped forward towards Frank. Frank was standing at his full height, all five foot four inches of him, and his face was screwed up in righteous anger. Frank was dressed as I was, although he had no weapons on him. Nate insisted people train with their gear on, since they needed to be able to know their limitations in terms of movement and speed. "What's up, gents?" I said, trying to defuse the situation before someone got hurt. Our doctor was busy with a small flu outbreak among the older people. She didn't need to deal with fist fights.

Everyone in the room stopped and looked at me. Some shifted nervously and grasped their training weapons tighter

Nate Coles just spared a glance in my direction but fixed his gaze back on Frank. "This useless piece of useless shit feels like I am picking on him and making him work too hard. Everything is 'too serious' or 'too hard'. I have been working with this fuckhead for the last month and he has complained every fucking second of it!"

I looked at the rest of the room. I needed to let Nate handle it, because I didn't want to undermine his authority in his training room. But I needed to get Frank out of there before Nate seriously lost it and lost credibility with the people he needed to teach. Jason Coleman, one of the people we rescued from the Big Circle, was there, as well as his wife. Dean Cotton, a former plumber was there, and Martin Oso, a financial manager who hated zombies with a passion nearly as great as Charlie's. They were all sitting on the floor against the wall, watching the exchange between Nate and Frank. Carl Witry was there, a former drama coach for the local high school, and he agreed to act like a zombie for the training classes. He was an average-size guy, but he could project his voice like nobody else. We used him for entertaining the kids and reading books to them. That was how he earned his keep. Nate believed in realism, and Carl was in ragged clothes and a fair actor. If you screwed up, Carl would actually bite you. He bit my hand once in training. After I thumped him for it, I thanked him for the lesson, and never got bit again.

Frank yelled back. "I don't see the point! Why do all of us have to train? Not all of us should go out on raids! Some of us are too valuable to risk!"

Nate's eyes turned deadly and things didn't look good for Frank.

I stepped in. I had my goggles and balaclava on, so it must have seemed somewhat intimidating, which was the point. "Why are you so valuable, Mr. Stearns?" I asked quietly as I stepped closer to Frank, casually placing my hand on my SIG.

Frank looked up at me. "I am the office manager for the executive staff of David McCormick, legislator for the 33rd district. Without me, his whole office will collapse, and the state legislature will follow."

I have no idea how I managed to keep from laughing. I stared at him for a full minute, and the rest of the room stared at him as well. Carl Witry had his mouth open, but I don't think he was playing zombie at this point. I finally made a decision.

"You're finished here. You don't have to take training any more. It's wasted on you." I said.

Frank smiled smugly at Nate, not fully realizing what I was saying.

"You're on search and rescue permanently, starting today with myself and Sarah Greer. If you haven't paid attention in training, you're going to die, and we will watch you turn into a zombie before we kill you permanently." My voice was cold as I had no pity for slackers or people who were useless. Nate did not need this garbage, and Frank was just going to get someone else killed. At least with me and Sarah, we knew he wouldn't be able to screw up and get us killed. If we bought it, it was because *we* screwed up.

It was Frank's turn to stare at me. He couldn't believe what I was saying. Nate just smiled and winked at me, his way of saying thanks. I didn't give Frank a chance to protest.

"Get your weapon and meet me by the side door in ten minutes. If I have to come looking for you I won't be happy." Frank scurried off to comply, but I could see in his eyes he hated me for it. I turned and left the room, feeling the eyes of the trainees on my back. No mercy for the people wasting space by existing.

I headed to the library and found Sarah reading by herself at a table. She glanced up as I walked in. "Busy?" I asked.

She closed her book after putting a bookmark in. "Not that busy." She stretched her back and I could hear the cracks from ten feet away.

"Want to go for a walk? I'll be at the side door in ten minutes" I asked as casually as I could.

"Sure. Give me five minutes." Sarah hopped out of her seat and brushed past me, her ever-present Ruger strapped to her side.

I headed back to the "school" and let the women know I was heading out, and could they look after Jake. They said not a problem, he was down for a nap. I could see his little body wrapped in a blanket in a secluded corner. I went over and touched him gently on his back, silently promising him I would be home soon.

I went back downstairs and got to the side door just in time to see Sarah checking Frank's pack and she was not too gentle about it. I think he came off the ground a little bit when she pulled on his straps. She tossed his weapon at him, a baseball bat with a huge spike through the end. He had a knife as well, although I had no illusions about him being able to use it. I didn't bother giving him a gun. I didn't feel like getting shot in the back.

"Got your supplies?" I asked Sarah.

She nodded, pulling down her goggles and winding her scarf around her face. She looked at Frank. "He's got his as well. Three days of food and water, and emergency supplies." She had a question in her eyes for me, but I stopped her with a small shake of my head. I watched Frank's eyes narrow and I could see the calculations going on. Perfect. Exactly what I wanted him to do. All I had to do was wait, and let his little thoughts take over.

We headed out the side door and started walking down the long driveway. I wanted to take a look at the main highway, and we had a good hike ahead of us. If what I had planned was going to work, I needed to be able to move as quickly as possible before the snow came down.

We reached the end of the driveway without incident, although Frank jumped a mile when a bird flew up in front of us. That was one thing I wondered about. Why didn't the virus kill animals and turn them? For whatever reason it was, I was grateful. Human zombies were hard enough to deal with. Zombie everything else was a world without a chance. If that happened, you may as well strip naked, cover yourself in barbeque sauce, and holler for the zombies to come to dinner.

We headed north towards the main road, and didn't see a whole lot of activity. I did see the telltale marks of infection throughout the neighborhood. White flags hung limply from scores of mailboxes.

Frank complained about the walk, the weight of his pack, the weight of his weapon. I didn't say anything, letting Sarah deal with it.

She was direct in her methods. She poked him in the back of the head with her rifle and hissed at him to be quiet. "A zombie can hear you a quarter mile away, dumb ass. If you want to die fine, go walk into that house and die." She pointed to a house on the side of the road. There had to be at least ten zombies inside, all of them clawing at the window, trying to get out. They were all in various states of decay, and more than once I wondered why we left them there and didn't deal with them. I guess since they weren't an immediate threat, they could stay there a while until we decided to root them out or burn the house down. Most of the houses in the area had zombies in them. Turns out when people got sick, they got their families sick and didn't even know it. Families died by the thousands, and those that didn't get sick, got killed by their revived relatives. The infected were effectively trapped in their homes unless they accidentally broke a window and got out, since they didn't know how to operate doorknobs.

Frank looked at the zombies and shuddered. "No thanks, I'll be quiet."

Sarah snorted "Right." She didn't believe him, but she didn't have to. I think she looked forward to hitting him again.

I kept us moving pretty well, we stayed in the center of the street. High fences lined each side of the street, but I did not want to be rude and rouse any zombie playing in its front yard. I didn't need a gauntlet of zombies to run through as we tried to make our way to safety.

After about an hour of walking and stopping, checking our surroundings and listening for ghouls, we reached the first crossroads. We were in a largely empty area, save for cars here and there, so anything coming after us would be exposed for along time. We rested for a moment and I used the time to look at the several five-story condo complexes near the road. They were relatively new, and still had fairly cleared fields surrounding them. An idea poked its way into my head, and I waved Sarah over. Frank was on his back, wheezing and making whistling noises with his nose.

"What's up?" Sarah asked, only her eyes visible on her head.

"Check out the condos." I said, pointing to the buildings.

Sarah looked. "What about them? They're nice and all, but what about them.?"

I pointed to the bottom of the structures. "They have no ground floor. You could actually sleep in peace there without worrying about an attack at night. All they have are garages down there. And look over there." I pointed to the small grove of trees and grass growing near the edge of the complex. "I'd bet my knife there's a water supply there."

Sarah looked at the complex and then back at me. "What are you saying? You want to move everybody?" She seemed incredulous, like I was crazy.

"Let's face it. We can't stay in that school forever. Sure we're there now, but it was never meant to be a permanent place. I think we need to seriously consider coming to this place, cleaning out the zombies, if there are any, and starting life again there."

Sarah shook her head. "Starting life again? John, this is about survival, nothing more. The world we knew is gone, and we're not getting it back."

It was my turn to shake my head. "I can't believe that, Sarah. Yeah, we've taken a hell of a hit, but this can't be it. We can't end this way. What about the kids following us, what about the world they inherit? They can't live the rest of their lives in a school. That's like living in a cave. What if the zombies last twenty years? Fifty? We have to take our world back. One way or another, we have to take it back."

Sarah looked at me for a second, then placed a hand on my arm. The physical contact was like a jolt, and I nearly jerked my arm away, I was that surprised. Sarah generally avoided contact with people unless she respected them, and that respect usually meant you had to kill around fifty zombies single-handed.

"I can see why they wanted you to lead them, John." She said softly.

"Oh yeah, why's that?" I was seriously curious to know why they wanted me to be the leader.

"You never stop looking forward, no matter what gets thrown at us, you keep going forward. Thank you." Sarah's voice was as gentle, and I was pretty sure she smiled behind her scarf. With Sarah you never could be sure. She could be pulling a knife on me as well.

"We need to get moving. We have about five hours of daylight left, and I want to see what I can see." I regretted ending the relatively nice moment I was having with Sarah, but I needed to do some things. I walked over to Frank and kicked him in the foot. "Rise up, Wheezy. We're not done yet."

Frank grumbled and rolled to his feet, but he was smart enough not to say anything with Greer standing behind him. We crossed the road and headed up to the overpass, figuring it to give me a good idea as to the nature of the road. Since a major intersection was just a few hundred yards away, that should give me clear idea of what to expect on the road.

We climbed the over pass and looked out on the interstate. For the most part, it was empty, with a few cars here and there. The cars were empty, and I guessed they just ran out of gas. The highway had a fence running alongside it, which limited access by the zombies. The problem came from the on and off ramps. There wasn't any real protection there and I could see even from that distance there were many cars that looked like they had been attacked. Not a pretty way to go. It seemed like a bunch of ghouls had just wandered into some stalled cars and the slaughter began.

I was looking east when Sarah, who was looking west, got my attention. "We've got movement." She said, pointing towards a car that was slowing moving down the road. I could see it had a flat tire and was not going to make it much further. It was being chased by a group of about six zombies, and they were going to catch it the second it stopped. I sighed. Here we go. Frank started squirming and grabbing at my pack. I elbowed him in the gut and he backed away.

"Come on, Frank, we have work to do!" I called as I jumped the guard rail. I slid down the hill, bumping my shin on a root that I didn't see. I could hear Frank groaning all the way down, muttering to himself and generally being a nuisance. He rolled the last five feet and landed on his face. I managed to see that and reminded myself to tell Nate when we got back. Karma's a bitch, Frankie. Sarah set herself up on the overpass, resting her rifle on the rail and providing cover for our efforts should it prove necessary.

The car was sliding forward, and I could see that two of the tires were gone, and the car was rolling on rims only. I could see three people in the car, and the vehicle wasn't going to make it another fifty yards. We were about three hundred yards away, so we were going to have to move. I ran forward, unslinging my carbine and making sure the safety was off. Frank stumbled along behind me, trying to keep up. I'm sure he would have stopped, but the fact that Sarah was behind him with a rifle trained on his ass probably motivated him better than anything I could have said.

As we ran the car finally came to a stop about a hundred yards ahead of us. The zombies, seeing their meal finally stop, let out a collective moan and shuffled a little faster forward. The people were about forty yards from the zombies and had about two minutes to live. I moved as quickly as I could, noting that Frank had fallen behind. The doors of the car flew open, and a man and woman got out. The woman dashed to the rear of the car and opened the door, intending to get the back seat passenger out and moving. The man never looked back, he just ran towards me. The woman screamed at him, but he ignored her and kept running. She struggled with the back seat, and I could see she wasn't going to make it. I tried to run faster, but I knew I wasn't going to make it, either. The man, a smallish specimen, ran right past me and didn't stop until he reached Frank, who was about twenty yards behind me.

The woman pulled on the seat belt, but it refused to budge. I was close enough to try a shot to distract them, but the odds of a hit at that distance were slim. Besides, the woman was between me and the zombies. I just kept running and hoped she could get the seat belt undone.

The woman screamed again and the seatbelt finally came free. She pulled her passenger out, and I could see it was a small child, maybe ten years old. She started to run forward when the first zombie hit her from behind. She went down to her knees, and screamed as rotten teeth sank into her neck. Blood spayed and another zombie came from behind, grabbing her arms and tearing into shoulder. She screamed at her child to run, then stood up and swung at her attackers, knocking one down and kicking at another. She didn't have a chance, but she bought enough time for the child, a small boy, to get to me. His face was streaked with tears and he was yelling for his mother. I grabbed him and started backing up; keeping an eye on the group as they took the woman down again and began feeding.

She screamed for a long time before she finally died. I was headed back when I head another groan behind me. I looked and saw the group had finished with her and what was left wasn't pretty. She had been completely gutted, and her blood stained the road. Long strips of flesh had been torn from her arms and legs, and I could see bits of flesh hanging from the ghouls as they began walking towards us. I could have killed them all, but I was hesitant about shots this far from home. I didn't feel like a running fight all the way back.

Scooping up the child, I ran back to Frank and the man who had run. "We have to get out of here. They aren't going to stop until they get us. Move."

"What about my wife?" the man squeaked.

I pointed down the road where his wife's body lay. "Not sure why you care now, but there she is. Help yourself. The zombies are finished with her. There might be enough of her to reanimate in a little while." I had a vivid picture of this man saving himself and leaving his family behind, and if it wasn't for the little boy I was carrying, I would cheerfully have left him for the zombies.

I didn't stay any longer. If he wanted to stay and die, fine. But this little boy didn't deserve that, just like he didn't deserve to have such a coward for a father. I ran to the overpass hill and scrambled up. The boy followed me without a word, and I could see his mind was retreating to a state of shock. That's fine. Shock works, as long as it's quiet. I had seen this before, and in time he would be better. But for now, we needed to move. Frank and his friend crawled up as well, and Sarah kept her rifle on the zombies the whole time. She had seen everything, and when the man reached the top, she fixed him with such a withering stare I thought he would catch fire. He was clueless, and chatted away with his new best friend, Frank. The boy came out of his fog enough to take Sarah by the hand, and I saw a slight shudder go up her arm when he did that.

Time for that later. The zombies were under the bridge, unable to climb the embankment to reach us. They reached up with bloody hands and opened blood stained mouths. I had the urge to throw the man down the hill at them, but I couldn't do that to the boy. I had killed in vengeance before, and I didn't like what it did to my soul.

I headed back to the school, moving quickly. The man complained about the pace, but I was deaf to him. I needed to get back to the school and talk to Nate about some plans for the future, and that couldn't get done out here. We moved swiftly, stopping only once to catch our breaths. The boy was a trooper, never leaving Sarah's side. His father went over to talk to him, but the boy jerked away and hid behind Sarah. The man looked angry and started to move for the boy, but Sarah brought her rifle up and shook her head. The man wisely decided not to push the point.

We made it back to the school as the sun started to head down, throwing long shadows across the ground. A cold wind came up from the north, stirring the leaves and reminding me that I was running out of time.

Nate was at the entrance to greet us, and raised his eyebrows at the fact that we had left with three, and came back with five. "Busy day?" he asked.

I glanced at him. "We need to talk about a few things." I looked pointedly at Frank, who was in an animated conversation with the man we had rescued. I could hear him say 'What could you do?' and making conciliatory gestures. The man hadn't gone near his son, and Sarah was still trying to kill him with her eyes. She walked off with the boy after shrugging off her gear.

Nate nodded and went over to Frank and the man. "Get yourself out of your gear, I'll take care of this." Frank clearly did not want to leave his friend, but Nate's look did not brook argument. Nate turned to the man. "Welcome to the fort. Who are you and how can you be of use to us?"

Nate's twist on words was lost on the man. He stuck a hand out and said "Kevin Pierce. Pleased to meet you." Nate shook his hand and I could see he wasn't impressed. I took off my goggles, gloves and balaclava, and reslung my rifle over my shoulder.

Nate gave him the standard speech. "We'll give you a room, you can decorate any way you like. We have clothes if you need them, and food is prepared three times a day. We eat together, and each person is responsible for cleaning up after themselves. If you have children, we have a sort of school..."

"I have a son." Kevin interrupted.

"...which meets for four hours a day. You are expected to attend training to defend yourself and the community. If you are worthless or useless, you will not eat. Any questions?" Nate had given the speech before, but I always found it amusing to hear.

"Who's in charge? Is it you?" Kevin wanted to know. "I was a superintendent of a pretty big district and can lend leadership advice."

Nate pointed at me. "He is. He's saved more than half of us. Fact is, this place probably wouldn't exist without him. Superintendent, huh? John here used to be a principal before the Upheaval."

Pierce actually tried to look down his nose at me. Which was tough, since at six-two, I was a full head taller than he was. "Just a principal, hmm?"

I looked at him. "What I *was* is irrelevant. What I *am* is disgusted by your presence. The only thing that is keeping me from throwing you to the zombies is the fact that your wife managed to save your son before she was eaten. If he had been killed as well, you wouldn't be here. I *saw* you leave them. I *saw* you run. You can't change that. What you *were* was a superintendent. What you *are* is a coward and a bastard."

Kevin actually took a step back under my onslaught. Nate's eyes hardened and he dropped a hand to his gun.

I spoke again. "We'll keep you safe only for your son's sake. But cross me, and I'll throw you out. Run from a fight in here, and I'll kill you." Kevin sputtered but I cut him off. "Learn the rules and don't speak to me. You might actually live. Right now you need to find your child and beg his forgiveness for leaving him and his mother to die."

I turned on my heel and left him, signaling Nate to follow me. Frank came scurrying up and he took Kevin away. Sarah had left with the man's son, and in all likelihood was getting him something to eat and drink.

Nate followed me up to the Day Care, and I picked up Jakey. I remembered that boy running from his mother's killers, and I gave him an extra hug and kiss. He grinned at me and buried his face in my shoulder, making squeaky baby noises. He noticed Nate standing there, and reached out to be held by the big man. Nate was Jake's guardian when I was not around, and I knew without hesitation that Nate would die to protect Jake. Nate tickled Jakey's chin, causing him to laugh and causing Nate's features to soften. I could see how good of a father Nate probably was, and I was saddened his children were no longer around.

We went back to my room and as I fed Jake his dinner, I outlined my plan. Nate asked a lot of questions, and we talked long into the night, poring over maps by candlelight and making adjustments. Tomorrow was going to be a long one, but it was the first step in taking back what we lost.

18

The next day, I called the community together in the commons. Since I had only done this a few times before to discuss rules and such, people tended to take these things seriously. Everyone showed up on time, except for Frank and Kevin. They strolled in five minutes late and huddled together in the back. Charlie James wandered over to where they were and casually sat down next to them. Frank looked at Charlie like he was a bug, and Kevin was talking animatedly and gesturing with his hands, his fingers sticking out at weird angles. It was so distracting that Nate had to bump me to get me started.

"Good morning. I'm grateful all of you came down to the meeting. First of all, I want to bring you up to speed on our newest members. Kevin Pierce, sitting there next to Frank Stearns, and his son Phillip, joined us yesterday. Sarah, Frank, and myself rescued Kevin and Phillip from the interstate. His wife did not make it." There were murmured condolences, and that bastard Kevin actually had the nerve to look sad. I considered spoiling the moment for him with the truth, but that wouldn't accomplish anything. The man's true nature was easily seen, and I doubted anyone would be fooled. Besides, Sarah and Nate had already spread the word about Kevin, so it was done.

"Second of all, we need to talk about winter. We are relatively sheltered here, but heating a place this size is going to be difficult. Food we have no worries about, thanks to our raid on the Big Circle," There were a few cheers at this. "But we need to think about leaving the school behind."

There was a stunned silence as people took in what I had told them. Then the questions began to flow and Nate raised his hands for silence.

"I understand you are reluctant to leave, considering what we went through to get to this place and what we go through to keep it. But in reality, what did we win? We bought ourselves a little time, that's all. We bought ourselves a little security. We can sleep somewhat easily at night, but we always have to be on guard, always have to be ready for the next attack. Ask yourself this question. Do you want to grow old here? Do you want your children to grow up here? We don't know how long the zombies will last, be it a year, two years, ten years? All the time stalking us and waiting to devour us. We've regrouped, yes. But we need to move out, reclaim the world that was ours, and tell the zombies we will not just lay down to be their dinner. We need to strike out and start taking it back. I have a feeling there are a lot of survivors out there, and they will not make the winter without help.

"Nate and I have been planning, and we think we have come up with a viable plan. First of all, we will move out of this building and into another facility. One that is more secure and allows us to move about freely outside." That struck home. Many people hadn't been outside in months, and they often talked about their yards, their gardens, whatever.

"We don't think it is possible yet for everyone to go back to their homes. If you did, you'd face the survival problem on your own. We think staying together as a community will ensure our success and survival." There were several nods at this.

"Secondly, we need to establish secondary posts, manned by essential personnel and self-sufficient. I have figured out one perfect location for such a post, and it is there I will be heading in the near future. We figure to have five or six of these posts set up next spring, and from there we will begin the final part of our plan, which is to begin clearing the area of zombies, securing it completely, and establishing ourselves in a permanent home to rebuild what was lost.

"It's going to take a lot of work, but right now time is of the essence. It's October now, and we all know what winters are like in the Midwest. I figure we have two months before the really nasty stuff comes after us. If we are really lucky, the zombies will freeze in the winter and allow us to establish our posts unmolested; however, nothing in our short history tells me we have much in the way of luck.

"I'm not asking you to believe in the plan. I'm not asking you to believe in me. What I am asking is this – In forty years when you look back on your life and the Upheaval, don't you want to be able to say to your children "I stood and fought. Not I ran and hid."

I didn't know what I expected. I half expected to have a lot of shouted questions and epithets. I half expected to be threatened. What I did not expect was to have one person, Jim

Bigelow, our oldest community member, stand up and address me personally.

"John, you've constantly put this community first, and many people have wondered why. You never asked for anything in return and you have fought for us at every turn. Some people here owe you more than they could ever hope to repay. You've never made a move you didn't think through first. If you tell me we need to move, then I'm with you. Where are we going?" He sat down and people started to clap. I have to admit I was touched. I never realized that people noticed what I did. I thought I was being selfish, doing what I thought was best for my son and his future. I guess everyone got caught up in that as well. That's okay, they can come with.

When the clapping died down, Nate stepped up and addressed the assembly. He had a map of Illinois tacked to a piece of cardboard, and there were areas outlined in red, blue and green.

"The red areas here, those are the ones John and I consider too hot to attempt any penetration. We just don't have the manpower or resources. Maybe later, but for right now, it's out of the equation. It is not, however, out of the realm of containment, and we can use natural terrain to our advantage. We will begin by sectioning off one area at a time, eradicating every zombie in the area, and moving on to the next area. We expect to increase our ranks as we find survivors. The blue areas are considered to be areas of little zombie activity, and the green areas are what we consider to be relatively safe zones. These are the rural areas and outlying towns and farms, and we think in all likelihood there are entire towns which have been spared the devastation. The end goal is self sufficiency, and we have the resources at our disposal to rebuild better than we had before. We just have to go and get them, and establish ourselves at points where we can support each other and combat the threat.

"I'm not going to lie to you. Not everyone will welcome our efforts with open arms. There are likely groups that are existing to take advantage of the situation and establish themselves as warlords or kings of certain territory. They will show no mercy and shoot first, without asking questions. We will deal with them when the time comes.

Nate paused to gather his thoughts. "We are going to head to the condos at the corner of the road. They are ideally situated, and provide a good measure of security. There is water there, and people can actually have their own condominium, not just a room in a school. They have no ground floor, and you won't have to worry about getting your ass chewed by a ghoul every day." People brightened at the thought of resuming some sort of normalcy. "We will still have school and training, we will just be in a different area. We will begin cleanup tomorrow. We want to be completely moved in two weeks. Any questions?"

The room was quiet, then Frank raised his hand. Before Nate could explode, I said "Yes, Frank?"

All eyes turned to Frank and I could see him reveling in the attention. "What if we don't want to leave?" He asked smugly, as if this was a revelation I missed.

I decided to burst his bubble. I addressed the group. "Does anyone wish to stay in the school?" No one raised their hand. I could not blame them. We had fought for this place, but it was time to move on and get busy living.

Frank looked defeated. I had no pity for him, or his new friend. "If you want to stay, you'll get two weeks of provisions, one firearm, one blunt weapon, and a hearty 'Good Luck!'" A huge part of me wished he'd stay, but I knew Frank would never be self-reliant. He preferred to live off the work of others. Hence his political career.

"Okay people. Let's get to work!"

19

The next five days were busy. We spent a lot of time casing the condos, and we had to be on the lookout for roaming bands of zombies as well. There seemed to be an increase in the number of zombies out for a stroll, and I wondered if the ones from the city were finally making it out to the 'burbs. We got lucky with the first building, as it was relatively empty, just stinky from rotting food. We did find a dead old woman in one of the bedrooms, but it looked like she died of dehydration instead of the virus. We moved five families into the condos, and set them up with provisions. Nate took on the task of securing the water supply, and after an interesting moment with a ghoul in the high grass, declared the water secure.

Charlie and Sarah were clearing out the second and third buildings, and it was rather entertaining to hear "Heads up!" as another zombie came flying out of a window to smack noisily on the ground below. We figured it was easier to toss them out the windows than drag them down the stairs and make a huge mess. It was tricky, killing them without serious fluid loss, but Charlie and Sarah were pros. Their backup teams were pretty good, too. Funny what it takes sometimes to have a successful career change.

The weather was getting colder, and I really didn't notice any difference in zombie movements. They were still trudging along, and there were the occasional faster ones, but nothing out of the ordinary. When you live in a zombie-filled world, that is.

I was taking the RC (Recon Car) down the interstate, checking on passageways and clearance for vehicles. Martin Oso was with me, but we didn't talk much. I needed to be able to move a semi truck, so clearance was a priority. Strangely, the freeway was mostly clear, and I was able to make extremely good time. I headed past New Lawrence and towards Joslin. There were more cars on the roadside, and I saw more than one which was occupied by ghouls. They looked to be in pretty sorry shape, having turned near the beginning of the Upheaval and been stuck ever since. One was barely able to lift its head to watch my car go by. Poor Stinky.

I crossed the river and from my vantage point on the bridge, I could see quite a few zombies wandering the streets of Joslin. They were kept in check by the river, but I was sure they had fanned out to the surrounding countryside. Martin stiffened a bit at the sight of so many zombies, but we were safe on the bridge.

We rolled past Casino Street, and I was sorely tempted to go take a look, but I had a feeling that place was wiped out by people having one last fling before the end. I spotted my exit and took it, keeping an eye out for the usual problems. Martin was curious as to our destination, since I had kept it from him the whole trip. I pulled up to a high gate, and stopped the car. The whole area was surrounded by a high man made hill, too steep for zombies to navigate and perfect for keeping safe what I considered precious cargo inside. There was a guard shack next to the gate, and a sign that said "NO ENGINE BRAKING" Moving out of the car, I approached the guard shack as Martin scanned the street we had turned off of. No zombies yet, but you could almost feel them coming out of hiding and shuffling in your direction.

The guard shack was empty and I approached the gate. There was a lock and chain on the gate, and I figured the key was long gone. I pulled out my crowbar and with a few yanks, broke the lock. I threaded the chain through the gate and it made a huge clanking noise. Martin jumped at the sound and there were several answering groans from the area. We had to move fast. I just hoped that I wasn't jumping into a yard full of zombies.

I pushed the gate open and Martin hopped back into the car. He drove into the yard and I closed the gate behind the car. I put the chain back and secured it with a karabiner. Easy on, easy off. Just as I secured the gate it pushed violently back at me. I stepped back and looked through the slits. Sure enough, there were five ghouls that wanted to party. *Not yet, boys, but I'll get to you later*, I thought. How, I had no idea, but something would come to me.

Martin got out of the car and looked around. We were in a storage facility for cargo containers, the kind you see stacked by the thousands by docks and rail yards. They were stacked up six high, about as tall as a five story building. There was a container fork truck over on the side, and we were looking at about a thousand containers, and I could see more down the hill. Perfect. All I needed now was a way to move them. There was a small parking lot of trailers to put the containers on, and an old truck ready to roll. Better and better. It would have been great if I had a clue how to drive the fork truck to move the trailers, and even better if I knew how to drive the truck to get them to where they were needed, but I didn't. I think Charlie knew how to drive one, maybe Tommy, but I wasn't sure.

Martin looked around and wondered why I was so happy. "What was the point of coming here? There's just a bunch of old containers."

I enlightened him. "How tall are the containers?" I asked him.

Martin looked closely. "About eight feet or so"

"Think a Z can climb one of them?" I asked cryptically.

Martin looked again. "Not really. Maybe one in a thousand might manage it."

"Could you walk on it, patrol on it?" I asked, looking at one nearby.

Martin finally got it. "A fence! Perfect! And if they tip it over, it still blocks them! Are we taking them back to the condos?" He seemed eager to get started.

"That we are, Martin, old son, that we are. But first, we need to figure out how to operate the fork truck. I have no illusions about the two of us able to lift one of those things." I said, pointing to the machine. "That's your job."

Martin grinned and hopped over to the cab of the fork truck. As he opened the door, a zombie fell out and landed on top of him. He shrieked and pushed the Z in the chest, narrowly avoiding snapping jaws. The Z was dressed in overalls and hardhat, and likely turned in the machine. It was pretty well decayed, and its skin slipped and tore off as it struggled to get closer to Martin and he struggled to keep it away from him. They danced back towards me, and I nearly drew my knife when I spotted the towing chain on the ground. I grabbed it up and looping around my hand, I swung it with everything I had at the zombie's head. He must have been more decayed than I thought, because his head came right off his body and sailed off into the weeds by the office trailer. The headless body dropped immediately, and Martin was nearly taken off balance since the thing still gripped his jacket.

"Jesus Christ! Where the hell did that guy come from?" Martin asked as he struggled for breath.

"We better keep an eye out for more." I said, shifting my weapon to the ready and moving towards the trailer. "See if that thing will start, and if it won't, jump it from the car. With luck, the gas hasn't turned bad."

I headed over to the trailer and looked through the window. I didn't see anything, but that didn't mean squat. I knocked on the door and listened carefully. Sometimes a ghoul will be sitting quiet, and will galvanize at a noise. But I figured if Martin's shriek hadn't roused anything, it wasn't there. I walked away from the trailer and felt something dragging on my foot. I looked down, and saw Martin's zombie's head attached to my heel. It had bit my boot heel and hung on like a pit bull. I dragged it over to a tire rim and stuck it under the corner of the rim. I rolled the rim over its head and forced it off. It continued to stare and snap at me so I picked up the rim and smashed it down on the head. Its struggles ended immediately.

I looked back at the fork truck to see Martin staring at me. I shrugged my shoulders and motioned him to try and start the truck. It turned over but didn't want to catch. He tried it again and it caught for a second then died. On the fourth try, it turned over and stayed running. I jumped up and gave him a thumbs-up. I ran over to the old truck and wondered if we would be lucky again. I tried the engine, but it refused to even turn over. Okay, time for plan B

I signaled Martin to drive the fork truck over to the side of the truck and see if we could jump the battery. He did, and I retrieved the jumper cables we had in the car. We hooked up the truck and tried to start it again. This time we got turnover, but no dice on the engine starting. I checked the gauges, and realized the truck was out of gas. Martin promptly pushed the truck over to the pump with the fork truck, and I filled the tank, thanking whatever god was still listening that the fuel tank was gravity –fed. I filled the truck and tried starting it again. Imagine my relief when the thing coughed and roared to life. Success!

We pulled the truck around and attached a trailer. It slid off a couple of times before we figured out how to do it right, and then Martin tried his luck putting a cargo container on top. It fell off the first time, but we got it right the second time. I secured it and turned off the truck. Martin turned off the fork truck and immediately we knew something was wrong.

There was a lot of noise coming from the gates, and I couldn't see through the zombies that were pounding on it. Thank God it was made of steel and the chain was holding. I went over to the Office and grabbed the ladder from the side of the trailer and placed it against the containers that were near the gate. Climbing to the top I hauled the ladder up and climbed up the next container. I stepped up the containers like this until I was on the top container that looked out over the gate.

"Oh, fuck me running." I said, surveying the scene before me.

"What do you see?" Martin called up to me. "How many are there?"

I looked out on a mass of about fifty of the nasty things, all in various states of decay. When they saw me standing on the top of that container, they set up a collective groan and reached for me. They were funneled into a relatively small area, thanks to the design of the yard, but there was no way we were going to get out of here without a fight. I checked the terrain and saw that they couldn't get in as long as the gate held, but we couldn't get out either.

I got back down to the ground and gave Martin the lowdown of the situation. Apparently our riding around had made enough noise to cause the locals to come see who the new neighbors were. Great. If we didn't deal with this soon, the noise *they* made was going to attract a whole lot more.

We could set up on a container and shoot them, but we may as well set up a flare for every zombie within a five mile radius to come a-looking.

I looked around and took stock of what we had. We could throw fuel on them, but we might need that for the truck. There were some lead pipes over in a corner by the machine shop, and a quick look in the shop showed nothing of use against a horde of the undead. Oh sure, if they stood still long enough we could use the grinders and such, but they seldom were so accommodating.

Martin came up with the best idea. "Why don't we drop containers on them? The fork truck can easily lift containers over the gate and we can crush them flat."

Brilliant. He went to work and managed to grab a container lengthwise and hold it over the teeming masses. We had a moment when we realized we couldn't just drop the containers. But Martin remedied that too, when he tipped the forks forward and the container slid off, crushing about twenty of them. Gross fluids squirted out from under the box. Martin went back for another container and repeated the procedure. The zombies had no idea what was happening, and just stood there to be crushed. There were about ten of them left that we couldn't reach, so I grabbed a length of pipe and rode the fork truck over the gate and onto the containers.

They were a little lopsided from the goo underneath, but I could still work. The ghouls reached for me and clawed at the top of the container. They couldn't get a grip, and those that did had no strength to pull themselves up. Perfect. I hefted my pipe and went to work. It was kind of like being at the driving range, in a way.

Martin hauled me back over and we opened up the gate. There was still movement under the containers, and Martin used the fork truck to push down on the containers. He was getting pretty good with that thing. I swear I could hear popping like bubble wrap, and I didn't want to know what it was. Martin pushed the containers out of the way, and blocked the road to the south. Greasy goo and body parts covered the driveway, and I was reluctant to drive over that mess time and again. Realizing the necessity, I poured gas into a container and covered the infectious mass.

Martin and I checked weapons and gear while the zombies fried. When the fires died completely, we got into the vehicles and headed back to the interstate, remembering to lock the gate behind us. We certainly were going to be back. This first container was the first step in securing our new home, and I was happy to get it there.

As I drove toward the exit, I realized we had no way to get it off the truck. Oh well, we'll think of something. We always do.

Even though we had a lot of trips to make, every one would make us more secure. I smiled to myself as the plan started to come together. Next step was moving to the new place, and setting up a second sanctuary. Things were looking good, and I worried more than ever. When things looked good, that was usually when the zombies came and bit your face off.

20

It took the best part of four weeks, but we managed to move enough cargo containers to completely encircle the condo complex, the water supply, and the empty acres to the north. I had insisted that one container be placed on its end every ten lengths, to give us a lookout tower. Martin and I spent long hours ferrying cargo containers, and when we managed to get two more trucks running, the process speeded up considerably. As an afterthought, I grabbed the welding supplies from the maintenance shack at the depot, and one of our survivors managed to turn the towers into covered shacks. I thought that was pretty nifty. On one of the return trips, Martin had a burst of inspiration and made a side trip to a boat storage facility. I thought he was nuts until I saw he had managed to secure another big fork truck to help with placing the containers.

The new fence had a profound effect on the community. People spent long hours outside, and our kids ran freely in the sunshine for the first time in months. It was gratifying to see smiling, running children in the midst of this messed up world. It didn't matter that it was getting cold, the kids still played and ran. For the first time in a long time, people could let their guard down, if just a little bit. Even Jakey perked up by being outside, and for a kid that was perpetually in a good mood, that was something.

People were immediately grateful for the change in living arrangements. We had enough condominiums for everyone to have their own, and the privacy this afforded had a positive effect as well. It was a small return to normalcy that two weeks ago would not have been considered possible.

We still had the occasional zombie wandering around, and they were dealt with pretty quickly. Our barrier was put to the test when a large group of about thirty of them showed up and began attacking the fence. They managed to move a container a few inches before they were stopped, so we decided to add weld points to the containers to prevent that from happening again.

In all, we had a good thing going at this point and were pretty well set up for the winter. All of the condos had fireplaces, so warmth was not going to be an issue. Nate had a group getting firewood from one of those nearby garden centers that had piled it up before the Upheaval, and they were bringing it back by the truckload.

With things pretty well set up, it was time for me to move on to the next part of the plan, which was to set up another safe zone. Nate was going to be left in charge here, and his goal was to expand the fence as much as he could as often as he could. The idea was to cover as much of an area as possible, taking back as much as possible, utilizing natural terrain and land features whenever possible to secure the safe zone. We needed to be self-sustaining for a while, since the zombie's rate of decay seemed to be up to the individual, we had no choice but to wait a bit. But I was anxious to see about other communities and survivors, and I needed to get going if we were going to have a chance at surviving the winter.

I had had a meeting a few days before, outlining the plan and asking if anyone was willing to come with Jake and myself. I certainly couldn't force anyone, and it was going to be difficult for anyone to leave the relative safety of the new community, but I had to ask.

To my surprise, Sarah agreed to go, along with Charlie and Tommy. Tommy said he would get lonely without me, and Charlie said someone had to watch my dumb ass. Duncan certainly was not going to get left behind without Tommy, and I was secretly glad the three of us were hitting the road again.

Jason Coleman and his wife Lisa agreed to come with us, and to everyone's surprise, Kristen Larkin wanted to come with, and her friend Chelsea Forbes wanted to go as well. I could understand it. When the condos were doled out, the girls in the little dorm room had been 'adopted' into other families, and I think these two were having the hardest time adjusting. No trouble to me, the more the merrier. I figured Sarah could look after the girls, and they would be well taken care of.

We spent three days getting ready for the trip, and I was vague as to the details of the location. I knew where I wanted to go, but I didn't want to get anyone's hopes up in case the place turned out to be a bust. If it was, I had a small backup plan, but that was for worst-case scenario.

We decided to take cars for the trip north, as the cold weather did not make taking bicycles a possibility. We had a lot of bikes, and used them frequently on foraging trips to the nearby homes, but no one wants to take a bike trip in snow. I was driving a small Honda CR-V, with Charlie riding shotgun and Kristen in the back seat with Jakey. Tommy and Duncan were in the next vehicle, a Jeep Cherokee, along with Jason and Lisa. Sarah and Chelsea brought up the rear in a Ford F150, with all of our clothes and personal stuff. Our weapons we carried with us, and we drove in full gear. We couldn't take the chance of not being armed. In a perfect, uninfected world, this trip would take us thirty minutes, depending on traffic. Today, I had no idea what I was going to hit, so I needed to be ready.

Nate caught up to me about an hour before we were supposed to leave. It was a cloudy day, with a brisk wind out of the West. The trees were devoid of leaves, and the ground was that light green color with a lot of yellow mixed in, letting you know that the world was going into hibernation. There were still some people out and about, and I could see two of the towers were manned. The fence was the only indication anything still was wrong with the world, its patchwork of colors and corrugated steel interrupting the landscape.

"You all ready?" Nate said gruffly, always getting to the point. His breath came out in a thick mist.

"Pretty much, just need to get people in the vehicles and rolling." I replied, checking my gear and clothing. I was grateful for the heavy clothing as the wind tried its best to find every way in to freeze me.

"You know you're leaving me the two biggest problems I never want to deal with." Nate said cryptically.

I knew what he was talking about. Kevin Pierce and Frank Stearns had taken up residence as roommates, and one could only guess at the depth of their conspiring. More than once I had regretted not letting the zombies kill Pierce and Stearns, but I wasn't one for outright murder. I shrugged. "Can't be helped. I can't take them with, as they are nothing but leeches, but I may offer you a solution."

Nate was all ears. I explained about how Frank seemed to be calculating when he learned what was in his pack, and I suggested that Nate send Frank and Kevin out on long-range recon. "Chances are, they will think they are being clever, especially if you and others ride them pretty hard here at home." I said.

Nate seemed to consider it. "What about Pierce's boy?" he asked.

I shook my head. "Not a factor. He knows his dad abandoned him and his mother, and wants nothing to do with him. He'll be glad his dad is gone. In all honesty, the way the boy has taken to training, I'd say he was looking to take dad out at some point."

Nate snorted. "Can't argue with that. That kid fights like he's possessed. More than once Carl has complained of bruises and cuts from that little guy."

"Just keep him focused and try to get him to forget about revenge. He'll only get killed." I warned, placing a second handgun in the door basket on the CR-V.

"Got it. By the way, I got something for you, if you want it." Nate reached into his rucksack and pulled out a radio. "I found these in that old guy's house we checked out last week. The batteries are good, and the range is supposed to be fifteen miles."

I looked over the radio. It looked like a Motorola on steroids. I tucked it into the center console. "Thanks, man. I was wondering how we were going to communicate. Hopefully it will work."

Nate held out his hand. "See you in the spring, Chief. Take care of my little buddy."

I shook Nate's hand. "You got it. Remember the plan. Push out the fence at every opportunity, and take out the houses one at a time. If the zombies freeze, hunt them out and kill as many as you can. With any luck, you'll be at the river before I will."

That was essential to the plan. Nate was to push out West as far as he dared, and I was going to make my big push in the North. The idea was to expand our bases as much as possible, clearing as much territory of zombies as possible. We wanted to have rivers as our borders, and it could be done, but in order to contain the contagion, we were going to have to implement a burning policy. Any homes not made at least half of brick were to be burned to the ground. There weren't enough people left to occupy them, and they were going to decay anyway. Removing the homes gave the land back to nature, which would provide us with food and materials we needed to rebuild. A pipe dream, but it was all I had. Homes were to be stripped of anything useful, but if they were filled with infected, they were to be burned immediately. Rivers were to be our highways, since most of the highways were choked with cars we couldn't get out of the way. We were lucky with the route to Joslin, but I doubted the way North would be clear. We would have to see.

I went to the condos and stopped at the second floor one. They were a family that was watching Jake for me while I was getting ready. I found him playing with a small set of cars, laughing as he knocked them together. He smiled as he saw me and offered me one of the cars.

"You ready to go, little guy?" I asked Jake as I picked him up. He smiled again and tried to eat the car. I snared his coat and thanked Mrs. Bose for watching him and headed out to the vehicle. Charlie was there, and the other vehicles were filling up as well. I buckled Jakey into his car seat and he squeaked when he saw his traveling companion would be his beloved baby sitter, Kristen. She smiled at him and made peek-a-boo motions, which made him laugh.

I waved at the other cars and the drivers waved back, indicating they were ready. I jumped into the driver's seat and headed out, waving at the people who had come out to see us leave. Everyone smiled and waved, except for two of them. Frank and Kevin were standing together near the gate, and they just glared at me as I drove past. I decided to stop the car and address the issue.

"So long Frank. I'll see you in the spring." I said.

"Good bye, Talon. Its been a slice." said Frank, snickering. Kevin giggled as well.

"Nate's in charge, Frank." I said, enjoying the look on his face. "I told him to keep order here any way he saw fit. Sucks to be you." I figured helping the cause a little wouldn't hurt.

Kevin and Frank didn't reply, they just turned away and I could see Nate glowering at them in my mirror. *Let the games begin*, I thought. I motioned to the gatekeeper, and he signaled the watchtower, who gave him a thumbs-up. The gate swung open, and we drove through, heading towards the interstate and hopefully a new home.

21

We drove out and I reflected on the past few months. Sometimes I joked with Tommy that had I known the world was going to end up like this, I would have just shot myself and saved myself the trouble. But I was never one to give up that quickly. Besides, I found myself thinking less and less about what life was like before and found myself looking forward to the challenges that faced me now. Gone were the tedious duties of school administration, gone were the meetings and parent phone calls and the conferences. We have been driven to the brink of destruction. The only question remaining was "Will you die today or tomorrow?" I thought about the rest of the world. I had no idea what had become of the government, the rest of the country, the rest of the world. For all I knew, we were the last.

We moved quickly down I-80 and I took the exit to I-355. I was taking a long detour, but the hope was to reach our destination quickly by avoiding population centers. The last time we moved through a town, a thousand ghouls followed us. I wasn't keen on a repeat.

We moved north and slowly came to a halt. The road was jammed with cars, running about a mile back from the toll booths. So much for the Open-Road Tolling concept. I looked left for a way around as Charlie looked right. He shook his head at me at the same time I shook my head at him. We would have to go back. There was no way to get through, and we could see many of the cars were occupied. It would be suicide to try and move through that mess. Maybe if I had an interstate snow plow, but not a mini-SUV.

We turned around and headed back down the on-ramp and back onto the west-bound lane of I-80. It still felt weird driving on the left side of the road, even though I knew no traffic was headed my way. I got back onto LaGrange road and headed north. Oh, well. Nothing is ever easy. Charlie had Kristen pass up his rifle, and he stuck it out the window to signal to the cars behind us that it was time to be ready. We were moving into potential hostile territory, and we needed to be prepared.

On my right was a subdivision, and we could already see dozens of zombies moving in between the houses. Many of the homes were burned out-husks, and many had windows broken in or doors torn from their hinges. I could see smoke coming from a few homes that were still smoldering. This neighborhood had been hit hard. I doubted anyone was alive in there. Nearly every home had a mailbox with a white flag on it. It made sense. Lots of these people commuted to the city where they likely picked up the virus. We moved by as quickly as we could, but we were running into some traffic that we had to go around. I angled onto the shoulder, and managed to avoid some of the worst snarls. But I couldn't avoid them all. A big SUV was jammed on the shoulder, and I couldn't go any further unless I moved the stupid thing. I parked the SUV and got out, Charlie coming with me. Jakey was sleeping, so I told Kristen to get in the driver's seat to be ready to move if needed.

There was a big forest preserve to West, and Charlie eyed it for a minute.

"If we had a place in the middle of that, the Z's wouldn't ever get close 'cause of the brush." he said.

I chanced a glance. "If you like that, you'll love where we are going." I said, moving towards the SUV. I was hopeful we could move it without too much trouble. I came up on the driver's side, unholstering my SIG, just in case. I checked the mirror, but didn't see anything. I looked over at Charlie, but he couldn't see anything on his side either. When I got within reach, I tapped the glass, trying to activate any "sleepers", zombies who had gone quiet and were just waiting for stimulus.

No response. I tried the rear door, but it was locked. I went to the driver's door, and was surprised when it opened. I was even more surprised when a female zombie fell out and started crawling towards me, scrambling to get to her feet. She had blood over her face and hands, and it completely covered her clothes. I could see a crude bandage on her arm, indicating how she got infected.

I danced back, bringing up my SIG. She followed me, rising to her feet and shuffling forward, her blood-covered mouth opening in a deep moan. She raised her hands towards me and reached out with blackened fingernails to rend and tear.

I sidled backwards and was about to fire when I managed to trip and fall on my butt. I kept my gun, but the zombie had closed in and was about to fall on me. *Shit and damn.* I thought. *Gotta move, NOW!* I hooked the zombie's ankle with my left foot while I pushed on her knee with my right. That was a trick they taught us in administrator's school to keep uncontrollable kids from getting on top of us. She fell backwards and gave me a chance to get to my feet and back away. I was about to shoot when Charlie stepped up and put a round through her head. Her face was a mask of rage and would stay that way forever.

"Graceful." Charlie said, lowering his rifle. "Can I get dinner with the show?" he asked.

I flipped him off. "Only if you kiss me first, sweetie." I said, smiling.

My smile faded as I looked at the subdivision across the retention pond. Zombies were literally pouring out from between the houses, falling over each other as they stumbled down the retention walls in search of prey. Their collective moan was disturbing to say the least, and we needed to get the hell out of there right now.

"Get the car, I'll move the SUV!" I yelled at Charlie. He bolted for the driver's side while Kristen dove for the back seat and I ran for the SUV. I jumped into the seat and looked for the key. Thankfully, it was still in the ignition. I turned it, not expecting anything, and was proven right. But the key allowed me to put the big vehicle in gear. I signaled to Charlie to push with the CR-V, and he bumped me in reply. I steered the vehicle while being pushed, and Charlie came to a stop and let me drift out of the way. I glanced at the back seat of the SUV as I climbed out and immediately wished I hadn't. There were two car seats back there and a lot of blood and bits of decaying gore. Two small heads were slowly rising out of the cargo area, and I wasn't sticking around.

No time for commiserating. I ran back to the CR-V and saw that the zombies had closed the distance and were starting to swarm through the cars at us. I shot one in the head that was too close to the car and shot another that was starting to pound on the windows of the truck. I missed his head, but hit him in the neck, severing his spine and dropping him in his tracks. A hit's a hit. I dove for the passenger door and managed to close the door almost completely. Another zombie got his hand in the door and was trying desperately clawing at me. I was holding the door closed and shouting at Charlie. "Go, go, go!" The zombies were starting to surround the cars, and I could see they had the numbers to overwhelm us and get a new meal. Charlie hammered the gas, and shot away, knocking over two smaller zombies and flattening a third. The other cars followed our lead and escaped through the hole we made. The swarm howled in protest and started a shambling pursuit.

We raced away as fast as we could, still dragging a corpse with us who refused to let go. I shifted in my seat until I was facing backwards, then pushed the door open. The zombie, a skinny kid in black clothing, hissed and snapped at me and tried to claw with his other hand. I shot him in the face and he fell away, spinning under the wheels of the Jeep behind us. Jakey screamed in protest at the noise, and Kristen had a time comforting him.

"Sorry, little buddy." I said, returning to my seat. I glanced at Charlie and he just shook his head. I told him to take the next turn left. We needed to avoid population centers as best as we could. I figured the side roads might be passable. If not, at least there was less chance of a swarm. I exhaled loudly and Charlie just nodded.

We headed down the side street and I motioned for Charlie to head north again at the second road. There weren't any cars there, and the community to the south was gated and fenced, so the zombies in there were effectively trapped. If anyone was in there, they were trapped as well. Not that we could do anything about it at this point.

We headed through a wooded area, and I once again hoped to hell I was right about where we were going. I had a backup, but it was going to be tight if it came to that. We passed several houses, and a few more high-end subdivisions. I could see several occupied homes, but none living.

I saw a small home tucked away in the woods and told Charlie to head for it. It was away from the road for a bit and something about it made me want to take a closer look. Maybe it was the handwritten sign that said 'If you can read this: Welcome.' The two vehicles behind us swung down the same driveway. The driveway was flanked and gated by two stone pillars, and the property was ringed by an unkempt hedge. It made as effective a fence as our cargo containers. Any zombie horde would never get through that, only adding to its strength with their numbers. Charlie pulled to a stop and turned off the CR-V. We all got out, and stretched a little. I used the small rest to replenish the magazine in my SIG.

Tommy and Duncan strolled up from the Jeep. "So what's up? You planning another gymnastics show?" Tommy said, punching me on the arm. Duncan snickered.

"No, moron, I just wanted a closer look here." I said, indicating the property with a sweep of my hand.

Duncan scowled. "Why? There's nobody here. Don't matter what the sign said."

I pointed to the chimney. "Then who lit the fire? Zombie's don't feel the cold."

That changed the equation. Duncan and Tommy went to alert and Charlie started a slow recon around the house, stopping when I held out a hand. "Wait here."

I walked toward the small dwelling, taking off my hat and gloves. I started whistling, and was rewarded with a moaning from out back. I looked back at Tommy, and he and Duncan circled around the garage, guns at the ready.

I continued walking towards the house, and when I was about fifteen feet away, spoke out.

"Hello the house! Anyone in there?" I didn't want to yell too loudly, but I didn't want to get shot by mistake, either.

The door opened and a woman stepped out. She was roughly fifty years old, wearing a big flannel jacket and work boots. Her hair was curly red, and she had calloused, work-hardened hands. A big smile lit up her face when she saw us, and she set aside the rifle she had been carrying.

"Hello yourself. Now who might you folks be?" Her voice had a slight Irish lilt to it, and her eyes twinkled a bit as she spoke, like she was the only one who was going to get the joke. I liked her immediately.

I introduced myself and the rest. "I'm John Talon, and that serious-looking gent over there is Charlie, those two coming around the corner would be Tommy and Duncan, and there's about six more of us in the cars behind us."

"Quite a group. I'm Dot. You all headed south for the winter?" She asked, putting her hands in her pockets. I thought I caught the outline of a handgun in there, but I couldn't be sure.

"No, ma'am, we're heading to a safe place for the winter." I replied

"Ain't no such place, son, you know that. But by the looks of you, I bet you could make near anyplace safe if you put your mind to it." Dot said, cocking her head to the side and seeming to look through me.

I looked down briefly and shifted my feet. "That may be true. Listen, we're just looking for a spot to rest for a spell before we push on. Do you mind if we stop here a bit? We just managed to wiggle out of a tough spot, and could use a little regroup."

Dot smiled. "No problem. Haven't had company in a while, and George ain't much for conversation." She picked up her rifle and came out to the cars to meet the rest of the crew. She spent the most time with Jake, who waved his hands at her. I took him out of the car seat and carried him towards the house.

"Would you mind if I borrow a chair? Jake needs his bottle and he's getting too heavy to carry while he eats." I asked.

Dot smiled again. "Help yourself. The green one is a good feeding chair."

We went inside and I saw the house was neat and tidy. Mementos lined the fireplace, which crackled with a warm fire. One wall of the small living room was lined with shelves overflowing with books, and a quick glance showed a variety of interests. The kitchen was lit by hurricane lamps, and the whole house just exuded warmth. If it wasn't for the need to move on, this would be a nice place to stay for a while.

Dot sat down to watch Jakey eat. "Been a while since I saw a baby. He's a beautiful boy." She said.

"Takes after his mother." I said, smiling at my son.

"You're a good man for remembering her like that." Dot said, reading me like a book.

"What do you mean?" I asked.

"What I mean is anyone with a good eye can see he looks like you, but you carry a good memory of your dead wife with you, so you see her in him. Nothing wrong with that, just shows you loved your wife and miss her. But it will pass. All things do." Dot said, reaching out and stroking Jake's hair, casting a knowing eye at Sarah, who looked away.

I didn't say anything, just committing every part of the scene to memory. Jake feeding quietly, the fire popping occasionally, my close friends relaxing nearby. I nearly jumped when Dot spoke again.

"Eventually I will have to kill George, but for now it's just too hard." She said.

I burst out of my reflections. "Wh-what?" I stammered.

"George. My husband. He's out back. He took the sickness that killed everyone else. When he turned I moved him outside." Dot said this as calmly as if she had said it was Tuesday.

Duncan spoke up. "No kidding. There's a zombie chained to the shed out back. He's pretty secured. Tommy got close enough to see his bridgework, and there was no danger."

Dot smiled at my reaction. "No, I ain't crazy. George and I had been married since I was seventeen, and it's hard to let go after so long. I've dug his grave and made his marker, but I just can't finish him."

As nutty as it sounds, I was actually sympathetic. I could see how someone would be hesitant to kill a family member, and in all likelihood, that reluctance got a lot of people killed or infected.

I finished with Jake, and gently burped him. He wiggled a bit and then leaned towards Dot. She smiled and asked to hold him. I didn't see a problem so I let him go. He immediately started playing with her hair, and her smile made him laugh. It was good to see Jake happy, and it was good to see him making someone else happy.

After a little while, I figured it was time to go. We had been here long enough, and if we had attracted the attention of local zombies, I didn't want to put Dot at risk.

I rallied the group and they headed out to the cars. Charlie asked me a question with his eyes and I put the question to Dot.

"Dot? I can't thank you enough for letting us remember what hospitality is like. Would you like to come with us? We're going to the office condos on 131st street." I asked, taking Jake back from her.

Dot smiled wistfully as Jake went back to is daddy. "No, I've lived in this house for thirty years, I'm not going anywhere soon."

"Is there anything we can *do* for you, before we go?" I hinted heavily in my question, and Dot picked it up immediately.

"If you're asking if you want me to let you finish off George, the answer...," Dot sighed, "...is yes. But, please, you can't shoot him. I don't want a gunshot to be my last memory of my husband."

"Will do. Thanks for everything, Dot." I said, heading for the door.

"John?"

"Yes, Dot?"

"Finish what you started." Dot looked at me seriously.

"What do you mean?" I asked, shifting Jake to my other arm.

Dot pointed to Jake and then to the window. "You got two things to do before you're done. Finish them both."

I only half understood what she meant. "Will do." I said, closing the door behind me.

Charlie stood before me and I nodded. He headed off to the back shed, and returned a minute later, wiping off one of his tomahawks with a bit of rag. I put Jakey back into his car seat and he promptly fell asleep.

We moved the cars out of the driveway and I waved a hand at the house. Dot did not come out to see us off, and I didn't blame her. I could see a still form lying out in the yard in the back, and another kneeling nearby, and I just shook my head. I thought about what she had said to me and slowly began to realize what she had meant. I did have things to do.

22

We headed out again, stopping when the road finally ran out of North. Charlie looked at me and I told him to head West. We were nearly there, and I was getting anxious. I did not want to have to do anything in the dark. We passed another subdivision. God, there was enough of the stupid things. This one had huge homes, any of them could pass for a fortress if the people had sense enough to barricade the first floorwindows. As I looked, I saw the inevitable white flags decorating several expensive mailboxes. We would have passed by if it hadn't been for a person standing on a second floor porch waving a pillowcase at us. Here we go.

"Are we stopping?" Charlie asked, slowing down the car. He had seen the pillowcase, too.

"Have to." I said.

"Why?" Kristen asked, making a teenage face.

"You never know who lives in these places. Maybe that's a surgeon or even better, an electrician. Be nice to have someone around to patch holes up or rig up some power." I said, trying to put the best face on what could become a difficult situation.

"Yeah, right." said Charlie. "You're just hoping to score some points to make up for that fall you took."

"There is that. But I am first a humanitarian." I said loftily. It was a good thing I couldn't see how much Kristen was probably rolling her eyes.

Charlie just snorted and pulled into the gated community. I could see we were not going to get out without a fight, as we had attracted the attention of about ten zombies loitering around two of the houses.

Charlie waved to Tommy and Sarah, and they pulled up alongside the car. "We got people who need help. Turn your cars around in case we need to get lost fast." Charlie said to the other vehicles. As they hurried to comply, I took a look at the situation. We actually were in a decent spot. The community was gated, and had a fence running along the outside of the subdivision. We were blocking the only access road, and there was a large pond to our right. The houses were up on a hill, and we had a clear field of fire across the fairway of the golf course that was on our left. Could be worse.

I hopped out of the car and got us set up. "Jason and Lisa, you watch the road and protect our exit. Chelsea and Kristen, you watch their backs and keep an eye on the cars. Kristen, Jake's your responsibility unless I say otherwise. Tommy and Duncan, you're to clear a path to the house. Charlie and Sarah, we're cleaning up and going in. Any questions?" All heads shook negative. "Let's go."

I headed towards the house while Tommy and Duncan lit up the zombies headed towards us. It would have been scary to have bullets whipping past your head to take out a zombie in front of you if you hadn't been through it before. I never slowed and reached the house in short order. The door had been caved in and I imagined there were several little sweeties waiting for us. Tommy and Duncan stayed out on the lawn, dropping the zombies that were coming from the other houses and covering our backs.

I moved in and aimed my gun left while Charlie slid in and went right. Sarah went in the middle and we all had targets. Eleven zombies of all shapes and sizes came shuffling from their various hiding places, and we had our hands full. I dropped the two closest ones to me, and Charlie's rifle cracked loudly in the small space. Sarah's rifle boomed once, and then again. We could hear loud moaning coming from all angles, so this was a heavily infested house. Great. The garden level of the house consisted of a central room, with hallways to the left and right. We were going to have to be careful, as more zombies started to come from the other rooms. We could wait for them to come to us, but there was a stairwell in the middle which made coverage difficult.

I motioned Sarah to the stairs and she took up a position to nail anything coming down. Charlie went right and I went left. I went to a bedroom door and checked the knob. It was locked. Good. No worries about something hitting me in the back. I moved down the hallway, the light fading as I moved away from the windows of the central room. It was quiet, and I could hear my own breathing as I moved slowly down the hall. God, I hated this. Give me a stand up battle every time. Hunting these bastards sucked. I moved down the hall and checked the last room. The door was open, and I pushed it further with my rifle barrel. It was empty.

I turned around and was confronted with the biggest zombie I had ever seen. He was six foot six if he was an inch, and was headed my way. His huge frame was dressed in torn sweats, and his face bore the marks of several confrontations. Dried blood covered his chin, and his lips curled back in a grimace as he moved towards me. I backed up and raised my rifle, but he brought up his hands to grab and knocked the barrel out of the way. I brought up the butt of the rifle as a barrier and shoved as hard as I could. I barely managed to slow him down, and he bore me backwards to the wall. His hands grabbed my shoulders and tried to bring me within biting range of his gaping maw. I pushed back and managed to keep myself from being bit, but I couldn't let go of the rifle, as it was the only thing keeping the teeth from me. The zombie's decaying face moaned into mine, and his graveyard breath made me gag. I pushed off the wall and we began a dance of death around the room. I couldn't afford to go down, as he was too heavy, and I couldn't draw my SIG as I needed two hands to keep this thing off me. I pushed it back into the bathroom in the room, and while I had the momentum, shoved it into the bathtub. The edge of the tub tripped the zombie and he fell with me on top. I used the opportunity to shove knee into his chest and rip away from him. I fell back and landed on the floor, with the zombie moving to get out of the tub. I shot it in the head from the ground, and nearly deafened myself from firing in such a small space. The zombie slowly sank into the tub, his big head coming to a rest on his big chest.

I took a moment to catch my breath and take stock of my injuries. My shoulders were going to be sore for a while, but I was alive, which was the important thing. I got up and headed back down the hallway. The locked door I had passed earlier was broken off its hinges, no surprise where Tiny had come from. I peeked in and didn't see anyone else, so I went back to Sarah at the stairs. Outside, I could hear an occasional shot as Tommy and Duncan honed their shooting skills.

"You okay?" Sarah asked, keeping her gun on the stairs.

"Yeah, I'm fine." I said, rolling my head and shaking my shoulders a bit. "Had a big son of a buck give me a moment, there."

Sarah shook her head. "I saw him head your way, but I couldn't help out. Sorry."

I understood. Sarah had her job and would do it, which was making sure we didn't get jumped by anything coming down the stairs. The small pile of corpses at the first landing was evidence of that. "No worries. Just inconvenient." I tried to make light of the fact that I nearly bought it. If it had been Sarah in there, the big Z would have easily overwhelmed her. Charlie came back from the other hall way, and I could see a zombie half in and half out of a back room.

"All clear?" I asked.

"Yeah." Charlie said. "You?"

"Just a big bugger that gave me a good run." I took a second look at the corpse in the hall. "Say, Charlie, is that your knife in his chest?" I inquired, smiling a little.

Charlie looked back at the body. "Uh, yeah, that's mine. Not sure how it got there." He wandered back to the zombie and pulled out his knife. Wiping it off, he came back to the stairs. Both Sarah and I were grinning at him. "What?"

Sarah broke the silence. "Did you miss his head?" she asked, giggling a little.

Charlie glowered. "He surprised me, okay? Sometimes when they're fresh you forget they're zombies."

I laughed. "Guess this lets me off the hook for falling on my ass."

Charlie refused to dignify me or Sarah with further comment.

I patted Sarah on the shoulder and brought my gun up to the ready position. I jumped to the landing, sliding a little on a spot of Z-goop, and aimed towards the top of the stairs. Charlie leapfrogged me and went to the top. Sarah jumped past him and I ran up to take a position on their left.

We had a minute to take in our surroundings before they came for us. The room was massive, with vaulted ceilings and a walkway on the second floor that opened out to the room. I could see some survivors up there, and reminded myself not to shoot too high. The kitchen was a mess, with tables and chairs thrown about the tile floor, and the hallways had blood smeared on the walls. A decomposing body was in the center of the room, and it was interesting that it had no head. I motioned to Sarah and she looked over.

"Great. Some idiot has a sword." She was not amused.

I smiled inwardly. We had run into a guy a while back who insisted he was the greatest zombie killer in existence, and his weapons were two cheap samurai swords. He didn't last long after he charged a group of five zombies by himself. We buried his swords with what was left of him.

I didn't have much time to reminisce. There were about fifteen zombies in various states of decay that were coming for us. A small woman was immediately in front of me and she was almost able to grab my arm when I dropped her. Sarah had slung her rifle and was using her Ruger to drop zombies. Charlie fired three times and took out a set of twins and their grandmother. I moved to my left and killed two more, an old man and young boy. I was moving towards the kitchen, clearing a path. I shot my last one and turned to see Sarah finishing off hers and Charlie using his tomahawk to take out a zombie that was crawling out from under the table where it had been feeding on what looked like a small dog or cat.

"Clear." I said.

"Clear." said Sarah.

"Clear." said Charlie

I looked around. The place was nice, but useless as a place of defense unless you shored up the windows. I motioned to Sarah. "Check for transportation for these people. We don't know how many there are or if any of them are infected, so I don't want them riding with us."

Sarah nodded and went off to find the garage. Charlie came over and I motioned to the stairs. "Go see what we have up there. See how they are provisioned for the winter, and see if they have anything of use. I'm going to secure the rest of the house." I could still hear shots outside from Tommy and Duncan. "We need to be out in ten minutes, max."

Charlie nodded and went to the stairs, where he had to navigate over a pile of debris and doors to get to the second floor.

I shouldered my carbine and unholstered my SIG. There were a couple of rooms to check and the front door to secure. I didn't need any leftovers ruining my day, or any wandering Z's coming to call. I went by the dining room and admired the chandelier in there before heading to the front door which was wide open. I checked the lawn and shot a zombie that was dragging itself across the grass, its lower legs having been torn off. I closed the door and locked it, noting that it was steel and could hold off quite a few zombies.

Oh well. I could hear Charlie talking to the people upstairs and heard more than one raised voice. Great. This should be fun. I headed towards the back rooms and checked the furthest one, finding nothing. The second one nearly drove me over the edge.

It was a nursery, with a changing table and dresser, and Winnie the Pooh was the theme. In the corner was a crib, and I could see movement under the blanket. I couldn't stop my feet from walking over to the crib, and my hand gripped my SIG like I was trying to break it. I looked over the side of the crib and saw the Winnie the Pooh blanket covering something alive. It wasn't crying or making any noises, so I knew what I was going to see. I reached out and pulled the blanket away, and had to turn away, nearly retching in my disgust. A baby was in the crib, roughly four months old, and it apparently had become infected and turned. Its skin was blue grey, and its eyes were milky like the rest. It saw me and reached out with tiny, grasping hands, its face becoming a mask of anger at the meal it couldn't reach. The mouth opened and closed, and I could see one small tooth coming through the gums.

I couldn't leave it there, and I couldn't ask anyone else to finish it off. I never asked anyone to do anything I wouldn't do myself. I've had so called leaders like that in the past, and I swore I would never be like them when I became an administrator. I raised my SIG with both hands, lined up the tiny head, and pulled the trigger. The blast was loud in the room, and my hands dropped to my sides. I closed my eyes and thought of Jake. *This will never happen to you*, I swore for the thousandth time. *Never.*

I holstered my SIG and used the blanket to cover the baby. I turned around and saw Sarah standing in the doorway. Apparently, she had seen me shoot the child. As I walked past, she reached out and touched my arm.

"You had to, John." she said softly.

"I know." I said. "But that doesn't make it easy."

Reading my mind, Sarah tried to reassure me. "I'm glad its not." She said. "It won't happen to Jake, John. I promise it won't."

I shook my head. "I need to get out of here." I moved past Sarah and stopped in the hallway. "Thank you." I said over my shoulder.

"You're welcome."

I headed back to the main area with Sarah behind me. A group of nine people waited by the stairs, in various states of disarray. There were three men, four women, and two teenage boys. One of the teenagers was carrying a sword. A Scottish Claymore reproduction, by the look of it. He glared at me as I walked past, challenging me silently with his hand on the hilt. Moron. A fourth man was engaged in a lively conversation with Charlie, who was not known for his people skills.

"And I do not see your point. Yes, we are grateful, but if you think we are going to leave the relative comfort of this home to go who knows where, you are crazy." It was a fat, balding man with a weak chin expressing his views. He wore a "tactical" vest, the kind many mall ninjas surely invest in. He had a handgun in the holster, what kind I couldn't tell. He had a Ruger Mini14 slung over his shoulder and what looked like several magazines in his vest pocket. He should have been able to clean house on his own. Something to consider. I stopped by Charlie and signaled Sarah to stand by.

"I'm going to check outside. I'll be right back." I said to Charlie in a low voice.

Charlie nodded and the look on his face clearly indicated he wanted to get away from his antagonist.

I headed downstairs and went to the door we originally came in. I could see Duncan and Tommy outside, and by the way they held their weapons, the immediate danger had passed.

"Heads up, gents. What's the word.?" I said, startling Duncan.

Tommy answered. "We're good out here. Some movement back down the street, but nothing to worry about. Jason and Lisa nailed a couple, and Chelsea shot one that came out of the water."

"Really?" I was impressed. "Wonder how it got in there?"

Duncan shrugged. "Probably saw a frog and went after it. Who knows?"

I had to admit it was probable. Zombies were the definition of stupid. Deadly, but stupid. I went back inside. I could hear Fatty raising his voice. Like that was going to improve his argument, whatever it was.

I headed back upstairs and asked Sarah about the vehicles. She told me that there were three cars in the garage and they were all working and ready to go. Finally, some good news.

I moved over to Charlie and tapped him on the shoulder. He looked at me and promptly walked downstairs, leaving the fat man sputtering at his loss of audience.

I decided to be direct. The baby was still on my mind and I was in no mood for bullshit. "Hello, all. My name is John Talon, and we're glad you folks are still alive. We have cleared the area for now, but the shots will attract more in a little while. You have roughly fifteen minutes to pack up and get out. We are leaving immediately. We're glad to have helped you all escape, but we need to leave. If you want to join us, you need to move *now*. I have been told there are three cars in the garage that are working and ready to go. Best take them and go."

Fat man stood in front of me. "I am Dane Blake, and these people have chosen me to represent them. I can assure you, we will not be going anywhere. Your help was not needed, and I see no reason to leave a comfortable position." His jowls wobbled as he spoke and it was distracting.

I was past caring. I went over to the group and asked them. "Anyone want to go?" All hands except the teen with the sword went up. I waved them to the garage. "Go now." They started to leave, carrying what small belongings they had with them. Dane Blake stood in the way, with his hand on his gun.

"Those cars are my personal property and I have not authorized their use." He said imperiously.

Authorized? I wondered why the rest of the group had not mutinied. Then I realized he was the only one armed save for the teen. I guess that makes sense. When one person has the weapons, that person makes the rules. Since I was armed, I decided to push the issue.

"Go to the cars, get in them, and get out. Your time is running out." I said moving towards Blake. Sarah moved in behind me.

"Stop where you are! You will not take my cars or leave this house!" Blake started to unbuckle the strap that held in his gun.

I stepped towards him placing myself directly in front of him. I put my hand on my SIG and stared into his eyes. "Pull it, bully." I said, my voice mean. "Pull it and see what happens. I have just rescued those people and that means I am responsible for them, not you. You've had a nice thing going here, I'm sure, stroking your ego and making those people miserable because of your power trip. They are leaving." My tone of voice made it clear to even the most stupid of individuals that I meant everything I said, and severe violence would follow my words if pushed.

Dane blinked and flicked his eyes over to the group. Then a small smile appeared on his pudgy face. I didn't blink. I knew what was happening and what was *going* to happen.

Sure enough, there was a loud crack and a cry of pain, followed by a metallic clattering on the floor. If I trusted my instincts, I would bet everything I had on the fact that Blake had given a signal to his trustee, the kid with the sword. The kid probably had drawn the sword, then Sarah made her move. I didn't look, not trusting to take my eyes off Blake, but I was sure the kid was now looking down the barrel of Sarah's gun. I gave a little smile of my own. Blake blanched and kept his hands away from his guns.

What I did not expect was one of the women to jump on the downed teen, who was holding his wrist and glaring at Sarah, who in turn was replacing her blunt weapon to its place on her pack, its purpose served. The woman landed on the teen's back forcing him to the hardwood floor. She pummeled him mercilessly, smacking his head to the floor and cursing him in a most inventive way. I didn't know you could use some of those words together. I took another look at the headless corpse and it dawned on me that it was not a zombie I was looking at, but an example, ordered by Dane and carried out by this sadistic teen with the sword. My estimation of Blake dropped even further, if that was possible.

I shook my head and motioned to Sarah, who pulled the woman off the teen. He was bleeding from several places and his face was a pulpy mess. He was making little mewling sounds, and curled up into a ball as soon as the weight was taken off his shoulders.

I pointed to the garage and the group headed there. Sarah pushed the woman along with the other survivors, then headed downstairs. I looked back at Blake. "We're leaving. You can have your weapons and your little buddy there. If you do anything stupid, I will personally hang you upside down from the nearest tree, call in the zombies, and watch them eat your face off. If you're lucky, you'll die before they're finished with you. Understand?" Blake just glared hatred at me. "I will take that as a Yes." I headed for the stairs, still keeping my hand on my gun. I had a feeling I would not see the last of Blake, but if I was lucky, maybe I would see him first.

I ran outside and saw my group was ready to go. I jumped into the CR-V and got rewarded with a squeak from Jake. I gave him my hand to hold, and I almost had tears in my eyes when I thought about that baby in the house. We headed back onto the road, and I could see in the rear-view mirror that the three cars from the house were following us. Good enough.

We headed West, and I saw less signs of violence and mayhem than I expected. In all likelihood, this extreme end of the suburbs of Chicago had been spared the devastation, but the virus had infected so many so fast. When it first hit, people were infected and didn't even know it. With the concentration of population in the cities, the virus could have been contained in the cities, but with the early long incubation period, and the commuter population, it was inevitable that it would spread to the suburbs. Once it got out of the confines of the population centers, it was over. Where we were was actually behind the wave of the dead, dealing with the ones that couldn't travel as fast or were trapped indoors. But there were still millions out there, and we had to deal with them all. You never knew where they were. You just had to keep your guard up all the time.

We reached another intersection, and passed by a burned out gas station. There were blackened cars in the lot, and a couple of shriveled corpses. Two of the cars had several bullet holes in them, but that could have been caused by anything. I had a suspicion about the holes, and glancing at Charlie; he had seen them and was suspicious about them as well.

No time for that now. We turned north and after a small subdivision we were flanked by forest preserve. I didn't need to see it, but I would bet there was a small smile on Charlie's face as we left most traces of civilization behind. Charlie had been born to the country, and in all likelihood grown up to farm like his father before him. But he managed to go to college, met a woman, married and settled in the 'burbs. But the call was still strong, and after all this, I expected him to head back home. The only thing stopping him was his sense of duty to the group. He would do the job until finished. I, for one, couldn't imagine any success of the plan without him.

At the next intersection, we turned right. I told Charlie that if pushed, our absolute last stand was down this road. There was a large lake just down the hill, and with boats available and several islands, we could make do for a long time. He just nodded and pointed at another car on the side of the road. This one had bullet holes in it, too. I nodded. "Once a coincidence, twice a pattern." I said, "We'll need to keep an eye open."

We headed down the road and finally managed to bring our little convoy to our destination. We parked the cars in the parking lot and looked at our new home. It was an office/condos building, sitting on an intersection. Across the street was the forest preserve, and across the second street was a small spring-fed pond. There was a small subdivision and town home complex around the pond, but I didn't think it would be a problem. The best part of the building was the fact it did not have a ground floor; the parking lot was under the building. There was a single doorway/stairwell that led to the upper floors. Properly provisioned, we could withstand the worst siege for years.

Charlie and I got out of the car and looked around. Our convoy had attracted a little notice, and a few lone Z's were coming to investigate. They were moving pretty slowly, so I was hopeful that the coming winter would make them nearly immobile.

Duncan and Tommy came over. "Nice digs, chief. How do we secure the stairway?" Duncan asked, eyeing the entrance. It was a glass enclosure, and several dedicated zombies could easily break in if they had reason. I pointed to the cars.

"We park those right by the glass, and that should hold for now." I said, indicating the larger vehicles.

Tommy looked around. "You know, I'll bet there is deer and rabbit in those woods."

Charlie nodded. "We'll be fine for food and firewood. What about water?"

I pointed to the pond. "Last I heard, that was spring-fed, so we're good there. Also, down the road that way," I indicated east. "There's two big grocery stores and a strip mall, as well as two gas stations and a drug store, about a mile away.

Duncan whistled. "You can pick 'em." He motioned to Tommy and Charlie. "Let's go check out our new home."

The other two nodded and Charlie patted my shoulder as he went past, the best compliment one could expect from the man. I took it for what it was and watched as the trio checked weapons, loaded magazines, secured masks and goggles, then headed for the stairs. I smiled to myself as I realized that this had become so routine, we never even thought about it anymore.

I went over to where Chelsea and Kristen were entertaining Jake. He was crawling around the bed of the Jeep, and standing on the side looking out the windows when he could. Chelsea was watching him while Kristen was keeping an eye on our slow-moving friends. I left them and went over to the group of survivors we had rescued. They looked to be in a depressed state, although that seemed to be improving. They huddled together, and Sarah was talking to a few of them. Several heads kept turning to look at the zombies, and I knew any discussion would have to wait until they were dealt with.

The zombies were about a hundred yards away, but moving slow enough that it would take a while before they were a threat. I held up a finger to Sarah and wandered out towards the zombies. It took a minute to reach the first one and he was in bad shape. His head was nearly devoid of hair, and his skin was stretched tight around his face. His lips were pulled back and his blackened teeth opened and closed as he worked to get to me. His right arm hung down uselessly, but he reached out with his left. I walked up to about five yards of him and shot him once in the head. He dropped with a grunt, and I moved towards the second, never breaking stride. This one was a female, but I couldn't be too sure. I didn't waste time and put a bullet between her eyes, knocking her backwards and onto her back. The third was a longer shot, but I figured it was worth it. I fired and blew the top of its head off. Lucky shot, but I would never admit it to Tommy or Duncan.

I went back to the group and addressed the people. I was sure Sarah had been filling them in as to what we were doing and where we were from. I wasn't going to waste time. "Good afternoon. I'm sure Ms. Greer has been filling you in and answering questions. My name is John Talon and I lead this little group. We survived the Upheaval and we are surviving the aftermath. We have a plan and this building is part of our efforts take back what we lost. If you want to stay with us, you're welcome. We will train you, find a place for you in our community, and use you if you have skills we need. We are going to take back our world and our lives. It will be a long battle, but if you want to be part of it, come along."

I winked at Sarah and went back to Jakey. I figured the group had some things to talk about, and I wanted to spend some time with my son. He was playing with a small pile of books, stacking them and knocking them over. I lost myself in his antics until Sarah came over.

"Want to talk about it?" Sarah asked, sitting down next to me.

"About what?" I knew what she was referring to, but I have been wrong before.

"About the baby in the house." Sarah searched my eyes, looking for who knows what.

"No need, really. I had a bad moment, let my imagination run away for a bit. But I'm fine. Really." I said.

Sarah's face said she didn't believe me. "Really? For a moment back there, I thought you were going to execute that Blake and his little toady."

I laughed. "I'd be lying to you if I told you I didn't think about it. Especially after that woman jumped that kid. I thought she was going to push his head through the floor. But he was no danger."

Sarah didn't say anything. She just looked at me.

I sighed. "Look. I just got twitchy when I realized that baby had been left to die and turn alone. That its last thoughts were of loneliness and abandonment. How long did it cry before it died? How long did it reach out for its mother or father who were not coming? Someone could have done something. That worthless piece of dog shit let that child die alone. If there is any justice, he's trapped again in that house, with just that little turd for company."

Sarah stood up and adjusted her jacket. She checked her Ruger and her pack. She leaned over and placed a hand on Jakey's cheek, earning a smile from him. Sarah then looked back at me and I could see a funny look in her green eyes. She leaned over and placed a hand on my cheek. "You'll do." she said, and walked away to talk with Jason and his wife Lisa.

Shaking my head at women in general and one in particular, my attention went to the stairs where Tommy,

Duncan, and Charlie were coming out of the building. They weren't dragging anyone or anything, so I guessed all went well.

Tommy spoke first. "Place was empty. We checked and double checked every possible hiding place and came up empty. Looks like it was cleared before the big mess hit and whoever worked here never came back. The offices look pretty new, and the condos look like they were furnished, but never lived in."

"Sounds good." I said. "What about numbers? How many per condo?" I was curious because we had picked up a few more people.

Charlie spoke up. "There's eight condos, and all of them are two bedrooms."

"That's not a problem then." I said. "Tommy and Duncan have one, Jason and his wife can share one with the teens who can share a room or one of them can bunk with Sarah, and Jake and I can share one with Charlie."

Duncan piped up. "When are we going raiding?"

I considered that. "We'll go once we're settled in. I don't want to get cocky and lose someone. There's another element out here that we need to be careful of."

Tommy frowned. "What do you mean?"

I explained about the cars with the bullet holes and Charlie backed me up on that information. "We don't know for sure, but I can personally vouch for some scumbags I dealt with a while back when everything was breaking." I didn't go into detail, but they got the hint. We would need to watch for others as well as zombies.

"Let's get unpacked." I said, picking up Jakey and my duffel bag. I had another trip to make for another bag, but these days we traveled relatively lightly.

Unpacking the cars and getting settled in took a very short amount of time. The condos were very nicely furnished, and as we discovered, furnished exactly the same. Even the colors of the furniture were identical. The offices were on the first two floors, and the condos made up the top four. Tommy quickly found the stairs to the roof, and set up an observation post. Old habits, I guess. The girls were happy to be sharing a bedroom, since it was just like old times, and Jason and Lisa were happy for the opportunity to be a positive influence for the girls. Jakey liked the new place and immediately began exploring. I was grateful to see that the condos had functional fireplaces, and Duncan had found the office copier paper supply, so kindling was taken care of. I had the odd thought that if the plague had hit later, the gas station would have a supply of those ever last logs that burn for hours. How inconvenient some viruses can be.

I got a surprise when I learned that only two of the couples we rescued wanted to stay with us. The other couple and the woman whose husband was beheaded, as well as the teen, wanted to head south for warmer weather. I tried to tell them that the zombies seemed to be slower in the cold and we could have a few months of relative safety as opposed to the warmer climes that favored the Z's. But they were having none of it, so I waved goodbye as they headed out. They didn't take me up on the offers of food and supplies, so I think they just wanted to escape this place and every memory associated with it. I could respect that.

I got another surprise when I went back into my condo. Charlie had apparently been strong-armed into trading with another crew member and was no longer sharing a place with me. I got a shock as I went into the condo and found Sarah playing with Jacob.

"Where's Charlie?" I asked, looking into the bedroom and seeing Sarah's gear.

"He and I traded. I figured Jake could use a woman's influence. Any problems with that?" Her tone held both trepidation and challenge.

I shook my head. I came to the realization that even though I was the leader, I really wasn't in charge.

23

I leaned to the left as Charlie's knife flashed past my neck. I lunged forward with my shoulder and knocked his arm up, while stabbing towards his midsection with my own blade. Charlie deflected the blow with his free hand while his knife hand stabbed downwards. Spinning away to the right I avoided the stab and backed away, forcing Charlie to come to me. His face was impassive, and moved fluidly towards me, his knife held low with the blade pointing upwards. My own blade was held the same way, and each of us looked for an opportunity to strike.

Charlie glided close and struck with the speed of a rattler. I stepped back just out of his reach and grabbed his wrist with my free hand. He pulled me in close in an attempt to free his hand and I released his wrist suddenly, causing him to jerk his blade back out of the way and stumble slightly backwards. I lunged forward and my blade tagged his neck, causing Charlie to grunt and swear.

"Dammit! I knew you were going to do something like that but I fell for it anyway." Charlie exhaled loudly and rubbed his neck. "Thank God we keep the sheaths on our knives. Did you have to stab so hard?"

I laughed. "Quit whining, you baby. I notice you didn't pull your stab when you nailed me in the kidney last time. I'll be pissing blood for a week, thank you."

Charlie grinned. "Best out of three?"

I hefted my knife. "Love to. Gun cleaning for the loser?"

"Deal."

Charlie and I had agreed that we needed to keep up with training, since we were going to be heading out later that day to clear out homes and hunt for supplies. Tommy and Duncan were gathering supplies for the winter from the nearby grocery store and drugstore, and Sarah was working with Kristen and Chelsea to get the new people to the community situated and up to speed with what we were trying to do. I accepted the fact that the world as we knew it was gone, and not coming back for a long time. But we had a chance to remake what had been lost, avoid the mistakes we had made, and use this plague as an opportunity to hit the Restart button on the world. That is, if we managed to live that long.

I had been in contact with Nate when we arrived here two weeks ago, and he had both good and bad news. The good news was the fence was being expanded very well, and they had begun firing the homes south of St. Andrews Road, a major roadway in that area. They had also made a push to the north and were firing the homes and subdivisions along the Route 45 corridor. He figured the burning would take at least a month, but thought winter was a fine time for a fire. I agreed, and was going to get started on some nearby homes today. The bad news though I am sure Nate didn't think so, was that my old friends Frank Stearns and Kevin Pierce had left the community, and were headed in my direction. Great. Maybe I'll just shoot them once and for all. Accidentally, or something. Of course, I could hope that the zombies get them, but since it was winter and we had managed to determine that cold weather effectively slows them down to the point of immobility, Kevin and Frank's chances were actually pretty good.

Charlie and I faced off again, and were grappling quite well when Sarah walked in on us. She was holding Jake, who looked like he had been crying. Sarah eyed the two of us, then asked "Who won?"

I rebuckled my knife onto my belt and attached the leg clip. I took my son from Sarah, and said "We both lost once. You interrupted the tie-breaker." I turned my attention to Jake. "What's the matter, buddy? You were supposed to be sleeping." I bounced him gently and he laid his little head on my shoulder. He was getting bigger all the time, and starting to pull himself up on the furniture. His favorite game was to walk around the coffee table, chasing his daddy who crawled around.

Sarah rubbed his back. "He seems more upset these days when you're gone, like he knows what you're doing."

I shook my head. "I know I should be spending more time with him, but it's critical we move as much as possible while the zombies are slow." I was actually looking forward to the deep freeze days of January when we could move in relative safety and clear out hundreds of homes and businesses. "Don't worry little buddy, Daddy will always come back."

Sarah looked at me. "You make that promise a lot?"

I glanced back at her. "Every time I leave."

"Thought so. When are we heading out?" Sarah was already dressed for success, having spent her morning in training with Kristen and Chelsea.

I thought about it. "We'll head out when Tommy and Duncan get back. I don't like to leave the place without a veteran around." It wasn't that I didn't trust the other members, but Tommy and Duncan had been through enough that they would be less likely to make mistakes. And since we still had no idea who was responsible for the bullet riddled cars we had seen on our way here, I didn't want to take any chances. "Where are the new couples? John and what's her name?"

Sarah smiled. "They are out getting firewood for the condos, and the other new couple, Ryan and Amy, are with them."

"Okay. Well, we'll head out when the boys get back. You want a crack at Charlie?" I asked, tossing a thumb towards the big lunk.

Sarah's eyes turned predatory, and she took a step towards Charlie, who retreated with his hands up. "No way, man. She's too fast for this old country boy."

Sarah turned on her heel and walked out of the office we used for training. She winked at me in passing and I laughed out loud. I left with Jake while listening to Charlie ask "What?"

Tommy and Duncan returned from their trip an hour later. They reported that the grocery store had been looted, but they still managed to get quite a bit of canned and dried goods. Duncan had found a decent amount of baby food for Jake, and a goodly supply of diapers, for which I was very grateful. They had also looted the pharmacy, grabbing whatever they thought would be helpful. I had told them to look for anything that had 'cin' or 'cillin' in the name, as chances were it was an antibiotic. They had also grabbed a bunch of aspirin and cold medicine. Although, when I thought about it, I hadn't had a cold in a long time, probably because the population had been reduced to the point where we didn't have the same contact with germs like we used to. Odd bonus, but there it was. They also had picked up some supplies for John Reef, one of our new people. He was a plumber and had an idea about using a reservoir tank and giving us running water. If it worked, I would personally kiss him.

With Tommy and Duncan back, Charlie, Sarah and I geared up for our excursion. We were heading to the subdivision which was north west of our current home. This was an older community, but it butted up against a forest preserve and a retirement community, so I wanted it out of the way as a possible threat. We were going to leave the town homes that were immediately to our north, as they could be used for any survivors we may come across this winter. I hoped to find many, but one never knew, and the old saying I needed to be careful of what I wished for kept running through my head. I snared Kristen to watch after Jake while I was away, and it pained me that the little guy cried as I left, but there wasn't anything I could do. I certainly was not going to send someone out in my stead. This was my job, and I had to do it.

We took the CR-V and headed out, moving north on 104th avenue until we reached two subdivisions, one to the east and one to the west. We passed a large 'active living' community, and I made a mental note to check that building out for supplies and such. I figured there might be some food stores in there, as most of those places had restaurants and such. Worth looking into.

We rolled into the west subdivision and stopped at the first house. It was one of those two-story cookie cutter homes that builders loved to charge too much for and were put together too quickly. They had interesting names for the things like 'The Appletree" or 'The Chesapeake' or some such nonsense. Right now, its name was Kindling.

The weather was cooperative, mostly sunny with a few clouds. There wasn't any snow on the ground yet, but we had a couple freezing rains. I had forgotten how much I had grown dependant on the weatherman, and trying to figure out what the weather was going to do sent me back to my days on the golf course grounds crew when we would gauge how much time we had before the rains would catch us too far from the garage. It was cold, around twenty degrees or so. There wasn't much wind, but what there was tried very hard to get into every opening in my clothes. Typical Chicago winter.

We stepped out of the car and checked weapons. I was carrying just my SIG and my trusty crowbar. I was getting low enough on ammo for the carbine that I was seriously considering a run back to my home to pick up the extra ammo I had left behind when Jake and I made a run for it. Sarah had her Ruger .22 and a long steel bar with a right angle bent into it. The end had been pointed but not sharpened, the idea being to crush the skill but not to open it to keep the infection contained until it could be burned. Charlie had his Glock and his tomahawks, as well as his knife.

I walked up to the front and checked the windows. I didn't see any movement, but that meant nothing. Charlie circled around back and when he came back reported nothing moving. I signaled to Sarah, who checked the front door and found it locked. That usually meant the people had left, but not always. Punching the glass panel next to the door with the end of my crowbar, I waited a minute to see if the noise had attracted any attention. One of our guys a while ago managed to get killed reaching in to open the door. A zombie grabbed his arm and had torn off huge chunks of meat before we could pull him out. He bled out screaming on the lawn.

No activity so I reached through and opened the door. Sarah went through first, her pistol sweeping the living room and stairs. Charlie glided past and headed down the hall towards the back, checking the rear family room and bathroom. I went upstairs, SIG at the ready. The upstairs was dark, and for the millionth time I wished I had bought a tactical light for my SIG. Oh well. I improvised with a small Maglite, and checked the bathroom at the top of the stairs. I didn't hear anything, but that wasn't a sign all was clear. The room at the back was empty, as was the small room at the front. The master bedroom door was closed, which was never a good sign. I kicked the door and heard a small shuffling sound. Contact. I waved down the stairs at Charlie who came up and crouched beside the door, tomahawk held to trip up anything that might come out of the door.

I nodded to Charlie and kicked the door in, the cheap hollowform door splintering around the handle. The door flew open and I got a quick look at the bedroom. It was indeed the master suite, and occupied. A single woman lay on the bed, her face grey and taut in the rigor of death. Her eyes were closed, and did not show any signs of violence. Her clothes were neat and tidy and her hands were folded across her chest. By the look of her, she had been dead for a long time. So what had made the noise?

I motioned to Charlie to check the closet while I covered him. He threw the door open and fell backwards as a dove flew out of its nest and into his face. His momentum carried him to the bed, where he fell onto the woman lying there. Jumping up like he had been stung, Charlie glared at me and said "Clear."

I calmly holstered my SIG, propped my crowbar against the wall, and then proceeded to laugh like I had not laughed in a long time. By the time I had finished, I had tears running down my face and my stomach felt like it had been subjected to a thousand sit-ups. Charlie had begun to laugh as well, and when Sarah came up to see what the hell was going on, the two of us were bent over at the waist, laughing our fool heads off. She shook her head at us and went downstairs to wait outside.

We went back downstairs and met up with Sarah, who had gone through the downstairs looking for anything useful. She had some foodstuffs, but nothing else. I left the door open and we went to the next house.

We proceeded like this down the street, picking up supplies here and there, a couple of rifles and shotguns, and batteries and tools. We did find zombies, but the cold weather had slowed them down so much it was almost ridiculously easy to kill them. They could barely move, and it was no trouble to smash their skulls and end their existence. After a few of these, Charlie and I started to get creative. I speared one using my crowbar like a javelin, and Charlie spent five minutes practicing throwing his tomahawks at a teenager who was stiff in a corner. With several of them, we practiced with our knives, perfecting the best way to kill them with a knife. Charlie liked the temple entry, while I was a proponent of the top of the head thrust. We argued the point until Sarah told the two of us to shut up.

We reached the last house on the street, and went through our routine of checking the windows. I noticed a lot of furniture had been moved around, and the kitchen looked like there had been a fight of some sort. I could see a blood trail leading out of the kitchen. Something had happened here, and recently. I signaled to Sarah and she tried the door. Thankfully it was unlocked, and the three of us slid silently into the house. Immediately it was obvious there was trouble here, and we spread out to check the downstairs.

Finding nothing, we met back at the stairs. Sarah and Charlie shook their heads at me and I returned the favor. It was in that moment I heard a long scratching sound, and I glanced upstairs. Charlie heard the same thing and put away his tomahawks, drawing his Glock and holding it ready. Sarah placed her bar against the doorframe and pulled her gun as well. I looked down at the blood trail that led out of the kitchen and up the stairs. Whatever was making the scratching noise was upstairs.

I drew my SIG and slowly went upstairs, Charlie watching my back and aiming at the top of the stairs. My flashlight illuminated the darkened hallway and as I stepped higher I could see two forms in the hallway. One was the body of a man who was clearly dead and the source of the blood trail. He had been torn up pretty badly, and I could see blood splatter on the walls and red handprints where a struggle had taken place. The man had fought to get to the door at the end of the hallway, and died trying to protect what was in it. The zombie on top of him, his wife, I guessed, was slowly scratching at the door with both hands, her fingers worn to the bone. Her clothing was covered in blood and gore, and when I hit her with the light, she slowly turned her dead head towards me. I could see stringy bits of meat hanging from her bloody mouth, and dried blood covered her face. She had so thoroughly torn apart her husband that he had no chance to come back as a zombie. She slowly rose to her feet and took slow, painful steps towards me. Her thin arms raised and her lips curled back as she moved closer towards the light that illuminated her.

I didn't waste time, I simply shot her in the head and dropped her next to her husband, the shot sounding unnaturally loud in the small hallway. I moved towards the door and stepped around the mess in the hall. I leaned against the door and listened carefully. I didn't hear anything, so I tried the door and found it open. I pushed it in and found myself in a nursery. *Oh, shit.* I thought. *Not again.* I looked around and saw that the nursery was for a little girl, based on the pink animals and yellow duck stenciling on the walls. I approached the crib, expecting the worst. There was a small form curled up in the corner of the crib, and I couldn't tell if she was dead, zombified, or other.

My heart was full of dread as I reached in and carefully turned her over. Her face was angelic as her head turned towards me. Her eyes were closed and she was dressed in one of those fleece sleeper blankets, and I guessed she was approximately three or four months old. I sighed and brought up my SIG, wondering again why God punished the little ones. I lined up her small head and stopped. For some reason, I couldn't pull the trigger. Charlie came up to the door and saw me pointing my gun at the crib.

"What's the matter?" he asked, holstering his Glock.

"Something doesn't seem right." I said, lowering my weapon.

"What do you mean?" Charlie stepped over the corpses and entered the room.

"Why was that mother trying to get in here?" I asked. "The Z's don't stick around after something is dead. They prefer live...Holy shit!" I exclaimed, staring at the crib.

"What?" Charlie hurried over.

I waved him back and stared at the little girl. Sure enough, I could see her little chest rise and fall as she breathed. My exclamation had caused her to open her eyes, allowing me to see her clear baby blues before she closed them again.

"Shit, she's alive!" I yelled, grabbing a blanket in the crib and gently lifting the baby out and wrapping her up against the cold. "Grab whatever supplies you can find in here and meet me outside. Sarah!" I yelled as I hurried down the hall and headed for the stairs.

"What?" came the reply form the kitchen area

"Grab all the baby supplies you can and get to the car right now and fire it up! Get the heater going full blast!" I hollered as I fairly jumped down the stairs.

Sarah, bless her, didn't hesitate and I could hear cans and things being dumped into a garbage bag. I made it outside with Charlie and Sarah right on my heels.

"Dear God, is that a live baby?" Sarah asked as she hurried past and jumped into the car, firing it up and cranking the heater.

"I don't know how alive she is, but we're going to give her as much of a chance as we can. Her father died for her, so we owe him at least the attempt to save her." I filled her in on what we had found upstairs and the zombie clawing at the door. Sarah shuddered and gunned the engine.

Charlie was strangely quiet as he sat in the back seat with me and stared at the little bundle in my arms. I paid little attention to him as I grabbed the small radio we kept in the car.

"Tommy or Duncan, you read me? Over." No response

"Tommy or Duncan, you read me? Over." I was starting to get impatient.

On the fourth try, Tommy's voice crackled over the small radio. "John, that you? What's up? Over."

"Tommy...get on the big radio to Nate and have him get the doc on the horn. I don't give a damn what she might be doing, he needs to get her to the radio *pronto*. Over"

"Will do. What's going on?" Tommy wanted to know so he could tell Nate.

"We found a baby in one of the houses." I responded. "She looks to be dehydrated and probably hypothermic. I don't feel any fever but it's possible."

"Holy crap. I'm on it. Out." Tommy signed off and I looked at Sarah and Charlie. *Please*, I thought. *Let us win this one.*

Charlie remained silent but his eyes were locked on the little girl. I idly wondered if he was thinking about his own daughter and was reliving that loss.

I didn't have time to dwell on it as Sarah careened into our parking lot. The tires squealed as she pulled to a stop. I was out of the car before it had stopped moving and rushing up the stairs. Charlie was right on my heels. I ran to Charlie's condo, which happened to be the closest one and brought the little bundle near the small fire that was going in the fireplace. The motion and warmth of the blanket and fire had stimulated the little girl and she started to open her eyes and began to give little rasping cries.

I motioned to Charlie. "Stay with her. I'll be right back." I ran to my condo and waved to Jason and Lisa, who were watching Jacob play on the floor. I briefly wondered at this as I had left Jacob with Kristen, but I didn't have time to question it. I grabbed a baby bottle and dumped some water and formula in it, then ran back to Charlie's place. As an afterthought I grabbed the tube of baby bottom cream from Jacob's bag.

Sarah was coming up the stairs with the baby supplies, and joined me with Charlie. She dumped the contents of the bags out on the floor and found some diapers and wipes. She quickly changed the baby and put some diaper rash cream on a very sore looking bottom. Sarah kept the baby in her little nightgown and picked her up gently. I gave her the bottle and she gave the baby a little sip. The tiny mouth immediately sucked down an ounce, but Sarah was smart enough not to give her too much at once. We were giving her a binky when Tommy came in the door with the radio.

"Doc's on the line." was all he said. His eyes got big when he saw the child, but he said nothing more.

"Doc?" I asked holding up the radio so we all could hear.

"I'm here, John. Nate told me you found a baby?"

"That's right. She looks to be about four months old, possible dehydrated, maybe a little hypothermic." I described as best I could.

"How's her color?" Doc wanted to know.

"Pretty good, actually. We've been warming her up, and Sarah is giving her sips of formula. Nothing dramatic until she gets used to it."

"Sounds like you have things in order. Make sure she takes warm water as well, and call me back when you have two wet diapers. If she doesn't produce a wet diaper in the next 12 hours, increase the amount of fluid. Call me immediately if she develops a fever." Doc didn't sound too concerned, so I took that as a good sign.

"Will do. Talk to you later, Doc. Out." I clicked off the radio and looked at the group. Sarah was giving the baby a little more formula and Charlie and Tommy were just watching. Tommy caught my eye and motioned me aside.

"I needed to talk to you when you got in, but obviously you were busy." Tommy looked like he had something on his mind.

"What's going on?" I had a sneaking suspicion it had something to do with the fact that Jason and Lisa were watching Jake, but I waited for Tommy to tell me what was up.

"We have a situation." Tommy was keeping something back and I was starting to get annoyed.

"So? What is it already?" I put enough impatience in my voice to make Tommy wince.

"Well, Duncan thought it would be a good idea to take Kristen and Chelsea out on a small supply run and get them used to working together and taking what's important and such. He decided to check out that small strip mall north of the gas station on the main road. No big deal."

I nodded but said nothing. I had dismissed the strip mall as irrelevant, but maybe something could have been salvaged.

"Anyway," Tommy continued, "they went into a store and had nearly secured it when a Z came out of the bathroom and landed on Chelsea. She was bit before anyone could do anything about it."

24

Something inside me fell. Every time I thought we had a hold on this situation and could move forward and start to show some progress, something like this happened. What made me angry was that it shouldn't have happened. Duncan knew better. Now I had to put down another member of our group, another child, no less, and I was starting to wonder why I bothered.

"Where is she now?" I wondered, checking my SIG.

Tommy caught the motion and looked down. "She's outside with Kristen."

I nodded and started to head for the stairs. Tommy called after me. "Duncan and I are going to that active community building you mentioned. Anything you think we should look for?"

My voice was barely audible. "Check for the usual. See if they have a generator. God knows we could use some power for a change." I didn't even look back, I just kept walking.

Sarah caught up to me and asked what was going on.

I stopped by the landing to the stairs and looked out one of the windows. I could see two figures sitting outside and it was hard to get my feet to move. "Chelsea got bit." was all I said.

Sarah's hand went to her mouth and she looked outside. We stood there for a minute, not saying a word, just looking at the small figure out in the brown grass. I barely noticed Sarah place her hand in mine, giving me a small squeeze. It was reassuring to a point, but I was still wondering whether this was worth all the effort.

"Why do I bother?" I said aloud, not really expecting a response. "What's the point? It seems like every time we make progress or get ahead, something kicks us back. It's like something is telling me just find a spot to lay down and die. Your time's done. Its times like this I wonder why I don't just pack up Jake and take off for parts unknown and take my chances in a zombie world."

Sarah didn't speak for a minute then said "If you want to go, then go. But if you leave, then everything you fought for was for nothing. Everyone you saved won't matter, and the world you want to take back will never recover. I can't see you wasting that much time."

I smiled inwardly and returned the squeeze and gave Sarah a grateful look, then went downstairs. Sarah followed me down and we went out towards the two figures on the grass.

Kristen was sitting down, hugging her knees and crying. She wasn't holding her friend, and it was easy to see that it was killing her not to comfort Chelsea. Chelsea was sitting cross-legged a few feet away, holding a bloody rag to a bite on her shoulder. She was staring blankly into space and I could only imagine what was going through her head. Her weapons and gear had already been removed, and she looked so small sitting there.

Kristen saw me and Sarah walk up and starting crying harder, knowing what was going to happen. Sarah knelt down to comfort Kristen as I bent down to one knee in front of Chelsea.

"You're here to kill me, aren't you?" Chelsea said without emotion. She never looked at me, she just stared down at the ground.

"Yes." I was never one to sugar-coat things. That trait used to drive the parents in my district nuts once upon a time.

She looked up at me with red-rimmed eyes. There were dark circles around her eyes and I could see her starting to sweat. The virus was moving fast. It was going to become dangerous to be around her in an hour or so. "I can feel it killing me." Chelsea said. "It feels like fire is creeping towards my head." She looked down at her arm. "I can't feel my hand anymore."

"Whenever you're ready. I can wait." I said, motioning Sarah to take Kristen away. They both said goodbye to Chelsea and Sarah had tears in her eyes as well.

"Why me?" Chelsea asked. "What did I do to deserve to die?" She held back a cough.

"You lived." I said. "That was enough. Eventually we all die, and sometimes we get to choose how we go out. Sometimes we don't." I pointed to her shoulder. "I hope you finished the bastard that got you."

Chelsea actually smiled a little. "I smashed his head so much it actually came off his shoulders."

I smiled myself. "Good girl."

"John?"

"Yes?"

"Don't blame Duncan. It wasn't his fault. I didn't check the bathroom the way you taught us. I thought I was ready, I thought..." Chelsea ran out of steam and hung her head.

"Don't blame yourself. It was just bad luck. Next time it could be me." I tried to be reassuring, although inside I was seething.

"No. You can't die. They need you..." Chelsea's voice was fading and she was starting to slump over. I had never heard of a case happening this fast, she had been bitten barely an hour ago. I moved back and watched as Chelsea slumped over, closing her eyes forever as the little girl we knew and cared for.

I waited, and while I waited I raged inwardly at what had happened. She was supposed to live, the children were supposed to live. I again wondered at what kind of God would allow this to happen to the children.

I stood by Chelsea for another hour, just letting the cold blow past my face. I watched the brown grass stir around her still face, knowing the virus was hard at work inside her. Her skin became pale as the blood drained away from the surface. Her bite wound looked blackish, and I could only imagine what kind of pain she was going through. Dark, spidery lines webbed out from the bite, indicating the spread of the infection. The thickest lines went to her neck and head, where they disappeared under the skin.

One hour and twenty five minutes after she died, Chelsea opened her eyes again. Her head lifted off the ground and she painfully got to her feet. She turned her head slowly, and caught sight of me. Her lips peeled back from her mouth, revealing her teeth, and she raised her arms towards me.

I raised my SIG, and with a final "Good bye, Chelsea." I shot her between the eyes. She crumpled to the ground again, and I holstered my pistol with a sigh.

I reached down and grabbed her ankle, and unceremoniously dragged her over to a field where we had burned other zombies. I placed her in the center of the burn ring, poured some gasoline from a can we had stashed there, and lit her funeral pyre.

I watched the flames for a while, then turned my back on the scene, heading back to the building. Sarah was waiting for me at the bottom of the stairs.

"Want to talk about it?" she asked carefully, reading the look in my eyes.

"Nothing much to talk about. She got bit, she got infected, and she died. That's all there is. That's all there ever is these days." I was suddenly tired and I wanted to see my son.

Sarah and I went back to our condo and I thanked Jason and Lisa for watching Jake for so long. They said they didn't mind, it was good practice for when they had children. I didn't say it, but I wanted to ask why in hell they would want to bring a child into this messed-up world.

I took off my gear and weapons, and sat on the floor with Jakey. It was nearly time for his dinner, and I was just enjoying some quiet time, something I hadn't done in a while. The sky was darkening quickly, as it was prone to do in the winter, and the waning orange light lit up the condo in a light amber glow. I lit a couple of candles and placed them in their holders

Jake pulled on my pants leg, and I picked him up. I carried him to the window and together we watched the sun set and I tried to ignore the dying fires of the tragedy of the day.

Sarah joined me a few minutes later, dressed simply in a sweat shirt and jeans. Jake saw her and leaned towards her, his way of letting me know he wanted to be held by someone else. Sarah smiled at Jake and took him from my arms, shaking her head at him and giving him Eskimo kisses on his nose, making him giggle.

We stood there for a while and it was Sarah who broke the silence.

"I was nineteen when I had my daughter Julia. She was Chelsea's age when my husband killed her." She said.

"I'm sorry." was all I could say.

"Don't get me wrong." Sarah corrected. "I don't blame him. The part of him that made him my husband was dead and gone, replaced by a mindless killing drone. I can blame the virus, but how far will that get me? The point is, we go on. We take what joy we can," Sarah emphasized this by tickling Jake and making him laugh, "and we take our sorrows as they come. But we can't dwell on what was, since that doesn't help us with what is."

I thought about that for a second, than put my arm around her and Jake. I didn't say anything, and judging by the way Sarah leaned into me, I didn't have to.

Our reverie was broken with the arrival of a caravan of cars and trucks.

"What the hell?" I said, belting on my SIG and knife and putting my coat on to head downstairs. "Tommy and Duncan must have found some people and brought them back."

Sarah looked out and nodded. "I see their vehicle. I'll stay with Jake and feed him."

"Thanks." I said and I gave her a quick hug to let her know I was disappointed our moment had been interrupted. Her smile let me know she was disappointed as well.

I headed down to the parking lot area where seven vehicles came pulling in. Tommy and Duncan came piling out of their car and headed directly for me. I stared hard at Duncan and he kept his eyes averted, knowing I was ticked off at him, despite what Chelsea had said.

Tommy spoke. "Hey Chief. You'll never guess what we found." I could see other survivors coming out of the vehicles, and it took a minute before it registered that all of them were women, fifteen in all. "They were living in that big active living center up the road, but they were starting to run low on supplies and stuff. I told them about us and our refuges, and they agreed to join up with us." He seemed a little out of breath and I had the sneaking suspicion he was holding something back on me. When Tommy did that it was never a good thing. Sometimes funny, but never good.

I took stock of the group and I noticed one stood out from the others. She was a tall blonde, with Nordic features that might have been considered attractive had she not had such a look of hatred in her eyes. I don't recall ever pissing off anyone that looked like her so I imagine it had to be for other reasons.

I stepped into the light cast by two of the cars' headlights, and addressed the newcomers. "My name is John Talon. I'm the leader of this community and all of you are welcome. The town homes behind you are empty and you are welcome to take any of them as you choose. We will provide you with firewood to see you through the next couple of days, and during that time we will assess what your needs are regarding food and supplies. We have a few rules in our community but the important ones are everyone works and everyone contributes. We will train you to fight and kill zombies, and we expect everyone to take a hand in defending our homes should it come to that. Right now, we have a need for a medical person. Does anyone have medical training?"

A small, mousy looking woman of about thirty raised her hand. "I'm a registered nurse. Is someone hurt?" she asked.

"We rescued a baby today who needs some looking after. If you go with Tommy here, he'll take you to her." I gestured to the stairs, expecting the two of them to head up.

Tommy started to move and so did the nurse, only to be stopped when a harsh voice said "Hold it!" It was the blond woman who spoke. "My name is Pamela Richards, and I am the leader of this group of women. I do not recognize your authority and will not allow a man to give orders to one of my women." She had an accent that was hard to place, although I would bet Eastern Block if I had to choose.

Today was not a day for this foolishness. "If you don't want to be here, go back. You have vehicles. Leave. If you choose to stay, I am the only leader and you follow my lead." My voice had become hard towards the end and I could see Duncan trying to signal to the woman to shut up.

She wasn't having any of it. "We fought hard for our lives and we have fought off men who would try and turn us into their slaves or worse. We came here because we have all lost something in the plague and thought the plan about taking things back sounded good. But I will not take orders from you." She walked towards me during this speech and stood about three feet from me. From this vantage point I could see she was armed only with a knife, although there could have been other weapons.

I was unrelenting and getting madder by the minute. "If you don't like it, *leave*. I didn't invite you, but I welcome you if you want to stay. I don't force anyone to do anything I won't do myself, and you are free to leave whenever you want. But while you are here you will take my orders, if and when I choose to give them. Do you see those two over there?" I pointed to Tommy and Duncan. "They have been with me since the beginning and we have been through more shit than I care to try and forget. They follow my lead, but I do not insist they stay with me. If they want to leave, they can go anytime."

"There is only one way I will follow you." Pamela said, squaring off and raising her hands. "We fight. You win, I follow your orders. I win, you follow mine."

I was incredulous. "Are you kidding me? This isn't some movie, you idiot. People die here. See that smoldering mess over there? That used to be a teenage girl who got bit. I don't have time for these games. Take your women and leave." I hooked my thumbs into my belt, leaving my hand close to my gun if things got ugly.

Pamela moved closer. "I'm surprised anyone would follow a man who would get a teenage girl killed. But what man would actually care?" She sneered in my face, and at that moment, the days events came at me in a rush. I'm not sure what came over me, but the cold fire of battle had been stirred and for once I welcomed it.

"You want to fight?" I snarled. "Fine. Head north and get yourself killed. I particularly don't care. You and yours mean next to nothing to me right now. The only one I have a use for is your nurse. She will stay and help that little baby we rescued. I'll pull a gun on her or you to get her to help if I have to, but it will get done. As far as fighting you? Dream on. I didn't get involved in this effort to rebuild what we lost to be ruled by the will of the strongest. I was elected to this position and any time these people want to replace me they are free to do so. I will not," and I got right up into her face as I said this, "reduce myself or those I lead to the level of some of the animals I have encountered since the world ended. If they are more to your liking, *get out now*. You're not welcome here."

I turned my back to her and faced Tommy and Duncan who looked at me like they had never seen me before. "Get the rest set up in the condos. Get the fires going and we'll see to their needs in the morning." I turned back to the group of women. "I don't have time for this nonsense. If you want to leave, go. If not, you know the rules." I pointed at the nurse. "Please go check on our little survivor. Tommy will show you the way."

With that, I went back to my condo, shaking my head all the while at the stupid turn of events. I went inside and washed my hands with the bucket of water by the sink. Sarah came in and asked what had happened. I told her quickly, sparing her none of the details. She was quiet for a moment, and then she spoke.

"You may have trouble with her later." She said.

I sighed. "Yeah, probably. But I will not let us fall to the level of uncivilized barbarians who kill each other for trinkets or status. Enough." I shook my head to clear it. "I've had too rough of a day to worry about it now."

Sarah smiled. "No kidding. Go play with your son. He wants his daddy."

I smiled and went to the living room, where Jake and I played tag until it was time to go to bed.

25

In the morning, I got a surprise as I passed Tommy and Duncan's condo. I could hear animated voices within and I swear I heard that Pamela's voice. Shaking my head I went down to Charlie's condo to check on our new arrival.

Charlie was feeding the little girl when I knocked and was told to enter. The nurse, whose name was Rebecca Maxwell, as I found out later, was going through some medication that Tommy and Duncan had taken from the pharmacy down the road.

"How's it going?" I asked Charlie, peeking at the little face that was feeding noisily.

Charlie smiled at the little face. "She's been up and down all night, getting water and formula. She hasn't gotten a fever, and everything seems to be normal." Charlie looked up at me. "I think we got lucky and got there just in time. Doc says if nightfall had come she would likely have died."

I nodded. "Given all that we have been through, I think we were owed a little luck. I'm glad it worked out in this case and we're able to give this little girl a chance."

Charlie gave a thoughtful nod and then asked, "Any idea what her name might be?"

I shook my head. "I didn't see anything as we got out of there. I guess it's up to you if you want to go back and see if you can find anything."

Charlie nodded again and said, "I'll go back today to get the crib and supplies, and see if I can find anything else. What are you up to today?"

"I'm in a mood to see if I can't find us a snow plow." I said watching Charlie's reaction. I wasn't disappointed. His eyebrows shot straight up and his mouth dropped open. He recovered quickly and returned to his usual stoic self.

"Why?" was all he said.

"I figure it might be a good idea to be able to move in the winter, and a plow will allow us to go wherever we want. We both know the heavy snows are on the way, and the fact that we haven't been hit with any yet just tells me we're in for it."

"Well, that makes sense. I'm going to take Jason and Lisa with me, and we're going to clear the rest of the houses and start firing them up." Charlie finished feeding the baby and motioned for the nurse to take her. After he had passed her off, he stood up and stretched.

"I heard about last night." Charlie said, looking at me as he belted on his gun and knife.

I snorted. "Bunch of crap. I don't have time for such stupidity. People like that have been reading too much End of the World as We Know It fiction."

Charlie laughed. "I used to read that stuff myself. Never figured I'd be living it."

We walked out of the condo together. "I try not to think about that too much." I said.

Charlie headed towards Jason and Lisa's condo while I went back to mine. I found Sarah up with Jake, who was trying his best to thwart her attempts to feed him oatmeal. I couldn't figure out who was wearing more, him or Sarah.

Sarah turned to me, with a big glob of oatmeal in her hair and said, "Next time, you're feeding him. He's faster with his hands than you are."

I laughed. "He is. I should have warned you. Listen, Charlie is heading to the subdivision we went through yesterday with Lisa and Jason. They're going to start firing it as soon as possible. I'm going to head to a Highway Department Facility and see if I can get a snow plow. I have no idea what Tommy and Duncan are up to, but I have a suspicion that Pamela Richards spent the night with them. Don't know if that is going to cause a problem yet, but we'll see."

Sarah finished with Jake and gave him some Cheerios to work on. "You're not that stupid are you?"

"What? What are you talking about.?" I was more than a little surprised.

"Let's do the math, shall we? Pamela does not like you and does not want you to be the leader. She hooks up with a friend of yours, and spends as much time as possible filling his head with bad thoughts about you, criticisms of your decisions and what not. Nothing out in the open, of course, but I would not be surprised if there is an election soon to replace you." Sarah stood there with her hands on her hips. It reminded me of my mother, for some disturbing reason.

I thought about it for a second. "You think so?"

"Of course. It's what I would do." Sarah said, giving me a sly smile and a punch on the arm.

I returned the punch. "Thank God you're on my side. I'm heading out soon, so if you want to come along, you'd better get off your lazy ass and suit up."

That earned me a glare from green eyes as Sarah stalked off to her room. I picked Jake up and got him dressed, and brought him to Charlie's condo. I asked Rebecca if she would be willing to watch Jake for a few hours and she readily agreed. I told her about his nap schedule and brought some of his favorite toys.

Kissing his little head and promising him I would be back soon, I went back to my condo and prepared for action. I put on my usual gear, checking my weapons and placing them in their usual spots. I had done this so often I could do it in my sleep. I grabbed my gloves and balaclava, the latter being used more for warmth than anything else these days.

I met Sarah in the hall and together we went down to the ground. Tommy, Duncan, and Pamela were already outside, engaged in conversation. I waved Tommy over, and the trio came as a group.

"I'm going to head over to a highway facility and see if I can't get us a snow plow. I figure when the snow hits, and it may be today, judging by that sky, we're going to need mobility and a way to get around if the snow gets deep. Anyone want to come along?" I was sure Tommy probably would, but Duncan was another matter.

Pamela spoke up. "Seems like a waste of time. Why don't we spend the time gathering supplies and cutting wood.?"

I tried to keep the irritation out of my voice. "If we can't get to the supplies, we can't exactly gather them, can we?"

Pamela seemed unfazed. "Still seems kind of a waste."

Tommy spoke up. "Makes sense to me. I'm in."

Duncan shook his head. "I'll stay here. I don't feel like heading out right now." His eyes drifted to the burn area, where Chelsea's body lay.

I nodded. "Fine. Do me a favor and make a check to see who needs cold weather gear and get them situated. Also, get some more people out to gather firewood. Check with Charlie and make sure he gets any useful tools before he fires the houses and especially extra coats and blankets. If he finds an axe, great."

Pamela shook her head and walked away. Duncan watched her go and Sarah ran out after her. I watched the exchange between the two of them, and the body language was interesting. Pamela first put her hands on her hips, then she crossed her arms. Next she leaned in towards Sarah, who didn't give and inch. Finally, she took a step back and her face was frozen in shock. Sarah left her like that and came back to the group, smiling that little smile of hers that let me know she just did something I likely wouldn't have approved of.

I didn't ask what had transpired, figuring Sarah would tell me in time. We climbed into pickup truck and fired it up. The gas gauge was at three quarters, so we were good for a bit. We were only going a few miles, so I wasn't worried about running out.

Turning east, we went past the grocery store and the gas station. Sarah wondered aloud if there might be any coffee left over in the coffee shop. I smiled but I was pretty sure I would cheerfully murder someone for a diet soda right about now. Alas for the little things.

We passed the drugstore on the corner and I could still see the cars from my last encounter there. The man's body had been pretty well picked over by animals, and I would bet the woman had been as well. I gripped the wheel tighter as we passed, and Sarah asked me what was wrong.

I told her and Tommy about the murders and what I had done in retaliation. I didn't hold anything back, as was my nature, and left people to judge as they would.

Sarah didn't say anything, and I was strangely afraid I had lost stature in her estimation, but Tommy seemed to empathize. "Good riddance. Scum like that are just opportunists. Kill 'em all, I say."

"Amen." was all Sarah said.

I smiled as we rolled down the street, past a golf course and another subdivision. This one was gutted, with skeletal remains of homes burned and others with windows smashed and doors torn off. From our vantage point, I could see that no house had been spared. Every mailbox had a white flag of some sort on it. This must be what the areas north of the river, closer to Chicago must look like. When the Z's headed south en masse, they overwhelmed everyone who tried to make a stand. Unless you were lucky enough to find a fortress, you were food.

Turning right along the valley highway, we skirted around a couple of abandoned cars and made our way to the next intersection. The dark grey sky was getting more ominous all the time, and I figured we had two hours maximum before the weather broke.

We drove up another street heading east and came to the entrance of the highway facility. The gate was open, but the garages looked like they had been left alone. Several vehicles were parked around the yard, and everything looked relatively calm. Usually that was when the other shoe dropped.

We got out of the truck and spread out. I headed for the office, as I figured that would be were the keys were. As cold as it was, I wasn't too worried about lingering zombies, but I still held my crowbar as a precaution. Sarah and Tommy went over to the smaller garage to see if there was anything useful.

The office door was locked, but opened quickly with some judicious persuasion with my crowbar. The office was in a little disarray, but I didn't pay particular attention to it since my own office often looked worse once upon a time. I checked the desk for keys, and finding nothing, went over to the lock box on the wall and checked it. My hopes were dashed when all that fell out were band-aids.

I went over to the smaller desk in the office and checked the drawers. I found nothing of interest except for an unusually large supply of chewing gum. Frustrated, I looked around and saw a door that led to the large garage next to the administrative building. Opening the door, I looked into the gloom of the garage and saw several plow trucks, so that part of the mission was accomplished. But the keys were elusive. Staying in the doorway, I looked around at what I considered logical places for keys. Finding nothing, I went back into the office and looked around again. I noticed something on the wall behind the open door of the office, a rack with keys. That made sense. The secretary and supervisor could see at a glance what trucks were out and what ones were still in the garage.

Grabbing three sets of keys, I went into the garage and started a slow recon of the garage. I stayed near the doors, as I could see better using the light from the windows in the garage. The plow blades loomed large in the waning light, the trucks waiting like dormant beasts. I couldn't hear anything out of the ordinary, so I used the tried and true method of throwing something and seeing if anything moved. Picking up a pop can from a work table, I tossed it towards the back wall. The can hitting the floor sounded like a shot, and I listened intently for any sound.

Sure enough, I heard some scraping and sliding on the concrete floor. Something was back there. But I wasn't going to go hunting in the dark, no matter how cold it was or how slow the Z's were. I went to the garage door and unlocked it, shoving the door upward with a grunt. God, I missed electricity.

The open door cast a lot more light into the garage, and I bent down to see underneath the trucks. There was something moving in the back, but the truck's tires kept me from seeing clearly what it was. I circled to the left and saw what was left of a man trying to crawl. He was wearing a blue jumpsuit, and when he raised himself up I could see CARL stitched on the breast pocket. His skin was nearly white, mottled with black streaks. His back around his kidneys had been torn out, and I could see his broken spine through the cloth. That would explain why he was crawling.

After checking to make sure he was alone, I hefted my crowbar and slammed Carl's head to the ground. His skull cracked like a coconut, and his movement stopped completely. I hooked his collar with the claw end and dragged him outside. A quick look around showed he was alone, so I checked my keys and went over to the truck that had the corresponding number.

I climbed into the cab and looked things over. It didn't seem too complicated, and I was thankful yet again that my parents insisted that I learn to drive stick shift when I was learning to drive. "Never know when a skill might be handy." My dad used to say. I hoped he was alright, but I didn't have much faith in that.

I put the key in the ignition and tried it. The engine coughed and turned over, but didn't catch. I tried it again and the same thing happened. Hoping the third time was the charm, I tried it again. No go. Okay, one last time and I would try another truck. Once again I was rewarded with nothing.

It wasn't until I tried the third truck that I actually got one running. It was a newer model, so I imagined it didn't lose power as fast as the other ones. I got out of the cab to let things warm up and ran into Tommy and Sarah. They were both grinning like fools and I wondered what was going on. They had to have found something pretty neat to be smiling like that.

"What's up?" I asked, giving the two of them a suspicious look.

Tommy nudged Sarah who smiled and pointed to the pickup. In the bed were two small devices, and it took me a minute to figure out what they were. When I did, I whooped and grabbed up Sarah, swinging her around in a small dance of joy. She laughed and it was a good thing to hear. For good measure, I grabbed Tommy and did the same thing to him. He didn't laugh.

"Where the hell did you find them?" I asked, walking over to the truck and resting a hand on two of the most beautiful gas powered generators I had ever laid eyes on.

Tommy came up and slapped me on the back. "We found them just sitting on the side of that small garage. There was a bunch of other tools, and another welding torch, but these were the prize. I hear you have a truck running."

I smiled. "Took me twelve tries, three trucks, and a crippled Carl to find it, but she's warming up now."

"Carl?" Sarah asked, arching an eyebrow at me. "Since when do we name these things?"

I laughed. "Ordinarily I don't. But it's on his coveralls, so he gets a name."

Tommy spoke up. "So what's the plan then? You want me to head back with the truck or the plow?"

I considered it for a moment, then said, "Take the plow back. I want to take the truck for a small side trip."

Tommy cocked his head sideways like a dog looking at something that doesn't seem right. "Where you going?" he asked.

I decided to add to his confusion. "Home." was all I said.

26

Sarah looked at me strangely, but she got into the truck's cab. I guessed she wanted to see what I was talking about. "I'll be back at the building in an hour, no later." I told Tommy as he jumped into the plow. I winced as he clanged the big blade on the ground, trying to figure out the hydraulics controls.

I climbed into the pickup and moved out to the gate. Sarah asked which way we were going and all I said was "Straight." Which was odd as the road only went left or right.

But it immediately made sense when I pulled into the subdivision across the street. I had driven this road so many times it was easy to forget the how the world was now. The homes I passed were as familiar to me as my own, and even though I saw the wreckage and decaying bodies, I didn't really see them. In my mind's eye I was looking at my neighborhood the way it was, the way it was supposed to be. Part of my mind warned me that this was a dangerous trek I was taking, that the truth might be harder to handle than anything I could ever have imagined. But the other part didn't care. I *needed* to see my house, I *needed* to see the place where I had built so many memories.

I turned the corner and went down the side street, my eyes taking in the broken homes and the smashed cars. This neighborhood did not seem to have suffered too much devastation, and I began to get the hope that I would find my house intact and unlooted.

Sarah was quiet the whole time I was driving, and I could see her glance at me from time to time in the corner of my eye. What she had to be thinking was anybody's guess. But with the events of the last day and losing Chelsea, something was pushing me towards home.

I turned around the bend in the road and I could see my house at the end of the block. From a distance, it looked untouched and I began to harbor the hope that it had been passed by looters and the waves of zombies looking for food.

I pulled up to the house and initially it looked okay. The windows weren't smashed, and the door was still in place. I looked at Sarah and she smiled, although I could see she was troubled by this visit, for some reason. I got out of the truck and Sarah followed, the both of us instinctively scanning the area and looking for threats. Seeing none, I went to the garage door and turned the handle. Still locked. I reached down to my knife sheath and unsnapped the small pouch that held the sharpening stone for the knife. Pulling out the stone, I reached into the pouch again and pulled out the key I had stashed there months ago.

Showing the key to Sarah, she just grinned and shook her head at me. I opened the door and let the light spill into the garage. My car was still there, the tires a little lower, but still drivable. I signaled to Sarah to pull the truck into the garage, as I did not want to leave it outside in case someone went by and decided he wanted the generators more than we did. After I had pulled down the door, I looked around and went over to the tool wall. Grabbing an axe and hatchet, as well as a hand saw, I put them into the bed of the truck. As an afterthought, I put in the kukri machete I had bought to control the runaway English Ivy that tried every year to choke out the lilies. Sarah eyed that machete, and decided she liked it better than her knife. I smiled and said nothing.

I went to the garage door that led to the house, and using the same key, unlocked the door. I hesitated for a second, more by habit than anything else, then opened the door. I had my gun out, because the experience of the last several months had conditioned me to distrust appearances. On the outside, my house seemed the same way I had left it. But the inside could house horrors and I was fooling myself if I didn't think it was possible.

I stepped inside and quickly looked around. The overcast skies did not allow much light in the best of circumstances, and my barricaded windows allowed even less. But even in the gloom, I could see that the house had miraculously survived intact. Everything was exactly as I had left it when Jake and I had fled, hoping to escape the worst of the zombie hordes. Looking at the house, I wonder if I had made the right decision.

I was prepared for the house to be destroyed, and I was prepared for the house to be looted. What I was not prepared for was the flood of memories and feelings that surged as I moved around the house. I went upstairs and looked in on the bedroom Ellie and I had shared. I gently closed the music box where she had always put her rings when she went to work. I stopped in Jakey's room, looking at the small crib and dresser, and the rocking chair that I had spent so many nights in. I looked into the front bedroom that Ellie and I had planned to give to Jake when he graduated to a "big-boy bed."

I went back downstairs to find Sarah looking around the family room, taking in the pictures and looking around.

"Nice place. Where did you find the wood for the windows and doors?." was all she said.

I sighed. "It was, once. I used the wood from my porch. There's a lot of memories here."

"I'll bet. Good idea, by the way. It explains a lot." Sarah said. She was being more quiet than usual, and I had a suspicion about what was bothering her, but I wasn't going to address it today. Not the time nor the place. But I did know what I needed to do.

"I am going to go downstairs and get what ammo and guns I left here when I bugged out. Do you want to come down and grab the food and water I left here?" I asked.

Sarah seemed to shake herself out of her mood. "Sure."

We went downstairs and it was so dark we needed to use a flashlight. I led the way to the back area, pushing the cabinet aside and revealing the opening to the room under the garage. I used my knife to scrape away the caulk I had put in, and Sarah looked over my tools as I worked.

"I didn't know you were handy." She said, running a hand over my tool belt and miter saw.

I answered from the floor. "Yeah, I picked up a lot from my dad and grandpa. I was taught to try and fix something myself before I called a professional and spend hard earned money. I had a lot of unfinished projects that used to drive Ellie nuts."

Sarah murmured to herself, but loud enough for me to pick up, "I never knew her name."

Finishing with the caulk, I removed the first piece of wood, then went to work on the second. It came out in a minute and I slipped into the gloom of the room, lighting my way with the flashlight. I showed Sarah the water bottle supply and she immediately began bringing cases up to the truck. I went to my safe and opened it, after spending a minute trying to remember what the combination was. Opening the safe, I pulled out the cases of ammo for the M1 Carbine, all of the reloaded ammo for the SIG, and the boxes of .22 ammo. I hauled it all upstairs, bumping into Sarah on the way down, whose eyes opened wide at the haul.

Passing Sarah again on my way down to the room, I went and grabbed my Walther PPK and my GSG-5 .22 rifle. Tucking the Walther into my pocket, I put the GSG-5 into a rifle case with its extra magazine, and brought it out, bumping into Sarah once again. I put it in the truck and went back to grab the plastic bins of clothes that Ellie and I had for Jake which we had inherited from my brother. Jake was running out of clothes and these would be just about ready for him.

I passed Sarah one last time, grabbing my Winchester and bringing up my extension cords. I had four of them, and they should be enough for our purposes. Heading out into the garage, I realized we had seriously loaded the truck. The bed was full and the back seat was full as well.

I went back into the house and stood in the kitchen looking around. Sarah came in from the garage and stood by the door. Her eyes met mine and I could see she was impatient to go.

I didn't want to leave, not yet. But I couldn't stay. There was nothing for me here. Sure, I could live here and survive, and Jake could survive, but that would be all we would be doing. We wouldn't be living, just scavenging an existence on the fringe of oblivion. And what would happen to Jake if I was to pass from infection or illness?

I looked at Sarah. "Anything you want from upstairs? You're about the same size as Ellie, except a bit thinner."

Sarah scowled for a minute, then a thoughtful look came over her face. She went upstairs and came down a few minutes later with an armful of clothes. I followed her lead and went and grabbed a lot of clothes for myself, mostly cold weather stuff, but also essentials like jeans and cargo pants and sweatshirts.

Heading out to the garage, I found Sarah stuffing the clothes into a garbage bag. Doing the same, we tossed our booty into the truck bed.

"We need to get going, the weather is getting bad." Sarah said, pointing to the large snowflakes that were starting to come down.

"You got it. I have one more thing to do." I said. I went back into the house with a puzzled Sarah following. I went to the fireplace and took down the picture of myself, Ellie and a two month old Jake. *What we didn't know then*, I thought, my heart suddenly heavy. I stared at the picture then replaced it with a sigh. I straightened up and took my wedding ring off my finger. I put it on the mantle next to the picture and patted the picture, much the same way my grandfather patted the coffin of my grandmother when she passed away. It was a final goodbye, and I was doing the same to the life I once had. This was my house, but it would not be my home for a long time, if ever. I had work to do. My dad hated funerals, his thought on it being *"The dead are dead. They don't care about us and we shouldn't cry about them."*

I turned around and Sarah turned towards the garage, but not before I could see her eyes were moist. I smiled to myself and noticed that my step was a bit lighter and I actually felt better than I had for a while.

27

Sarah was in the passenger seat and I went to the garage door. Opening it, I got a shock when I saw 6 people standing in my driveway. I recovered quickly and swiftly drew my SIG, taking a bead on the closest male. He was carrying a pump shotgun, and though it was pointed downward, I was taking no chances.

His eyes got wide and he threw up hand, the people behind him putting up their hands as well. Sarah had seen me throw down in the mirror and was out of the truck in a flash, drawing her gun and aiming at the group as well.

"Whoa! Whoa! We're friendly! Don't shoot! Don't shoot!" he cried, stepping back and getting in front of the woman next to him. The family behind him tucked their children away and looked fearfully at Sarah and I.

I have to admit, we probably looked pretty fearsome in our gear, with knives and guns and backpacks with blunt weapons. I held my gun on the man with the shotgun, and looked him over. He looked to be about five ten, roughly forty-five or fifty, with a lean look about him and asked "Who are you and what do you want?"

The man with the shotgun swung it down so it was hanging by his side. "My name is Mark Wells, and this is my wife Teri." His wife smiled weakly. "The family behind me is Bill and Sally Kowalski, and those two youngsters are Jenny and Tim." Bill looked like he had held a desk job all his life, with a slight paunch and balding head. His wife was thin and haggard, like she carried the weight of the world on her shoulders. Their kids were thin and scared, and their clothes looked like they had been salvaged from a person two sizes bigger than they.

I lowered my SIG but kept it at the ready, Sarah following my lead. "I'm John Talon, and next to me is Sarah Greer. You're not from around here, are you?"

Mark looked at me and said. "No, we're from Chicago, and we've been on the run for a while. The cold weather seems to have slowed down our little friends, so we were going to be heading out again, but our vehicle died. We've were looking for another when you drove in."

"Chicago, hey? Well, Mr. Wells, you and I have a lot to talk about, but now is not the time." To accent the point, the wind picked up a bit and more snow swirled around. "Sarah and I need to get back to our base, but I will send a couple of vehicles to pick you up immediately. Good enough?"

Mark shrugged. "Don't have much choice, do we?"

I shrugged back. "You could refuse and I could leave you here to fend for yourself."

Mark smiled ruefully. "Getting a little tired of that. What cars do we look for?"

"It'll be a couple of SUV's. The lead driver's name will be Duncan Fries. Don't be offended by anything he says, he's just a goofball." I said climbing into the truck and firing it up. "Get out of the wind but stay visible. If anything besides an SUV shows up, it's not us."

The group waved as we pulled away, and I drove as quickly as I could back to the compound. The snow was coming down thickly, and I was more than glad we had made the effort to secure a snow plow. I was even happier about the generators we had found. God knows we needed them.

I pulled into the compound and saw the big plow parked underneath the building. I pulled the truck up and honked several times. Tommy, Jason, Duncan, Pamela, and Charlie all came out to help with the load. Charlie's eyes lit up when he saw the generator, and he and Tommy wrestled it upstairs. We would figure out where we would put the things later. Jason and I pulled the other off the truck and Sarah began taking the personal items up to the condo. I waved Duncan and Pamela over.

"We found six more survivors in the subdivision. Apparently they're from Chicago and have managed to live this long. They're two couples and two kids. I need you and Pamela to take the Honda and the Ford and go pick them up." Duncan nodded and to my surprise, Pamela nodded as well. I gave them directions and told them what to look for. "You've got about thirty minutes before things get really ugly." I said looking at the sky and watching the flakes coming down. Off to the northwest, I could see a small glow where Charlie had been at work getting rid of homes and zombies.

Duncan and Pamela went off to the vehicles and I watched them roll away. I grabbed the rifle case, ammo, and headed upstairs myself. I had been away from Jakey too long and needed to spend some quality time with him. I needed to make another trip for his clothes, but I wanted to get in quickly.

After the clothes and everything we had pulled from the house had been brought into the condo, I stoked the fire and helped Jake walk around. He was shaky, but he was getting better, although when I let go of his hands, he would stand for a second, then plop back down on his butt. He was very happy, since in addition to his clothes I had grabbed a container full of baby toys that we were waiting to give him. When I originally left the house, there was no way I could have taken them with, so they waited there. I was just glad he could play with them.

Sarah watched me play with Jake for a while, then asked "What do you have in the cases?"

I looked up from Jake and said "The brown case has my old Winchester, and the tan case has a gun for you."

Sarah's eyes lit up and she went into my bedroom. Coming back out, she was cradling the GSG-5 like a kid at Christmas. Checking the action, she swung the gun up to the window to sight the red-dot scope I had mounted on it once upon a time. Smiling at me, she took it into her bedroom and I could hear her loading the magazine.

Coming back out into the living room, she bent down and kissed me on the cheek. "Thank you very much." She said

"You're welcome very much." I said, picking up Jake and bringing him over to the window to watch the snow come down. What I could see was already blanketed in snow, and I thought about all the zombies we might miss under the snow that we may have to deal with in the spring. I had no hopes that the virus would die in the cold. Viruses are so resilient it wasn't funny. But I was getting the feeling we were actually getting a handle on things and could move soon to a much more permanent place.

Sarah sidled up next to me and watched the snow with us. Jakey noticed her and leaned over, wanting to be held by her. She took him with a grin and we all watched the snow for a bit.

Sarah broke the silence. "My husband and I were in the process of separating when the virus hit. We got married so young and we had a lot of dreams that over time became burdens. I would have left a while ago except for the children. Sometimes I think maybe the girls would have lived had I divorced him. Who knows? All I know is I'm alive when a lot of people aren't, and maybe I can make up for that mistake by saving a few here and there."

I didn't say anything. I knew the need for release.

"You know what's funny?" she asked

"What?"

"I didn't like guns a year ago."

We stood in silence for a while, then Jake started to fuss. We smiled at each other and went to feed the baby and ourselves. Today had been a decent day.

Outside, the snow continued to fall.

28

The next morning, I met with Mark Wills and Bill Kowalski. There hadn't been time to talk yesterday with getting them in and prepared. The ground was covered in about 6 inches of snow, and the sun was amazingly bright on the white ground. The world seemed so fresh and new it was easy to forget what we were about or how we got there. The conversation with the two men from Chicago reminded me soon enough. We used a conference room in one of the offices.

"I was on a call for the north side when things suddenly turned over." Mark started. "We had been listening to the reports and such for a week, but we weren't getting much information. The mayor had been on television a couple of times telling us to go about our lives as usual, but you could see the strain on his face. It was like he knew something was up but couldn't talk about it. I guess it made sense. If he came out and said the dead were walking, we would have had anarchy sooner than we did. There was stuff all over the internet, so people were pretty well informed, but all of a sudden it came to a head." Mark paused to collect his thoughts. "I got a call from my supervisor that a transformer had blown in Wilmette, and I needed to get up there. No big deal, standard stuff, thinks I. Well, I get there and there's this weird silence, like the world had paused to take a breath before it screamed. I changed the transformer and got back in the truck. I radioed my dispatcher and got no response. Heading back, I see swarms of cars trying to get out of the city. There's smoke everywhere and I could see lots of fires. Sirens are going off, and over it all I could hear screams and moans. Screams and moans."

I nodded and urged him to continue.

"I drove my truck into the city and I could see them everywhere, attacking and eating, breaking into houses, tearing people apart. I felt like I was moving in slow motion. I ran into a couple of them and they got right back up after they bounced off the fenders. I saw cars smashed in, and people just running. One woman was on the twentieth floor of an apartment building and I saw her hold her baby as she jumped to her death. A second later, about five of those things were at the window, reaching for the meals that chose to die instead."

He shook his head at the memory. "I managed to get home and told my wife we had to get the hell out of there. I didn't know where to go, or how we would live, but I knew if we stayed, we were dead. It just happened so fast. I guess so many people were infected at the same time, and turned all at once. There was no preparation, no nothing. I could see my neighbor trying to protect his wife from his turned teenage children, and get killed for his trouble. I watched a police officer empty his gun at a group of those things and they ripped him to pieces in seconds. There was nothing left to reanimate."

Mark paused and Bill started talking. "My story is pretty much the same. But I think I was lucky in that I hadn't gone to work in several days due to a round of the stomach flu rolling through my house. I think that may have saved my kids, too." He stared off into space, thinking about what might have been. Bill continued. "I wanted to run, but I didn't know how. I didn't know what I was going to do with my family. I could hear the sounds of death all around our apartment as the infected fed on the living. The old woman living upstairs had her head ripped off her shoulders, and two toddlers hiding on the fire escape screamed for a long time before they died at their parents' hands."

Mark nodded and continued his story. "Teri and I grabbed what we could and headed for the lake. I figured our best bet was to try and get a boat and at least sail away from the mess. We made it about a block and a half before we were spotted and had to run for it. We made it four blocks to an apartment building and hid there. That happened to be where we hooked up with Bill and Sally and the kids."

Bill took up the story. "We had abandoned our apartment after the neighbor was attacked. We went down the emergency stairs and luckily no one was there. We were hiding in the maintenance room when the door crashed in and Mark and his wife tumbled in."

Mark smiled. "We had three of them sniffing for us, and we just managed to fall in out of sight. Luckily the smell of chemicals masked our scent and they left us alone. Of course, back then, we didn't know how good their sense of smell had become. Sometimes I wonder how many hiding places were discovered by the smell of fear?"

I remember thinking the same thing when I was trying to figure out how the enemy operated and their strengths and weaknesses.

"Anyway," Mark said, "We found ourselves stuck in a basement with nowhere to go. But we got lucky. Bill's son found an access panel behind an old mattress to the electric tunnels under the city. We had a way out, but if any of those things were down there, we were dead for sure. We moved as best as we could, checking every place we came to for a way to get out and to find food and such. We had a close moment when we were discovered at a business, but we gave them the slip in the tunnels. We headed south as best as we could, and then we ran out of tunnels."

Bill and Mark looked at each other, then Mark continued. "We spent a lot of time moving from place to place, avoiding not only zombies but other predators as well. I picked up the shotgun from a home we broke into, but it wasn't good for much against the dead. Everywhere it was the same. People dead or dying, walking dead trying to eat the living, fires, looting. I saw a man running down the street from a pack of zombies carrying a plasma TV. Dumbass."

Bill picked up again. "We managed to find a car and we headed south, but the roads were choked with cars and dead people. We heard the announcements about the state centers, but we had no way to get to them. In hindsight, I'm glad we didn't, when we heard they had been overrun with infected. Anyway, we moved as quietly as we could, at one point floating down the canal to escape zombies. We found a car in what used to be Westchester, and headed south again. Everywhere was death."

Mark started again. "It took us 9 months to get that far, hiding and scrounging and living in fear. We were at the end of our string when we saw your truck pull up to that house. I was scared stupid when you pulled that gun on me." indicating my SIG.

"Why?" I asked. "You had a shotgun. You could have nailed me when I opened the garage door."

Mark looked sheepish. "I was out of shells. I had been out for a month."

I shook my head. "Good way to get killed."

Bill smiled. "Looks like you have things under better control out here."

I smiled back. "You have no idea. This is a small group. To the south, there's another community of over a hundred people." I enjoyed the look that showed up on both their faces. "We're making a push to the river, then we'll hook up and the real work begins."

Mark asked, "What's the real work?"

I stood up and answered simply. "We're taking it back."

I left them wondering about that and went out into the main office area. Charlie and Sarah and Tommy had gone on a recovery mission. I had sent them to the small gun shop that was several miles to the west, in a town that was right on the river. They took the plow and cleared the road, since we were going to need it later this winter. Duncan and Pamela and several others had taken the axe and tools I had brought from my house and were making serious piles of firewood for the winter.

The truck pulled up and Charlie swung down from the cab. Sarah scooted out the other side and ran towards the building, carrying something long. Charlie motioned me to the back of the truck. Stepping back there, I whistled when I saw what he had found. Ammunition of all types was back their, in boxes and crates. Apparently, the locked storage room had been left alone. I had a lot more ammo for my carbine, and there was a lot more ammo for the AR's we had, as well as plenty of ammo for the handguns. Hell, looking at the stuff, we were ready to go to war.

Charlie spoke up after I had whistled my appreciation. "Storage room was right where you said, still padlocked and everything. Everything else was pretty much looted. There weren't any guns to be found, but we did find a lot of cleaning supplies and extra magazines." He handed me three additional magazines for my SIG. "P226, right?"

I gratefully accepted the magazines and put them in my pockets to be filled later. "Anything else?"

"Not from the shop, but we found something weird."

"What's that?"

"We were headed back and Tommy thought he saw something in a subdivision we passed. We went back and there was a pile of zombie corpses in the middle of the street."

"Really." That was interesting. Maybe were not alone out here.

Charlie nodded. "Really. Want to hear the weird part?"

"That wasn't the weird part?" I asked, perplexed.

"Nope. The weird part was all of the corpses were headless." Charlie waited for my reaction.

I scowled. "What?"

"Want to hear the really weird part?" Charlie seemed to be enjoying himself.

"It gets weirder?" I was almost afraid to ask.

"We found no fewer then eight piles of zombie corpses, all of them headless. I figure there had to be over three hundred zombie heads missing."

I was stunned. No wonder the activity around here was less than I expected, environment not withstanding. Somebody had been hard at work and had been really effective. But why remove the heads? The heads were still alive and still able to bite and cause infection. Something was definitely wrong here, and I said as much to Charlie.

"Definitely need to keep our eyes open. I'll radio Nate and give him a heads up." I said.

Charlie nodded. "Good enough. I'll take this stuff upstairs and distribute as needed. I heard we have an electrician?" he asked hopefully.

I nodded. "Grab him and see what he can do with our generators. I'm looking forward to a meal not cooked over a fire."

Charlie laughed. "Amen, brother, amen.

I went upstairs to find Sarah playing with Jacob. She had a funny look on her face when I came in and I asked her what was up.

"Got a present for you." She said, indicating with her eyes the bundle on my bed.

Curious, I went over and undid the towel that had wrapped what appeared to be a rifle of some sort. When the towel fell away I was holding a beautiful Springfield M1A rifle. .308 caliber with a twenty round clip. A very effective rifle out to 600 yards or better. I couldn't imagine a better rifle to go into battle with.

My expression must have revealed how I felt. Sarah just called from the floor "You're welcome. There are extra magazines and ammo

I was speechless for a moment. "Where did you get this? Charlie said you didn't find any firearms." I checked the action and found the gun to be in excellent working order.

Sarah laughed. "I told Charlie to lie to you. He was very accommodating."

I put the gun down and kissed the top of her head. "Thank you very much. I've always wanted one of these but never could justify the expense."

Sarah changed the subject. "Charlie tell you about the heads?"

I grimaced. "Yeah. That's a new one. We'll have to see where it leads."

"So what's the plan for today?" Sarah wanted to know.

I shrugged. "Beats me. I'm staying home today. Jake has been without his daddy for a few days and I need some baby time."

Sarah smiled. "Sounds good."

I smiled back, but I had a strange feeling it was going to be a wild spring.

29

The coldest days of winter were the hardest. The sun would be out but the bitter north winds would rip at clothing, and claw at exposed skin with fingers of ice. We stayed indoors for the worst of it, but we went out at every opportunity because this was our one chance to drastically impact the zombie population. A small part of me thought about the city and the area to the north of the canal, but I realized that the zombie population up there would be in the millions, and I realistically could not hope to finish all of them in one winter.

If all went well, maybe next winter, when I could return with a larger contingent of people and weapons, but right now, that was impossible.

We cleared out several subdivisions and homes and we warmed ourselves on several burning homes. We stayed away from the city of Oakland Park proper, working at the fringes and gathering supplies where we could. I absolutely forbade anyone from trying to go to the mall there, as I figured the cavernous building might have enough residual warmth to keep hundreds of zombies moving.

The winter wasn't all work. Jake had his first birthday, and Sarah and I invited everyone to the party. We managed to put together quite a feast from the food and supplies we had scrounged, and the generators provided us with light and music for a while. Jake loved the attention, and Sarah even managed to get him a present. She and Charlie found a baby store and picked up a little walk-behind car. Jake was moving around pretty well, and the car let him practice his walking skills. He gave a squeal of delight when he used it, and Sarah said it was the best 'thank you' she had ever received.

The party was a welcome relief from the stress of our situation, and it was also the opportunity for Charlie to bring out the little girl he had unofficially adopted. She had recovered remarkably well, and her brilliant blue eyes took in everything around her. Jake was fascinated with her, and was constantly trying to give her toys to play with. Charlie had decided to name her Julia, which Sarah received with a small smile. I gave her a hug and she assured me it was all right.

Julia had a host of admirers, not the least of which were the women from the adult center, most of whom had lost a child or more in the Upheaval.

The winter brought out some interesting changes in our group as well. I was as surprised as anyone when Pamela moved into Duncan's room, and Tommy began hanging out with a young widow named Stacey Wood. Charlie was getting friendly with Rebecca, our resident nurse, and Kristen was complaining about her lack of prospects.

A week later, I decided it was time to hit the town of Leport. It was a river town and older than most towns in the area. As a river town, I wanted to make sure it was going to remain intact, as it was going to be another community after we had cleared it out and declared it safe. I just hoped we had the population around to make it work.

Charlie came with me, as well as Tommy, and the three of us rode in silence, taking in the snowy landscape and each of us lost in our own thoughts. As we passed the forest preserves, I could see several herds of deer moving like ghosts among the trees. The lakes were frozen and swept by winds that created drifts like whitecaps on top of still waters. The road was clear, since we had been this way several times with the plow, but a drift or two was still blocking the way, making travel difficult as usual.

We passed a subdivision of enormous homes, an area we had already been through. We had managed to secure a large amount of supplies from several of those homes, as well as some interesting vehicles. Tommy found a Mercedes convertible he was proud of until Charlie asked where he was going to put the supplies. We didn't burn any of the homes, as they were made of brick and likely able to survive for a while. There was a huge estate on one side of the road, and we decided to stop for a look. Charlie navigated the truck into the driveway and Tommy whistled at the size of the home. We got out of the truck and spread out. I took the front door while Charlie checked the windows and Tommy started towards the back. I checked the door and found it unlocked. Pushing it open, I held my new M1A rifle at the ready, not expecting trouble, but not relenting in my vigilance, either.

The place was huge, and expensively furnished. Polished hardwood floors peeked out from beneath oriental-style carpets, while a marble fireplace commanded attention in the ornate living room. High ceilings added to the overall effect and the whole place reeked of money. Nice digs in a regular world, not so great in the current one. The only detriment to the place was the fact that the expensive furniture was tossed around, like someone had been stumbling around in the dark, bumping into things.

Movement out of the corner of my eye showed Charlie making his way to the front door, and I expected Tommy to come rolling in from the back. What I didn't expect was gunshots from the side of the house. It was too cold for zombies to be moving quickly but this was something else.

I ran past Charlie, and he looked at me in askance. "That wasn't Tommy's gun." I said as I flicked off the safety of my M1A and followed Tommy's footprints to the side of the house.

I could hear the snarl of engines as I raced to the edge and rounding the corner, the distinctive whine of snowmobiles. Tommy was taking cover behind the fireplace and getting ready to engage when I burst around the corner. Swinging wide, I circled out into the lawn and was able to see three snowmobiles racing away, two of the riders with rifles strapped to their backs, while the third had a large duffle bag. They were roughly two hundred yards off and moving fast, but I decided to take a shot anyway. Bringing up the barrel, I sighted in the retreating figure and pulled the trigger. The rifle punched the air with sound and I was rewarded with one of the retreating figures swerving sharply and nearly colliding with a tree. But he corrected in time and sped away.

Bringing the gun down, I went over to where Charlie was helping Tommy to his feet. "Did you get hit?" I asked, checking him for any blood.

"No, they missed me by a mile. More like surprise shots, than anything else. I came around the corner and we stared at each other for a second. I was about to hail when one of them whipped up his rifle and fired at me. I dove for the building and was getting ready to return the favor when you came around. Wonder who they were?"

"No clue, but I actually am surprised we hadn't run into some other survivors like that until now." I said, looking off to where the snowmobiles had gone. Southeast, by the look of it, and if memory served, there wasn't anything really off in that direction except a couple of home improvement stores.

Charlie broke off our reflection with his usual charm. "I'm going inside, you two hens can talk out in the cold all you want." He said and stomped off towards the front door.

Shaking my head, I followed him, with Tommy coming in behind.

We went back inside the house, but with the likelihood of the place being already visited, we didn't expect to find much. Tommy went to the kitchen, while Charlie headed to the basement. I decided to take the upstairs and look around. Maybe I would get lucky.

I went upstairs and checked the rooms to the east of the main stairwell. There was a nicely furnished library and I picked up a few books to take back to the condo. Many books were on the floor, as if someone was looking for a safe or something, but nothing serious. Another room had a home theater set up in it with a huge plasma television mounted on the wall. Useless now, but fun when it was working, I'd bet. There was a nice suite near the stairs that looked like a guest area, and it was nicer than any hotel I ever stayed at. It even had its own small kitchen.

I moved to the bedrooms and checked them out one by one. The first two were unremarkable, just your standard bedroom with a sofa, television, and bathroom. After seeing the other rooms, I was actually looking forward to the master bedroom.

I opened the door and immediately when into combat mode. There was blood splattered over the walls and furniture, and I could see a pair of legs sticking out from around the corner. They weren't moving, but I took nothing for granted.

Checking behind the door and moving in with my rifle up, I edged around the body and looked at the rest of the bedroom. I cursed when I saw what was on the bed. A woman in her late forties had been stripped and tied spread eagle face down on the bed. Her husband had apparently been forced to watch her be raped by her attackers until they were both killed. Seems like they had been caught trying to survive here and paid a brutal price for it.

The way they had been killed struck a familiar chord in my memory, but I brushed it aside and cut the woman's bonds. I turned her over and saw the bruises and scratches that mapped a horrific experience. I laid her to rest and struggling, managed to heave her husband up next to her on the bed. I then covered the two of them with a sheet and looked up to find Tommy staring at me.

"What happened here?" he asked, looking around.

"I'm not fully sure, but I would guess these two were trying to survive and happened to get in the way of a few animals who relished the idea of a lawless nation." My voice was grim and hard, thinking of the others I had encountered who used the Upheaval as an excuse to satisfy their baser instincts.

"Well, that matches what Charlie found in the basement." Tommy said, stepping out into the hallway.

I followed him. "Why? What did he find?"

Tommy shook his head. "Charlie found three bodies down there, two of them children, the third likely a teenager. All of them had been killed, none of them infected."

I felt a familiar rage starting to build, frustrated that I had no one to vent it on. I headed downstairs and stopped at the landing. Tommy bumped into me. "What's going on?"

I pointed at a portrait on the wall. "If there was a family here and they have been all killed, then we're one short." The family photo showed four children, two teenagers and two kids under twelve.

Tommy looked thoughtful and we mulled that one over in silence as Charlie came up the stairs. He was holding a small hatchet which was covered in dried blood, which he held up to us.

"I'm guessing this was what killed the kids in the basement. Came from a McCard's home store." Charlie said without preamble.

"We're missing one." Tommy said, pointing to the wall portraits.

Charlie's eyes narrowed and he looked at me. "Parents?"

"Dead upstairs." I replied. "Mom worked over pretty badly, looks like Dad was forced to watch."

"What do you want to do here?" Charlie asked.

I looked around. As nice as this place was, it was a tomb. "Light it up."

Tommy and Charlie nodded and went to work. Twenty minutes later, we were driving away. In the rear view mirrors, I could see flames starting to lick at the edges of the windows. *Rest in peace.* I thought darkly.

We pulled into the outskirts of Leport and immediately could see that there was something wrong. The first subdivision had another pile of headless zombies, and all of the houses had been broken into. We split up and checked a few houses each. I found a few corpses in a couple houses, and none of them had been infected when they were killed. Charlie and Tommy reported finding similar things. The three of us looked at each other and it was pretty clear what we all thinking. There was a group out there that was not only killing zombies, but killing survivors as well.

We got back into the truck and proceeded into the city proper. Devastation was all around us, and we had a difficult time navigating around some of the blocked intersections. Many of the homes had been burned to the ground, and large swaths of devastation covered much of the town. We passed a grocery store but didn't even bother looking in, as the doors had been smashed in long ago. We headed down the hill towards the river, and could see from the top of the hill the line of cars that choked the road and doomed many people to the rampaging dead.

Turning down the side road to the older part of town, we parked the truck and got out. There were several streets but oddly there were no cars. I wondered if they were on the road above us but was shaken out of my reflection by Tommy jostling my arm.

"Look over there" he said, pointing to the river.

I looked and smiled back at him. A small marina was tucked up next to the river, and a boat landing was evident. There weren't any boats, and I hadn't expected any, but we had our waterway access. Looking back to the town, I realized that the older homes and businesses had been spared the devastation, and the newer part of the town up the hill had been destroyed. A cathedral was still standing, as well as a large school. Either would make a good defensive point if necessary, and the bell tower was perfect as a watchtower. The lands around would do nicely for farming and raising animals, if we ever found any, and the woods would provide shelter and materials.

All right, then. I waved Charlie and Tommy over and we spent the next two hours going through businesses and houses. We found no survivors, but we did find quite a few zombies frozen in the snow and ice. We dispatched all that we found, fifty-six total. We found signs of violence here and there, but this part of the city seemed to be mostly abandoned. Charlie found a child's clothing store, and came out with armloads of clothes for little Julia. Tommy checked every bar he found, but there wasn't a drop of liquor in the town. I happened across a construction company and found a back hoe and a bulldozer, which would be useful later if we could get them running.

Getting back in the truck, we headed back to the condo complex. Our mood was sobered when we passed the burning mansion but lightened as we came within sight of our condo complex. I wouldn't call it a good day, but it was productive.

Sarah and Jake met me and I told Sarah about the mansion and what we had found and what had occurred. She looked thoughtful for a second, and then asked, "Do you think there might be a connection between this incident and the one you had at the drugstore last year?"

I thought about it and realized that was what had been nagging at my mind when I came across the scene. "Now that you mention it, it does seem similar. I guess it would be too much to hope for that I had stopped them back then, wouldn't it.?"

Sarah nodded and handed me a hot cup of coffee. "Nate called in and wanted to know how things were going. I told him you would get back to him later tonight."

I sipped the coffee and nodded. "I made it to the river today."

Sarah suddenly smiled. "You did! I knew you would! How did the town look?"

I turned serious. "There's a lot of work to do, but it will serve. It most certainly will." I spent the next hour talking about what we had found and what we were going to do before Jake demanded to be fed and played with. Duty called.

30

The next month was a whirlwind of activity as we cleared the town of Leport and started to move ourselves in that direction. I decided to use the big school on the hill as a temporary base, as it provided the best source of protection in case of attack. We had found several more homes that had shown signs of violence, and many individuals who had died of gunshot wounds, not infection. We found a large population of zombies in the upper west neighborhood, and Duncan concluded that these must have come from the freeway that was near that area. We killed them all, and dumped them in houses that we set on fire. By the middle of February, we had cleared the area around the old part of town and were just about ready to start our move.

Charlie had come up with an interesting idea. He had found a chain link dog pen around four feet by six feet by six feet tall. He secured it to the ground using some tent pegs and chain, and disappeared for the day. When he came back, he surprised all of us by dragging and tossing in the cage a zombie popsicle that hadn't been neutralized yet.

When I asked him about it he just shrugged. "I figure the best way to know when these things are thawing out and moving again would be to have one nearby and when it starts to get active, that's when we know the rest are likely active as well and had better be ready once again."

I just shook my head once again at what Charlie called 'country-boy-brilliance' and let it go. I did call Nate and tell him about it and was rewarded with just one word. Nate then said he would be heading out to do just the same thing in the morning. I also told Nate about what we were finding, and he said he had begun to find similar things to the south. I started to wonder if perhaps there was a group operating right in between us, but I didn't have the resources to go checking thoroughly. Any group that could behead as many zombies as we had seen was one to use caution with.

March brought warming weather, and keeping an eye on our imprisoned friend, we started to see increased activity. At around thirty degrees, our pet Z's movements were slow, but definitely dangerous in a swarm. At forty degrees, the movements became faster, and on a particularly warm day, one of those rare sixty degree days we sometimes saw in March, our zombie friend was moving quite well and seemed back to normal.

About the second week in March I decided that the threat was real enough, the zombies were able to revive after being frozen, and we needed to be on the lookout once again. The areas around us had been cleared and could be counted on to be relatively safe, but after three months of being frozen, I figured the little critters were going to be hungry as hell and would be on the roam worse than they had been before. I warned my people to be as on guard as they had ever been, even with areas that had been cleared; if there was any chance a zombie could have gotten in, treat it as a hostile environment.

On the morning of the third week of March, Sarah, Kristen, and Jason were out on a search for a boat or something for the river. I had directed them towards the town of Freeport, as I figured there would more likely be a boat in that direction. I was helping John Reef, our resident plumber, with a water system that would allow us to have running water. The good news was we could still use the sewer system in place, although at some point things were going to get ugly, but we would cross the bridge later. This was going to be a trial run for the condos, but we would move the system to Leport when we moved out there permanently. John said if we could get a power source to the pumping system, we could have running water for a lot of homes, but since that required a foray into the city, I opted for local control.

Charlie was spending the day with Julia and Rebecca, and it was amusing to see the three of them outside walking around, with Charlie armed to the teeth. Tommy and Duncan were hunting a couple of ghouls that had been spotted in the woods, and Pamela was helping Mark Wells, our electrician, re-wire some of the lines so we could have electricity on a fairly regular basis.

I was wearing about thirty feet of garden hose and wet up to my knees when the Honda came rolling in. I could immediately see something was wrong. One tire was flat and there were bullet holes in the windshield. I dropped my hose and ran over to the vehicle as it limped to a stop. Charlie saw me running and came over to see what was going on.

I pulled open the driver's door and jumped back as Jason fell at my feet. He had been shot twice, and how the hell he managed to make it back here was a mystery. He rolled onto his back and I yelled for Rebecca, who came running over with Julia.

"Jason! Jason! Can you hear me? What happened?" I didn't see any other signs of violence in the car, except for where Jason had bled on the upholstery. I had a sneaking suspicion about what happened, but I needed to hear it from Jason.

Jason looked up at me, his eyes cloudy with pain. His breathing was labored, but his mouth was not bloody, so at least he hadn't been hit in the lungs. It took a huge effort, but he managed to speak.

"Came out of nowhere...we were securing a boat when they attacked." Jason coughed thickly. "Sarah shot one of them, but they overwhelmed her and Kristen. There was six of them..." Jason's voice faded and I was afraid he was going, but Rebecca was working on him feverishly. Lisa had been called and she was kneeling by his side, tears running down her face.

Jason shook himself and continued. "They grabbed the women and carried them off to their truck. One of them knocked me to my knees and then shot me. He laughed as he shot me..." Jason looked into my eyes. "I couldn't help them...I should have helped them...." His voice faded away as he fainted. I squeezed his shoulder and motioned for Charlie to help me get him up to his apartment.

We carried Jason to his bedroom and Rebecca worked on him with supplies we had retrieved from an ambulance. I got on the radio to Nate and had the Doc talk to Rebecca to walk her through some of the harder procedures.

I left the room and looked at Charlie. The cold fire of battle had started again, and this time I welcomed it. I allowed my rage to extend itself into every corner of my being, and breathed deep the air of revenge.

"What's the move?" Charlie asked, already knowing my answer.

I looked at him slowly. "We go hunting." was all I said. I turned on my heel and went to my condo. Jake was playing with Julia, and Amy Strickland and Sally Kowalski were watching them both. A sense of urgency had descended upon the complex, and everyone stepped up to help however they could.

I didn't say a word as I belted on my knife and SIG. My extra magazines went into my holder and two more went into my jacket pocket. I loaded up my M1A magazines and placed them in my outer pockets of my jacket. I put an extra box of cartridges in a pocket of my backpack, and made sure my supplies were fresh and ready. I opted not to bring my crowbar, instead bringing a hand axe that had a long handle. I didn't have any real reason for choosing the axe or the heavy rifle over my crowbar and carbine other than I thought they would hurt more. My mind was filled with images of the woman at the drugstore and the family at the estate, and my rage increased with each passing minute. I passed Jake and he smiled up at me. I smiled back at him and said "Daddy has to go take care of some bad men. I will be back. I promise." I looked at the women with the children and they nodded at me, giving me silent consent to the violence I was about to do.

I met Charlie in the hallway and he was geared up as much as I was. His AR was on his shoulder and his tomahawks were secured. His knife was on his belt along with his Glock. I was sure he had plenty of ammo with him, and I could see the rage was in him as well. Sarah and Kristen were more than friends, they were family, and we were not about to let their kidnapping go unanswered. Jason was just hanging on, and if he died, I would not let it be in vain. If he had not managed to make it back to us, we might not have known for days.

We ran into Tommy and Duncan in the office area, and they were dressed as we were. They didn't say a word as we passed, they just fell in behind as we headed down to the cars. We were grim men as we climbed into the truck, and the holes in the CR-V and Jason's blood on the parking lot pavement pushed us on.

Duncan was driving. "Where to?" he asked, firing up the truck.

I thought about that. Where would they be? What clues were right in front of my face that I was not seeing? Thinking back, I realized I knew where they were, the evidence given to me by Charlie at the estate house.

"McCord's" I said, indicating the road west.

We drove in silence, the only sound was the click of ammunition into magazines as Tommy topped off his rifle and handgun. Charlie topped off Duncan's magazines and handed them back to him. Charlie then tapped me on my shoulder and I handed my knife back to him. Charlie sharpened the knife slowly with a small whetstone he carried in his pouch for his tomahawks, the rasping sound stroking the fire of revenge and nearly causing me to urge Duncan to drive faster. We wanted to fight, to kill, but we also wanted to come out alive.

We turned south on Bell Road and when we came to the top of a hill, I motioned Duncan to pull over. I got out and pulled my binoculars out from my pack. From behind a tree, I looked out towards the massive home improvement building. I could see several vehicles, including a small fleet of snowmobiles and motorcycles. That in itself was not an indication that Sarah was there, but it did give me enough to investigate further. I didn't see any guards or watchmen, so I figured it was safe to proceed.

Going back to the vehicle, I directed Duncan to drive slowly down the hill, so as to attract as little attention as possible. There was a house on a small bit of land next to the store, so I told Duncan to turn in there. It was about a hundred yards from the building, and would serve as a rally point. I looked at the building again, and still didn't see any lookouts or guards. Strange.

I got out of the car and the other men did the same. We passed out the radios and I signaled for Tommy and Duncan to scout the back of the building while Charlie and I headed for the front. The garden center seemed to be the place where they came and went, so I wanted to see about alternate entry.

Moving quickly, Charlie and I crossed the parking lot and worked our way to the front of the building. A pile of bricks and paving stones covered the exit doors, so there was no worry of being seen from there. We went over to the front door and found it to be similarly blocked. I hunkered down and used the radio.

"Tommy, do you read, over." I clicked the radio twice.

"Loud and clear, over" came the reply.

"The front is blocked, how's the back? Over." I asked.

"Same. Looks like the only way in is through the garden center. Over."

"Right. Meet you in five. Over." I motioned to Charlie and we made our way to the Garden Center exit. Waiting a moment, we saw Tommy and Duncan come around the corner and join up with us. I motioned Tommy and Duncan to move to the right while Charlie and I would move to the left.

We slid into the Garden center and worked our way along the wall. Nothing seemed out of the ordinary except for an odd lack of garden tools along the south wall. We reached the interior door and waited for Tommy and Duncan to clear the other side. The door to the inside was a large garage-type door, and very effective against zombies. But not so effective against people who retained their fine motor skills.

Charlie tested the door and found it to be locked. Moving to the other door, he tried it and it was open. Not wanting to announce our presence just yet, we conferred briefly and decided to try stealth and see if it worked. Opening the door slightly and with as little motion as possible, Charlie and I pulled up the door about three inches very slowly, with Tommy and Duncan on their stomachs with their rifles at the ready in case of detection.

Getting the thumbs up, Charlie and I raised the door a few more inches. We waited for the signal from Duncan, then raised it another few inches. Not arousing any undue attention, I bent down and looked to the right while Charlie checked to the left. I didn't see anything and Charlie signaled he didn't see anything either. Nodding, we rolled under the door and into the building. Coming up into a crouch I covered the right while Charlie covered the left, and Duncan and Tommy rolled out from underneath the door. We could hear a large number of voices, and they seemed to be coming from the center of the building. We moved along a storage corridor which ran the length of the building, edging closer to the source of the noise. There was a lot of trash and discarded items littering the walkway. There was a humming noise coming from somewhere which sounded familiar, but I was uninterested in anything but getting Sarah and Kristen back.

We moved towards the back of the dark building and heard a cheer go up from the voices. A scream sounded briefly and I could hear cursing. Gritting my teeth I moved forward to an opening in the wall which led to the main floor. I looked around the corner and got my first look at my enemy. It was a group of teenagers, roughly 20-25 of them. They were wearing the most outrageous collection of clothing I had ever seen. The girls were wearing loops of necklaces and fur coats, while the boys wore leather coats and designer jeans. Abercrombie was well-represented, as was Hollister and GAP. They were standing on a platform that overlooked the store, and were cheering on some sort of dispute happening on the floor. Hawaiian torches lit the scene in grim shades of orange and red. I heard a smacking sound, another curse, and then a thud like someone being hit in the gut. Another cheer arose and then a voice rang out, silencing the group.

"Enough! Enough! She will be judged and sentenced in due time. Your vengeance will wait, Devon. Move away. Bring the other up here."

I couldn't see the speaker, but he sounded young like the rest of the group. I began to wonder about what was happening here and how all these kids managed to assemble in one place and survive. We slid out slowly, keeping to the back wall and working my way through appliances. If everyone was gathered at the center platform, then we could move undetected until we were in place. I hunkered down and outlined a plan to the other men. It was bold, it was crazy, and would likely get us all killed, but I didn't have any choice. These kids had degenerated into beasts, and I would treat them as I would any other rabid animal.

We split up and I headed towards the tool section, being careful not to knock over anything or cause any noise to attract attention before I was ready. When I reached the end of the aisle, I had to be careful, because I would be in sight of the teens. I kept hearing an odd clicking sound, and it sounded eerily familiar, but I couldn't figure out what it was. I was about to make my move to cross the aisle when I heard the leader speak again.

"It's time for punishment!" This elicited a chorus of cheers. "We found this man stealing from us. His partner we killed, but this one we caught! He has been judged and found guilty!" Another cheer. "Have you anything to say?"

"You can't do this! I have rights! You can't do this to me!" came the squealing reply.

I was stunned. I knew that voice. I leaped across the opening to give myself a better view from another aisle. I slowly raised my head until I could see the platform. Standing on what looked like a plank from a pirate ship was none other than Kevin Pierce. His hands were tied behind his back and he looked much worse for wear. His face was cut and he was only wearing his boxers. So his partner Frank was dead, hmm? Even in this situation good news could be found. I made a mental note to call Nate when we finished here. I looked down to what he was standing over and my blood froze in horror. In a ten foot by ten foot by six foot pen of chain link fencing, surrounded by a second, smaller fence to keep people from accidentally bumping into it was a nightmare. Zombie heads filled the pen, and because the brain was still intact, they were still alive. Their grotesque mouths opened and closed, and their dead eyes darted around. Those on top of the pile stared at the meal suspended before them, those on the bottom were twisted into horrible, contorted faces as the crush pressed on them. The teeth of the zombies clacked together, causing the clicking sound I had heard earlier.

Like a pool full of piranhas, I thought, starting to bring up my rifle. I hesitated, though, because I didn't know if the other men were in position yet and I didn't want to start the ball without them being ready.

A scream caught my attention and I looked up at Kevin being pushed out further onto the plank. He was being shoved by a long pole, and his tormentors were clearly enjoying what they were doing. Kevin knew what awaited him in that pen, and I could see the tears running down his cheeks as he cried for mercy. "I know who you want! I know where he is! You have his woman! He'll come to you! You can kill him! Don't let me die! You need me!" Kevin's voice started to crack as he pleaded with his captors, who jeered and laughed at him.

"Silence!" The leader's voice broke out amid the din, and the noise subsided. A tall, skinny kid of about nineteen years old stepped forward and grabbed the pole from his minion. He looked familiar, but I couldn't place where I might have seen him before. "I know what I need to know. And I don't need you." With that he swung the pole, smashing Kevin across the back of his knees, causing him to buckle and fall onto the plank. He tried to grip the board with his legs, but he slipped and fell headfirst into the pit of heads. He screamed for a long time as the zombie heads slowly tore him apart. It was particularly gruesome to see the ones on the bottom lick the blood off their faces and see their eyes dart around for the source. I saw a head chewing on a piece of meat, swallow it, and the next head below it eating what came out of the severed throat. This process continued until the bits of chewed flesh were ground up to fine bits of pulpy mess. Kevin's bones were attacked until there was nothing left on them.

The crowd on the platform watched the grisly scene in captivation. Then they turned to each other and started gyrating and making out. I shook my head and moved to another aisle, confident I would not be seen.

When I cleared the next aisle, I saw another pen, this one holding a single figure. She was standing with her arms at her sides, and even from behind I knew that pose. Sarah. I thanked God and every other deity I could think of that she was still safe. I wondered briefly where Kristen was when I felt my radio vibrate. I smiled to myself. Tommy, Duncan and Charlie were in position. Time to get moving. I almost stood up when I heard the leader start to shout.

"You see that pit, bitch? You want to join your friend? I want to know where your people are and you're going to tell me!" I heard the sound of a slap and a quick intake of air. "You're going to die, bitch, and your little tough-guy bitch friend as well. But we're going to make you two suffer first. Put her on the rack!" I heard a scream and another slap, followed by some more cheering. I heard a girl's voice snarl and a thump like someone had been hit on the head.

I needed to let Sarah know we were there and to get down when the shooting started, because it was going to start soon. But how would she know we were there? Think, think, think. I was running out of time. I was hearing cheers again and the leader yelling "I will choose who is first!" I quickly got out a picture of Jake I kept with me and folded it in half, then half again. It was small to begin with, but I needed to make sure it would go unnoticed when I threw it.

Saying a small prayer I tossed the picture at the defiant figure in the other pen, clearing the side of the cage and dropping it in front of her. I saw her body twitch at the intrusion and saw her slowly bend down and pick up the picture.

I nearly shouted with the success but I had to save Kristen first. I moved to the front of the aisle and looked up again at the platform. The fire that had been inside suddenly burned brightly as I saw Kristen, the little girl who I had trusted to watch my son with, was tied to a large "X" made out of timbers. Her head was hanging down and the leader was slowly striping her clothing off with a large knife. I could see a trickle of blood running down her cheek from a cut on her head. She seemed to be unconscious, which seemed to add to the enjoyment by the group.

I checked the availability of my magazines and made sure the safety was off on my M1A. My original thought of just getting the women back was replaced with another. I was going to kill every one of these sons-of-bitches.

The leader was yelling at Kristen as he cut her clothes. "Where's your precious leader? Who's going to save your sweet ass? *Where, bitch?*" he screamed into her unresponsive face.

"Right here." I said loudly, stepping out into the open and aiming my rifle at the leader, who jumped and nearly dropped the knife. He regained his poise quickly enough, and turned to face me.

"So you're the famous John Talon everyone seems to think so highly of." He paused to cut away another piece of Kristen's clothing. "I was hoping you'd come to call. I was looking forward to coming to you, but this works, too. Where's your brat?"

Apparently, Kevin had been talking quite a bit. Likely Frank had, too. "None of your business." I said. "You have three seconds to cut down that girl and release my other friend or I will open fire."

"Johnny!" The kid said disapprovingly. "We don't need to have such hostility. We haven't even been introduced. My name," he paused for effect. "Is Cole Tieman. These are my people." He gestured behind him and I was greeted with a chorus of jeers and one fingered salutes. "My woman, Tina Reyes," Cole held out a hand and a pretty dark haired girl stepped forward. "My lieutenant, Devon Hunter and his woman Rayanne Davis." Cole gestured with his other hand and a tall black teen stepped forward, glaring hatred at me. His girlfriend was just as hard.

"Forgive my lieutenant's demeanor. He is upset at your woman killing his brother. She is your woman, correct?" His voice was oily and I was irritated at the sound of it.

I flicked my eyes to Sarah, who was looking at me with a mixture of relief and fear from the pen. "Yes." was all I said.

"Devon will kill her, when I let him. You understand that, don't you Johnny?" Cole handed the knife to his woman who resumed the removal of Kristen's clothing. "My own brother was killed last year, shot down like a dog when all he wanted to do was to have a little fun at the end of the world." Cole held a slender hand to his head and I began to realize why these people followed him. He was clearly unstable.

Cole continued. "You understand, don't you Johnny? You understand my loss?"

I nodded. "Yes, I do."

Cole sighed from his perch. "I knew it." came his breathy reply.

I finished my sentence. "Because I'm the one who killed him. Large bullet wound to the chest? Was that how he died? I know that because it was my gun that killed him. He was scum who deserved to die for what he did to that family. Just like you're scum for what you've done to the people of this area."

Cole shuddered at the revelation. "You! You! I'll kill you! Kill Him! Someone kill him!" Cole screamed at his people. Several of them started pulling weapons out from belts and pants pockets. He grabbed the knife from the girl and before I could shoot him, plunged it deep into Kristen's chest. She raised her head briefly, then dropped it again as the life left her body.

"No!" I roared, firing my rifle. My bullet went high as Cole ducked to the ground. Charlie and Duncan chose that moment to open fire as well, dropping several of the teens who started firing wildly. Sarah dove to the ground and ducked under the platform, trying to present as small of a target as possible. I backed into the aisles and ran towards the pen where Sarah was being held.

As I rounded the corner I saw someone else had gotten there before me. Devon, the lieutenant of Cole, was striding purposefully towards the pen, his gun swinging in his hand. His back was towards me and he didn't see me moving up behind him. Sarah saw me, but to her credit, did not give away that she had seen me.

Devon only had eyes for Sarah. "I wish I had more time to make you suffer, bitch. But I have others to kill today. For my brother." Devon raised the gun and took aim at Sarah.

"Join him." I said as I stuck my SIG in his ear and pulled the trigger, splattering Devon's brains all over a display of decorative wallpaper. Devon dropped lifeless to the floor, and I heard a shrill scream from somewhere, then a bullet whipped past my arm. I could hear gunshots and screams, and figured my men were doing just fine. At the moment, I was focused on someone else

Sarah's eyes were wet as I worked on opening the pen. It was crudely lashed together with zip ties, but effective. I cut through them and opened the door. Sarah fairly jumped into my arms and I hugged her fiercely, holding her as tightly as I could.

"Your woman?" she breathed into my ear, turning her head to look into my eyes.

"Yes." was all I said, before kissing her deeply. It was ludicrous, taking this private moment in the middle of a firefight, but I didn't care. If I died here, I was going to make it worth my while.

Sarah returned the kiss with as much emotion, grabbing my head and holding me close. After a second we broke apart and ducked as bullets whined past our heads to slam into the shelves behind us. We grinned like teenagers at each other then got down to business. Sarah had a bruise on her cheek and what looked like the remnants of a bloody nose, but she seemed fine, otherwise.

"Charlie, Duncan, and Tommy are with me, hook up with one of them. Take the rifle until you can find your weapons. Watch the kick, it's worse than the AR's. I'm going to find that bastard Cole." I gave Sarah my extra magazines for the M1A and a quick kiss for luck. She gave me another in return and headed off to the sound of firing. I figured Cole had headed for cover the same way Devon had gotten down from the platform, and was hiding out somewhere. He wasn't going to be able to leave the building, we had cut off his exits too well for that, but leaving that lunatic alive was inviting trouble. I intended to cut this cancer out once and for all.

Circling to the back of the aisles, I headed for a clearer part of the store. Tall shelving units effectively blocked my view, so the little rat could have been anywhere. Firing on the other side of the store began to taper off, and I could hear the heavy sound of the M1A as Sarah took her anguish out on her attackers. I could see Kristen still on the elevated platform, but several bodies lay around her feet. Her killers had paid a heavy price for her death, and I meant to add to the tally.

The light was getting darker, the deeper I went into the store, but I needed to make sure Cole didn't get around me. Moving quickly towards the lighting department, a figure suddenly popped up from behind the Returns desk. I ducked and fired quickly, striking the figure in the chest and knocking them back against the counter. Moving quietly, I looked over the edge and saw I had managed to kill Tina, Cole's woman.

Well, that ought to piss him off. Deciding to add fuel to the fire, I picked up the body and dumped it into a shopping cart, arranging it like a drunk sorority girl. I moved it to the main aisle and shoved it down, moving to a side aisle to see if it had any effect.

I heard a small voice whisper "Tina?" and then a shadowy form moved toward the slowly rolling cart. A thin squeal of anguish came from the figure, and I could see him turn his head my way to try and discern where I was. I caught a flash of something in his right hand, and figured it was the knife he had used to kill Kristen.

I stood up and moved to the center of the aisle, keeping my SIG centered on Cole. I didn't say a word, I just moved steadily towards Tieman.

For his part, Cole just stood there, staring hate at me. I could imagine his frustration. I had killed his brother and now I had just killed his girlfriend. For someone with an unbalanced mind to begin with, I'm sure it was thoroughly scrambled in there right now.

Cole stretched out the knife and I could see a feral gleam in his eyes. I stopped about fifteen feet away and kept the gun on him.

Cole surprised me with his next move. He dropped the knife on the floor and spread his arms wide. "I am unarmed, hero. You can't kill an unarmed man, can you?" His voice was a purr and he looked at me sideways, grinning slightly.

"Your brother was unarmed." I said coldly. "So was Kristen." I fired rapidly, sending five rounds at Kristen's killer. The bullets slammed into an incredulous Cole and threw him backwards, cartwheeling him over a low shelf and sprawling him spread-eagled on the ground. In the darkening light I could see a darker stain spreading out from underneath him.

A shrieking form burst out of the appliances section and hurtled towards me, screaming epithets and waving what looked like a branch trimmer. I ducked back in between aisles and holstered my SIG, pulling out my hand axe and waited for the next attack. I stood there for a second and didn't hear anything.

Risking a peek around the corner I saw a sprawled figure lying on the ground with a tomahawk sticking out of the back of its neck. A closer look revealed that it was Rayanne, Devon's girlfriend, who had been killed. Her weapon had been tossed when she fell to the ground. Charlie was walking down the aisle to retrieve his weapon.

"Thanks, man." I said, clapping him on the shoulder. "I didn't know you could throw those things, too."

Charlie shrugged. "I didn't either. I figured if it didn't work, at least she'd be distracted and you could take her out."

"Are we finished here?" I asked, looking into the gloom.

"Yeah, we're done. Tommy took a bullet to the arm, but it's nothing serious. Rebecca should get him moving in no time. Sarah found her guns, and is right now scared silly you're hurt or something. What did you do to that woman, anyway.?"

"I kissed her."

Charlie raised an eyebrow at me. "About time." he said wryly.

I smiled. "*I* thought so."

Charlie turned serious. "Sorry about Kristen. Duncan brought her down and wrapped her in a blanket. Nothing you could do, man." he said.

I looked at him. "I know. But it doesn't make me feel any better. Even wasting the bastard that killed her won't bring her back. She didn't deserve any of this, Charlie. She was just a kid."

Charlie didn't say anything; he just walked alongside me as we worked our way to the others.

Duncan and Sarah were kneeling beside a wrapped form, and Tommy was standing out of the way. Sarah saw me, stood up and wrapped her arms around me. I held her for a moment then gently moved away. I reached down and picked up Kristen's body, and walked over to the doors. I had a long walk back to the truck, but I didn't care. I'd carry her if my legs fell off. Sarah moved in behind me and the rest of the men followed suit, forming a small funeral procession out of the store.

I walked to the truck, and gently placed Kristen in the bed. We climbed into the truck and headed back to the complex, none of us saying much of anything. Sarah put her head on my shoulder and I could feel the occasional tear hit my sleeve. I was angry at what had happened, angry at myself that I hadn't seen what Cole was about to do and stop him. Part of me wanted to burn the building to the ground, but a larger part reasoned that it was not my fault, and I had actually managed to save Sarah and Kristen from worse fates. I didn't regret killing Cole, unarmed though he was. He was a blight that needed to be eradicated, and I was assigned the job.

When we got back to the complex, there were more tears shed for Kristen. Charlie and I assigned ourselves the duty of digging her grave. We buried her next to her friend Chelsea, and said a small prayer for her eternal soul.

When the sadness of the day passed, I sent Charlie back to the McCord's with Mark Wells, our resident electrician, and John Reef, our plumber, to look for supplies and things they might need to make our lives a little easier. They also had the job of burning that grisly pile of zombie heads. Charlie reported they popped like acorns. I was pleasantly surprised when they returned with a huge generator. Apparently the teens had no idea a large power source was right outside their lair, and instead had relied on sunlight and flashlights. Charlie pulled up with it, and Mark went to work immediately attaching the lines and seeing how much power could be had. In short order, we actually had working lights in the condos. We took the smaller generators and brought them over to the town homes, where they provided welcome relief from the darkness.

I spent the evening with Jake and Sarah, just taking in the activity and staying relatively quiet. Sarah and I didn't speak about what happened, but we both were thinking about it. Part of me felt guilty, but I was reminded by a little voice in my head to *Get busy living*. Part of me was concerned about Sarah, but I wasn't sure how to approach the subject. We went to bed in our separate rooms without a clear answer.

I got my answer about an hour after the lights went out. A soft rustling alerted me to someone in my room, and I saw Sarah moving towards my bedside.

"Your woman?" she asked again, with a sly smile.

I held out my hand. "Yes." was all I said as she took my hand and climbed into bed.

I didn't feel the need to say much else after that.

WHITE FLAG OF THE DEAD

Book 2: Taking it Back

Joseph Talluto

Available from Severed Press 2011

As John Talon and his small band of survivors struggle to come to grips with the aftermath of the Upheaval, questions arise. What happened to the government? What happened at the state centers? Was anyone else left alive? What happened to Mike Talon, John's brother?

John discovers that the answers to these questions might take more from him than he had planned on, and that worse things are out there than the living dead.

For John Talon and his crew, one question overrides them all. What is the difference between being alive, and living?

www.severedpress.com

DEMONMACHY
Brant Danay

As the universe slowly dies, all demonkind is at war in a tournament of genocide. The prize? Nirvana. The Necrodelic, a death addict who smokes the flesh of his victims as a drug, is determined to win this afterlife for himself. His quest has taken him to the planet Grystiawa, and into a duel with a dream-devouring snake demon who is more than he seems. Grystiawa has also been chosen as the final battleground in the ancient spider-serpent wars. As armies of arachnid monstrosities and ophidian gladiators converge upon the planet, the Necrodelic is forced to choose sides in a cataclysmic combat that could well prove his demise. Beyond Grystiawa, a Siamese twin incubus and succubus, a brain-raping nightmare fetishist, a gargantuan insect queen, and an entire universe of genocidal demons are forming battle plans of their own. Observing the apocalyptic carnage all the while is Satan himself, watching voyeuristically from the very Hell in which all those who fail will be damned to eternal torment. Who will emerge victorious from this cosmic armageddon? And what awaits the victor beyond the blood-drenched end of time? The battle begins in Demonmachy. Twisting Satanic mythologies and Eastern religions into an ultraviolent grotesque nightmare, the Messiah of Death Saga will rip your eyeballs right out of your skull. Addicted to its psychedelic darkness, you'll immediately sew and screw and staple and weld them back into their sockets so you can read more. It's an intergalactic, interdimensional harrowing that you'll never forget...and may never recover from.

THE DEVIL NEXT DOOR

Cannibalism. Murder. Rape. Absolute brutality. When civilizations ends...when the human race begins to revert to ancient, predatory savagery...when the world descends into a bloodthirsty hell...there is only survival. But for one man and one woman, survival means becoming something less than human. Something from the primeval dawn of the race.

"Shocking and brutal, The Devil Next Door will hit you like a baseball bat to the face. Curran seems to have it in for the world ... and he's ending it as horrifyingly as he can." - *Tim Lebbon, author of Bar None*

"The Devil Next Door is dynamite! Visceral, violent, and disturbing!." *Brian Keene, author of Castaways and Dark Hollow*

"The Devil Next Door is a horror fans delight...who love extreme horror fiction, and to those that just enjoy watching the world go to hell in a hand basket" – *HORROR WORLD*

The Official Zombie Handbook: Sean T Page

Since pre-history, the living dead have been among us, with documented outbreaks from ancient Babylon and Rome right up to the present day. But what if we were to suffer a zombie apocalypse in the UK today? Through meticulous research and field work, The Official Zombie Handbook (UK) is the only guide you need to make it through a major zombie outbreak in the UK, including: -Full analysis of the latest scientific information available on the zombie virus, the living dead creatures it creates and most importantly, how to take them down - UK style. Everything you need to implement a complete 90 Day Zombie Survival Plan for you and your family including home fortification, foraging for supplies and even surviving a ghoul siege. Detailed case studies and guidelines on how to battle the living dead, which weapons to use, where to hide out and how to survive in a country dominated by millions of bloodthirsty zombies. Packed with invaluable information, the genesis of this handbook was the realisation that our country is sleep walking towards a catastrophe - that is the day when an outbreak of zombies will reach critical mass and turn our green and pleasant land into a grey and shambling wasteland. Remember, don't become a cheap meat snack for the zombies!

Lightning Source UK Ltd.
Milton Keynes UK
UKOW051814100712

195774UK00001B/179/P